A WORLD TO WIN II.

Vincent G. Wald
14 November 2005

TIMELINE

World's End	1913 - 1919
Between Two Worlds	1919 - 1929
Dragon's Teeth	1929 - 1934
Wide is the Gate	1934 - 1937
Presidential Agent	1937 - 1938
Dragon Harvest	1938 - 1940
A World to Win	1940 - 1942
Presidential Mission	1942 - 1943
One Clear Call	1943 - 1944
O Shepherd, Speak!	1943 - 1946
The Return of Lanny Budd	1946 - 1949

Each book is published in two parts: I and II.

A WORLD TO WIN II.

Upton Sinclair

Simon Publications

2001

LCCN: 46003965

ISBN: 1-931313-22-9

Dis tributed by Ingram Book Com pany

Printed by Light ning Source Inc., LaVergne, TN

Pub lished by Si mon Pub li ca tions, P.O. Box 321 Safety Har bor, FL

An Author's Program

From a 1943 article by Upton Sinclair.

When I say "historian," I have a meaning of my own. I portray world events in story form, because that form is the one I have been trained in. I have supported myself by writing fiction since the age of sixteen, which means for forty-nine years.

… Now I realize that this one was the one job for which I had been born: to put the period of world wars and revolutions into a great long novel. …

I can not say when it will end, because I don't know exactly what the characters will do. They lead a semi-independent life, being more real to me than any of the people I know, with the single exception of my wife. … Some of my characters are people who lived, and whom I had opportunity to know and watch. Others are imaginary—or rather, they are complexes of many people whom I have known and watched. Lanny Budd and his mother and father and their various relatives and friends have come in the course of the past four years to be my daily and nightly companions. I have come to know them so intimately that I need only to ask them what they would do in a given set of circumstances and they start to enact their roles. … I chose what seems to me the most revealing of them and of their world.

How long will this go on? I can not tell. It depends in great part upon two public figures, Hitler and Mussolini. What are they going to do to mankind and what is mankind will do to them? It seems to me hardly likely that either will die a peaceful death. I am hoping to outlive them; and whatever happens Lanny Budd will be somewhere in the neighborhood, he will be "in at the death," according to the fox-hunting phrase.

These two foxes are my quarry, and I hope to hang their brushes over my mantel.

Author's Notes

In the course of this novel a number of well-known persons make their appearance, some of them living, some dead; they appear under their own names, and what is said about them is factually correct.

There are other characters which are fictitious, and in these cases the author has gone out of his way to avoid seeming to point at real persons. He has given them unlikely names, and hopes that no person bearing such names exist. But it is impossible to make sure; therefore the writer states that, if any such coincidence occurs, it is accidental. This is not the customary "hedge clause" which the author of a *roman à clef* publishes for legal protection; it means what it says and it is intended to be so taken.

Various European concerns engaged in the manufacture of munitions have been named in the story, and what has been said about them is also according to the records. There is one American firm, and that, with all its affairs, is imaginary. The writer has done his best to avoid seeming to indicate any actual American firm or family.

...Of course there will be slips, as I know from experience; but *World's End* is meant to be a history as well as fiction, and I am sure there are no mistakes of importance. I have my own point of view, but I have tried to play fair in this book. There is a varied cast of characters and they say as they think. ...

The Peace Conference of Paris [*for example*], which is the scene of the last third of *World's End*, is of course one of the greatest events of all time. A friend on mine asked an authority on modern fiction a question: "Has anybody ever used the Peace Conference in a novel?" And the reply was: "Could anybody?" Well, I thought somebody could, and now I think somebody has. The reader will ask, and I state explicitly that so far as concerns historic characters and events my picture is correct in all details. This part of the manuscript, 374 pages, was read and checked by eight or ten gentlemen who were on the American staff at the Conference. Several of these hold important positions in the world of troubled international affairs; others are college presidents and professors, and I promised them all that their letters will be confidential. Suffice it to say that the errors they pointed out were corrected, and where they disagreed, both sides have a word in the book.

Contents:

BOOK FIVE

A Tide in the Affairs of Men

———————— o ————————

16. 'Gainst Female Charms

I

ON THE day that Lanny left England, the newspapers featured
the startling tidings that Rudolf Hess had dropped down upon the
soil of Scotland, but not one word about what he had come for, or
what was being done with him. So all the imaginations in the world
were turned loose. Was he fleeing from the wrath that he saw was
to come? Had he quarreled with his Führer, and was he now revealing
his Führer's secrets? Did this mean a break in Nazi morale, and was
it the beginning of the end? Or had the Führer sent him? Had the
accident of a sprained ankle been the means of unveiling efforts of
the old-time appeasers of Britain to make terms with Germany?
There were nearly as many guesses as guessers.

And when Lanny's plane had flown him through the springtime
fogs of the far north and landed him safely on Long Island, he bought
more newspapers and discovered that it was the same in this half of
the world. The British authorities had had no more to say; the Nazis
had announced officially that the Deputy Führer had for a long time
been suffering from a nervous disorder and that his unauthorized
flight meant that he was definite'v irresponsible. Could that be true,
or was it just Hitler's alibi? And   at would be the effect of it upon
the German people? Certainly it must leave them bewildered and
anxious; it must be a great blow to their cause. A madman can talk,
and may reveal secrets. What was the Führer's most trusted friend
saying to his captors?

Lanny's duty, as always, was to phone Washington for an appointment; while waiting for it to be arranged he was free to call his father and report that he was safe. Robbie took only enough time to say how glad he was to hear Lanny's voice, then asked: "What on earth does this news from Scotland mean?"

"It means that the Nazis were trying to make a deal, and they got fooled."

"Did Mr. Big know about it?"

"It is possible that he did; I can't say. I'll tell you when I see you." That was all, over the telephone. When the father heard that Lanny was going to Washington, he said: "Don't fail to stop off and see Reverdy on your way back. We have gone into big business together. He will tell you about it." Lanny smiled, knowing what "big business" he, Lanny, was supposed to do in Green Spring Valley!

His appointment with the President was for the usual hour that night, and he had barely time to call a taxi and get to the airport. Some large magnificent businessman had been thrown off, and stood there by the plane, fuming and fussing, for he thought that *his* business was important too, and who the devil had taken his place, and was this a free country or wasn't it?

That was the way with travel between New York and Washington in these days of undeclared war; the twelve billion dollars voted by Congress had completed a job which the New Deal had begun, of shifting the capital of America from Wall Street to the offices of Washington bureaucrats, and traffic between the two cities had outgrown all the existing facilities. First Lanny couldn't get a taxi, and then he couldn't get a room in the Mayflower Hotel, where he usually stopped. After he got a room in a smaller place, he had barely time to bathe and shave, and to get a bite to eat before it was time to go strolling on the street and be picked up by those two men in a car. When he remarked to Baker: "These must be strenuous times in Washington," the heartfelt answer was: "You said it!"

II

So Lanny entered once more that bedroom which had come to be the most interesting spot in the world to him. If it had not been for pictures he saw in the papers, he might have believed that Franklin Roosevelt spent all his time reclining in an old-fashioned mahogany bed with a blue spread, a reading table beside it with a lamp and a stack of documents, a smaller stack on the bed, and often one on the occupant's lap. Lanny might have believed that the "Governor" never wore anything but a blue-and-white-striped pongee pajama suit, and either a crew-necked sweater or a blue cape. Always he leaned over and held out a firm right hand, and always there was a grin on his features and some joshing remark. He loved his friends and enjoyed seeing them, and he never put on any "side," or looked solemn unless it was a truly solemn occasion.

This time there was a joke about Lanny's covering so much of the earth. "The only man in the world who travels more than my wife!" Then the Chief said: "Shoot the works!" and Lanny opened up like one of those "Chicago pianos."

First, about Hess. Lanny had reported to F.D. that the flight was to take place; in fact he had been the only one—not even Churchill had known it, and so it was a great feather in a P.A.'s cap. The story he told now fitted perfectly with what F.D. already knew, and the great man said: "You get one hundred per cent score on that job." When Lanny told how he had been bounced from Britain, the President threw back his head and gave one of those hearty laughs which had helped to keep him alive through eight years of political and military conflict. "Golly!" he exclaimed. "I'll have to tell Winston about it!" Then he added, seriously: "I'll fix it so that you can go back and have your dinner with Mr. Fordyce."

Lanny said: "I hope you can, for England is a sort of base of operations for me. Also, I pass on a lot of news to my friend Rick, and he gets it into the papers in various quiet ways."

"I talked with Winston just a while ago; he's an owl, you know, and stays up till all hours. You provided me with a ten-strike on the old boy. I told him two or three weeks ago that Hess was going to fly to England, and he replied that it was a crazy report, and he didn't even bother to check on it with his secret services. So the news knocked the wind clean out of him."

Said Lanny: "I take it I'm correct in my idea that his B4 had planned the whole thing from the beginning?"

"Absolutely! They had been writing letters to Hess in the name of Ivone Kirkpatrick, the Duke of Hamilton, the Duke of Bedford, and Lord Beaverbrook, and other important Englishmen. And did Winston give his Intelligence a dressing down when he discovered what they had been up to!"

"Not on behalf of Hess, I hope."

"No, but of the Englishmen. It wasn't considered to be cricket to use their names."

Lanny knew that his Chief liked to talk, so he ventured: "Tell me what has happened since. Has Rudi talked?"

"He's been interviewed by several of the men who were supposed to be writing to him. They have all been told to play the game, so Hess thinks he is in the midst of important diplomatic negotiations. That is why the matter is being kept so closely under wraps. Don't you say anything about it."

"Surely not," Lanny replied. "It would be bad policy for me even to know about the case—or any case that gets a lot of publicity. Some reporter might get the idea to trace me down!"

III

The most urgent subject at the moment was that of Russia. Lanny reported that it was taken for granted by all the Nazis he had talked to that the attack would begin in about six weeks. F.D. said that his own information confirmed this, the German armies were being mobilized all along the border between the two countries. "I got your message," he said, "and I had it passed on to Oumansky. He pretended not to believe it, and he still keeps up that bluff; but my guess is he has a bad case of the jitters when he gets alone by himself in the Embassy. Tell me what you think about how that attack will go."

"Hitler is absolutely certain that he can roll over the Red Army in a month, or two at the outside. I am told that the *Oberkommando* is divided. Some talk about the enormous size of Russia, and the mud, and then the snow and bitter cold. They remember Napoleon, and have nightmares. Hitler, of course, is the gambler, the plunger—and he is the one who has the last word."

"What do you think yourself?"

"Your guess is better than mine, Governor. The Red Army men hate the Nazis and will fight like the very devil. But I am worried about their transportation, and about their staff work. So few of their commanders have had experience; and you know, they didn't show up very well in Finland."

"They killed off so many of their best commanders, I am told."

"It's hard to know what to believe about that. If you accept what the Communists tell you, the men who were shot were German sympathizers, and wouldn't have been of much use to Stalin in the coming crisis."

"The Soviets will hold out, whatever happens?"

"Hitler has made that certain by his denunciation of Bolshevism; it's a life and death matter with every Red leader. They will fight a defensive war, and fall back—all the way to the Urals, if necessary. They will surely not give up."

"That is what Oumansky assures us. Do you know him?"

"I can't afford to associate with the Reds any more. I'm a Nazi-Fascist, and believe me, Governor, I couldn't stick it out if it wasn't for these visits to you."

"Well, come whenever you feel like it; the latchstring is out. And by the way, Lanny, didn't you tell me that Jesse Blackless is your uncle?"

"Yes, my mother's elder brother."

"Did you know that he's in this country?"

"I haven't heard from him since he skipped out of France."

"He's been in Russia. The State Department didn't want to let him come here, since it appears that he had taken French citizenship in order to get elected to the Chamber of Deputies."

"I knew that."

"The case was appealed to me, and I said: 'Let him come.' I decided largely on your report that Hitler means to attack them. That will make them a sort of left-handed allies, and we shall have to get our public used to them."

"Every Communist in the world will be for the war, Governor. I can speak for Uncle Jesse on that, I am sure."

"He was in New York the last I heard, and I had somebody talk with him. It might be a good idea for you to have a meeting on the Q.T. He would probably tell you more than he would tell a stranger."

"He always has," replied the nephew. "He's a rare old boy, and I got my start in social thinking from him. He's something of a saint— though he wouldn't take that for a compliment."

"We shouldn't like the saints in the least if we met them at a Washington cocktail party," remarked F.D. with one of his grins.

IV

The busy man wanted to know about his agent's program. The answer was: "Unless you have something urgent in mind, I'll wait until Hitler makes his next move. That will make a lot of difference in the world situation." When F.D. said: "All right," Lanny replied: "I'll have a talk with my Red uncle and if he has anything of interest, I'll send you a report in care of Baker. Also, I'll see Forrest Quadratt and tell him a little about Hess. That will impress him greatly and he'll tell me what he is up to. Do you want me to do anything about those rascals who are plotting to put you on the shelf?"

"No," was the reply, "I think I have them under observation. Europe is still your field."

"I promised the Lord of San Simeon that I would keep him informed as to how that little matter was progressing. I might run out there again and see what his mood is."

"California is a pleasant place to visit," replied the other, smiling. "But I think that old alligator has passed the age where he talks frankly to anybody on earth."

"He knows his own heart too well to believe that anybody on earth can be trusted."

Lanny had his orders, and it was time for him to depart, but the

Boss wouldn't have it that way. "You only come about once in six months," he said. "Stay and entertain me for a while."

"I see that stack of documents—" began the visitor, apologetically.

"I can't tell you how I hate them!" exclaimed F.D., and gave them a little push. "Bureaucrats squabbling over power and precedence! You have to try to administer something on a large scale before you really know human nature: how almost impossible it is to find a man who will do his job and not get into a row with other people who are trying to do theirs."

"You are doing new things, Governor, and you have jostled people out of their old ruts. It takes time to get them settled in new ones."

"That's it. But meantime all they can think of is to come running to me to settle their disputes. They send me long arguments to show why they have to have control of a certain department, and then somebody gets wind of it and rushes to explain why *he* has to have it."

"Everybody marvels about the way you manage to keep cheerful, Governor!"

"That's the audience that sits out in the soft, plush-covered seats and enjoys the show. But when you get back into the dressing-room of the star you hear a different story."

"The show must go on, Governor! And for you there is no 'stand-in'—as they call it in Hollywood. Surely not now, in the midst of this crisis."

"My enemies accuse me of loving power, of wanting to be a dictator, to perpetuate myself, and all that stuff. Do you know what I would really like to do?"

"I suppose it would be to retire to Hyde Park and grow Christmas trees."

"That as a sideline; the real thing would be to write history. I said that to Winston the other night, and he has the same dream. Also, he likes to build brick walls!"

"And Hitler! Do you know what Hitler is longing to do?"

"What?"

"To design beautiful buildings. The only trouble is, they are all big buildings—so big that there wouldn't be room enough for them all in Germany."

"I suppose that is what he means by *Lebensraum*," countered the President.

V

Next morning Lanny telephoned, as was his duty, to Baltimore, and was assured that the doors of the Holdenhurst home were open to welcome him. He took the train, and was met by the talkative chauffeur, who told him on the way the news of the family and the neighborhood. Most improper, but then Lanny invited it by sitting alongside the man, and by being genial in manner, whereas he should have "frozen" the fellow at the first sign of presumption. But there were big factories in Baltimore, including an airplane plant, all busy with war work and clamoring for more labor; so even the richest and most important people tried to keep friends with their "help." That twelve billion dollars was making a great difference in American society. And there were more billions to come!

It was the top of the season in Green Spring Valley; the trees had on their bright new costumes, and the rolling hills were green to match. The little brook which ran through the Holdenhurst estate sang gaily, and the fish leaped in the little pond in which you could catch your own breakfast if you had the notion. The red brick mansion appeared to have had its walls washed, and the white wood-work had been freshly painted, as if in Lanny's honor.

Certainly it was that way in the heart of Lizbeth—not the paint, but the honor. The smiles were fresh, and the gleam in the lovely brown eyes. She had grown more mature in the two and a half years Lanny had known her; he had to admit that nobody could be nicer to be with. Her whole manner seemed to say: "What is the matter with me?" His manner would have been churlish indeed if it had not responded: "Nothing whatever, my dear."

The most pathetic thing you could imagine; she had evidently been trying to figure the matter out, why it was that her *beau idéal* and ideal beau was behaving so abnormally. She had decided, perhaps with the aid of her father, that she was frivolous and ignorant, whereas he was a serious and learned gentleman. He read books and thought about the problems of the world; and how could she interest him with chatter about the parties she had been to, and what the members of her "younger set" had said and done? She had decided to try to be worthy of him; she was listening every day to radio commentators on what was happening in the world, and she was looking at the war maps in the newspapers, to learn where Bulgaria was, and Abyssinia, and Libya, and all the other queer-sounding places. More significant yet, she had employed a lady teacher from one of the art schools, and they had been going to lectures on art and visiting the Baltimore galleries together. *Les Femmes Savantes!*

Now she wanted, not to display this learning, but just to have it certified by a real authority. Instead of taking Lanny to the Country Club to show him off to her smart friends, she drove him in to the galleries and invited him to turn loose that flow of discourse which had earned him over a period of some eighteen years close to half a million dollars. It was the best way in the world to make an impression

on him; it was like saying: "I am ready to be whatever you want; and
if you marry me you won't be dragged to dinner dances, but will
have time to meditate and rehearse what you are going to say to Mr.
Winstead or Mrs. Ford the next day!"

Lanny found it deeply touching; and of course it made him think
about her. Why on earth had she chosen him, over the many swains
who were besieging her from every noon to every midnight? It must
have been a case of that alarming thing called love at first sight. Since
she had met him at Emily Chattersworth's luncheon at Sept Chênes
she had apparently never wavered in her determination that he was
the man for her. Then he had had more than twice her years, and as
they stood at this moment he had almost exactly twice. He had a
previous marriage to his discredit, and would make her a stepmother
—but apparently she was too young to realize the perils of that
relationship. No, Irma Barnes in her eyes had been a selfish woman
who had wanted to become a countess, and it couldn't possibly have
been any fault of the kind and genial and wise Lanny Budd.

This kind and genial and wise one had sat in at enough family scenes
to be able to imagine what had gone on in the Holdenhurst family:
the efforts of the parents to dissuade her, and her counter arguments,
her defense of a much-traveled and widely read man who knew all
the great people of the earth and was so much more interesting than
anybody who had ever lived in this overgrown port on an estuary of
the Chesapeake Bay—famous for oysters and shad and deviled crabs,
but less so for musicians and poets and painters, and never for dukes
and duchesses! Lanny had never seen Lizbeth in a tantrum, but he
could guess that she had a fountain of tears; and then, when she had
got her own way with two fond unhappy parents, she would wipe
her eyes and emerge as the debutante heiress, waiting for her chosen
Prince Charming to step from his horseless chariot.

VI

Lanny told himself that his predicament was owing to the uncomfortable business of politics, and to the war that was going on in the
world, not merely the war between Germany and Britain, with the
United States as a lend-lease adjunct, but the class war that was rend-
ing modern society, and of which the armed conflict was but an
early stage. Lanny had pledged his faith and his hopes to the workers,
the disinherited of the earth. And where would the daughter of
Reverdy Johnson Holdenhurst stand in that battlefield? Would she
follow him there as humbly and as cheerfully as she accepted his
judgments concerning Rembrandt and Turner, van Gogh and Matisse
and the rest? Or would she be horrified and outraged, as Irma had

been? Would she weep and exclaim: "You have cheated me! You should have told me! It was my right to know!"

Of course it was her right; it is every woman's right to know what she is marrying, and what her future life is to be. Lanny couldn't tell her; but in his imagination, he could go through a number of scenes in which he told her. In most of them, she assured him that she would follow him in whatever he believed to be right, regardless of its effect upon herself and her fortune. But even that didn't satisfy him, for before he had asked Irma to marry him he had told her that he was a Socialist, and she had said that that didn't worry her. Irma had been at that time just about Lizbeth's age—far too young to realize what it would mean to be the wife of a well-to-do friend of the workers, a "parlor Pink" as they were derisively called.

It meant having unpresentable friends who had the right to come to your home at all hours of the day and night, sometimes fleeing from the police, and invariably wanting money for "the cause." Many of them were far from being pure idealists; on the contrary, they were jealous and embittered personalities who would bite the hand that was in the act of feeding them. It took a lot of social insight to understand the system which had produced these distorted souls. Was it possible to imagine Lizbeth Holdenhurst as ever possessing such understanding?

In one of these imaginary scenes Lanny explained matters to her, and she told him frankly that she didn't think she could stand that sort of life; she hadn't been trained for it, and she didn't like dirty and ill-bred people—especially when they promised to deprive her of her money and reduce her to their own level of servantless and undignified commonness. But she respected Lanny's right to try to reduce himself to that level if he wished, and she promised to keep secret the fact that he was doing it. He went off—still in his imagination—wondering if she would keep this promise. Might she not decide that he was a traitor to his class, an enemy of public safety who deserved to be exposed? Might she not at the least decide that it was her right to explain to her parents the sudden change in her attitude and hopes? There is nothing more humiliating to a rich and somewhat spoiled daughter of privilege than to be turned down by a man; and was it human to imagine that Lizbeth would keep hidden from her most intimate friends the fact that it was she who had turned Lanny down?

The standard accepted way to worm the truth out of secret agents is with a woman; and Lanny Budd, who prided himself upon being a super-spy, so high-brow, so haughty, was about to fall for the cheapest and commonest of enemy devices. He decided, for the tenth or twelfth time, that he was playing with fire in a powder barrel; he must stop driving with this daughter of the Holdenhursts, looking at

pictures with her, playing tennis with her, even talking to her; he must
stop showing human interest in her or kindness to her! And straightway his imagination carried him off into a scene in which he told her
that he couldn't see her again, that he could never marry her, nor
even tell her why. She burst into tears and flung herself into his arms
and told him that she could not live without him, that if he left her
she would kill herself, or go into an Episcopal nunnery. There had
been many such scenes in Lanny's imagination, and it was getting
quite dangerous; he was convinced that the real one might break at
any moment, and how the devil would he meet it?

VII

He had a long talk with Reverdy, and told him about conditions in
Europe and in Britain; what Hitler and Göring and Hess had said, and
what Lanny thought the Hess flight meant—but not saying that Hess
had told him. Hitler was undoubtedly going to invade Russia next
month—but again Lanny didn't say that Hitler had admitted it. The
P.A. had learned a lesson in Toulon, and another from Mr. Fordyce,
and from now on wouldn't talk quite so freely in polite society,
wouldn't be quite so brilliant, such a shining mark for underground
partisans and B4 agents and other people on his own side!

It was safe for him to tell this Baltimore capitalist that it was going
to be a long war, and that nobody was making a mistake in putting
money into fighter planes. A huge war machine was going to be constructed, the greatest the world had ever seen; America was going to
become the great arsenal of democracy—never knowing who had
invented that phrase! Lanny had come to understand his host by
now, and was not deceived by his manner of placid indolence, or by
his valetudinarian talk. Before Reverdy went off on one of those
half-year sea jaunts, he made sure where every dollar of his money
was placed and what work it was going to perform in his absence.
Quietly, carefully, he studied market conditions and world prospects,
and made up his mind and placed his investments.

He had devised an armor-clad device for thwarting the income-tax
laws, by dividing his fortune among a carefully selected group of his
future heirs, some forty of them; they owned the securities and
received the income, but did not have the use of it; they left it for
Reverdy to reinvest for their benefit after his death. By this means a
supposedly retired semi-invalid accomplished two purposes: he avoided
the higher tax schedules, the so-called surtaxes, which he considered
outright confiscation, a devilish device to break down the "private-
enterprise system" in America; and he kept for himself the control of
more fluid capital than any other person he knew, or whom Robbie

Budd or Lanny knew. As a rule it was only banks and insurance companies that disposed of so much money nowadays.

This yacht-sailing bank and insurance company was turning the money over to Budd-Erling Aircraft. All summer long he would study its reports, balance sheets, contracts, payrolls, bank statements—everything; then for the winter he could go off in peace of mind, receiving only a few cablegrams at ports where he put in. This arrangement served both men, for it reduced the amount of government funds which Robbie had to accept, and both were united in fearing the Roosevelt administration as much as, if not more than, they feared the Nazis. In his youth Lanny had made jokes about the firm of "R and R," consisting of his father and Johannes Robin; now the firm had come to life again, only this time it was Robbie and Reverdy! And always it had made money faster than any other firm of which the son had knowledge.

VIII

Lanny made excuses—he hadn't seen his father yet, and he had picture business which must be completed without delay. Reverdy respected such excuses, even if his daughter didn't. Without taking a chance of being alone with Lizbeth again, the art expert took the train to New York and from there to Newcastle. He shut himself up in his father's study and revealed everything he knew that would be of any use to that "merchant of death." Lanny wasn't going to tell a single person in America about his Toulon adventure, nor about his pre-knowledge of Hess's flight, nor of the part which B4 had played therein. But he could say it was certain that Hess had come seeking peace with Britain; and he could say that the Wehrmacht was moving to the east, and what for. He could say that Britain was going to stick, beyond any question; that Churchill's position was secure, the appeasers having been driven underground. He could say that the R.A.F. had won out, and that Britain wasn't going to be invaded within any foreseeable time. The war was going on and on, and every dollar that Britain could scrape up would go into it, and every pound of steel and explosives that America would furnish on lend-lease or lease-lend. That was all the President of Budd-Erling Aircraft needed to enable him to eat heartily and sleep soundly.

He would, of course, like to have his firstborn marry the right girl. He and Esther must have talked it over in advance and decided that they had said all they could; now they just asked how he had found matters in Green Spring Valley, and when he said that everybody was well and seemed reasonably happy, and that he had taken Lizbeth to art galleries to look at paintings, they knew that he hadn't popped the question, and they didn't ask further. He was going to stick around for a while, he said; he had brought two small paintings with him and had offers of others. He would use the car, if it was all right. The father said: "Always."

Lanny had to see the new plant, of course, and express his pride in it. Such an amazing country, in which new factories arose like Jack's beanstalk or the products of Aladdin's lamp; buildings standardized, built in sections all uniform, prefabricated and put together by gangs of men with riveting machines and welding torches—three gangs, working around the clock, at night by glaring electricity. The men and women appeared from nowhere, as if they, too, were products of Aladdin's wonderful lamp; they crowded themselves into somebody's attic, or fixed up somebody's cow shed or chicken house, or worked overtime and constructed homes out of old pieces of tin and tar paper. Robbie said that getting them wasn't as simple as it sounded; he had agents at work, north, south, east, and west, telling people of the wonders of airplane fabrication—you had just one little thing to do and you could learn it in an hour or two, and you got around two dollars an hour even while being shown.

IX

Also, there was the matter of Esther Remsen Budd's niece; such a lovely young woman, and rich as cream, and she was going to learn to be an art expert and run a museum, not because she hoped thereby to catch Lanny, but because she thought every woman ought to have a career and not be an idler and parasite. Of course it was from Lanny that she had got the idea of old masters as a profession; but she had dug up for herself information about the wonderful Fogg Museum of Art at Harvard where they turned out art experts on the production line, just as Robbie turned out Budd-Erling 17Ks—that being the Army's new designation. Not quite so fast, of course; there wasn't the same demand for museum directors as for fighter planes, but it was part of the same American efficiency.

Lanny could imagine his father and his stepmother discussing this case, too. Since he obviously wasn't going to marry Lizbeth, it would surely be all right to let Peggy Remsen have her chance. But there mustn't be any hint that anybody had this idea; they must be all wrapped up in old masters, and perhaps Lanny would drive Peggy to New York and escort her through the Metropolitan Museum of Art, which she knew well but could always know better. For that reason it would be worth while for her to take a couple of days off from school, and let Esther invite her to lunch while Lanny was there, and see what the signs were. That is the way the marriage market is conducted in refined and elegant circles; there are no schools where it is taught, but ladies manage somehow to get a sound education in it, and conducting it is the first business of all mothers, grandmothers, and aunts. "Doänt thou marry for munny, but goä wheer munny is!"

If Lanny wanted to visit his father's home and drive one of his father's cars—or indeed if he didn't want to be a hermit entirely—he had to play his hand in this game. He was as nice as could be to Peggy, who had everything that a modern young woman ought to have—looks and clothes, manners and speech, even a sense of humor. When her watchful aunt suggested that Lanny might give her the benefit of his point of view on what the Metropolitan contained as against what it ought to contain, Lanny felt duly honored, and they made an extensive date; he would drive her to New York next morning, and they would spend the day in the museum, then have dinner and go to a show, and he would put her on the night train for Boston. After the lunch, when Esther got her stepson off by himself, she pressed a fifty-dollar bill into his hand and wouldn't take it back. This was her party, she insisted; she had planned it, and he would have to buy Peggy's ticket and sleeping-car berth, as well as all the other expenses. "Isn't she a nice girl?" asked the aunt, and when translated into good society it meant: "Why don't you marry her?"

Marry, marry, marry! Nobody would let Lanny alone! Here was a young woman with whom it might be a pleasure to look at paintings, provided she would be content with that. She had been well drilled, and her opinions were those generally received, but she was open-minded and could be taught; it was a pleasure to stroll with her through the long galleries of New York's immense treasury of art. This museum as a rule bought the works of dead artists, and that was a way of playing safe; they had to pay higher prices, but avoided bad guesses, and perhaps it paid in the long run. Lanny would ask his companion's opinion of this work and that, and then would gently suggest a new point of view and observe her reaction. Even though she might never become a museum curator, she would be a collector and a patron, so it was worth while to guide her and give her courage to use her own judgment.

But did lady curators and art patrons have to be married? Apparently so! Lanny could be sure that Esther had discussed him as a possible match, and that Peggy was looking him over and searching his mind, just as he was doing with hers. Life was real and life was earnest in New England, and the arts of painting and drama were vain things except as they contributed to the founding of a family and the bringing of a new generation into the world. If Lanny thought that he could be a good pal to his stepmother's niece and never contemplate matrimony, he would find that he had made the same mistake as in the case of Lizbeth Holdenhurst.

He played the perfect gentleman and poured out the treasures of his knowledge. He fed her and took her to a proper play, not so easy to find in New York. Of course it dealt with love and marriage, and they discussed it in the light modern manner. Lanny said: "I was married once, you know; my former wife is now a countess, which suits her much better." When his companion asked: "And how does it suit *you?*" he replied: "We have a lovely little daughter, and when I go to visit the Castle, we talk about the child, and about world politics— never about the past." It was a gracious way of dodging, and Peggy had sense enough to observe it. She would call him "impenetrable," and decide that he was an intriguing personality.

A taxi took them to Grand Central Station—no use trying to use your own car in that theater jam. Lanny saw her on board her train; a friendly handshake and assurances that they had both had a delightful day—and then he strolled out, thinking how it would be as husband of Peggy Remsen. Where and how would they live? And what would she make of his long journeys on art missions? And would he entrust her with his political secret? And what would she make of his Pink opinions?

X

On his way to the street was a newsstand loaded with every sort of reading matter that might tempt the public. So many new magazines that one couldn't remember the names. The June issues, just out, new and neat, multicolored traps for the modern eye. Lanny stopped and glanced over the contents tables. There was a *Bluebook*, and he thought of Mary Morrow. Sure enough, there she was, the leading story, a title half English, half German: "The *Herrenvolk*." He purchased a copy and carried it to his hotel room; before undressing he sat in an easy chair and read it through.

Another of those biting satires on the Nazis at home. Again the scene was a *pension* in a provincial town. This time the narrative centered about a peasant girl, the slavey of the establishment; her name was Greta, and Lanny could guess that she might be that kind-hearted girl who had risked her life by stealing out of the Pension Baumgartner and letting Laurel Creston know that the Gestapo were raiding her room and examining the contents of her *Schreibtisch* and her *Gepäck*. But Greta was merely a glass through which we could look into the souls of half a dozen greedy and jealous members of the master race who drove this poor creature about. They were hateful and they were cruel, and each and every one was imbued with the conviction that he or she was the most perfect product yet thrown off by a blindly functioning universe composed of material atoms in perpetual inevitable activity. (There was a professor who explained this while he grabbed the last slice of *Leberwurst* off a platter.)

So Lanny stopped thinking about a prospective museum curator and thought instead about a present fiction writer. Here was the woman who was intellectually his mate, and whom he ought to be thinking about marrying if he was going to marry at all! This woman had the real stuff in her, and she was doing her work in her own way, not asking anybody to teach her or to help her. She hadn't waited for Lanny to reveal to her the fact that the world was out of joint, that it was full of parasites and exploiters, and that some of them had organized a criminal conspiracy against the modern world. This was the woman who deserved the prize—if Lanny was going to distribute prizes—or to *be* one!

So there started the old arguments all over again. If he should ask Laurel Creston to marry him and she consented, where would they live, and how? Where was the place in which Lanny could visit her with the certainty that nobody would recognize him? Where could she live and have any friends who wouldn't be curious about a fashionable gentleman who might or might not be her husband? Here in this vast megalopolis was the best of all places to get lost in. But where would she get her mail and how would she cash her magazine checks? Was it conceivable that the Nazi agents who swarmed all over this city would permit a story like "The *Herrenvolk*" to appear in a popular magazine and not set out to locate the writer and find out where she got her material? Wouldn't they find a way to get her address from the magazine and wouldn't they trail her wherever she went? Of course they would; and of course they would find out who her lover was; and if he turned out to be an intimate friend of *Nummer Eins, Zwei, und Drei*—well, the things that had happened to that man in the back country of Toulon would be child's play compared to what would happen to him the next time he set foot across the borders of Germany.

But even so, before the P.A. went to sleep that night he decided that, since he had spared a full day for Lizbeth Holdenhurst and one for Peggy Remsen, common decency required that he should spare one for Laurel Creston!

XI

Next morning he called her on the telephone. "No names," he said, knowing that she would recognize his voice. "Am I interrupting a writing job?"

"Nothing urgent," she replied.

"Come out and stroll on the avenue—on the same side as your apartment house, going north. Say in an hour." He knew that ladies have to dress.

He did not take his father's car, but a taxi—and not from in front of his hotel. He told the driver where to go, and not too fast. "I am looking for a lady—rather small size." All taxi drivers understand these matters and take an interest in them.

"There she is!" Lanny said. The cab stopped, and she stepped in without a word. "Drive around the block," he said, and made sure that nobody was following them. Then he ordered: "Take us into Central Park." When they were just inside he paid off the driver.

"Forgive this Sherlock Holmes business," he said when they were alone. "I got into serious trouble through being spied upon in France, and there are special reasons why I have to be careful in New York."

"I understand," she said, for she had guessed a lot about him. "I surely do not want to be to blame for anything going wrong."

"I read 'The *Herrenvolk*' last night, and I know that you must be a marked woman. That's why I had to make sure that neither of us was being followed. I have my father's car, and would like to take you for a good long drive, but I was afraid somebody might make note of the license number. If now you don't mind sitting on a bench for a while, I'll bring the car here."

"We had pleasant times sitting on benches in the Tiergarten," she reminded him. "All these subterfuges and stratagems will serve me some day when I want to tell a spy story."

In half an hour Lanny was back with the car. "Where would you like to go?"—and when she replied that she had no choice, he said: "We'll go north and see what we see." They followed the east bank of the Hudson, and when they came to the village of Croton they struck into the hills. There was a great curved dam, part of the city's water system; the road wound past the reservoir and on into the hills. Nature was at her loveliest, and they admired the scenery now and then, talking between times about the world at war.

Lanny told her that he had been back in Hitlerland, and had met the Führer and his Deputy. Laurel was relieved, having feared that her own misadventure in Berchtesgaden might interfere with his work; but he told her no, he had visited Hitler's office and Hess's home, and they had not mentioned her. He gave his interpretation of the flight, the world's number-one mystery, but not saying that he had known about it in advance. He told of the coming attack upon Russia, and they discussed for a while what that was going to mean to Russia, to Britain, and to America.

Then their personal affairs. He reported on Beauty, and Baby Marcel, and Emily and Sophie and the rest of the gang. And then

Green Spring Valley, and how Lizbeth and her mother and father were. Laurel said: "They have invited me there for a couple of weeks this summer, but I'm not sure if I'll take the time off."

"It gets pretty hot in New York in midsummer," he commented.

"I stay in my little apartment under an electric fan. I am doing some . writing that I hate to interrupt. Did you say anything about me to them?"

"No, I thought they might consider it strange that I hadn't mentioned you before."

"It is just as well. They would surely not approve of my getting into trouble in Germany, and probably not of what I am writing. If we ever happen to meet in their presence, let them introduce us and we'll start all over."

"Very well," he replied. "I shall be pleased to meet you."

That bit of gallantry sufficed to pass off a delicate subject. It would have been easy for her to make some remark: "Lizbeth is a very lovely girl, don't you think?" or even: "Has Lizbeth found herself a beau yet?" But no, she accepted his casual remark that her Uncle Reverdy was putting a lot of money into Budd-Erling, and left it to be supposed that that was sufficient reason for Lanny's visits. She carried reticence to an extreme, but he had to admit that he found it convenient.

XII

They had a large subject of conversation in her writings. He did not have to be reticent in regard to the "The *Herrenvolk*," nor would she wish him to be. She told about other sketches she had written or had in mind. Knowing the Nazis as he did, he could suggest details, and was pleased to do so; she asked if she might make notes, and he said: "I shall be proud." She told him that her subject had become popular, and the editors were eagerly buying what she wrote. "The bombs over London have waked them up," he commented.

A still more important revelation: she was trying to get up the courage to spread her wings; she aspired not merely to sketch individual Nazis but to write a novel with a conflict of characters embodying the old and the new Germany. What did he think of the idea? Of course he thought well of it, and she invited him into the machine-shop of a fictionist's mind. He had had the same adventure years ago, when Rick had been a budding playwright; he helped her, as he had helped Rick, by suggesting types and traits. They became excited, and forgot about the landscape, and got lost on country roads, but it didn't matter, for they had no special goal. He was heading toward the east because the Berkshires lay that way, and he knew they were lovely.

They found a roadside inn and had an acceptable lunch; nobody knew them, nobody was concerned about their affairs. How pleasant if life had been all literature; if you could fight your enemies with a pen, and annihilate them with a witty sequence of dialogue! But the enemies wouldn't be satisfied with what William Blake called "mental fight"; they were dropping bombs over London, and *Der Dicke* had made a grinning remark to Lanny: "Tell your friends in New York we're going to have a way to reach them before long."

"What could he mean?" asked the woman. "Just a bluff?"

"It isn't safe to be sure that anything the Germans say is bluff. I know they are working at what is called jet propulsion, that is to say, rockets. That device is just in its infancy, and when it grows up, three thousand miles may be as one."

"But could they aim anything at that distance?"

"Who can guess what modern science may do? They might have some sort of telephoto device, and when the picture of a city comes onto the screen the bomb would be released automatically."

"Are we all going to have to live underground like the gophers?" she asked, and he answered: "Either that, or else we have to abolish competitive commercialism, and build a world on a basis of co-operation."

"Don't let my Uncle Reverdy hear you say that," she warned. "What he calls private enterprise is the only god he has."

"All right," countered Lanny with a grin. "His private enterprise shall be to put Green Spring Valley underground. The new bombs will be no respecters of class."

XIII

Another subject of conversation they would never neglect. Laurel had discovered that she was a medium, and that was the strangest thing in the world to her, and a matter for investigation in her spare time. She had a woman friend, somewhat older than herself, whom she had met in a boardinghouse where she had stayed when she had come to the city in search of a career. This friend came to see her now and then in the evenings, and Laurel went into a trance, and the friend made notes of what happened. How the P.A. would have liked to be there!

The one-time international banker, Otto Kahn, had become Laurel's "steady company" in the spirit world—or the world of the subconscious mind, or whatever you chose to call it. She had never heard his spirit voice, but her friend Agnes had listened to it for long periods and made elaborate notes of what he had said. He presided over the séances with the same easy grace that he had been wont to display at social functions in New York not long before. He had a keen sense of humor, and was immensely amused by the idea of being in the spirit world; of course it couldn't possibly be true—every enlightened person knew it was nonsense—but here he was, and what were they going to make of him? He didn't know how he had come to be here, just as he hadn't known how he had come to be on earth. His body, of course, had been born; but where had his mind come from? And where had it gone to? No place he could describe to anybody; but since he was here, they might as well enjoy the fun.

He knew a lot about what was going on in the world. How would an alert mind like his consent to be left in darkness? He made fun of the banking business, as he had done in real life, even while making millions out of it. He admitted that the game was about played out; he compared it whimsically to "freeze-out" poker; the game went on until one player had got all the chips, and that was the end. He laughed at the idea that the war debts would ever be paid. What with? Even the interest, paid in goods, would wreck the home industry of the country which received them. ·

Agnes had rebuked him: "You talk like a Red"; and he had answered: "I always enjoy their company." Even so, Lanny found it suspicious, for he had the idea that something deep in Laurel Creston's subconscious mind was inventing Otto Hermann Kahn out of a girlhood memory, plus some of Lanny Budd's own ideas. If her conscious mind was impelled to create Gauleiters and their cousins, why might not that same activity be going on in her "memory mind"?

But then, there was the problem of the facts which this spirit mentioned—facts that Laurel was ready to swear she had never heard and couldn't have heard. This "control" informed her with mock solemnity that he was to be treated with respect, for he had been and still was a Commander of the Legion of Honor of France, a Knight of the Order of Charles II of Spain, a Grand Officer of the Order of the Crown of Italy, a Commander of the Order of the Crown of Belgium, and an Officer of the Order of SS. Maurizio e Lazzaro of Italy. "And believe me," he declared, addressing the unknown Agnes Drury, "those things cost more money than you will ever see in all your life."

How had the subconscious mind of Laurel Creston found out all that? Assuredly her conscious mind had never heard of any except the first of these ancient and honorable institutions. Was it likely that the dignified Jewish banker had ever recited the list in the presence of a young niece of one of his clients? Here was one of the most fascinating of life's mysteries, and the two friends talked about it for a long while, exchanging experiences and theories.

With such conversation, and the viewing of a panorama of western Massachusetts, the afternoon slipped away pleasantly; they had dinner at a roadhouse, and got back to the city late at night. After Lanny had left her, as usual, near her apartment house, he drove away, reflecting: "If I should marry her I should have not merely a wife but also a first-class medium." It would be almost bigamy!

17. The Darkest Hour

I

ON THE North Shore of the Sound, half way between Newcastle and New York, the Hansi Robins had their modest home. The flowers were blooming in their garden, and tiny little sparkles were dancing over the blue water. They had two lovely children, one of them dark like the father, the other blond like the mother. They had just come back from a concert tour of the Middle West, where large audiences had applauded them. They had all the money they wanted, and more to give away. They were young—Hansi only thirty-six and Bess thirty-three. They had health, and a great art which they practiced with religious devotion. Everybody thought they were a happy couple, if such existed in the world; but apparently it didn't, for they were a tormented couple.

Lanny went to spend the day with them; they loved him, and made a holiday of his coming. He told about his travels, and a good part of what he had learned. They asked questions about Bienvenu and Wickthorpe, and about the friends they had in common. They asked about the wicked Nazis and the cowardly French collaborators, but they made few comments; they sat tight-lipped and tense, knowing that if they expressed opinions they might get into an argument, and an argument would turn into a quarrel. They lived together under the terms that never, no matter what the circumstances, did they discuss the subjects which were of the greatest interest and importance to them both. They read newspapers and magazines, but rarely spoke of what they read. If one came upon something in the way of news or opinion which seemed to him of significance, he dared not even call the other's attention to it, for that might be taken as a challenge to the other's opinion, and so might lead to controversy. Just wall yourself and your ideas off and live with them alone; when you were with friends, let the friends do the talking!

The only thing that was really safe was music. The notes were

there and offered no chance of disagreement. What would Lanny like
to hear? He asked what they were playing, and Hansi said they had
been featuring Saint-Saëns, especially the *Rondo Capriccioso*. Lanny
said he hadn't heard it for a long time; so they played it, and those wild
skipping notes which make a test of violin technique expressed all the
joy which the Hansibesses had ever felt or imagined in youth and
nature and love. But in the midst of the piece would come little hints
of melancholy, and Hansi's fiddle would wail, saying plainly to his
brother-in-law's ears: "Oh, why, why cannot human beings understand one another, and be tolerant and kind?"

II

There was nothing unique about this family situation; on the contrary, it was typical of what was going on in many homes, and in jour-
nals of opinion in every country where free expression was permitted.
It was a split which ran right down the center of the leftwing movement, and which, in Lanny's opinion, was responsible for the triumph
of Nazi-Fascism. It was a difference of human types, set forth by the
psychologist William James long before this split had occurred. There
are tough-minded people and there are tender-minded people, and
they do not agree about what is to be done in the world.

The tender-minded among the leftwingers called themselves So-
cial-Democrats; they believed in social justice and hoped to get it by
the patient labor of education, through the democratic process of political struggle and popular consent. But the tough-minded said: "It is
a dream and will never come true; the capitalist class will never permit
it to happen." They would cite cases of the politicians who had risen
to power through working-class activity, and then had turned conservative and betrayed their followers: Ramsay MacDonald and Philip
Snowden, Briand and Viviani and Daladier and Laval, the vile Mussolini
—a long list. No, the overthrow of the exploiters was a grim business;
it would have to be done by fighting men, and the dictatorship of the
proletariat was the only way. Prior to 1917 that had been just theory,
evolved by Marx and Lenin; but now the world had seen it in action.
"I have seen the future and it works!" Who now, after nearly a quarter of a century, could doubt that the Soviet Union was the workers'
Fatherland, and that the protection of that Fatherland was the first
duty of every worker's friend?

Such was the faith of Lanny's half-sister, the surprisingly rebellious
daughter of Esther Remsen and Robbie Budd. When the rich go over-
board, politically speaking, they go all the way and with all their
clothes on. They have been used to having what they want, and patience is apt to be the least of their virtues. Bessie Budd had joined the

Communist Party, and she followed the Party line, keeping her eyes fixed upon it so closely that she couldn't even see how it wobbled, and would be greatly irritated if you called her attention to the chart. This was a capitalist war, and the Soviet Union was keeping out of it, and it was the duty of every class-conscious worker in the world to uphold that attitude. Whichever side won, the workers of that side would gain nothing. Efforts to make distinctions between capitalist nations were just propaganda of the ruling classes; in the long run all nations would become the same, for when the workers got strong enough to threaten the power of their masters, the masters would put an end to the so-called "democracy." That was how Fascism, Nazism, Falangism, had come, and it was an inevitable stage in the development of the proletarian revolution.

Hansi took his brother-in-law off and said, with tears in his eyes: "It's utterly hopeless, Lanny. I can't stand it much longer. Bess has got so that she puts words into my mouth; she knows what I am thinking and takes offense at that. It is like walking in a field that is sowed with mines; you never know where to put your foot."

"You must make allowances for her, Hansi. History is being pretty hard on the Communists just now."

"It would be hard on anybody who tried to fit Russian theories into an American mold. Imagine having to believe that there is no difference between the filthy Nazis with their torture camps, and the police and public authorities here in America, who leave Bess free to get up on a public platform and denounce them all she pleases! And when she knows that the Nazis murdered my harmless brother and robbed my father of everything he owned! When she knows that they are torturing and killing millions of good Germans for no crime save that of belonging to my race—and the race of our children—for you know that under the Nazi theories if you are half Jewish you might as well be all Jewish."

"Bess insists that she hates the Nazis just as much as you, Hansi."

"I know. In theory the Communists do; but in practice they save all their denunciation for those who are fighting to end Nazism. To hear Bess talk you would think that Roosevelt, the warmonger, is the most dangerous man in the world."

"Yes, Hansi. I, too, have to live among wrong-headed people, and learn to bite my lips and keep silent."

"But not the person you love most in the world, Lanny!"

"Even that—when I was married to Irma. And I was prepared to stick it out. It was she who broke it up."

"I sometimes wonder if Bess is not planning to break it up, Lanny. She has been so impatient of late. We made a bargain, but she can't stick to it."

"You know the old saying, that the darkest hour is just before dawn; and I've an idea this may apply to your case. Go to your study and fiddle, and leave Bess to me for a while. I have some news for her."

III

There was a summer house on a little point of land facing the water. It had seats inside and out, so that when the weather was cool you could sit in the sunshine and when it was hot you could sit in the shade. On this afternoon of late May the sun was welcome, flinging showers of gold over the blue water. Lanny led his half-sister there, saying that he had family matters to talk to her about.

When Lanny first met his half-sister she had been a child, round-faced, gentle, and trusting, full of the wonder of being alive. Because Lanny, seven years older, came from abroad, and could speak French and German fluently and played piano music tumultuously, she had thought him the most wonderful person in the world. Later, when she had fallen in love with Hansi, Lanny had advised and helped her, and for that she owed him a debt she could never repay. But as the years had passed she had been disappointed in him; she thought him a dilettante, a playboy of the arts, making money out of trading in the labors of Marcel Detaze and other men of genius. She was sure he did not really hold Fascist ideas, but she thought he put on that coloration in order to frequent moneyed circles in Europe. If it had been any other man, she would have considered that this placed him beyond the pale.

For herself Bess had developed two life goals: the first, to become a worthy accompanist for Hansi's virtuosity; and the second, to put an end to the exploitation of man by man everywhere over the earth. In the first effort she had done reasonably well, according to the critics; the general tendency was to patronize a wife, but they didn't say that she spoiled the rendition. In the second goal, alas, it was hard to see that she had made much progress to date, and worry over this had caused her face to become thinner and her expression serious, even stern. She dressed simply, even for the concert stage, and did nothing to attract attention to herself. Her flaxen hair she made into two long braids and wound them about her head like a crown. She received a share of the concert earnings, and the greater part of this she gave to the Party. Lanny had called her a granddaughter of the Puritans; he said it playfully, but he really meant it.

When they were seated beside the summer house, looking over the Sound dotted with white sails, Bess began with her characteristic impatience. "I know what you want to talk to me about, Lanny. My husband is getting ready for war in his soul, and he expects me not to be unhappy about it."

"A lot of people are getting ready for war, and not only in their souls, Bess."

"I know. The whole country is being made over for war, and I hate it, I hate it! I'll never compromise with it!"

"Listen, dear," he said. "I have some information that you ought to possess. But you'll have to make me a promise and take it seriously. It must be for yourself alone. You will not be at liberty to pass it on."

"I, too, have sources of information, Lanny; and it may be that I already know what you are about to tell me."

"I am quite sure you don't. If it isn't new to you, then of course you are free. But if it is new, then you have to wait until you hear it from other sources than me. I am not at liberty to tell you my reasons, but I cannot take the risk of having my sister become the fountainhead of this news—and especially not while I am here or have just been here."

"You sound very mysterious, Lanny. I will promise, of course."

"Very well. The news is that Hitler is going to attack the Soviet Union in a little more than one month."

She stared at him, and the blood was drained out of her face. She clasped her hands before her so tightly that the knuckles were white. "Oh, Lanny! How horrible!" And then: "How do you know that?"

"Hitler told me, and discussed his plans in detail. So did Hess; and Göring practically admitted it. The plans have been made to the last item, and the armies are now being moved to the front."

"But Lanny! What excuse can they have?"

"Hitler doesn't wait for excuses. He takes what he wants."

"But he has a treaty of non-aggression with the Soviet Union!"

"That means nothing to him. That is just to keep the Russians quiet until he is ready. What Hitler has to have is oil; he cannot win this war without it."

"But, Lanny, the man is mad! The Red Army will be a stone wall!"

"That may be, but he does not think so. He expects his Panzer divisions to break through and surround whole corps, whole armies at a time, and chop them to pieces. We shall have to wait and see."

"The Red Army has its plans also, Lanny. I have been told about them. They will fall back and go on fighting—all the way to the Urals, if necessary."

"Certainly I hope so, but also I am afraid. I just don't know what will happen."

The look on his sister's face was that of one enduring physical agony. "Oh, Lanny, what a dreadful thing! All that wonderful country the Soviets have been working to develop! The three five-year plans! The great dams, the bridges, the mines, the factories! Lanny, I have felt that I owned that country and everything in it! That has been my Socialist Fatherland, the workers' homeland!"

"I know, old dear. You will have to wait, and keep up your courage. What has been built once can be rebuilt more easily."

"Look, Lanny! You put a restriction on me, but this is terrible. The Soviets should be warned!"

"You don't have to have that on your conscience. Oumansky has been told."

"Who told him?"

"That I am not free to say, but it was somebody far more credible than you or I. That I can assure you positively."

"And how did he take it?"

"He refused to believe it. That was some two months ago, and I have no doubt that he has changed his mind now. The matter has progressed to a point where all the insiders know it. Armies of several million men cannot be assembled over a front of a thousand miles without spies being able to find it out. You must understand that the front is no longer the German border; it has been advanced everywhere into foreign territory, and the peasants come and go—you can safely count upon it that no German division is shifted without the Red Army staff knowing when and where."

"I suppose that is true, and of course they will have to fight. But the thought of it makes me physically ill."

"You will have to face it sooner or later, old girl; and I think it had better be sooner, on Hansi's account."

IV

Lanny sat for a while looking out over the peaceful strait of water, which makes a playplace as well as a channel of commerce for the great metropolis. He knew well the tumult of fear and grief that must be in this woman's soul. Rightly or wrongly, she had centered her hopes upon the social experiment being tried in the Soviet Union, and it was her fond dream that this might go on uninterrupted while the capitalist world tore itself to shreds. To face this new situation meant turning all her thinking upside down.

At last he said gently: "You know, Bess, you have a great man in your keeping. You have to think not merely of *his* happiness but of the happiness he gives to millions of others."

"Yes, I know that." There was a chastened tone to her voice.

"You remember, some two years ago, when I told you there was a possibility of a deal between Stalin and Hitler, you laughed at me, and even became a little angry. Now there will have to be another change in the Party line, pretty nearly a rightabout face. I thought it might help you if you had time to adjust your mind, and especially your emotions."

"Lanny, we have to stand a lot of ridicule for having a Party line and sticking to it. That is easy enough for café celebrities who earn their sumptuous livings writing for the capitalist press, and owe no allegiance except to their latest wisecrack. But the Communists have been at war ever since the Party was founded; and when you are at war you have to have discipline, you have to obey orders even though you may sometimes think they are wrong."

"I know all about that," he said, for his Uncle Jesse had explained it to him when he was a boy. "If that's the way you feel you can work best, it's all right with me. What I'm concerned to do is to save Hansi's happiness, as well as yours. You're going to have to come around to his point of view, you know."

"I suppose so," she said—very slowly, reluctantly. "I can't make it real to myself."

"Face up to it, like a good soldier. You are going to become a warmonger. You are going to think that Roosevelt is the greatest President this country has ever had. You are going to become a pal and bosom friend of good old Winnie."

"Don't tease me, Lanny! This is a ghastly tragedy."

"Yes, old dear; but we might as well get a little fun out of life as we go along, and the spectacle of the Duke of Marlborough's seventh lineal descendant co-operating wholeheartedly with the shoemaker's Red bandit from Tiflis is one which ought to afford you a smile now and then!"

"Is that really going to happen, Lanny?"

"Understand, all this is under the seal of secrecy. The reason that Hess flew to Britain was to try to persuade Ceddy Wickthorpe and other appeasers to make a deal with him on the basis that Germany was going to conquer Russia and that Britain would stand by and keep hands off."

"That is what I have been dreading, more than anything in this world."

"I know, bless your heart; but it didn't work out according to the class-struggle formula. It appears that your English forebears have certain moral standards, even older than capitalism, and Adi Schicklgruber has failed to conform to them. The British refuse to trust him an inch farther."

"But will they trust Stalin?"

"This much I know: they have Rudi Hess under guard and are pretending to negotiate with him, thus worming out of him all the secrets they can. And meantime, good old Winnie has the speech all written which he intends to deliver the day Hitler moves into Russia—and it's a speech of brotherly welcome to a partner in a righteous war. The

Hess part I really know; and Rick says he has heard about the speech and believes it. Churchill is wearing out the patience of his friends, making them listen to him rehearsing his periods."

"Lanny, that takes a terror out of my soul."

"Yes, dear; and you can get busy and adjust yourself to the brave new world. My suggestion is that you don't tell Hansi what I have told you. Play a little game with him, for the sake of your love; let him think that he is converting you, little by little, and it will make him the happiest man on the Connecticut shore."

Bess couldn't keep from smiling. "Lanny, you are a rascal—the shrewdest one I know, and the dearest."

"Don't jump all at once, you understand, for that might awaken suspicion. Get into an argument and let him convince you, step by step. Admit that there are such things as moral standards, even in the class struggle. Admit that Hitler may be a little bit worse than Roosevelt. Admit that there is more free speech in America than in Nazi-land. Admit that America has to arm in a world where all Europe is an armed camp. Admit that you hope to see Britain win, and next day you are ready to allow that lend-lease may not be the very worst of crimes. Easy does it, little by little—it's like bringing a big transport down on a landing field!"

V

Lanny had asked his half-sister about Uncle Jesse. She had been to a meeting where he had spoken; he was old and withered, but still full of fire. She had had a few minutes' talk with him, and she gave Lanny his address, which was an obscure hotel in the Gramercy Park section, not far from Union Square where the "Commies," as they were called, had their headquarters. When Lanny returned to the city he called the number, and there was the mocking voice which he had not heard for more than a year. Lanny said: "This is your friend from Bienvenu. Take a walk around the park and I'll pick you up." These two were old hands at dodging the cops and their spies.

The little park, which is smaller than a city block, has an iron fence all around it and is reserved, apparently, for the nursemaids and children of the residences which front it. Lanny didn't think the Nazi agents in New York would be keeping track of all the Communists, so he was satisfied to drive once around the park and make sure that his car wasn't being followed. There was the tall erect figure, defying age, and the perfectly bald scalp defying the weather. Lanny drew up, and the lively old man hopped in, and away they went.

"Well, Uncle Jesse! I missed you in Paris, and then in London, I believe."

"You should have come to Moscow. There is the city worth seeing —where the world's decisions are going to be made."

This pair had been arguing with each other for almost a quarter of a century. It was much the same controversy as between Hansi and Bess, but here it was carried on with a sense of humor. Lanny, the tender-minded one, believed, or at any rate hoped, that mankind might be influenced by reason, and that social changes might take place without slaughter and waste; Jesse, the tough-minded one, told the fond dreamer that mankind wasn't made that way, and that history was written in blood, not in ink. Bourgeois politics was a farce—and surely he ought to know, having been in the French Chamber for more than a decade.

If you asked why he had stayed, he would answer: it was a platform from which he had been able to tell the people of France about the crooks who were representing them, and about the great interests which were putting up the money. If you asked about the position of France at present, Uncle Jesse would say it was doubtless worse from the material point of view, but better intellectually, for at least the French people weren't being fooled any more—they knew who their enemies were. If you asked what the French could do about it, you would start an exposition of Marxist-Leninist theories. Lanny didn't ask the question, because he had heard it all before, and had told his propagandist uncle that it was like putting a phonograph record on a machine.

What Lanny talked about was the folks at Bienvenu, and how they were getting along under the Vichy regime; then about Newcastle and the people there. He hadn't mentioned Jesse to Robbie, because Robbie hated and feared his near-brother-in-law like the devil, and had no sense of humor concerning him. It was all right to mention Robbie to Jesse, because Jesse did have a sense of humor, and took Robbie's hatred and fear as a matter of course. "I suppose he is making money by the barrel," the uncle remarked, and the nephew replied: "By the hogshead." He didn't go into details, not wishing to supply material for Jesse's Red speeches in New York.

VI

The Red deputy told about his adventures, getting out of Nazi-occupied France and into Russia. He and his wife had not dared to travel in company, so she had gone to join some relatives who were peasants in Normandy. Presumably she was still there; he had no way of communicating with her, and could only hope that she was not among those who had been "surrendered on demand" to the Nazis. Millions of families had been broken up and scattered like that all over Europe: Poles and Czechs, Belgians and French, and above all Jews and Leftists, who had no idea if they would ever again see their husbands or wives, parents or children. If it is true that misery loves company, Jesse Blackless could have found plenty of it among the refugees right here on Manhattan Island.

He told about his life in the Soviet Union, the land of his dreams, and all the dreams had come true. Everybody was working, and every day's work brought them that much nearer to the goal of Socialism. Everybody was poor by American standards, but that was not because the Soviet system couldn't produce goods; it was because the accursed Nazis made it necessary for everything above a bare subsistence to go into military production. Jesse himself hadn't been idle; he had been taken in as an adviser to the Foreign Office on French affairs, and he had read proofs for the French language edition of *International Literature*. Also, he had done some painting, which the Russians had been generous enough to praise and to exhibit. Their love of art was deeply rooted, and they made the most of every talent, whether manifested by a native child or a Franco-American refugee in his seventies.

In short, here was the same old Uncle Jesse whom Lanny had known for the past twenty-seven years and who hadn't changed a particle, except that he had fewer hairs on his head and many more wrinkles in his lean face and scrawny neck. He was still the incorrigible idealist professing a philosophy of cynical harshness. Human nature was unevolved, and it had to be disciplined and drilled, especially in wartime. The war in which Jesse was interested was not that between capitalist states, which had been going on for centuries and might go on for a thousand years without bringing any progress to humanity. Uncle Jesse's war was the class struggle, which was going to end in the victory of the proletariat of all nations and the establishment of a classless society. Workers of the world, unite; you have nothing to lose but your chains; you have a world to win!

Jesse didn't know whether or not the Nazis were going to attack the Soviet Union. "Such matters are known only to the leaders," he said, "and you don't ask questions, especially if you are a foreigner. But from questions they asked me I gathered that they fear it, and are straining every nerve to prepare themselves."

"I can tell you they had better," responded the P.A. He didn't say: "Hitler told me." He didn't even say: "I know positively." If Constantin Oumansky, the personal friend and confidant of Stalin, had been told, there was no need for Lanny to make himself conspicuous wherever he went. He remarked: "I find it generally taken for granted among the people who are on the inside. It's obvious that Hitler has to have oil, and the Ukraine is the nearest place."

Said the Red painter: "You can tell the S.O.B. that he won't get any oil out of the Ukraine—at least not for several years. The Russians won't leave a peasant's hut or a blade of grass for the enemy. The oil fields will be completely demolished, and every hole filled solid with concrete. The Nazis will have to start all over again."

"That is very important, Uncle Jesse, for it will give Britain time to arm, and this country time to help her."

"It happens that I know about it through friends. The Russians are preparing to move whole factories to the Urals, and even to Siberia, and set them up and have them started again in a few weeks. The procedure has been planned to the smallest detail; everything will be put into trains, not merely machinery but office equipment and records. Hitler will find nothing but empty shells—and these will serve as forts until he blows them to pieces with bombing planes or artillery."

VII

There was so much to talk about when you had several families in common, and so many friends. Jesse wanted to know all about Paris, for which he was homesick. He wanted the news of everybody Lanny had met there, and what they had said. What were the newspapers like, and who was writing for them? What was playing at the theaters, and on the screen? Goebbels stuff, of course! And what were the people saying and thinking? Lanny couldn't tell much about that, but he had a fascinating story about Vichy, which Jesse had visited. In fact, the deputy had been all over France, painting pictures, agitating against the bourgeoisie, or just enjoying life on his small income. He had gone to Paris some fifty years ago, when his grandmother had died and left him the income; he had written such exciting letters that his sister Mabel had not rested until she got a chance to join him. When he saw her, at the age of seventeen, he called her "Beauty," and she had liked that name and kept it; also, she had liked Paris, and had never gone back to a preacher's home.

Jesse wanted to know about her now; and about Sophie and Emily and the other ladies of the Côte d'Azur. Could they get money from America, and was there food enough, and mail, and telephones? Was Beauty still suffering from *embonpoint*, and still talking about dieting? And that marriage of hers, to the funniest thing that had ever come down the pike! The very word "spirituality" was a red rag to this Blackless bull, and the idea of his worldly and fashionable sister taking up with such notions moved him to chuckles. It was like going back to the Baptist parsonage in which she had been born and from which she had been so eager to escape. But Lanny said, no, it wasn't at all like that; Parsifal had no creed and no congregation; he just loved you. The Red deputy said: "I'd as soon be dead as be that bored."

But five minutes later he was telling about the little bootblack whom he had picked up in Union Square, and who came three times a week to have his portrait painted. The smartest little *gamin*, with such shiny black eyes as you never saw, even in a Dago face. The first time he had come the face had been newly scrubbed, and Jesse had had to send him away for a week to get it normal again. He told some of the charming remarks this model had made, and Lanny said: "You see, Uncle Jesse, you love your little Dago exactly the way Parsifal Dingle loves everybody at Bienvenu. The only difference is that you 'class angle' your loves. They have to be proletarians with smudged faces."

The Red deputy's answer was: "Oh, fudge!" He was willing to be sentimental, but not to admit it. And least of all would he have anything to do with religion, the opium of the people. If you really wanted to get a rise out of him, just tell him that Communism was the newest crusading faith of mankind! Compare his dogmatism with that of Paul, the apostle to the gentiles, and his speeches in the Chamber with those of James, the brother of Jesus!

Not even the members of Jesse's own family could escape this evangelical zeal. "All joking aside, Lanny, you really ought to visit the Soviet Union. The things you would see there would be a revelation to you. One of the newer collective farms has all the co-operative services. They even have soda fountains and ice-cream parlors!"

"I'm told they're not welcoming tourists just now, Uncle Jesse."

"Naturally, they have to be careful whom they let in. But you don't have to worry, I can fix it for you any time."

"All right," smiled Lanny. "Maybe I'll take you up on it. But first I'll wait and see how your friend Uncle Joe behaves when his friend Adi Schicklgruber jumps on his neck."

VIII

Lanny went off and wrote a report on the items of importance he had picked up in this conference; and then he called the home of his friend Forrest Quadratt. He was told that the Nazi agent was out at the place in New Jersey where he had set up a publishing business. Lanny phoned there, and drove out on a rainy afternoon. When he arrived he was surprised to have the door opened by Forrest himself; and instead of inviting him in, the suave and soft-voiced agent asked: "Will you take me driving?" Of course Lanny assented, and when they were in the car the other explained: "Some government snoopers have been devoting time to me lately, and I thought it might be better for both if we talked where we couldn't possibly be overheard."

"That is very wise of you, Forrest. I have a lot to tell, and I should hate to have the F.B.I. on my trail."

"They are trying their damnedest to get something on me, but I don't think they're getting very far. Believe me, I keep my tracks covered!"

"I hope you don't talk about *me*, Forrest. It might play the devil with my ability to get passports."

"Trust me; I am an old hand. It seems marvelous, how you have been able to visit Europe, and I'll surely never do anything to imperil it."

Right there Lanny decided that he wouldn't tell this Nazi propagandist about having gone into Germany. If Quadratt had heard of it, all right; but otherwise Lanny would talk about Vichy France, where his mother lived, and London, where his daughter lived. He would talk freely—just enough to inspire a German-American propagandist to reciprocate.

At this time the Nazis and their friends were carrying on a desperate campaign to keep America from giving any more aid to Britain. Their broadcasts were beamed to this country day and night, boasting of the havoc their submarines were wreaking and of the gains their armies were making in the Near East; they had Crete and Libya; they were ready to take Syria and Suez; the British no longer dared use the Canal, but were obliged to route their ships all the way around Africa, a fearful tax. "Beware, beware!" intoned Dr. Goebbels; and of course Quadratt had to write like all the others.

But he was a shrewd fellow, and privately he made it plain that he was not fooling himself. Perhaps being distant from the scene enabled him to see things in better perspective. Anyhow, he admitted: "I am worried, Lanny; this war is dragging on far too long. Almost a year has passed since we entered Paris, and we have made no vital gains since then."

"We have taken the Balkans, and that's a huge territory."

"I know, but it isn't territory that counts."

"It's wheat from Hungary and oil from Rumania—"

"Yes, but not enough."

"It's lumber and minerals, a tremendous mass of resources."

"But England continues to hold out, and to keep the blockade that strangled us last time. And meantime, this country is getting ready for war. We mustn't fool ourselves, Lanny; that is what's happening. We must do something about it!"

"What *can* we do, Forrest?"

It turned out that what the ex-poet wanted was for the son of a great airplane manufacturer to come out publicly against the militarists. Lanny, and Lanny alone, a sort of Superman, was to reverse the trend of American thinking! His friend became eloquent on the subject of the wonders he could achieve by coming out on public platforms, in the style of Congressman Fish and Senator Reynolds and

Charles A. Lindbergh. Announce a crusade, and make a tour of the country! "Incidentally you could make a lot of money, Lanny—much more than by dealing in paintings."

The other had quite a time explaining that he couldn't possibly do it; he was no speaker and would be scared to death on a platform; he would forget every idea he ever had. This attitude of excessive modesty he persisted in maintaining, in spite of all his friend could say. He was not a public man; what talent he had lay in his ability to meet key persons and put key ideas into their minds. The Führer himself had recognized this, and had definitely commissioned Lanny to say certain specific things. Lanny had met Kurt Meissner in Paris and received fresh requests, and he was at this moment on the point of setting out on a trip to comply with them. The marketing of pictures, while profitable, was really a blind for the advancement of National Socialism.

IX

Forrest Quadratt had no authority to compete with that, so he gave up his scheme. He asked about the Hess matter, a subject on which he was completely in the dark. Evidently the pipeline between New York and Berlin worked only in an easterly and not in a reverse direction. Lanny said he was quite sure that Rudi would never have done anything without the Führer's approval; he believed the flight to Scotland was a last effort to make friends with Britain. There must be some big summer campaign about to start; Lanny didn't know, but he thought it might be through Spain.

Quadratt suggested Russia, very warily, and Lanny guessed that he knew more than he was telling. They discussed the prospects, and the ex-poet revealed once more how greatly he was worried; Russia was so vast and so formless, it would be like hitting into a feather pillow. The real reason, as Lanny made sure, was that Quadratt hated Britain so intensely he was reluctant to see any part of Germany's force expended elsewhere. "Britain is the enemy, and until we have conquered her we have done nothing."

Lanny said: "Yes, but you must see that if we conquer Russia this summer, we can turn all our forces westward—something we dare not do at present." So much pleasure it gave him to be a German, and to dispose of the Wehrmacht's vast resources while motoring through a New Jersey rainstorm!

Quadratt talked freely about his own activities: his book-publishing business, his magazine articles, the speeches he wrote for senators and congressmen, the mothers' crusades he was helping to keep alive. The ladies came to Washington and besieged the offices on Capitol Hill;

they screamed and had hysterics in the rotunda—some of them were "nuts," the agent cheerfully admitted, but all were useful. He had done everything he could think of, but he had to admit that he was losing out, alas. The warmongers were on top, with Roosevelt at their head; and how Quadratt hated him, and what language he used!

Lanny went to see Heinsch, and told how Kurt Meissner had been tremendously interested in the idea of getting That Man out of the way, and had promised to pass on the word to the Führer. Perhaps Heinsch had received some message about it. Heinsch said it was difficult to send messages on that subject; they would have to be brought personally by some trusted friend. He said that his own reports were vague; the men who were working on it had their lips tightly buttoned. Lanny couldn't drop any more hints without risk, so he turned the conversation to the Lord of San Simeon, who had recently started a personal column in his chain of papers. Lanny said: "I count that a feather in my cap, for I suggested the idea to him. But doubtless others have done the same."

"I have been disappointed in the column," declared the other. "The old man rambles, and talks about nothing a good part of the time."

"I can't say I agree with you," was Lanny's response. "I have been reading the column whenever I could get hold of it, and I clipped some of those that I liked, because I knew it would please Mr. Hearst to hear what I thought of them. You are a psychologist, and will get the idea."

This was in the steamship office, and Lanny carried a portfolio—he had brought it along for the sake of its effect on Heinsch. He extracted a folder, and from the folder a bunch of marked clippings. "This is the way to coddle the rich," he said, with a grin which his companion shared. "Imagine that we are in San Simeon. This, Mr. Hearst, is my idea of statesmanship." Lanny read:

"Winston Churchill, premier of England, has repeatedly declared that he will agree to no peace except a peace of victory.
"What victory?
"Whose victory?
"England was unable to achieve victory when it had Poland and Norway and Holland and Belgium and France on its side. . . .
"England has been offered a peace which would respect and insure the integrity of the British Empire. Would that not be the equivalent of a peace of victory? Does he mean that there will be no peace until England has conquered the continent of Europe and the Axis powers have bent the knee and bowed the neck to another Versailles treaty?

"Yes, Mr. Hearst, that is my idea of farsightedness, as well as of vigorous writing. It is absolutely correct and according to fact, as I know because it is what the Führer himself told me to say, and what I have been saying to all his friends in France and Britain and the United States for more than a year. And then this about the Japanese:

"We in America brought about the alliance of Japan with Russia, just as England brought about the alliance of Germany with Russia. We limited more and more our trade with Japan. We made it impossible for Japan to get from us the products and materials that were absolutely necessary for her survival. . . . We have only to treat Japan in fair and friendly fashion to establish firm peace between Japan and the United States. We have only to stop sticking our intrusive nose into her affairs to prevent our nose from being tweaked. We have only to mind our own business and keep out of other people's business to be at peace with all the world.

"That, too, I know to be correct, Mr. Hearst, for it is what the Japanese representatives in Lisbon said to me just a few days after your column appeared; only, of course, they used more polite language—they are a people who will never fail in courtesy. I am sure that in future years you will be proud of those utterances. You might put them at the masthead of your papers, for the world to read for the rest of time. Or perhaps you might have them engraved on your mausoleum, like the Gettysburg Address in the Lincoln Memorial."

Concluding this oration, Lanny remarked: "That may be somewhat exaggerated, but you see what I am driving at."

The Nazi replied: "For God's sake, go out to California and try it on him! It might be worth a million dollars!"

X

So much for politics; and there was business, too. Lanny got a stenographer and wrote letters to his various clients, telling what he had and what he had seen and got prices on. He planned a trip to several cities, because in this profession you had to exercise the mysterious attribute called charm; you had to make the wealthy art collector realize that he was performing a public service and was being appreciated by a few discriminating souls. Otherwise he might buy jewels for his wife, or his son might get the money and spend it on chorus girls, or his daughter on a gigolo or night-club band leader! Competition is keen in these modern days, and the world is so full of rackets.

Also, being a man and not a machine, Lanny Budd ate and slept, and went with his colleague Zoltan Kertezsi to look at what the new men were doing with the art of painting. The expressionists, surrealists, and abstractionists were doing their worst to confuse the public, but they left this fastidious pair quite cold. Here and there Lanny ran into some of his old friends, those he had met in the days when he was "Mister Irma Barnes." There were beautiful women among them, and these too had learned to exercise the mysterious attribute called charm. It was no longer necessary for them to wait to be invited; they had their own money, and they asked for what they wanted. Thus, inevitably, Lanny had to think a great deal about women—no matter how firmly he might resolve to think about saving the world from Nazi-Fascism.

He thought about Lizbeth. He knew that he had made her unhappy, and he was sorry about it, and would have liked to run down to Baltimore and tell her that he wasn't what she had imagined him to be, and that the *grand monde* in which she aspired to live was far from being the shining elegant place she imagined it. He thought about Peggy Remsen, and firmly resolved not to make the same mistake with her. More frequently still he thought about Laurel, because she was right here, and all he had to do was to dial her telephone number and say: "Come take a walk." It was a moral struggle to keep his hand from reaching out and performing that easy operation.

He had told himself that he owed her one day, and he had given it. But why should he limit himself in that arbitrary fashion? Why was one day a duty, and two days a sin? She had had a good time and had showed it; and certainly he had. Was she now waiting in the hope that he would call her again before he set off for unknown parts of the world? Was her hand moving toward the telephone with the idea of calling him? Never once during their friendship had she done that— except in Berlin, when her life was in danger. She was an old-fashioned lady, and if a man didn't want her she would never want him. The idea that she might be wanting him at this moment set warm currents running all over him.

Then, too, there was the matter of the novel she was planning. He was interested in it, and couldn't help thinking about it. Ideas would occur to him; wouldn't it be an act of kindness to put them at her disposal? Wouldn't it even be unkind not to do so? He knew Germany so much better than she; he knew every sort of German, Nazi and anti-Nazi and pre-Nazi, from long visits since boyhood. Surely he ought to put that knowledge at her service! At just what point does kindness turn a sin into a duty, or a duty into a sin?

Also, at what point does the exercise of the imagination become a sin? Lanny was going on a tour; and what was to prevent his imagination from taking a lady along? He couldn't introduce her to his exclusive clients; but why couldn't he leave her in a comfortable hotel while he transacted his art business, and then pick her up and speed away to the next city? He knew so many pleasant places in which to sojourn, and so many interesting things to talk about! If Laurel would go along, he might even go as far as California; he couldn't take her to San Simeon—

but what lovely times they could have at those "motels" along the way and in the rest camps of the wonderful national parks!

Yes, there were many ways to have a vacation, and even without going so far! Lanny had sailed a boat along the Côte d'Azur, and also in the Newcastle River and the Sound. He imagined a cabin catboat in some place where nobody knew either a presidential agent or a magazine writer; say in Barnegat Bay—what a series of picnics they could have! Or they might go camping in the Adirondacks; the weather would soon be warm enough, and he had vivid recollections of visits to the elaborate "camp" owned by the Harry Murchisons there. On one of those lonely lakes whose shores were covered with pine and fir trees, they would paddle a canoe and catch trout and take them ashore and fry them with slices of bacon; they might rent what was called an open camp—a shelter facing the lake, and with a log fire blazing in front to keep it warm at night. Lanny lacked practice in chopping logs, but guessed he could manage it if he tried—and certainly he had no trouble being an expert lumberjack in his imagination.

This fact was notable, that on all these tours it was Laurel Creston he took with him. The reason was that he knew so much to talk to her about, whereas when he was with Lizbeth the imaginary conversation died quickly. He could be interested in the daughter of the Holden-hursts only so long as he was in the presence of her young fresh beauty, and his blood told him to take her in his arms. He was interested in Peggy Remsen only so long as he was in an art gallery, or in the home of his stepmother, who wanted him to be "nice" to her. But with Laurel there were always fireworks going off, intellectual skyrockets and verbal Roman candles. His choice of her companionship was a part of that process of natural selection and the survival of the fittest, according to which in the course of some hundreds of millions of years mind has won out over body, brain over brawn.

XI

All this in the realm of the dream; but when it came to reality, what Lanny took was his customary chaste and solitary tour. He spent several days with his friends the Murchisons, and inspected a new stream-lined plant for the swift production of a hundred different kinds of glass; he had not dreamed there were so many. He visited also a plant where alloy steels were turned out; he had learned from his father how many new kinds had been invented, and how many strange purposes they served. He walked the length, about three-quarters of a mile, where an endless sheet of steel was swept along at a speed of some forty miles an hour, but so smoothly on roller bearings that you hardly realized it was moving at all. Everywhere in this vast Allegheny inferno the mills were pouring out products, working in three shifts. Of the depression which had caused such panic among the New Dealers barely three years ago, there was no longer a trace.

And it was the same all over America; the god of war had waved his magic wand over the land. In Cincinnati Lanny's friends the Timmonses proudly showed him a huge hardware plant which was still making hammers and saws, but had been extended overnight to include metal parts for warships and planes and artillery. In Louisville his friends the Petries of "Petries' Peerless" were now distilling alcohol by the tens of thousands of gallons for war purposes. A marvelous sensation to any sort of producer to be turned loose to make all he could; it was a new sort of game, and he played at it as he had played football at college. The money was a matter of no consequence, he would say—though Lanny didn't meet anybody who was refusing it.

So it was in Detroit, and in Chicago, and even in Reubens, Indiana, where old Ezra Hackabury's sons were enlarging a soap plant, for it appeared that the British people had to keep clean, even under the bombs; the Tommies had to shave every morning, even amid the sandstorms of North Africa. Also there were new buildings going up far out in the farmlands, and this was supposed to be the most closely guarded of secrets; but old Ezra said it appeared that if you could make kitchen soap you could also make kinds that went off with a loud bang—preferably not in your kitchen.

You might have thought that all this material activity made a poor time to sell works of art; but Lanny found it otherwise. All these people were feeling good; they were sitting on the top of the world, and without any of the discomfort and danger. Old masters? Sure thing! If they are really good, they belong over here. Lanny had only to mention the fact that a Corot, superior to any in the Taft collection, or great examples by Constable and Bonington were now available in England. If you knew several millionaires, you played one against another. Alonzo Timmons, one of good old Sophie's many nephews, had built a wing of his country home just to hang paintings in, and he took his aunt's word that Lanny Budd was the fellow to fill the blank spaces. Lanny told him about Ezra Hackabury, thus playing the state of Indiana against the state of Ohio.

The old soapman, to whom Lanny was still the gay and eager little boy who had sailed on the *Bluebird*, had decided that he wanted all the paintings that Marcel had made on board the yacht and all that he had painted later as a result of the trip. That was a way to bring back old times, and to leave something for people to remember you by. Much better than a lot of jealous and quarreling inlaws! The soapman wanted to spend the money quickly, before the inlaws got wind of it.

Lanny had brought a complete set of photographs, with the prices on the backs; Ezra marked those he wanted, and it figured up to something like two hundred thousand dollars. Without batting an eyelid he wrote a check for the amount, dating it three days ahead so he could have time to market some securities and have the money in the bank. Lanny was to employ Zoltan Kertezsi to travel to Baltimore and get the right paintings out of the vault and have them shipped; meantime Ezra would start the building of a proper fireproof gallery in the center of the town. "Imagine putting Reubens, Indiana, on the map!" chuckled the old codger. Lanny thought he got more fun out of disappointing his sons' wives than he did out of looking at Marcel's paintings of Greek and North African ruins.

XII

So passed very pleasantly the early weeks of June. Morning and afternoon Lanny read the newspapers of the town in which he found himself; they were pretty much alike, for their foreign news came from central agencies, and the only difference was in what the local editors chose to headline. Also there was the radio, the same in its main features all over the country. Day and night he turned the dials, and held his breath as the news period began.

On the evening of Saturday the 21st of June, he attended a dinner-dance at the mansion of old Mrs. Fotheringay on the North Shore Drive of Chicago. The affair was in honor of a visiting niece; dinner was at eight-thirty and dancing began two hours later. At one in the morning Lanny strolled into one of the rooms where a large group of the older people were gathered about a radio "console." They were getting the news which Lanny had been expecting for the past three months. The German Armies were invading Russia, all the way from the Baltic to the Black Sea.

Interesting indeed to see and hear the reaction of this fashionable company! Here was the stronghold of isolationism, within the very shadow of the *Tribune* tower, where for more than two decades there had been a veritable arsenal of machine guns, awaiting an expected attack by the Reds. Now these gloating ladies and gentlemen seemed to have but one thought—that the news would destroy at one blow the wicked cause of their enemies, the "interventionists." Now everybody would believe in Hitler, and help him! Now even Britain would have to make peace with him! Now it was unthinkable that any American would wish to send arms to the Führer's enemies!

Later that same morning Lanny was motoring eastward, and over the radio in his car he listened to the rolling periods which "good old Winnie" had been rehearsing before his friends for the past couple of months. A speech in which he pledged full and complete solidarity with Stalin! Lanny would have given a lot to see the faces of the Chicago ladies and gentlemen. He would have liked to be with Hansi and Bess, with Rick, with Raoul, with Bernhardt Monck; but not with the Führer, not with fat Hermann, not with the grim Rudi, wherever the British were putting him up!

To himself Lanny said: "The Nazis have committed suicide!"

XIII

On these tours the P.A. made it a practice to keep in touch with Newcastle. His mail came to Robbie's office, and Robbie would forward it by air. It was while Lanny was in Cleveland, finishing up a deal, that the father phoned him and said: "There was a call for you from Washington. The man said 'government business,' but wouldn't give his name. I promised to tell you to be in your hotel at two this afternoon." Robbie asked no questions, having long ago learned to keep his own secrets and let others keep theirs.

At the hour appointed Lanny was in his hotel room, and there came a voice which he had not heard for quite a while. "This is your old employer from Paris. No names, please."

"Well, I'll be switched!" said Lanny. "How is the world treating you?"

"Keeping me much too busy. It is a cause of stomach ulcers. I want to see you about a matter of number-one importance. How soon could you meet me in New York?"

"I could fly, if necessary. I have a car belonging to my father, but he could send a man for it."

"How soon if you drive?"

Lanny figured quickly. "I could do it in a little less then twelve hours, starting in five or ten minutes."

"Drive until midnight, then get your sleep, and finish in the morning. You remember the hotel in New York where I met you and your father?"

"I do."

"I'll expect you there tomorrow forenoon. When you are an hour or two from New York, phone and leave word for me."

"O.K.," said Lanny.

"And take care of yourself on the way. I have something that will interest you very much, I am guessing."

"O.K.," repeated Lanny, and hung up.

He phoned the hotel desk to have his car at the door; he phoned a client to say that he had to leave unexpectedly; he put his belongings into his bags, paid his hotel bill, stepped into the car, and sped away eastward on Euclid Avenue, which had once been the fashionable boulevard of the city, and now, like Fifth Avenue in New York, had been encroached upon by business. He drove as fast as the law allowed; and while he drove he thought about what lay ahead of him.

A call from Charlie Alston, the one-time "barb" in Robbie Budd's class at Yale, was the same thing as a call from F.D.R.—even more so, because F.D. liked to gossip and tell stories, whereas Professor Alston, as Lanny called him, never summoned anybody unless it was in very truth a "number-one matter." Lanny's "old employer in Paris" had been at that time a humble geographer on President Wilson's large staff at the Peace Conference; but in the past twenty-two years he had become, first a close friend and adviser to the Governor of New York State, then a member of the "brain trust" which that Governor brought with him to Washington.

In short, he was one of those New Deal college professors whom Robbie Budd had so abhorred and feared, until a couple of years ago, when Charlie had summoned him to New York and "put him on the dole," as Robbie phrased it. All the way on that drive, the son of Budd-Erling was wondering: Was he, too, going to be ordered to take a job? And would he be paid out of the Fish Hatcheries Fund, or the Tennessee Valley Authority, or would it be by the Librarian of Congress?

18. A Furnace for Your Foe

I

NO MORE than two years had passed since Lanny had last seen Professor Alston, but they had been hard and wearing years for this political man. It is no job to be taken lightly—one in which you have a hundred million masters, and a large percentage of them hating you actively, watching day and night to find something wrong that you are doing. The hair of this slender little man had grown grayer and thinner, and there were many more lines in his face. Yet the eyes behind the gold spectacles still had their twinkle of fun, and the kindness in the voice never failed, except when he was talking about the Nazis and their American abettors.

Of Lanny Budd he had only the most agreeable memories. The grandson of Budd Gunmakers had been the perfect model of a

secretary-translator at a world Peace Conference. He had been completely wrapped up in his job, and had never once had to be rebuked
for neglect of duties. He had been entrusted with many secrets of state,
and though he had met reporters frequently, no one ever wormed
anything out of him, unless it was something that Alston wanted
wormed out at that precise hour. In fact, this socially trained secretary
had become so expert that he had known when his employer wanted a
"leak" to occur, and could spare the employer the embarrassment of
having to say so. The only blunder Lanny had committed was one of
which the geographer had never got a hint—his helping Kurt Meissner
in Paris to escape from the French police. In view of what Kurt had
since become and what he was now doing, Lanny knew that this had
been a serious blunder; however, Alston would have excused it, because he, too, believed in friendship, and had known what it was to
trust a friend too long.

Here they were, after exactly twenty-two years, and they were still
master and loyal servant; or so Lanny felt in his heart, and so he
guessed it was going to be in action. The New Deal "fixer," as was his
custom, wasted little time on preliminaries. He said: "You got some
sleep?" and then: "You feel fit?" Lanny, smiling, replied: "Go to it!"
and the other said:

"What I am about to entrust to you is beyond any question the most
important secret in the modern world. The fate of the war and of the
whole future may depend upon it. You know that I don't use words
lightly; I will add that the President agrees with me and that the words
are his as well as mine. I was with him yesterday morning, and suggested you as the man to receive the offer. If you accept, you will still
be working for F.D. It is a proposition for you to go into Germany
again and bring out certain information. You will need considerable
training before you go, in order to understand the information and to
be able to remember it, since not a word of it may be put on paper. The
man in Germany from whom you will get the information is one whom
we have every reason to trust, and I do not think you will run any
greater risk than you have been running in the past; but there is always
the chance of a slip, and nobody can guarantee safety in such work.
That you will understand without my telling you."

"Of course, Professor Alston." Lanny gave a sort of gulp inside him,
remembering things that had happened to him in Germany, to say
nothing of France and Spain; things that this quiet little "fixer" had no
idea of. Lanny hadn't enjoyed them then, and didn't enjoy remembering them ever.

"Let me make it plain—you don't have to accept this commission. I
don't put the slightest pressure upon you. The Governor agrees with
me that what you have done for him is plenty; and if you have other

things that you want to do, you have only to say so. All I tell you is that you may have a chance to do more than any other one man to help in knocking out the Nazi-Fascists. I don't say it will work out—nobody on earth can say that—but I say there is a first-class chance."

"That is enough, Professor Alston." Lanny said it quickly. Perhaps he was afraid that if he hesitated at all he might hesitate too long.

"Think it over and be sure," said the tempter.

"If it was anybody but you and the Governor, I might want time, because it would seem too much to be true. But I know you well enough, and don't have to delay. I am ready for the job. I'll do my best."

II

Before Alston had a chance to continue, Lanny got up and opened the door of the suite and looked outside into the passage. Then he looked about the room. There were doors which might lead into closets or into an adjoining suite. Lanny said: "Have you searched this place thoroughly?" When his friend replied in the affirmative, Lanny asked: "Do you mind if I turn on the tap in the bathtub?" He turned the cold water at full force, without the stopper in the tub. "That is a trick my father taught me," he said. "It makes things a little less easy for a keyhole listener."

Alston drew his chair close to Lanny's and began, in a low voice: "A half-dozen trusted men share this secret, and others know only parts. You will know only such parts as are necessary to your own job. Every person who is entrusted with even the smallest detail has had to give his word of honor never to speak of it to anybody else, except to others who know, and then nothing except what is necessary to the work they are doing in common. It is absolutely the most hush-hush matter in the whole world."

"I understand, Professor. You have my word of honor."

"Not to your father, not to your mother, not to your dearest friend, not to the woman you love. Tell me, Lanny, have you married again?"

"No."

"Are you in love?"

Lanny couldn't keep from smiling. "I'm in the uncomfortable position of not being sure which of two women I should like to love; and I can't love either, because I couldn't explain my job to them."

"Well, leave it that way for the present. Have you anything of your own that has to be done?"

"A couple of picture deals to be closed, but that can be attended to by mail."

"Keep your picture business going, because it is an essential camouflage. The point is, are you free to go and stay for a while in a place I name, and then to go into Germany as you did before?"

"The first part is O.K., but getting into Germany may not be so easy. It was Rudolf Hess who invited me last time. I don't suppose anybody is blaming me for what has happened to him—I certainly made it plain to him that I was afraid of his scheme. But still, I can't be sure how matters will stand. If the Wehrmacht goes on advancing into Russia as it is now, the Number One will be feeling fine; but nobody can guarantee how it will be in a month or two. My best bet is Göring, who always likes to talk about paintings, no matter what is happening to his Luftwaffe. He has promised to put me at the head of his art museum which is quite literally to end all other museums in Europe."

"And now tell me this: do you know anything about modern physics?"

"I have read a little of Jeans and Eddington—just enough to know that the subject is a thousand miles above my head."

"That's just about my measurement, too," said the ex-geographer; "but still I have to help with this project. In the present emergency we have to crowd whole graduate and postgraduate courses into a few weeks. So you will have to boost yourself up that thousand miles. When some very learned physicist gives you a formula, it must make sense to you, and you must be able to learn it and repeat it a week or two later. This secret of all secrets—"

Lanny broke in. "Listen, Professor—I don't feel happy talking in a hotel room. It is something I have never done if I could help it. There are such tricky listening devices nowadays, and you are a person whom everybody knows. I have a car, and I take the trouble to make certain that nobody has installed any recording device in the trunk. Motoring is the one way to talk with real security. We can drive as long as we please in Central Park; or we can go out into the country, have lunch in some small place where nobody knows us, and come back whenever you say."

The mousy little man stood up. "All right. Let's go!"

"I'll go first," said Lanny. "Give me five minutes to get the car. Then you walk north on the east side of Park Avenue and I'll slide by and pick you up."

III

"Out of the city," said Alston; so they proceeded north, and across one of the bridges into Westchester County. The sound of a purring motor is much better than water in a bathtub for the covering of a human voice, so now they could talk freely about the secret of all secrets. "Do you know any higher mathematics?" inquired the ex-geographer, and Lanny replied: "It seemed frightfully high to me at

St. Thomas's Academy, but it was only algebra and trigonometry. Today I'm sure I couldn't solve the most elementary problem."

"This time you will begin at the top. You are going to Princeton and cram the mathematical formulas and experimental techniques of nuclear physics. You will have a competent teacher, and your work will be under the personal direction of Professor Einstein."

"Oh, my God!" exclaimed the P.A.

"It sounds rather mad, but this is the situation we face: there are many physicists who know the subject, but they are known to be physicists and they don't happen to have access to Nazi Germany at war. We can't advertise for such a man, we can't even talk about the problem except among a very few persons. The only solution we could think of was to pick out a man who does have access to Germany and then make a physicist out of him."

"But, Professor, an utter ignoramus, an illiterate in the subject—and a man who has never applied himself to study!"

"You are surely wrong about that, Lanny. I saw you apply yourself to the world situation in 1919, and work at it faithfully for six months. Also, I am sure you didn't learn to play the piano as you do without applying yourself."

"Yes, but those were things that I loved!"

"All right; you will learn to love the nucleus of the atom, because you will know that it may afford you the means of blowing Nazi-Fascism off the face of the earth."

"Of course, if you put it that way, I'll work like a man possessed; but I can't promise that I'll be anything but a dud."

"This is the situation, Lanny. We have in Germany one absolutely priceless man: a physicist, one of the greatest in the world, who is believed to be a loyal Nazi and is trusted as such, but who is really an anti-Nazi. This man is working in the very heart of the most important war project now known to science. It is a race between the Germans and Italians on the one side, and the British and ourselves on the other. Whichever side wins this race has won the war. I am not speaking loosely, but precisely; whoever solves first the laboratory and then the production problem will wipe the other off the map of the world. This man I speak of is willing to tell us everything the Germans have learned and are doing on the project; the only difficulty is how to contact him. If he puts it on paper the formulas are instantly recognizable and point directly to him, with only two or three colleagues as alternative possibilities. If he entrusts it to a messenger in Germany, there is the problem of how that messenger is to get out, and the possibility that he might prove to be a Nazi agent. You must get it clear that the Nazis realize the importance of this secret exactly as we do and are taking every precaution they can think of."

"Have you any idea how I am to meet this man—assuming that I get there?"

"That problem is one which will tax all the ingenuity you possess. But first you have to prepare yourself, so as to be able to understand what is being told to you. It is conceivable that a man with a remarkable verbal memory might learn mathematical formulas and repeat them *ad litteram*, but the slightest error might be ruinous to the whole thing, and anyhow, there are questions you will have to ask, and you must understand the answers so as to know what additional questions may be necessary. There seems no way out of it but for you to cram like the devil."

"You've got me badly scared, Professor. All I can say is, I'll do my best. I have read somewhere that Einstein said there were only half a dozen men in the world who understood his relativity theory."

"That was some time ago, and a lot of men have been studying it since. But you don't have anything to do with that; what you have to understand are certain definite problems and their suggested solutions. You will be told exactly what you need to learn, and there will be somebody to answer your questions."

"Well, that sounds a little better," sighed this suddenly grown-up playboy.

I V

Alston talked for a while about the practical aspects of his proposal. "You will go to Princeton, prepared to live for a month or two. Professor Einstein will talk with you and assign somebody to take charge of your studies. Your mode of living will be arranged. It will be better for you not to take any part in social life—you won't have time, and you don't want to attract attention. I suggest that you do not speak about your past life at all. You know French and German, which will be useful; but don't mention how you came to know them, or the fact that you have been in Germany, or know any of the Nazis."

"All that is reasonable enough, and I'll conform to it gladly. But I am troubled about the idea of a place like Princeton, which is so well identified with Einstein, and probably with this project. Have you considered the possibility that the Nazis may be watching the laboratory, or wherever it is that he works?"

"His work is entirely theoretical, and his office is in the Institute for Advanced Study. You are not to be seen there. I have an appointment late this afternoon with a gentleman of Princeton who has an elaborate estate, and I am going to ask him to take care of you. He is an art patron, and you may possibly have heard of him—Mr. Alonzo Curtice."

"I know him by reputation."

"My idea is for you to go there, ostensibly to assist in preparing a catalog of his collection. No doubt he has some cottage or retired place which he can assign to you. His servants will attend to commissions for you, and it will be better if you do not go off the estate. As to your mail—how do you get it at present?"

"It comes in my father's care."

"Then you might ask your father to put it in a second envelope and address it to Mr. Curtice. I suppose it will be all right to tell your father that you are doing a cataloging job?"

"Certainly, if the gentleman is willing to be put to all this trouble."

"In times like these, Lanny, we put things up to people in such a way that they cannot refuse; at least, so far we have never encountered a refusal. You must understand that I am no longer the crackpot college professor, the boondoggler squandering public funds and undermining the American business system. I am a man who is helping to save the Royal Navy and the Royal Air Force—and I deal with persons who consider that a worth-while enterprise."

V

They stopped at a roadside place and had a light lunch, and then turned back toward the city. Having settled the practical details and made certain that they were acceptable, Alston talked for a while about the man who was to take charge of Lanny's mind.

"Albert Einstein represents one of Hitler's worst blunders—perhaps it may turn out to be a greater blunder even than the invasion of Russia. Einstein was deeply absorbed in his duties as director of the Kaiser Wilhelm Physical Institute; but, since he is a Jew, Hitler deprived him of his post and thus gave him to America. It appears to be a stroke of divine justice that this would-be pacifist is the man who, in the course of keeping watch over the progress of physical science, made note of the fact that two professors in a certain laboratory were on the verge of an achievement of enormous importance in military affairs. He wrote a letter to the President, pointing out that these men ought to have the immediate and full support of the government in their work. He sent this letter to F.D. by a friend; and it is part of the kindness of fate, or perhaps of Providence, that we have at the head of our government a man who understands the importance of scientific knowledge, and who saw to it that the advice of Einstein was immediately heeded."

"Oh, lovely!" exclaimed Lanny. "If we had had the making of world events we could not have devised anything more pleasing to the moral sense."

"It has now come about that a dozen of our greatest laboratories are working day and night on this project, and there is a supervising group, known as the Advisory Committee on Uranium. Does that suggest anything to you?"

"I've been trying to guess what I am getting in for, and it occurred to me that it must be what is known as splitting the atom."

"That is the point. Do you know much about it?"

"Only what I have read in the papers."

"You have noticed, perhaps, that you haven't read anything for some time. The subject has dived underground. But those who are in on the secret know that both sides in this war are straining every resource they possess. Among ourselves we speak of it as 'the battle of the atom.'"

"Tell me what you can about it, so that I may not be an utter ignoramus when I meet this learned man."

"When we are dealing with a man like Einstein, the difference between what you know and what I know is hardly noticeable. However, I have had to learn the A-B-C's and I can tell you that much. You are familiar with Einstein's discovery that mass and energy are the same?"

"I have read the statement."

"He worked it out mathematically, as a matter of pure theory, and it was left for the physicists to substantiate it, which they have done. All forms of matter, which appear so solid to us, are manifestations of electrical force. Einstein's formula reads $E = mc^2$, which tells us that the energy locked up in matter is equal to its mass multiplied by the square of the speed of light. The speed of light being 186,000 miles per second, you multiply that figure by itself and have something close to thirty-five billions. Thus it appears that we have in the atom a degree of energy almost beyond comprehension; wholly outside and beyond the scale with which we usually deal, of coal and oil and water power."

Lanny said: "I am familiar with the idea, but vaguely."

"We are approaching a time when it will no longer be vague. I stopped trying to learn the figures because they increase every time I talk with one of the uranium men. It appears that the heavy atoms are the easiest to split and the heaviest of all is this rare metal, uranium, which we get from pitchblende ore. The energy of the atom is contained in the center, which is called the nucleus, and when the nucleus is split, a part of the energy is released; but until lately the amount of energy expended to split the nucleus is greater than the energy obtained. What I have called the great secret is the fact that laboratory workers have found a way to release two hundred million electron volts of energy by the expenditure of one electron volt."

"That certainly sounds like a good business deal," commented the listener.

"It is less simple than it sounds, because laboratory conditions cannot always be reproduced outside, and as the scale of the work increases so do the difficulties and dangers. These are the problems upon which our best scientific brains are working, and they will be explained to you in detail by someone who really understands them. Give him your best attention, and while you listen bear in mind that upon your understanding may depend the question whether we shall wipe out Berlin or whether Berlin shall wipe out New York."

"God help us!" said Lanny Budd. "And especially me!"

VI

They came back to the great city, which Lanny saw with new eyes; a scene of ruin and desolation such as he had observed in London, only thousands of times greater. He delivered Alston to the neighborhood of Alston's hotel, and was told: "If Mr. Curtice comes on time, I'll be ready to phone you at your hotel in about an hour."

Lanny replied: "Meantime I'll visit a bookstore and see what I can find on the atom."

This he did, and when his telephone rang he had already learned the difference between electrons and protons and deuterons and neutrons, and was beginning to tear his hair over some of the formulas. Alston said: "The matter has been arranged, and our friend is telephoning to his home to have everything made ready for you. How soon can you leave?"

Lanny replied: "In fifteen minutes."

Two hours later he drove his car past the gates of one of those dignified estates which tell you that the owner and his father and his grandfather before him had money. It was an old-fashioned two-story house, painted white, with tall columns going up to the height of the roof; wings had been added, and one of these, as Lanny discovered, was the art gallery. There were old shade trees, and lawns which made him think of England; peacocks, some of them snow-white, and lavender-gray lyre birds strutted on them, and there was an enclosure with deer ready to nibble bread or lumps of sugar out of your hand. In short, it was an entirely suitable place for an art expert making a catalog.

A polite steward received the visitor and showed him to a little cottage which would be his home. It was remote enough so that he wouldn't be in anybody's way; apparently someone had been moved out at two hours' notice, for not all the bureau drawers were yet emptied. Remembering his camouflage, he asked how soon he could view the paintings; he was taken there at once, and spent a pleasant hour studying the best collection of English portraits he had ever seen. One could not have lived in the same house with these august and stately ladies and gentlemen and not have proper manners. When his hostess came to join him, Lanny was not surprised that she looked and acted as if she had stepped out of a large gold frame. In the two months that Lanny spent in this gray-haired lady's home he never saw her looking otherwise, and she never asked him a single question about himself, his past life, his family, his friends, or what he was really doing over there in the cottage.

The master of the estate returned from New York the next day. He was somewhat shorter than his wife, dapper and cheerful. He was an investment banker, now semi-retired, as he phrased it. He wore a white mustache, and his manners reminded Lanny of Otto Kahn in the spirit world. But Mr. Curtice was pure "Aryan," from a long way back. He must have recognized Lanny as a fellow-member of the ruling caste. What he thought about the invasion of his ultra-fashionable university by Jewish refugees from abroad was a subject that he never referred to. The institution, like most in the country, had gone in heavily for war work, and about this the visitor heard much.

Princeton is an old town, English in its culture and sympathies. Lanny might have met agreeable company here, but that wasn't in the cards; his breakfast and lunch were brought to him at the cottage and he dined with the family only when there were no other guests. Art books and catalogs from the library were brought to him and he spread them ostentatiously on his work table; but they were not what he worked at. There was a radio set in the living-room, and a New York paper was brought with his breakfast each day. The colored servant who brought it asked for a list of his wants, and whatever they were, the articles appeared with the lunch.

In a period of two months Lanny went off the estate only once; he got his exercise walking on the extensive grounds, generally after dark, and most of that time he was repeating atomic formulas in his mind. It was the life of a monk—which is what many of the worshipers of scientific truth are. They are permitted to marry, but often their wives are worshipers also, and work side by side with them in the laboratories, sharing the thrills of the discovery of truth, perhaps the greatest which can come to man or woman. There are no more continents or islands left for a Columbus or a Captain Cook, but there are universes of the infinitely vast and others of the infinitely small; also, as Lanny Budd knew well, there are universes inside the mind of man, waiting for generations of explorers.

VII

Next morning came one of the great adventures of a P.A.'s life—or so it seemed to him. Soon after he had finished breakfast there came a light tap on the cottage door and when he opened it there was an old gentleman. He was shortish and slightly plump, and had a round cherub's face which all the world knew and either loved or hated. He had a gray mustache and a generous thatch of gray hair, and apparently the latter was difficult to subdue so he just let it alone. He wore no hat, and his clothing consisted of a white shirt open at the throat and a pair of trousers which bore no signs of a pressing iron. He was one of the sights of this decidedly prim town and he must have known it; he watched it through a pair of twinkling brown eyes, and greeted it with the happiest and most charming smile that anybody on earth could imagine.

"Mr. Budd?" he inquired, and then: "Good morning. I am Professor Einstein."

"Oh, come in, Professor!" exclaimed Lanny. He was overwhelmed by the honor, and said so, whereupon the great man replied: "I am the one to say that, for they tell me you have the courage to go back into Nazi Germany, which is something I could never do. Both our services are needed, so we shall be friends."

"Thank you, with all my heart, Professor."

"*Ja wohl*—to work! I am going to try, in the fewest words, to give you an outline of the problem we are seeking to solve. It is too bad that we have to use these giant forces to destroy life instead of to build it up; but that has often been the way in the history of science, and it is tragically so now. We confront a situation where Germany will get the atomic bomb if we do not. That is our only possible justification. I take it we agree that the National-Socialist terror has to be put down, and that everything else has to wait upon that."

"Certainly, Professor."

"I want to begin at the beginning, and I do not want to speak one word that you do not understand. Will you promise to interrupt me the moment I say anything that is not perfectly clear to you?"

"Yes, Professor."

"When I was a youth, my teachers were all certain that the atom was a tiny lump of solid material, and that nobody could possibly divide it —I was rebuked for suggesting such an idea. Today we know that the atom, so small that its nucleus is estimated at two and one-half trillionths of an inch, is a miniature solar system, reproducing the phenomena and obeying the laws which govern all the universe. We have, of course, never seen an atom, or any of its parts; we have only seen their effects. We do not know whether they are really particles, or waves, or what; we can only call them manifestations of energy, apparently electrical. Around the nucleus revolves a cloud of electrons, and between electrons and nucleus appears to be empty space, just as in our solar system. The number of the electrons determines what we call the atomic number, and this varies from hydrogen, the lightest of all substances, which has one electron, to uranium, the heaviest, which has ninety-two. You will not need to learn the table, because you will be dealing for the most part only with uranium. That will be a relief to you, I am sure."

"Yes, indeed, Professor," said Lanny, as humble as any schoolboy. At the same time he smiled, for it was not easy to resist the elderly cherub's warm kindness.

VIII

This patient great man went on to explain the elementary principles of his science. Lanny thought, it was as if Shakespeare were teaching the alphabet to a child. But the pupil didn't have time to worry about it, being too busy trying to make sure that he understood every one of the twenty-six letters. He learned how it had been found possible to detach portions of the atomic nucleus by bombarding it with particles; great machines called cyclotrons had been built for this purpose, and a long series of experiments had been conducted. A particle of the nucleus, called the neutron, had been discovered which, having no electrical charge, could slip through the defenses of the nucleus. With these it had been found possible to bombard the uranium atom and tear it apart.

"So," said Einstein, "in the last couple of years we have been able to think of making some practical use of this most tremendous of all forces. We are dealing with an extremely complex situation. There are species of atoms having the same atomic numbers, but different mass numbers, and these we call isotopes; the uranium isotopes are still uranium, but different in mass. One is U-238, so named because its nucleus contains 92 protons and 146 neutrons. Another has lost 3 neutrons, and so we call it U-235. This is highly unstable, that is, easy to set off; on the other hand, U-238 refuses to go off, and it puts out the fire, so to speak. Thus we are in the position of a man driving an automobile; we have the fuel which makes the car go and we have the brakes which stop it; the problem is to learn how to use each in the right quantities and at the right time. But instead of having a tankful of gasoline which may burn up the car, we here have forces so terrible that a handful might blow up a city. When a nucleus of U-235 breaks up, it throws off one or more neutrons, and these, when slowed down, break up new U-235 nuclei, and so on. This is what we call a 'chain reaction' and you can see how dangerous it might become; we might be in the position of the sorcerer's apprentice in Goethe's poem, who commanded the imps to fill the bathtub and then couldn't remember the formula to make them stop."

Lanny ventured: "Might it not be that we could set all the atoms in the world to going at once?"

"Theoretically, yes; but it is enough to make sure that we do not explode the laboratory and the investigators."

"So far I think I understand, sir. But Professor Alston mentioned a new element, plutonium."

"We have succeeded in making various artificial elements. This one we named neptunium; then, very soon, we discovered that it changed into another element, which we called plutonium. This is 'fissionable,' as we say, meaning that it can be exploded. Not being an isotope of uranium, it can be separated from uranium by chemical means. We are now seeking what we call a 'moderator,' some substance with which we can surround plutonium, and which will slow down the neutrons to speeds at which they are more likely to cause fission. We have reason to think that the Germans are using heavy water for this purpose. Do you know what heavy water is?"

"I believe I have read that it is water whose molecule contains a heavier hydrogen isotope than normal water."

"It is called deuterium oxide. One of the things our British friends would like very much to know is where the Germans are making this heavy water, so that they could bomb the plant; also, of course, the place where their atomic work is being done. It is desired to know the techniques they are employing, and what progress they have made; whether they are still in the laboratory stage, as we are, or whether they have reached the production stage. Every smallest indication is of importance, because it will help to give us our time scale: how many weeks or months or years we may expect before an atomic bomb is carried to New York by a rocket, or by a plane launched from a submarine near by."

"I understand that part, Professor," said the humble neophyte, "and I can only assure you that I will study as hard as I can and do my best."

"Let us make a little test of your aptitude. I should like you now to recite to me the lecture you have just heard."

"Oh, Professor!" exclaimed Lanny, quailing; then, with the tact he had learned among the diplomats: "It will hardly be a test, because Professor Alston has already given me an outline, and I have been dipping into books last night and this morning."

"Never mind that," said the teacher, whose appearance of simplicity possibly was deceptive. "Just repeat to me everything you can remember of the words I have spoken to you."

Lanny began, and the patient great man listened attentively. Lanny did well, because he had really put his mind on it. He overlooked a few details, but when the teacher asked about these he was able to answer. To his relief Einstein said: "You have a passing mark. If you study conscientiously you should be able to understand the questions our scientists wish to have answered, and to remember the answers correctly."

"I promise to do my very utmost, Professor."

"I have asked one of my assistants, Dr. Braunschweig, to come to you this morning, and he is about due. He is in touch with this uranium work, and will give you confidential material to study; he will answer your questions and keep track of your progress day by day. Hereafter it will be better if he comes in the evening, so as to attract less attention."

"Thank you, Professor."

"And now, you tell me something, Herr Budd."

"If I can, sir."

"What do you think are the chances of the Russians being able to hold out?"

IX

Dr. Braunschweig was another of Adolf Hitler's gifts to the United States of America. He was slender, pale, dark-haired, and wore nose-glasses. He was about thirty, and Lanny, discovering what was inside his head, was awe-stricken. Oddly enough, he came to realize that the young scientist was in awe of him, presumably because Lanny was Anglo-Saxon, and elegant, and proper in every way. The younger man had evidently suffered greatly, but he did not talk about it; he took a strictly professional attitude, and did his job with thoroughness. He went through the atomic story again, with much more detail; he opened up a large brief case and produced books, pamphlets, technical publications, mimeographed documents. The formulas were appalling, but Lanny said: "I will learn them. I will work the way you have worked." He remembered, but did not repeat, the story of the Boston aristocrat who said to his indolent son: "If you don't brace up and do something I'll send you to Harvard to compete with the Jews." Lanny knew that was the real reason why the Nazis hated the Jews—they were so hard to compete with.

The P.A. buckled down to work. He ate his meals and then for half an hour or so he listened to the radio or read the newspapers; then he studied until he was dizzy. He would go out for a stroll, and feed the deer, or watch the peacocks and lyre birds and think how much they resembled in their manners the ladies and gentlemen he had known in the *grand monde*—the generals with their gold braid and precedence, the statesmen and plutocrats with their orders and sashes. Thus meditating, he would return to his task of undermining this world—for that was what the war was, now that the Reds were on the right side and it was another war for democracy.

At first it was very hard, for there was a new and highly technical vocabulary, and Lanny had forgotten what the symbols meant, if he had ever known. But every evening the faithful young doctor answered questions and explained what the neophyte had marked; and of course each thing the neophyte was able to understand made it easier to understand the next. "Don't worry," the tutor said, "you are making progress. As a rule it takes years to master this subject." He would comfort the distracted pupil by setting aside whole sections in the books and publications. "You won't need that; it's theoretical, and we are concerned with practice."

To an active mind it is fascinating to solve any problem, even a purely artificial one, say a cross-word puzzle, or one in chess. Other minds have taken these steps before you, but you, following them, feel that you are the pioneer, putting this and that together and drawing a conclusion, seeing one vista after another open before you, leading into regions where you, at least, have never been hitherto. Alston had said: "You will learn to love physics," and so it proved. Lanny was fascinated by the order he perceived in this infinitely complex universe, and the time came when the "fissionating" of the atom became to him a game, a hunt, a race—even without the thought of the Nazis to be beaten, even without the thought of having Berlin blown up ahead of New York!

X

So passed the warm summer months; pleasantly, so far as bodily affairs were concerned, but with heavy strain of the spirit, because of the dreadful duel of death going on in Eastern Europe. There had never been a battle like it in all history; some nine million men, fighting day and night over a front of eighteen hundred miles. It went on for weeks, for months . . . it might go on for years. And so much depended upon it, everything that Lanny Budd cared about—the future of mankind. It was a constant temptation to turn the radio dials and hear the latest bulletins. Lanny kept himself at his studies only by saying: "If we can destroy Berlin, the Germans will have to fall back, no matter how far they have got!"

The Germans were on the offensive, so they had the advantage of knowing where the next blow was to come. They could prepare a blow at one place and then at another; they could feint, make it appear that their purpose was to take one fortress, then drive heavily toward another. A great wilderness in Eastern Poland, the Pripet marshes, divided their forces into halves. And where would their heaviest blows come, toward Leningrad or in the south? The heaviest blows seemed to come everywhere. The Panzers rolled, and crashed through the Russian lines; the Russians fell back; everywhere it was withdrawal after withdrawal, defeat after defeat, and that is the most discouraging kind of warfare.

Very soon the Germans were on Russian soil; and the Russians were following their promised "scorched earth" policy, as they had seen the Chinese doing for many years, leaving no food, no shelter for the foe. The Nazi radio blared proclamations of tremendous victories, the surrounding and capturing of whole armies. You had sworn never to believe anything that Dr. Goebbels said, but you could never quite stick to the resolution. Even the worst liar in the world might tell the truth when he had everything going his way.

But this much was certain: the Soviet Armies were fighting. They fought all through that summer; and every time they killed a Nazi, it was one who would never invade Britain; every time they shot down one of Göring's flyers, it was one who would never bomb London. The Soviets appeared to have an endless supply of men; and they had materials—what Uncle Jesse had said was true, they had been starving themselves to make munitions, because they knew they had a deadly foe on their doorstep, and the time allowed them was short.

The northern half of the Wehrmacht headed for Leningrad, and with the help of the Finns they got to the very gates. Then began one of the most dreadful sieges of history; a whole population of a great city, half starved and fighting for their lives, bombarded day and night, not merely by planes but by heavy siege guns. Workers in factories were turning out munitions even while the roof of the building was falling about their heads. What helped to save them was the fact that their half-mad Peter the Great had built this city in a marsh, and all around it was soft ground, impassable for mechanized armies, at least until it was frozen.

But in the south were the dry rolling steppes and the farmlands of the Ukraine, which Hitler had publicly announced as one of his desires. Nothing to stop him but rivers, and these are easily crossed by modern armies. So all those collective farms which Lanny had read and heard about were now being laid waste; those mines and bridges and dams—the great Dnieprostroy, which had been to the Russians, and to friends of the workers everywhere, a symbol of hope, a promise of a new society. "Collectivism plus electrification equals Socialism" had been Lenin's formula, and the Russians had starved and toiled to attain this goal—the only case in history in which a nation had managed to industrialize itself without foreign loans. Britain and America had had a century and a half in which to do it, but the Soviet Union had had less than two decades. And now it was all being laid waste—great gaps blown in the dam, and the waters rushing down into the Black Sea, which did not need them. For these losses men and women wept in their hearts all over the world.

XI

Would the foe press on toward the southeast, to get the oil of the Caucasus, or would he turn northward and take Moscow? This was one of the questions of the hour, and another had to do with the undersea war in the Atlantic. In the spring the British losses had been a hundred thousand tons a week. Now all ships traveled in convoys, and Churchill claimed that the losses had been greatly reduced; but was he telling the truth? It was a secret widely whispered that American naval vessels were escorting the convoys far out from American shores; the isolationists clamored, charging one more crime against That Man in the White House. How long would it be before the U-boats sank an American warship, and the fat would be blazing in the fire?

Professor Einstein would come over about once a week, always in the evening, and hear his pupil recite. He would lecture and answer questions for a while, always lucidly, and exactly at the level of the pupil's understanding. Then he would say: "Enough for tonight!"—and suddenly the roles would be reversed and Lanny would be the teacher. Einstein knew that Lanny's father made warplanes, and he knew that Lanny had been in Europe recently and had many connections there. He never asked a question about these, but he would ask Lanny's opinion about the prospects, political as well as military, in the different lands.

The P.A. was delighted to discover that they were completely at one in their ideals and hopes, for this great scientist had not been content to limit himself to his specialty, he was a humanist as well as a physicist. He loathed war, as every truly intelligent man must do, but he saw that this war had to be won and Nazi-Fascism uprooted from the earth. He agreed that nothing would come from the victory unless an international government was formed; unless the nations would surrender some of their sovereignty, as the states had done when the American union was formed. He was a believer in the people, a fundamental democrat who knew that democracy in politics was good, but that it was not enough; before there could be any real freedom there must be democracy in industry, the worker must be the master of his job. In short, the greatest thinker of modern times was a Socialist; and when he admitted it to Lanny he didn't say: "Don't mention it!"

XII

Once they had an adventure. Lanny had been working especially hard, and had triumphantly recited several formulas without an error. Suddenly the master of all formulas grinned and said: "Let's play hookey!" When Lanny asked: "What shall we do?" he replied: "Alston tells me you play the piano. I play the fiddle; let us have some duets. You come to my place—it is late and nobody will notice us. I'll lock up the house and we won't answer the bell."

So they went, by unfrequented streets, as though they were two burglars. The great scientist lived in an elderly undistinguished house which had doubtless been the first he looked at, and which he would probably occupy for the rest of his days. "One room is as good as another to think in," he said, "provided that nobody disturbs you." As he led the guest into the old-fashioned parlor he added: "But some music is better to play than others. What do you like?"

"Anything that pleases you," replied Lanny, "provided it is not too difficult."

"What do you say to Mozart's sonatas?"

"Fine! I have played them with Hansi Robin."

"Oh! You know him?"

"He is married to my half-sister."

"Oh, then you are one of us! Why didn't you tell me?" He put his arm impulsively about his pupil's shoulders and led him to the piano. "You must be a real *Musiker*. We shall have an *Abend!*"

He got out the music and spread the piano volume on the rack. "Where shall we begin? With the *Number 1?* They are all delightful. They take me back to my happy youth." As if eager to get there quickly he took out his fiddle, tuned it, and set the music on the stand. "I almost know the first one by heart, but not quite." He tucked the instrument under his chin with a silk handkerchief; then: "Are you ready? One, two, three"—and they were off.

There is no adventure more delightful in all the world; you skip and you dance and you sing in your heart; and always there is another voice answering your singing, another pair of feet skipping and dancing in time. You race through the meadows, and the flowers nod and bow to you, the wind sweeps over the fields of waving grain, you hear it soughing in the pine trees, or maybe roaring on the mountaintops; you hear the birds singing, you see little waves dancing, and the sunlight strewing showers of golden fire upon the water. Then suddenly you realize that all this is going to die, and you grow very sorrowful, and walk mournfully for a while; but even your sorrow is made beautiful, deprived of all disharmony. Then the sun comes out again, and it is springtime, and you realize that life renews itself; you skip and dance faster than ever, and it becomes a race, most exhilarating; you rejoice in your powers, the fact that you are equal to all emergencies, even to *allegro assai*.

When they had finished *Sonata Number I* the entranced fiddler asked: "Shall we have another?" (Just like many a toper whom you have known!) Lanny said: "If you will," so they played another set of movements, repeating the same emotions, but with endless variety, like life itself. Nearly two centuries ago there had lived in old Vienna a child prodigy who had played the clavichord, and had been taken by his money-hungry parents to exhibit his skill in most of the courts of Europe. Melodies of unimaginable loveliness had been born in his soul, and he had labored incessantly, composing more than six hundred works of every classification. He had died young and poor, after the manner of genius in a heedless world; but his printed notes lived on for the delight of gentle and harmless souls through all the ages.

"Shall we have another?" asked the toper; and so they played the *Number III.* When they finished he sighed, as one coming down from heaven to a distracted earth. His usually pale cheeks were flushed and his eyes were shining. Said he: "That is enough. We are a pair of bad boys. Nobody has a right to be so happy until this war is over."

Lanny went back to his cottage, thinking that this elderly Jewish cherub was one of the most delightful human beings he had yet had the fortune to meet.

XIII

In mid-August President Roosevelt went on what appeared to be one of his customary vacation cruises off the New England coast. Swimming was the only form of exercise he could take; and also he liked to catch fish, or to try. This time he was after unusually big ones; he boarded a Navy cruiser at sea and was carried to Newfoundland, where he met a British battleship with Winston Churchill on board; also Harry Hopkins, who had been flown to Russia for a series of conferences with Stalin. Various other Americans, including Charlie Alston, had managed to disappear from Washington and to show up in what Churchill called "this Newfoundland bight."

Discussions went on for several days, and when all those concerned were safely back home the news was given out. They had adopted for the future world a series of eight principles which came to be known as "the Atlantic Charter." Lanny listened to them over the radio and wished that he could have known about the matter in advance; he would have tried to persuade the Chief to include a forthright statement in favor of an international government, the measure upon which Einstein was so insistent. But Lanny couldn't be everywhere and couldn't do everything; just then he was studying processes and formulas having to do with the production of uranium isotopes.

New documents were brought to him almost every night; he kept them locked in a suitcase out of sight. Early in September there came from New York a messenger with a brief case chained to his left wrist and fastened with a padlock. The messenger had the key, but was pledged not to use it until he was in Lanny Budd's presence; the padlock was to make sure that he didn't forget the brief case in a train or restaurant. Inside were carbon copies of material, and a memorandum of instructions, telling Lanny that he was to make no notes, but to learn the material by heart and then never mention it except as per orders.

While he studied, the messenger went into town and saw a motion picture; when he returned and found that Lanny was not yet through, he went to another theater and saw another program, a total of eight hours spent, including time for a meal. At the end of that time Lanny knew the formulas and processes for the large-scale production of plutonium, and the results of various experiments in use of graphite and of paraffin as "moderators" of the too-great ardor of neutrons. The unsigned memo from Alston read: "This is for England, not elsewhere. Will explain later."

That sounded immediate; so Lanny was not surprised when Professor Einstein came in next evening, and remarked, quite casually: "Mr. Budd, I think you now know everything about the subject of physics." He said it with a twinkle in his eyes, of course, and Lanny received it with a grin. The great thinker was as full of fun as F.D. himself.

"You mean that I know enough for this job?" asked the pupil, and the reply was: "I award you a diploma, *summa cum laude*."

Lanny responded, without smiling: "This has been the most interesting thing that ever happened to me, Professor; and when this war is over, maybe you will let me come back and really learn something."

"I'll let you come and play duets with me every night," replied the author of *The Special and the General Theory of Relativity*.

19. Even to the Edge of Doom

I

CHARLES ALSTON had come to New York again, so Lanny met him there and took him for another ride, this time in Central Park at twilight. The car rolled in a stream of fast traffic, along a winding drive with vistas of trees on the one side and tall buildings making a background of lights on the other. Lanny listened, first to thanks for his diligence as a student, and then to an outline of his future tasks.

"The man you are to interview is Professor Heinrich Thomas Schilling. He is, as you may know, a Nobel prize winner in physics and one of the greatest authorities in the world. When last heard from he was at the University of Berlin. Now we have reason to believe that he is in a laboratory near Oranienburg. It is your problem to find him and devise some inconspicuous way of interviewing him. To this end you will go first to London and consult with the English physicist, Professor Oswald Hardin, who has been in contact with Schilling and knows more about the situation than anyone else. Hardin was in Berlin for several years and is Schilling's friend. By the way, the details I sent you the other day may be given to Hardin; but you are not to give any information to Schilling, only to get it from him."

"Suppose he questions me?"

"You will pretend that you are ignorant. We are told that Schilling is completely anti-Nazi, but there is no use trusting any German more than we have to. If Schilling is on the level he should not ask questions. Your impression of his character and attitude is one of the things which will be of importance to us when you come out."

"If he is double-crossing us, there wouldn't be much chance of my coming out, I should think."

"That does not necessarily follow. He might be told to give you misinformation, with the idea of causing us to waste time and money on false leads. This much is certain—he will know that you are not coming into Germany out of unselfish love of scientific truth."

"How will he know who or what I am?"

"Professor Hardin will give you a password."

"And how will Hardin know me?"

"He will be expecting you."

"Let me point out, Professor: so far nobody has been allowed to know that I am a P.A. except the Governor himself. I wasn't even sure that you knew it. And I know from all three of the top Nazis that they have agents in England and are sending instructions and getting information all the time."

"We have to take chances in this case, Lanny; you cannot just go into Germany and look up this Schilling and say: 'I am an agent of President Roosevelt; tell me about the uranium project.'"

"I grant you that; but certainly I ought to do everything I can to keep my tracks covered."

"You can take precautions to meet Hardin secretly, as you have done with me. He will certainly understand that."

"How am I to get into England this time?"

"F.D. told me he would arrange it personally with Churchill."

"Understand, Professor, I'm not trying to welsh on this job; but I want to succeed and not fall into some Nazi trap. I don't like the idea of having my name discussed over the transatlantic telephone."

"You may count upon it that the Governor has made sure his conversations with Churchill are not being listened in on."

"I don't doubt for a moment that he thinks he has made sure. But I know something about the tricks of our foes, and the years they have been getting ready for what is happening now. They have planted their agents all over the world, and have tapped a lot of wires and broken a lot of codes."

"Well, take that up personally with the Governor and if you have precautions to suggest, do so. He may have information that he wishes to entrust to you and you alone. He is going to be at Hyde Park this week-end, and you are to get in touch with Baker in Poughkeepsie."

Lanny was required to repeat the names of the two scientists, and the details about them. He added: "I will look them up in the library and learn everything that is available. When I get to Berlin, I'll use the library there to the same end."

Said Alston: "It may be that you will get enough from Hardin. What you need especially is a pretext for meeting Schilling. It may be that he has some interest in art; he might own a painting worth viewing, or some relative might have one. It might be that you have a suggestion about having his portrait painted. Do you know anybody in Germany who might perhaps care to paint a Nobel prize winner?"

"I might think of somebody," replied the P.A. "I have met all sorts of art people in Berlin."

"All right; and now, one final word, Lanny. You must remember that you may be carrying the fate of the democratic world in your keeping. If your mission should fail, if you should discover that you have walked into a trap, you must deny that you have any knowledge of what we are doing with the nucleus of the atom. You must stick to that story through every cross-examination, and even through torture. You must remain the art expert and nothing else. You have been in Princeton making a catalog of the Curtice art collection, and your only dealings with Albert Einstein were Mozart duets."

"All that goes without saying, Professor."

"You must realize that you will face frightful tortures. The Nazis will use every device in their catalog to break your spirit. I want you to carry with you this tiny glass capsule. It contains cyanide, and if you bite it and swallow it quickly, you will be out of their reach in a minute or so. That will save you a lot of misery, and save the rest of us the possibility that in some moment of delirium you might blurt out a word or a phrase—say 'graphite moderator,' or something like that."

II

Lanny had two days' vacation before his appointment at Hyde Park, and he planned that to the best advantage. He drove to Newcastle to say good-by to the family. They found nothing strange about his having been cataloging an art collection, and were interested in what he had to tell about life in the Curtice family. They found it less easy to understand why and how an art expert should be returning to Europe in wartime; but they had long since learned not to ask about this. Robbie revealed that he had a business appointment with Reverdy Holdenhurst in New York for the following day, and the son accepted an invitation to join them at lunch.

On his way back to the city he paid a visit to the Hansibesses. Very touching to see what had happened to them; it was as if a wet sponge had been passed over their recent unhappiness and wiped out everything at a single stroke. Bess's beloved Soviet Union was in peril of its life, and nobody with any trace of social feeling could doubt which side he was on. Hansi was completely at one with his wife, and both of them ashamed that they had quarreled. Lanny said nothing about the part he had played in this domestic dénouement.

Bess told important news; they were going to Moscow. She had made the offer to Oumansky, the Ambassador in Washington, and he had cabled, suggesting the invitation. "We are to be honored guests of the Soviet Union, and will play for the people in all the cities. That may not do much to win the war, but it will at least tell them where our sympathies are."

They turned on the radio and listened to the news. The Germans were within a couple of hundred miles of Moscow, and had got east of Kiev, the capital of the Ukraine; things looked black indeed. With all three of them it was as Bess had said about herself—everything within the limits of that vast land was their personal property and its destruction their personal grief.

III

Back in the city, Lanny dined with Zoltan Kertezsi, and told of his picture deals; Zoltan reported on the job of getting the Detazes out of the vault in Baltimore and having them packed and shipped to Reubens, Indiana. Later in the evening, the P.A. dropped in on Forrest Quadratt. Things were getting hot for a registered Nazi agent; the F.B.I. was hounding him, he reported, and he might soon be needing help from his friends. This clearsighted man wasn't fooling himself; he said the situation was bad in the United States, and he wasn't alto-

gether happy about the Russian campaign either. "Our friends count
the number of miles we advanced and the number of prisoners we take;
they fail to realize the number of miles that barbarous country has,
and the endless masses of human cattle. Also, the dreadful winter is
coming on."

Lanny didn't want to appear too mournful, so he refrained from
repeating what the Führer had predicted, that the campaign would be
over in one month, or in two at the outside. Instead, he remarked: "It
may be that the Wehrmacht is prepared to fight in the winter. They
have uncorked so many miracles."

"We shall need them," declared the German-American. "If anybody
had told me that it would be possible to line up the British and the
American governments in support of the Red terrorists, I should not
have believed it."

"Nor I, Forrest. But at least we have learned who our enemies are."

"You are telling me! We won't need much research when we are
ready to compile a shooting list."

Lanny went to Baldur Heinsch, and carefully dropped a hint, but
the other failed to take it. Presently the P.A. ventured: "By the way,
what about those important persons who were going to rid us of that
worst enemy?"

"They seem to have all dived underground. I don't hear anything
of what they are doing."

"It would seem that this is their time, if ever."

"I agree with you. I was hoping that you might have news about it."

Lanny was disappointed, but it wouldn't do to pursue the subject.
Could it be that the steamship man had become suspicious? Or had
he made up his mind that the son of Budd-Erling wasn't going to help
anybody to kidnap the President of his country, but just chat about it
amiably?

The way to meet such a situation was to give news, not to seek it.
Lanny remarked: "By the way, Herr Heinsch, you know my father
sometimes drops hints about the airplane industry. He knows I am not
especially interested in the subject, but I hear him talking to others,
and what he says might be of value to you without doing any harm to
him."

"By all means tell me," adjured the other. It was amusing to see how
quickly the conversation came to life.

"It appears that several companies scattered over the country are
working on projects for rockets that will carry bombs; also they are
designing planes that will fly by means of the rocket principle—'jet
propulsion,' they call it. They are expected to attain unprecedented
speeds."

"Thank you, Lanny; that may be very important indeed." The P.A.

smiled inwardly, knowing that the Germans were working on such plans, and their men must know that the British and Americans were not entirely asleep. But evidently a steamship man hadn't been told!

IV

Next morning there were letters to be written, and a bank to be visited. Then came lunch in the dining-room of the Ritzy-Waldorf, and it turned out that Reverdy knew Alonzo Curtice—such an inconveniently small world it was! Reverdy was a Princeton man and knew about life there, including the fact that German-Jewish refugees were being harbored by this fashionable university; Reverdy considered it a somewhat unfortunate precedent. Usually the Baltimore capitalist was a tactful person, but this time he overlooked the fact that Robbie Budd's only daughter was married to such a refugee!

He was greatly interested to hear that Lanny had been making a catalog of the Curtice collection, and asked if the expert would consider his own collection worthy of such an honor. Lanny took this as one more effort to lure him into Green Spring Valley. He remarked that the collection would make a rather small catalog; something which the collector was free to take as a hint if he chose. Let him commission a competent expert to find more old masters on his next trip!

The collector said: "I am starting my cruise the first of November. Don't you want to come with us?" This was the third time he had made the same suggestion; both of them knew what he meant by it, and each knew that the other knew, which made it slightly awkward.

"It would be great pleasure," replied the younger man, "but unfortunately I have made commitments. I may be flying to Britain any day now."

"We are going to see a bit of the Orient. My wife has a friend, a woman physician, whom I have undertaken to deliver to her post in South China. Then we plan to spend a while at Bali, one of the loveliest spots in the world."

"It sounds most tempting," remarked the polite Lanny. "But aren't you the least bit concerned about war conditions?"

"We didn't have any trouble last winter. I have the American flag painted large on each side of the vessel, also on the deck, and I keep everything well lighted at night. The German raiders have been pretty well cleared out of the South Seas by now; and anyhow, they are not interested in a private yacht."

"I'd hate to take a chance on it, Reverdy, if they happened to be short on food or fuel."

"They'd leave us enough to get to the nearest port. If you ask me, Lanny, I'd say you are running more risk in flying to Britain."

Lanny let it rest there. Courtesy required him to mention the family, so he asked: "Is Lizbeth going with you this time?"

"She hasn't made up her mind," replied the father. "If you'd go, she'd come; and I'd be happy to invite anybody you'd like to have along."

"You are too kind, really. I can think of nothing I'd rather do, but I have engagements abroad that it wouldn't be decent to break."

His thought was, this persistence was in the worst of taste. It was a phenomenon he had noticed among the very rich, and especially the sons and daughters of the very rich; they were used to having what they wanted, and took it as a right; they gave up with extremely ill grace. It didn't seem probable that Reverdy Holdenhurst himself admired Lanny Budd extravagantly; they were too different in tastes and activities. But Lizbeth wanted Lanny, and Reverdy wanted Lizbeth to have what she wanted; he *had* to want it, because otherwise she would give him no peace—she wouldn't even come on his yachting cruises! Lizbeth was a third generation of the very rich, and it was even harder for her to endure the outrage of not being able to satisfy her heart's desires. Lanny decided that this family which thought itself so very elegant was in reality somewhat crude.

V

These thoughts led his mind to Laurel Creston, who had to make her own way in the world and was doing it. Surely it wouldn't be a sin to have another drive with her, before departing on a dangerous errand. Lanny called her on the telephone, saying: "I am going on a journey, and I wonder if I might have a chance to say good-by."

"By all means," she replied cordially.

"I have a peculiar proposal. I have a client who lives up the Hudson, a two or three hours' drive. He has asked me to be there at nine this evening. He usually keeps me a couple of hours, and then I drive back to New York. The place is near a town, and it has occurred to me that you might take the drive with me, and spend the interim in a picture show. One can always learn something from a movie, even if it's only how bad the movies can be."

"It's a date," she said. "When and where shall we meet?"

"The usual place," he said. "We'll leave early and have dinner on the way. Say five o'clock? And bring something to read, so that if the show is too bad you can sit in a hotel lobby."

VI

Having a couple of hours to spare, Lanny telephoned his Uncle Jesse. They met in the usual way, and drove up Madison Avenue and into Central Park. Inevitably they talked about the Soviet Union; the older man was not above saying: "I told you so!" He was extremely proud of the show his adopted Fatherland was putting up. "You see, they fall back, but they do not run away."

"You are right, Uncle Jesse." Lanny knew what pleasure it gives people to hear that. "I hope they will be able to keep it up."

"What is to prevent them? The farther they retreat the shorter their lines grow, while the farther the Germans advance the greater their difficulties. They have to change the gauge of the railroads and they will surely not be able to do it before winter."

"I agree with all that, Uncle Jesse."

"Also, you notice that the Soviet staff work is not so incompetent as you feared. There's a reason which I pointed out to you long ago. You were shocked by the purges, but now you see what they meant. There are no Quislings in the Red Armies, and no traitor groups among politicians and journalists at home. Compare that with France!"

"I must admit the totalitarian system is more convenient for war, Uncle Jesse. But I am one of those tender-minded fellows who don't like to see people killed."

"It has been going on for a long time in the world," said the tough-minded one, "and never faster than now."

"Well, you may join me in grief for all the young Russians who are dying."

"It has been happening on those vast steppes for many centuries, Lanny. It will not matter in the end, for they have not yet lost the courage to breed—as has been the case with the French for the last century, and nowadays in this classic land of capitalism. I observe that my nephew has reached the age of forty, and has contributed only one little girl to posterity."

Lanny broke into a laugh. "And how about my Red uncle? Has he got some posterity hidden away?"

"I am a freak, Lanny; one of those fanatics who dream of changing the world, and I cannot do a double duty."

"Don't worry, Uncle Jesse. Your nephew also has a duty, and some day he may have the pleasure of telling you about it. How long do you expect to stay here?"

"Not more than a few weeks. Then my address will be the Kremlin."

"So, you are going back! Are you expecting to join the fight?"

"Old men for counsel, young men for war. The Soviet authorities think I can give them advice about the building of the underground in France, and also in their dealings with their new ally, the U.S.A."

"I find it encouraging," ventured the P.A., "how this country has rallied to the support of the Soviet Union in peril. In future it will not be so easy for our journalists to lie about the Reds."

"It is like spring sunshine after a long winter," agreed the ex-deputy. "But don't let it fool you. Capitalism will always find ways to lie, for that is its nature. When it has no enemies abroad it lies about itself and the members of its own family. Every manufacturer lies about his product, every salesman about his sales. The whole system of competitive commercialism is built on falsehood and couldn't survive without it."

"I see the old phonograph records haven't been cracked by the war!" Lanny smiled. "Are you certain that nobody ever lies in the Soviet Union?"

"Come and see!" challenged the other.

"Do you suppose they would let me in? A bourgeois person who lives by selling the products of other men's genius?"

"Joking aside," declared the other, "you ought to get some idea of what the new world is going to be like. I'll vouch for you and get you a permit."

"Joking aside, Uncle Jesse, that's very kind. But I have a job to do, and some day you'll admit that it was worth doing. Meantime, don't mention me to anybody. Good luck to you and your Red Army!"

VII

The place agreed upon with Laurel Creston was a street near her apartment house. She took seriously Lanny's desire not to be known as a friend of "Mary Morrow," and walked around the block to make sure that no one was trailing her. It was a cloudy afternoon, with a touch of autumn in the air, and her cheeks were flushed, whether from the exercise or from the pleasure of seeing him. When she had stepped into the car and they had exchanged greetings she said: "I hope it is not too dangerous a mission you are going on."

"Not especially so," he replied. "I shall probably be flying to Britain."

She told him: "I have another short story coming out next week."

"Too bad that I shall miss it."

"I have a carbon copy with me. You may read it, if you have time, and then destroy it. I shall have no use for it when it is out."

"Keep it until this trip is over," he replied. "I'll read it in my hotel room and then make a little bonfire."

They were driving on upper Broadway, once the old Albany Post Road; they crossed a bridge and passed through a village with the odd name of Spuyten Duyvil. Laurel was answering his questions about her novel; she had not started it yet, but she had some ideas and told them. The subject had become dim in his memory after two months of nuclear physics, but it came back quickly and he was interested again. He remembered suggestions which had occurred to him before the atomic bomb had exploded in his mind.

Later he told her that he had had lunch with her Uncle Reverdy, and she said: "I am to lunch with him tomorrow. It will seem strange not to mention this drive, but I think it will be better so."

"Have you told him that you are Mary Morrow?"

"I don't think he would be interested in my stories; I'm not sure that he approves of women writing at all, and certainly not of their finding fault with the social order. You know how conservative he is."

"Indeed, yes. I think he has the general idea that it is dangerous to find fault with any government anywhere, because the Reds might profit from it."

"My Uncle Reverdy is a strange man. Underneath his reserve he is extremely unhappy, and his mind is a mass of frustrations. Do you know the sad story of his marital misfortune?"

"Yes, my mother told me."

"It was your mother who told me, also. I had to go to the free-spoken Riviera in order to find out about my own family."

Laurel herself was by no means freespoken, in spite of her best efforts. She did not put into words anything about the "misfortune" of a man whose wife had found him in the embrace of a maidservant; she just said: "Aunt Millicent cannot forgive him, and he cannot forgive her for not forgiving him; so they go through life with the doors of their hearts locked, never speaking a word of their real thoughts. I cannot imagine anything more destructive to the human soul; I sometimes think that Uncle Reverdy cannot forgive society for having let him be born, or God for having made him what he is."

"Tell me what you think of Lizbeth," ventured the man.

"Lizbeth is a child, and will remain that so long as she is sheltered from all experience and handed everything she wants on a silver platter. What chance is there for her to develop any of her faculties? I sometimes think that the child of indulgent parents is more unfortunate than an orphan. They ought to be taken away from their parents and raised in communities where other children have a chance to give them social discipline."

Lanny added: "It seems to me especially bad where two parents are competing for a child's favor."

"Exactly so! Uncle Reverdy and Aunt Millicent have done their best to keep Lizbeth from knowing about the disharmony between them, but of course she must be aware of it. When she decides to go on a yacht cruise or to stay at home, she is taking part in a family war. It would have ruined any child who wasn't naturally so gentle and kind."

Lanny said: "Some day you should write a story about such a family!"

VIII

In the city of Poughkeepsie they found a motion-picture theater with a hotel near by. Lanny told her where to sit in the theater so that he could find her; if she was not there he would come to the hotel. Then he drove a short distance, parked his car, and promptly on the minute strolled past the corner appointed. A car halted at the curb, and Lanny stepped in. As a rule there were two men in the car, but this time Baker was alone. He flashed a torch upon Lanny, and then the car sped northward up the river road.

They did not enter the Krum Elbow estate by the main drive with the sentry box in front; they went in by a lane through a grove of trees ready for the Christmas market. A sentry stopped them, but Baker had the entrée and they approached the house by a rear door. Here was another sentry—Lanny would have been happier if there had been half a dozen, but he knew that America wasn't used to war and didn't yet realize that it was at war. American destroyers were being attacked by German submarines, but the American public hadn't been told.

The visitor was escorted by a rear stairway, and into the comfortable bedroom with the chintz curtains and the grate fire; it was a chilly evening and the Boss had on his blue crew-necked sweater. But there was nothing chilly about his mood; he welcomed his caller with a grin, and when the door was closed he said: "Hi, old atom smasher!" He would always have some fancy greeting like that; he would carry with laughter the most crushing burdens of state. A P.A. would be invited to recite the formula for the production of plutonium—not because F.D. would recognize it, but because it was fun to pretend to.

But don't imagine that he wouldn't get down to real business. It wasn't more than a minute before he was saying that this was the most important errand upon which he had ever sent a man, and that P.A. 103 might count it a compliment. "The task will call for all the discretion you possess, Lanny; and if you bring home this piece of bacon you can have pretty nearly anything you ask for."

"All I'll ask is another assignment, Governor. I'm not planning anything else until we have knocked the Nazis out."

"You won't let me put up your expenses for this trip?"

"I have just sold a bunch of my former stepfather's paintings and

I am flush. What troubles me is how I'm going to get into Britain without making myself known as your agent."

"You won't need to be in England more than a day or two, and I am having Baker provide you with a passport under an assumed name."

"But, Governor! The photograph and the fingerprints!"

"We have ways of arranging such matters. We may have to tip off one person."

"What worries me is that you think it is only one person, but in practice there will be a clerk or a secretary, and perhaps a sweetheart. Let me remind you that there is a B4 man by the name of Fordyce who has me on his very special list; he's bound to have my photograph and fingerprints available."

"If he catches on, it will probably be after you have left, and that will be all to the good for you; he will be certain that you are a Nazi agent who has managed to slip through his net. If he does happen to catch you, you will have to tell him that it is top secret and that he is to go directly to Churchill."

"Churchill knows about me?"

"I have told him that a man will call. He has something to tell you that he doesn't want to mention even over our telephone."

"But how can I get access to Churchill without other people knowing it?"

"That is something we have to work out. I will give him your code name, Zaharoff, when you are due in England. Is there somebody you trust who could go to Churchill and say that name?"

"I have a boyhood friend in England, the playwright Eric Vivian Pomeroy-Nielson. I have never mentioned you as my Chief, but he knows that I am getting information for some high-up person, and I'd be surprised if he hasn't guessed it is you."

"Would he have access to Churchill?"

"He is rather too far to the left. But his father, the baronet, would certainly have it. He has several times helped Rick by getting some vital news to the papers without its source being known. He did that with the set of proposals that Hitler was trying to force upon Prague in the spring of 1939."

"All right then, your baronet goes to Winston and says: 'Zaharoff,' and Winston arranges for him to bring the mysterious person to him at night, just as you have come here."

"You understand that Churchill knows me. We saw quite a good deal of each other at Maxine Elliott's, on the Riviera, in the winter before the war."

"A delightful person," said F.D., who had just come from a three-day conference with His Majesty's First Minister.

"Didn't you find that he talked too much?" inquired the P.A. with a grin.

"Sometimes," was the reply; "but you know that I, too, have a weakness for telling stories."

"Personally I didn't mind, because I had come to hear him. I did get a chance to warn him concerning Hitler's purposes, and I found that he had made up his mind at long last that Hitler was a more dangerous enemy than Stalin. But he was quite sure that he personally would never have to deal with the problem; he described himself as a 'political failure,' and said that the Tories had put him on the shelf to stay."

"They have dusted him off," said F.D. "He is an extraordinary figure, and the man for this hour."

"He knows it," ventured Lanny. "He is playing his role as consciously as any other stage star. I think I told you of the report that Rick gave me—as early as last spring he had made up his mind that Hitler was going after Russia, and Churchill had written the speech he was going to deliver and was boring his friends making them listen to it."

"Well, it was worth the trouble," declared F.D. "I have to admit that it sent shivers up and down my spine."

IX

The arrangements for a P.A.'s job having been completed, the "Governor" talked about the Atlantic Conference and the making of the Charter. He had recognized in the Duke of Marlborough's seventh lineal descendant another master showman, a worthy companion at political arms, and now told about him with gusto. Inside that pudgy round body was a stout heart; he was the British lion incarnate, and roared at the foe in language the like of which had not been heard since Shakespeare had put words into the mouth of King Henry the Fifth. Roosevelt described him on board the cruiser *Augusta* smoking his big cigars—and Lanny didn't have to imagine F.D. matching him with several cigarettes, for here he was, half sitting and half reclining in bed, and slipping one after another into the long thin holder which he tip-tilted when he wanted to assume a jaunty air.

He listened for the second time to Lanny's description of the British leader wearing a worn red dressing gown over his white body and a floppy straw hat over his red hair; sitting by the blue-green swimming pool of a retired stage queen and discoursing on the conflict which then loomed so darkly upon the horizon. The P.A. said: "He pumped my mind dry about Hitler and Göring and Hess, everybody in Germany I knew. Beaverbrook was there, and I saw that he, too, was getting ready to break off his love affair with Nazism. I remember that he questioned me especially about Hess; he knew that Hess professed to be a Buchmanite, and the Beaver seemed to have the idea that this movement was going to save Britain from having to fight a hard war."

"That is interesting," commented F.D. "Beaverbrook joined us on the *Augusta*, and had a lot to say, as you can imagine. He told me that he had been one of the first to interview Hess after the landing in Scotland."

"I suppose Hess knows by now that he's not negotiating to get Britain into the war against Russia."

"He was allowed to hear Winston's speech over the radio."

"What a story!" exclaimed Lanny. "If a playwright had invented that, we should call it melodrama."

"They say it has thrown Hess into a spell of melancholia, and it is doubted if his mind will stand the strain."

"Poor Rudi!" exclaimed his false friend. "In a happier world he might have been a useful man. He isn't especially bright, but he was capable of complete fidelity, which you must know is not the most common of virtues. The code name I gave him was Kurvenal, who was the friend of Tristan in Wagner's opera and was described as 'the truest of the true.' I should be interested to have a talk with him now."

"You might suggest it to Winston, and ask him to arrange it."

"I am afraid it wouldn't do. Whatever the Nazi agents in Britain are doing, they can hardly fail to keep track of what is happening to their Deputy Führer."

"You might think up a plausible pretext for having been allowed to see him. You might be going to Hitler with some message from Hess."

"I'll think about it," Lanny said. "But I am afraid this war has long since passed the stage of negotiations. Churchill has committed the unimaginable crime of supporting the Bolsheviks; and so have you."

"You like my speeches better now than you used to?" inquired the genial great man, with a smile.

"Indeed I do, Governor!"

"You recall what I told you the first time you came to me. I couldn't go any faster than the people would let me. I had to wait, and let events change their minds."

"No kidding," said Lanny, "I think your handling of this crisis will be studied as one of the miracles of history. I have been tempted to despair many a time; but you seem always cheerful and sure."

"Ah, my lad, that's because you're not here after you leave the room!"

X

Lanny observed the customary stack of documents on this busy man's reading table, and he took it as a silent monitor. But he permitted himself one question before offering to depart. "Governor, you have so much better sources of information than anybody else. Tell me one thing: will Russia stick it out?"

"There is no question that she means to; the only question is, will she be able."

"What do you say about that?"

"Harry Hopkins has just come from Moscow, where he spent several days with Stalin. He is convinced that Stalin means to fight it out to the end, no matter how bitter. He has given positive assurance that they will hold out, even if it means giving up the whole of Russia; they will retreat into Siberia and continue the struggle with whatever they have left. They ask us for supplies, of course, and we shall do everything in our power to meet their needs."

"Does Hopkins think they can hold out?"

"He has no doubt about it. He says they are only in process of mobilizing their immense reserves. They are moving their machinery eastward and their manpower westward. The old men and the young and the women will do the work. Stalin says they will bleed the Wehrmacht to exhaustion, and in the end they will overwhelm it."

"All right," Lanny said. "On that basis I can go ahead with my job. By the way, I had another talk with my Red uncle. He says just what Hopkins says, but of course in his case it may be wishful thinking. He tells me he is going back to Russia—they will make an elder statesman of him, a foreign office adviser. He invites me to come there and says he can get me in. It might be that you will some day have an errand for me there."

"I'll bear it in mind," replied the Chief. "For the present you have your hands full. Take care of yourself, for you are one man I should hate to lose."

"Thank you, Governor; I'll do my best to come back." Lanny was conscious of the tiny capsule which he had sewn into the lining of his coat; but he didn't mention it. "I know you have several men's work to do, so, unless you have something else to tell me, I'll toddle."

"You might give my personal regards to Professor Hardin when you see him. I met him shortly after the last war, when I was in England, but he probably doesn't remember it."

"I'm guessing that he may have recognized your picture in the papers," said Lanny with a chuckle. He received a clasp from that large strong hand, and then went out into the hall.

XI

F.D.'s Negro attendant sat dozing in one chair and Baker sat in another. He rose and escorted Lanny downstairs. On the way back to Poughkeepsie he said: "I have been instructed to get you a plane reservation to Scotland by way of Newfoundland. I will have the ticket tomorrow, and your plane leaves Port Washington airport the day after tomorrow at 10 A.M. I was told to choose a name for you, so the ticket reads Richard Thurston Harrison. I hope that doesn't happen to be a real person."

"I don't happen to know him," replied Lanny. "And what about my passport?"

"I will attend to that in the morning. Professor Alston gave me your real name, Mr. Budd, and instructed me to arrange these matters for you. You need not worry about my having your name, because I am a man who keeps his mouth buttoned tight."

"That's all right, Mr. Baker; but won't you have to tell somebody in the State Department?"

"No, because the President has ordered that in case of need I am to receive passports already stamped, and I am to fill in the name, the fingerprints, and the photograph myself."

"But then the records in State won't contain anything about me."

"That is true, but it won't matter unless you lose the document, or unless someone becomes suspicious of you. In that case you will have to cable or telephone to me, and I will fix it up with the right party."

"Have you been told of the fact that Lanning Prescott Budd has been put out of England by B4 and forbidden to return?"

"Yes, and that's an awkward matter. I take it that you don't want to tell B4 that you are a presidential agent."

"Surely not, if it can be helped."

"I suggest a scheme that may work, and can't do any harm. I will provide you with a second passport in your own name, and you may sew it in the lining of your coat and not use it until you are landing on the Continent."

"It's hard to see how that could work, Mr. Baker. There are the fingerprints and the photograph."

"There are little tricks that can be tried, and that may work. The fingerprints on your false passport can be slightly blurred—a bad job, but you wouldn't be to blame for that. The photographic negative can be doctored—it is you, but it is not entirely like you and can hardly be recognized by anyone who knows Mr. Lanning Prescott Budd. The official on duty at an airport is not apt to know you, I take it."

"That is true, but if they have any suspicion of me, they will search me and find the second passport."

"In the first place, I don't think they will bother with details, because you will be arriving on a government transport. Civilian service has been ended over that route and the planes are carrying only persons whom the government sends. So the stamping of passports is pretty much automatic. If it comes to a showdown, you will have to say: 'This is an Intelligence matter.' There will be a secret mark on the passport which their top man will know about."

"Well, of course," said Lanny, "if you have magic like that!"

"We have it," replied Baker. "We have a great many men working on the Continent for one purpose or another, and the British pass them through. The code is changed now and then, but your mark will be fresh. When you leave England you will destroy the false passport. I take it that you can come home by way of Lisbon and the Azores, and not by London."

"If I can get passage."

"Tell me, is your father in on your secret?"

"Only to the extent that I am doing some government work. He doesn't know for whom."

"The name of Baker won't mean anything to him. When you reach Lisbon, telephone him to wire me at my street address. As soon as I hear from him I will get busy and make the reservation at this end and notify your father and he can notify you. Enemy agents won't find anything suspicious about your communicating with your father about coming home."

"I don't see any flaws in that," said Lanny. "Where shall we meet tomorrow?"

"I will come to New York and get a hotel room and ask you to come to me, if you don't mind. That will be less conspicuous. Hartley Robinson will be my name for the purpose; and you are Richard Thurston Harrison. Don't forget it."

"I have a lot to remember," said Lanny with a smile. "But I guess I can add that, Mr. Robinson."

XII

Lanny had himself set down on a street in the city of Poughkeepsie, which had once been an Indian village, "the Reed-covered Lodge by the Little Water Place." He strolled to the theater and had no trouble in finding his lady, who had taken a seat in the location agreed upon. Said she: "I have witnessed a terrible murder, and now I shall never know who committed it."

"There are millions of murders nowadays," he replied, "and no one but God will ever know who committed them."

He would have liked to tell her where he had been and what he had learned—about the Soviet Union, especially. She would have got a thrill out of it. But he couldn't afford even to let her guess, as she might easily have done, knowing that Hyde Park was only a few miles away. Complete silence wouldn't have been either plausible or polite, so he thought it wise to make up a story to account for his evening. He took one of his Chicago clients and moved him to the Hudson River valley, and told her a strange tale about an elderly gentleman who passionately loved beautiful paintings and yearned to possess them, but only now and then could buy one, because most of the money belonged to his wife and it always meant a quarrel.

"What does the woman want to buy?" asked Laurel, and he told her that the woman didn't want to buy anything, she wanted to build up her fortune. She had inherited it from her father, and she thought that she was honoring him by following in his footsteps and becoming richer every day.

This led to the subject of the strange distortions which money causes in the personalities of human beings. "Money is power," Lanny said. "Money commands respect and obedience from other people, and not everybody has the strength of character to carry such a responsibility. The very rich discover that all the world is trying to get some of their money, and they become haunted by fears, they conceive irrational hatreds and shut themselves away—their hearts and sometimes even their bodies."

He told about old Miss van Zandt, whose Fifth Avenue mansion had been gradually surrounded by the clothing trade, and who lived in constant terror of the Jewish workers who paraded up and down the street at noontime, eating their sandwiches; in her sight they were all Communists, so she gave fortunes to Nazi-Fascists who came along and promised to put down this enemy. He told about a wealthy gentleman who was certain that the revolution was just around the corner, and who spent all his money for things and hid them away in safe places—any sort of things, for only things would have value. This gentleman saw a vision of himself peddling his possessions in a black market in order to buy food to keep alive.

Laurel in her turn told about one of her relatives, whom she did not name. An elderly lady who entertained with great liberality and enjoyed the presence of her friends; but her daughter could not bear to see money spent on other people, even though the daughter had her own fortune. She had figured it out that one ought to be able to entertain guests at dinner for a cost of not more than seventeen cents per person, and she tried to limit the servants to that. The result was that the mother was very lonely, and all the servants were occupied in cheating the household. Things mysteriously disappeared, and whenever the daughter went away the mother had a party.

"What is your remedy for such things?" inquired Laurel, and Lanny answered: "The abolition of inheritance. I have come to the conclusion that it is the most evil force in human society. It poisons the lives of most of the wealthy families I know. Even where they do not openly quarrel, the children are sapped of all vitality, all initiative. Our conservatives talk glibly about 'free enterprise'—I should like to tell them that the first step to preserve free enterprise is to make it plain to every young person in the world that when his education has been completed he has to go out into the world and make his own way, and that he can never have a chance to spend a dollar that he hasn't earned by his own efforts."

Thus easily solving human and social problems they drove back to the great city in the small hours of the morning. Only when they were close to Laurel's apartment house did the conversation take on a personal tone. She asked him: "Is this really not a dangerous mission you are going on?"

He thought that he noticed a trembling in her voice, and it was like an alarm bell to his ears. He would only have had to say: "Does it mean so much to you?" and the fat would have been blazing in the fire. But F.D. had bade him use discretion; so he replied: "It is hard to be sure. We cannot be less willing to take risks than our enemies." Then, after a little thought: "Write me some of that novel in the meantime."

XIII

After a sleep, Lanny got in touch with Baker again, and the two passport books were prepared. "I, the undersigned, Secretary of State of the United States of America, hereby request all whom it may concern to permit safely and freely to pass, and in case of need to give all lawful aid and protection to"—this much in Gothic type. Then came his name, and the customary thirty-two pages, including five to identify him and tell him what he must not do—to enlist in foreign armies, and so on. The document was invalidated for countries at war—a long list—but Lanny meant to go into some of them, even so.

He wondered: did Baker know where he was going and what for? In all probability not. This man with the tight-buttoned mouth asked not one question, and the only personal remark he made was: "I have been in this business a long time." That was after the passports were completed, and Lanny had expressed doubts as to his skill in sewing one of them into the lining of his coat. Baker offered to do it; he had learned that art, along with the retouching of photographic negatives and the sandpapering of fingertips in order to reduce the clearness of prints.

Lanny had the rest of the day free; and just as he had made up his mind to visit the library and look up Professors Hardin and Schilling, the telephone rang. It was Laurel, saying: "Can you spare me a few minutes? It is something important."

Of course he said he could, and met her on the street as usual and drove her into the park. He had not seen her so troubled since the night in Hitler's Berghof, when she had come to his room and told him of the Führer's alarming advances to her. This time it was the spirits who were troubling her; less than an hour ago she had been in a trance, with her friend Agnes sitting by making notes. Otto Kahn had announced himself, and reported the presence of an old gentleman with a white beard who said that his name was Eli Budd. "Did you have such a relative, Lanny?"

"Yes," was the reply. "He was my great-uncle. I met him several times in my youth."

"Did you ever tell me about him?"

"I don't remember; I probably did, because he left me his library, and it's in my studio. I generally tell people how I got all those fine books."

"Did you ever show me his picture?"

"It is hanging on the studio wall, and I may have spoken of it."

"That tends to spoil things; but I don't remember it consciously. He was described as having a thin, ascetic face; a tall old man, slightly stooped, and with a gentle voice."

"That is correct. He was a Unitarian preacher."

"What he said was: 'Tell Lanny to postpone that trip. A calamity confronts him.' He repeated three times: 'Danger! Danger! Danger!'— and then faded away."

"That is very interesting indeed, Laurel."

"It frightened me terribly. I made excuses to Agnes and came out and phoned you from a pay station."

Again Lanny might have said: "Does it mean so much to you?" But a voice said: "Danger!"—and more than three times. What he said was: "Here is one of those cases where you don't know what to think. You were contemplating trouble that might come to me—you spoke of it last night. And of course all those facts about Great-Uncle Eli may have been in your subconscious mind; certainly they were in mine. You go into a trance and your subconscious makes a little drama out of it."

"You don't believe in premonitions, then?"

"I am forced to believe in them; I have read of so many cases—they are as old as history. But that doesn't mean that every fear is a genuine premonition. If we believed that, we should have a hard time living at all."

"You can't postpone this journey?"

"Not possibly, Laurel. You can't imagine how hard it is to get plane reservations these days."

"But even for a day or two?"

"Listen, my dear. Did that voice say *how* I was going to be in danger?"

"No; only what I told you."

"Well then, what can we conclude? We are in danger of a collision here in Central Park. I might be killed on the way to the airport. I might easily be killed trying to get about in the London blackout. An astrologer once told me I was going to die in Hongkong, and I am surely not going to Hongkong on this trip. Why shouldn't his premonition be as good as Otto Kahn's? The psychical researchers have collected statistics as to premonitions that came true, but who has ever counted those which failed to come true? My guess is, they might be ten to one, perhaps a hundred to one."

Thus cheerfully he tried to console her. He took her to dinner in a small obscure place, and made himself as agreeable as possible—as if that would help! When he left her, just around the corner from her home, he said: "I cannot cable you from England, but I will send you a postcard to let you know I am safe. I mustn't sign my name—I'll make it 'Brother,' which may touch a censor's heart."

"Good night—Brother," she said. He wondered: was there a faint touch of irony in her voice?

20. *Those in Peril on the Sea*

I

ROBBIE sent his man in to town, and Lanny drove him to Port Washington on Long Island, then turned the car over to him and saw him depart. When he was out of sight there occurred a metamorphosis of Lanning Prescott Budd into Richard Thurston Harrison. The traveler had left his old suitcases in the car because they bore his initials; he had left in them every piece of paper which might have identified him; he had even removed from his clothing the cleaners' marks which sometimes contain initials. He stepped aboard the plane a new man; and several hours later he stepped out upon the soil of Newfoundland, at the Gander airport near the long lake of that name.

This was a military airport of immense size, built jointly by British and Canadian air forces. Now America was sharing the use of it—part of the strange process of getting into a war by walking backward, with her eyes fixed upon peace and her voice loudly declaring that she was not taking a step. Here were Pan American Airways employes still wearing their blue serge uniforms, very natty, but civilian service was suspended and they were carrying only such passengers as Army and Navy and State requested, and the government paid the bills. There was a field of large drums full of gasoline, arranged in rows, and vast new construction going on, which visitors were not encouraged to inspect.

This village by a cold blue northern lake had become one of the greatest air centers in the world; large planes of many types assembled here from all over Canada and the United States; they flew away, and only a small percentage came back—just enough to return the pilots for the next flight. The plane which was to convey the mysterious Mr. Harrison was drawn up near the entrance to the field, with the steps in position against it. A Boeing four-engine transport, it looked weather-beaten but substantial; Lanny guessed that it was one that would bring pilots back. His baggage was put on board, but he was told that there would be a delay, the weather conditions were not satisfactory. Some distance from the field were radio towers, and in the office building men sat with earphones and got reports from weather stations half way round the world. Storms were definite things and their paths could be charted; they were especially common at this equinoctial season, and upon them depended whether the plane would fly to Greenland, Iceland, or Scotland.

Such matters were in the hands of the higher powers. Mr. Harrison strolled about for a while unlimbering his legs; then he found a seat on a bench and became absorbed in an exercise which had become second nature—the recital of the formulas and techniques of atomic disintegration. But he didn't continue this very long; the place beside him was taken by a blond young man in the navy-blue uniform of Pan-Am. He lighted a cigarette, took a couple of reflective puffs, and remarked: "Lots of fog these days, and how we hate it!"

Lanny was willing enough to chat; there would be time for mental recitations during the flight. The man, in his early twenties, said that he had left college to become a navigator during this crisis. He was not the navigator of Lanny's plane; he had come in early that morning and had a sleep and would be going out in a couple of days. "A lonesome place," he said, "and nothing to do. The natives don't get enough to eat, or perhaps they don't know how to cook it."

He discussed the life of these new style "ferrymen." Nothing about the number or types of planes, or anything that could be a military secret, and he didn't even ask the name of his auditor. He just told human stuff; a funny life, for you lost four hours every time you went east, so you were never hungry at mealtimes or sleepy at bedtime; then, just as you had started to get used to it, you flew west and gained four hours, and then you were hungry before mealtimes and sleepy before bedtime. You were a man without a country and your watch was always wrong. You could stand it, because they paid you eight hundred a month and expenses; the pilots got a thousand.

Then he talked about the route, which had no land and a superfluity of weather—that surely was no military secret. There were fogs, and all your pilot could do was to follow the beam. There was a robot pilot to help him; the Americans called it the "Iron Mike," the British called it "George." There would always be ice, and the radio would give you a "freezing level" below which you had to fly. Pan-Am had a flying system of which it was proud; the engineer plotted at brief intervals what was called "the Howgozit curve," a synthesis of five curves showing the miles flown versus the number of gallons of gas consumed, the number of gallons versus the hours of flying, and so on. On the basis of that chart the captain determined the so-called "Point of No Return," and if the figures were not right he turned back before the point was reached.

"Were you ever in an accident?" inquired the traveler.

"I was in the drink once. I spent seventeen hours in a rubber boat before the Dumbo found us."

"What is a Dumbo, if it is not a secret?"

"Didn't you see the motion picture of the elephant who learned to fly by waving his ears? A flying boat has a big awkward body and we make fun of it, but believe me, it looks perfectly wonderful when you are soaked to the skin and your fingers and toes are beginning to freeze."

"Do you keep this route going all winter?" the traveler wanted to know.

"We didn't think we could, but now we're doing it because we have to. We have a plan that we call 'pressure pattern.' We don't try to follow the great circle route; we don't bull our way through storms; we get continuous information as to high- and low-pressure areas and work by chat. We have learned that wind in a low-pressure area blows counter-clockwise into the middle of the area, while it blows clockwise out of a 'high.' So we sneak to the place where the wind will boost us along."

The traveler said: "Some two hundred years ago there was an English poet who predicted something like that. He was writing about the Duke of Marlborough, who was Winston Churchill's ancestor:

> "Calm and serene, he drives the furious blast,
> And, pleased the Almighty's orders to perform,
> Rides in the whirlwind and directs the storm."

"Swell!" exclaimed the navigator. "Where do you find stuff like that?"

II

The sociable airman got up, remarking that he had come west and was hungry ahead of time. He strolled away, and his place was taken after an interval by a tall gentleman of about Lanny's age wearing a· brown business suit somewhat rumpled. He was chewing nervously on an unlighted cigar; now and then he spat, and then swallowed, and his Adam's apple rose up out of the collar of his blue shirt. "I don't like this damn weather," he said. "Look at that"—and he pointed to the low rocky ridges of Newfoundland, from which the morning fog had only just been dissipated, and where already the evening fog was drifting in.

"Yes," Lanny replied. "They have the Gulf current and cold air and that makes lots of fog."

"Do you mind if I talk?" inquired the stranger.

"Not at all."

"My name is Aglund."

"Mine is Harrison."

"Do you like this flying business?"

"I've sort of had to get used to it."

"I've never been up, and I'd have sworn I never would. They wanted me to fly here from Cleveland, but I came by train and boat— The damnedest jerkwater railroad across this island or whatever it is. And the poorest country and people I've seen since I left Georgia."

"They live by fishing and lumbering, and those are hard trades."

"I suppose so. They tell me they haven't been able to meet the interest on their bonds, so they are in hock to the British government; they have lost their constitution."

"Indeed?" Lanny said. "I hadn't heard that. Money talks."

"Money wouldn't get me to come up here to this God-forsaken icebox and fly away into a snowstorm."

"What does it, then?" asked Lanny, smiling amiably.

"I'm a specialist in machine tools, and they told me to go and help the British learn to work one of our heavy presses. Am I bothering you?"

"Not at all, if it's not a military secret."

"It's no military secret that I'm nervous as a wild colt. You'll think there's something wrong with me, but I had an experience last night that has given me a bad case of the jitters. I had to sleep sitting up in the train, and maybe that had something to do with it; anyhow, I had a nightmare and I can't seem to shake it off."

"What was it?"

"Did you ever hear of dreams coming true?"

"Yes, of course. It's a common idea, as old as history."

"Then you won't think I'm some sort of a psycho?"

"Not at all. I have read about such subjects and they interest me."

"Well, I dreamed that I met my mother. She's been dead about twenty years, but it was just as real as if I had been a boy at home. I put my arms around her and gave her a hug, and I felt her firm solid body—she was a chunky, hard-working woman. I kissed her on the cheek, and then she whispered in my ear: 'Son, don't go on that plane! Don't go on that plane!' I woke up in a cold sweat and I've hardly been able to think about anything else since. Have you ever had an experience like that?"

"Yes," Lanny said. "I have had them, and I know others who have. A strange thing, I had something of the same sort only yesterday. I have a woman friend who is a medium and goes into trances. Yesterday afternoon she came to me in a state of excitement, to tell me that someone claiming to be the spirit of my great-uncle had appeared and given a warning for me not to take this journey. He said the word 'Danger' three times."

"Jesus!" exclaimed the man. "And you are going on that plane?"

"I *have* to go," Lanny said.

"Well, *I* don't! Look at that old crate!"

"It looks like a pretty solid one to me."

"They are using everything they can lay hands on, and they drive them till they fall to pieces."

"That one needs a coat of paint," Lanny ventured. "Otherwise it may be O.K."

"Have you thought of the possibility that somebody may be doing a bit of sabotage at these bases? There are Germans all over this country, and why shouldn't they be trying to help their own side?"

"I don't think they'd do anything more than once. Not in this place."

"Well, once would be enough for you and me. Brother, do you know what you and I ought to do?"

"What is that?"

"Go for a walk and get lost in those pine forests that I saw a hundred miles of—or maybe it was five hundred. After a couple of days we could come out and it would be some other plane."

"What good would that do?" inquired Lanny. He couldn't keep from smiling, even though he, too, was troubled in soul. "Maybe the danger our ancestors were warning us about was of getting lost in a pine forest and starving to death."

Mr. Aglund had risen to his feet and was looking about him nervously, as if he thought someone might try to put him onto a plane by force. The unlighted cigar was beginning to fall into shreds from the violence of his chewing. Suddenly he turned upon Lanny and said: "Whatever kills me, it won't be that old crate. Good-by, brother, and good luck to you!"

He turned away and strolled casually toward the entrance gate. He passed out of sight behind one of the buildings, and that was the last Lanny ever saw or heard of him.

III

A bell clanged. One bell meant for the crew to go to the plane, and Lanny stood and watched them do so. The four engines began their "revving," and there was a lot of noise, and dust flying away from the plane. After a while two bells clanged, and that was for the passengers; half a dozen men, some in military, some in civilian garb, gathered at the steps. The captain took their tickets, checking from a list. Lanny, very polite, was the last; and the captain noticed that one was missing. "Aglund," he said, and looked about. "Where's Mr. Aglund?"

"He told me he wasn't going," Lanny volunteered. "He's afraid of storms."

"Well, I'll be damned!" exclaimed the other, and stared. Apparently it was something new in his experience. "Where's he gone?"

"He said he was going to get lost in the forest. He thought that would be safer."

"Well, I'll be *God* damned!" declared the captain. Then he shrugged his shoulders. It wasn't his responsibility to keep bloodhounds and hunt fugitives. "What'll I do with his baggage?"

"I suggest you put it off; he'll come back for it."

A valise and a duffelbag were set off, and Lanny entered the big transport. It was like no plane interior that he had seen before. All the comfortable seats and other appurtenances of luxury had been removed, if they had ever been there. The space was packed pretty nearly solid with crates and bundles covered with heavy canvas and bound tightly in position to rings in the floor and the struts. There were ropes enough to make a regular spider's web. Barely enough room had been left for the six passengers; Lanny wondered where they had expected to put Mr. Aglund. You could sit on a camp chair, or you could fold it up and lie on your back, with your feet stretched out if you didn't mind having them walked over. For anyone who objected, the answer was becoming more familiar every day: "Don't you know there's a war on?"

There would be no heat in this transport, so everybody had to put on a soft flying suit, like overalls, and over that a waterproof and windproof sort of jumper, and over that a life jacket, called a "Mae West." There were parachutes, also, but what good would they do in the middle of the North Atlantic? Nobody put them on.

Lanny, the last man to enter, had barely space enough to sit in. Crates were on one side of him and on the other a man whose name had been read off as Carlton; he must have been six-foot-four and broad in proportion, by his dress a lumberjack or some sort of outdoor man, perhaps a horse breeder going over to take charge of army mules. One by one the passengers were fastened to the wall by heavy leather belts, and while this ceremony was going on Lanny remarked: "I hope these crates don't roll over on us." Seeing the grin on the other's face, he added: "Don't *you* roll over on me!" The man said: "I'll try to keep underneath," and that was all there was to the conversation, for at that moment the four engines started full speed. There were no soundproof walls to the plane, so nobody tried to talk unless he had something important to say. Carlton smiled at Harrison and Harrison returned the smile. Looking back upon this afterwards, Lanny wondered if it had been those friendly words and looks which had been the cause of his life being saved.

The wide curved door was shut and fastened and the plane was in motion. It rocked and bounced on the runway, and then suddenly these motions ceased and you knew it was airborne. By-and-by one of the crew came and made signs indicating that the passengers were free to unstrap themselves, and they did so, and made themselves as comfortable as possible on a floor of aluminum alloy. Four of them elected to play cards, with their feet tucked under them Buddha fashion. Lanny elected to stretch out and close his eyes and recite atomic formulas until he fell asleep.

IV

The flight was to Iceland, which lay to the northeast, a matter of sixteen hundred miles. It would take somewhat less than eight hours, though you couldn't be sure, because of this new method of "pressure patterns." Since all the flying would be by instruments, day and night were the same; "blind flying," it was called, and every pilot had had to learn to trust the instruments and not try to use his eyes. Presently they were in a storm, and the plane began to buck and dip; somebody became airsick and had to use his can, which was unpleasant in these crowded quarters. Lanny wondered: had the pilot failed to find the right pressure area, or was this part of the program? Nobody had told him anything at the outset and nobody told him now. In civilian flights, for which you paid your good money, there was a charming stewardess to murmur assurances into your ear; but now that the government paid, you were just one more package to be delivered to a certain destination. Six boxes containing supper were handed out, but only two were opened, and Mr. Harrison's box was not among them.

Lanny dozed, he didn't know for how long. Then he was startled into wakefulness by a terrific lurch of the plane which slid him along and pressed him against the crates; it slid Mr. Carlton on top of him, in spite of all promises. And hardly had the man wriggled off before there was another yaw and they were sliding in the opposite direction. The freight creaked and groaned and the ropes that bound it appeared to stretch and strain. The thought came to Lanny: what would happen if those ropes should work loose or break? Human bodies might be pounded to pieces by that heavy stuff. He recalled a scene in one of Victor Hugo's novels, about a cannon breaking loose on a frigate in a storm, and racing here and there like a live thing gone mad.

The passengers stared at one another, and shouted their doubts and fears. Lanny, who had never encountered anything like this, wondered if it was a consequence of letting a storm carry you, or something extra and unforeseen. Was it possible for pressure areas to sneak in and escape the vigilance of weather observers? He knew that there were sudden local tornadoes in Alaskan waters; they were called "williwaws." Did they have these on the way to Iceland, and keep them secret on account of "military security"?

It seemed as though the great plane had been seized by a giant hand and was being hurled this way and that; sideways, and then up and down. Suddenly it seemed as though you were being pressed hard against the floor, and then as though the floor were disappearing beneath you—the strange feeling you get when an elevator in a tall office building suddenly starts down. A man's insides became displaced and his diaphragm refused to work. The lights wavered, and the six passengers caught hold of one another in the effort to keep themselves steady. Lanny locked hands with the big outdoor man and was impressed by the warmth and firmness of his clasp. It was reassuring, in conflict with the blind forces of nature, so powerful, so utterly irrational. A high wind is a lunatic turned loose upon the surface of the sea. An earthquake, a volcano, is a madhouse turned loose beneath the earth's surface. What a pitiful thing is man—and what a tragedy that he should destroy himself in war, instead of turning his efforts against these cosmic energies!

This couldn't go on very long; no construction made by man could stand it. There was a cracking sound, and suddenly the lights went out.

The plane tipped crazily, and one of the crew rushed into the compartment, shouting into their ears: "Put on your lifebelts! We are going down!"

Lanny had read that a drowning man reviews all the incidents of his life. Now, told that he was facing a horrible death, nothing of the sort happened to him. His thoughts were few and simple. The first was: "This can't happen to me! Out there in that storm, that blackness and waste of icy waters!" Then he thought: "My job! My message! All the work I did, the lessons I learned! No, I must get to Germany!"

It was not true that his thoughts came any faster. He had no track of time, but he thought of those formulas, all that study, and for nothing! They would have to get somebody else, and three months would be lost! A maddening waste of life! And could it be sabotage? Had something been done to the plane? Had it been sent off on false information? And then thoughts of the warnings he had received! The psychic researchers had been right after all! There were such things as premonitions! And after studying the subject for so long, he had refused to heed the warnings! If only he had gone off with Aglund—for a day, two days—until the omens were right. "*Absit omen!*" the ancients had said; but Lanny, super-sophisticate, hadn't paid even that slight tribute to the fates and the furies!

V

Buffeted this way and that, members of the crew dragged in a rubber life raft; it had a device which would inflate it automatically in a few seconds, and the passengers had been told how to work it. Lanny, who had read and heard much about planes, knew that everything depended upon how this transport hit the water; if it came down at a steep angle they would all be crushed, but if the pilot still had control and could level off at the surface, the plane might stay afloat for several minutes and they would have a chance to get out. Lanny threw himself onto the floor, face down, with his feet toward the front of the plane and braced against the cargo. That was the way to break the shock and save one's head and neck.

He was just in time. There was a terrific shock, and it seemed to him that his body collapsed like an accordion; an agonizing pain, and screams—he didn't know whether they were his own or other persons'. Everything was dim from that moment; he was dimly aware of blows, seeming to come from many directions; it was the plane, hitting wave after wave before it slowed. Men were thrown this way and that, and on top of one another. Lanny heard them shouting, trying to get the door open. Apparently they succeeded, for there was a rush of wind and water. He tried to drag himself; his legs were helpless, but with his arms he got near to the door; then he became aware of a pair of strong hands seizing him and a voice saying: "Come on, now!"

He must have fainted; the blackness of the night and the blackness of his soul became one. Afterwards he thought he could recall a few moments of consciousness; of lying in the darkness with icy cold water being hurled over him, and forces tossing him this way and that; his pain was so great that he didn't want to know about it, and perhaps that was why he sought refuge in unconsciousness again.

Looking back on it afterwards, he decided that for all practical purposes he died that night; the experience taught him that he need never be afraid of death. There could be pain before it, but there was no pain after it; when you were dead you were dead. You didn't find yourself transported to glory, no angel handed you a golden harp and invited you to play or sing; you didn't meet the spirits of your ancestors—Great-Uncle Eli Budd talking New England transcendentalism, Grandfather Samuel Budd laying down the law from the ancient Hebrew Scriptures. There came no Tecumseh, grumbling at "that old telepathy," no Otto Kahn, making sophisticated fun of himself, no Zaharoff, "that old man with guns going off all round him." Maybe your subconscious mind went back to join these other subconscious minds, but your conscious mind didn't know anything about it, or about anything else. Such, at any rate, was the conclusion the amateur philosopher drew from the experience of that night. "A sleep and a forgetting"!

VI

The faint beginnings of new consciousness were among the strangest experiences of this philosopher's life. They came and went, and appeared to be a bewildered effort to catch hold of themselves, to make sure if they were there and what they were. Voices, dim and wavering, seemed as though they were floating in air and had no connection with anything else in the universe. That was the way it might have been in the spirit world, and Lanny's thoughts began to shape themselves around that idea; he was dead, and was coming slowly to consciousness in a new world. Would he meet people he knew there, and how would he know them? Was he himself, or was he some other person, or several persons? He felt pain, and why was that? What had happened to him? Slowly it came back to him: oh, yes, a plane, a wreck! And a mission to Germany! He had failed, and he shrank from the thought— he lost consciousness again, because he could not dare to face the terrible fact of his failure.

But the voices continued, floating in infinite vastness. He couldn't make out the words, but some of the tones were familiar; somebody in the spirit world whom he had known well. It was like groping his way in darkness, and there would come tiny gleams of light. He decided that the tones were Robbie's; undoubtedly, a man would know his own father's voice anywhere. But then, Robbie wasn't in the spirit world, so it couldn't be so. Lanny found the mental effort too great and gave up; the little spark of consciousness faded out. Perhaps he fell asleep, perhaps he swooned, perhaps he died again—who could say?

The spark came back, however, and Lanny remembered that it had lived before, and what he had thought—that his father had joined him in the spirit world. Now he could make out the words, and unquestionably it was Robbie saying: "You are all right, Lanny. This is your father. This is Robbie." Then it came to him—a truly startling idea— that maybe he wasn't dead, and that his father was with him, somehow, somewhere. The idea was too confusing and the spark failed again— for a minute, an hour, a day—Lanny had no means of judging the intervals.

As the awakening continued, little by little Lanny came to realize that the voice was really his father's, and it was his father's hand touching him. He opened his eyes, and it was his father looking at him and smiling. The effort was too much, and he had to close his eyes, and again there was a period of oblivion. He still had so much pain that he didn't want to face it, and not even the pleasure of seeing Robbie could compensate for it. He became aware that people were feeding him things through a tube, and that was unpleasant, too; however, Robbie kept assuring him that everything was all right, and that he was going to get well. Lanny would think of the mission to England and to Germany, and all the formulas, and how urgent it was; he would start shuddering with anxiety and grief, and again he would fall back into oblivion.

VII

What had happened Lanny found out later, a hint here and a hint there. He had been dragged out of the plane and onto the life raft, along with two other passengers and two members of the crew who had survived the crash. Apparently the fury of the tornado had been higher in the air; the sea was not too rough, and somebody had lain to leeward of him and kept him from being washed away. The crew had had time to radio their position before the crash, and search planes had come even before daylight, looking for flares. In the morning the survivors had released a dye which colored the water about them—that was one of the devices which were strapped to the raft. About noon a "Dumbo" had found them and taken them aboard and flown them to a hospital in Halifax.

Lanny was suffering from both shock and exposure, and in addition he had both leg bones, the tibias, broken below the knees. The hospital authorities considered it a miracle that he survived; they attributed it to a sound constitution and a temperate life, plus modern remedies which are so close to miracles. When this battered body had been carried in they had searched the clothing, and found a passport in the coat pocket and another sewed up in the lining. Manifestly, this meant some sort of secret war work, and since he didn't look like a Nazi, they guessed that he was an American agent. They sent two telegrams, one addressed to the next of kin of Richard Thurston Harrison at the New York address in the passport; since it was a fictitious address, this telegram was reported undeliverable.

The other was addressed to the next of kin of Lanning Prescott Budd, care Budd-Erling Aircraft Corporation, Newcastle, Connecticut, and that brought a result startling to a hospital superintendent. A voice over the telephone said: "This is Robert Budd, President of Budd-Erling Aircraft. Lanning Budd is my son. How is he?" When the answer was: "His condition is critical," the voice said: "I will fly immediately. I should be there in a few hours." Then, being a businessman, Robbie added: "I will pay all his bills, and if you save his life I will contribute two thousand dollars to your hospital fund." That is one way to assist a miracle, if not to cause it!

So Lanny was in a comfortable bed in a private room, and his father in the room adjoining. That busy man had shown where his heart was; he had dropped everything and come to sit by Lanny's bedside and whisper to him that everything was all right and that he was going to live. Robbie didn't know much about the subconscious mind—they hadn't mentioned it at Yale in his day—but Lanny had done a lot to educate his old man over the years. Robbie had heard it explained that you could give suggestions to the subconscious mind and that they would "take"; it might even be possible to do it without talking, mind to mind. Perhaps that was what made prayers work, for surely they did. Robbie didn't know whether he believed in God or not, and certainly if He existed He had made a lot of miserable people for no reason that a rational mind could discover; but if sitting there and whispering to Lanny that he would get well would help him to get well, Robbie would try it. The hospital had a chaplain, a Church of England priest, who came and did the same thing, and Robbie found him a very decent fellow; they talked it over, and Robbie raised his bid—he promised the church a stained-glass window if his eldest son lived.

Somebody once asked Voltaire whether it was possible to kill a cow by enchantment, and that cynic replied: "Yes, provided you use strychnine, too." So the hospital doctors used not merely prayer but the new sulfa drugs, and blood plasma, and other remedies of their *materia medica.* Lanny was made as comfortable as a man could be who has each of his legs enclosed in a heavy plaster cast, from the upper third of the thighs down to the toes. (He had what the surgeons called a "spiral fracture," and they had performed an "open operation," putting stainless steel screws through the fractured part of the bone.) Little by little he came back to life and memory; the fever diminished, but still he babbled in his sleep, and it was all about the nucleus of the atom, and its positrons and neutrons and deuterons and what not. When the patient was well enough to be asked about it he whispered: "It is a mission, Robbie, and it is so urgent! I must get well quickly."

The father could do some guessing, for he had a lot of technical men on his staff and he listened to their conversation. When men are talking about jet propulsion they can hardly fail to mention atomic energy and the possibility that the Germans might get it ahead of anybody else. Robbie said: "Take it easy, son. It'll be a long time before you can travel again, and somebody else will have to be doing your job."

The sick man insisted: "Write a note to Professor Alston and tell him what has happened." That wasn't revealing any secret, for Robbie had long ago come to the idea that "Charlie" was the government authority who had charge of Lanny's comings and goings. In the old days this would have exasperated the father, but now it was all right. Anything to win this war—even the boondogglers!

When it was certain that Lanny was past the crisis, Robbie returned to his own job, and his place was taken by Cousin Jennie Budd, a member of the clan who was a confirmed old maid and lived in Robbie's household as a sort of upper housekeeper. She came by train; nobody was ever going to get her into one of those flying contraptions. She took the room next to the patient and read to him, wrote letters for him, smoothed his pillow, and told him stories about their numerous and eccentric New England family. Cousin Jennie didn't have the least hesitation about praying; she had been brought up to it, and never found fault with God, but told Him plainly what she wanted and overlooked those cases in which He did not see fit to oblige her. She assured the son of Budd-Erling that some day God would let him know why He had allowed that plane to be wrecked. Something that Lanny was doing, or that somebody else was doing, that God didn't happen to approve! Thy will be done, on earth as it is in heaven!

VIII

This two-thousand-dollar patient received the best of care. The superintendent did not fail to stop in each day and study the chart. The doctors, even those who had nothing to do with the case, stopped by to try out their bedside manner. The severe head nurse shepherded her flock and made sure they overlooked no duty. Each of the nurses, young or middle-aged, had her own career to think about, and no one of them overlooked what might be the chance of a lifetime. The story of the father's offer was known and it was reported that the family was fabulously wealthy. Suffering had not destroyed the patient's good looks, but had lent them a tender quality. The two passports also were talked about, and it was taken for granted that the injuries had been incurred in the service of Britain and Nova Scotia. While Lanny lay unconscious the nurses stroked his forehead and prayed for him; when his consciousness returned they found him delightful, and prayed for him in a different sense of the words.

He was polite to everybody, but reticent, and soon they realized that he was tormented in mind. Asleep, he murmured a strange gibberish which nobody recognized, and sometimes he had nightmares, cried out, and struggled to lift his plaster legs. Something was preying on him, and the doctors feared that he might die of worry instead of shock. The superintendent, a man of experience, tried to probe his secret, but all he got was: "I have an urgent duty. How soon shall I be able to walk?" The superintendent could only reply: "You can delay your recovery by impatience."

Matters got so bad that Robbie Budd came for another week-end. It was easy for him because, as he said, his place was lousy with planes. Budd-Erling was now making a two-seater pursuit job, and for these Halifax was practically in the backyard—a matter of a couple of hours' flight. Robbie had had a talk with Charlie Alston over the telephone, and brought the message: "Tell your patient not to worry. We are sending somebody else." All Lanny would answer was: "Oh, Robbie, it's *so* important, and nobody else can do it! Anyhow it will take months to prepare!"

"But look, son," the father pleaded. "You are setting yourself back. You can't mend broken bones with tears."

Lanny moved his head from side to side in helpless grief. "It ought not to have happened, Robbie! It's like a death—it's like thousands of deaths—millions of them!"

"You don't want to tell me about it?"

"I can't tell a word. I am on my honor."

"Well, there's nothing to keep me from trying to guess."

"No, but whatever you guess, don't say it here, don't say it anywhere. People here know too much already. What happened to my passport?"

"They found two of them."

"I feared they would. Did they find the capsule?"

"I didn't hear about any capsule."

"Well, forget it. Some day I'll tell you the story. Has anything been in the papers?"

"They don't publish much about the Ferry Command, Lanny. And certainly nothing about accidents to it."

"Thank God for that! Don't tell anybody whom you don't have to. Understand, I'm not worrying about myself, Robbie, it's the country."

"Now is the one time when you ought to be thinking about yourself and nothing else. You know so much about auto-suggestion—why don't you try it?"

"I'm doing my best. I'm fighting to reconcile myself to what has happened. It's the hardest job I ever had."

I X

The President of Budd-Erling went back to his own urgent tasks, and Lanny lay on his back—he could not turn over. It causes eyestrain if you read in that position, so the kind Cousin Jennie read aloud in a slow inexpressive voice whatever he asked for: newspapers, magazines, any novel that he could be sure was proper. But fiction seemed empty and thin; all he wanted was the war news, and especially Russia, which the prim maiden lady considered slightly objectionable. The Germans had about surrounded Leningrad and were drawing inexorably nearer to Moscow; this two-thousand-mile battle was beyond the scope of human imagination.

Robbie had brought a radio set, which could be used in a hospital room if it was kept very low. The Canadian radio, government-owned, is free of commercials, which is a blessing to any man, sick or well. There was plenty of news, and Lanny fed on this. The trouble came when the impatient patient closed his eyes and tried to sleep; then his mind went over the duties he had planned, the schemes he had evolved —for Britain and for Germany; then he was like a wild lion in a cage, or a skylark beating itself to death against bars overhead.

Writing materials were brought, and with a pillow for support he managed to scribble notes on a pad. Mail out of Canada would be censored, he knew, so he wrote with caution. He doubted if a letter would go from Canada to Vichy France, so he had asked Robbie to write to his mother. To Rick he wrote: "I had an accident somewhat like your own, but at sea. I am going to be all right, but it will take time." Almost a quarter of a century had passed since Rick had crashed, but he had surely not forgotten it. To Zoltan he wrote: "I met with a serious accident, but am getting well." He wrote the same to Laurel Creston, and added the sentence: "Your fears were justified and I wish I had taken your advice." He signed that one "Brother," and hoped the censor wouldn't take it for code. To Lizbeth he didn't have to mention the accident, since Robbie had told her father about it. "Just a line to let you know I am getting along and will soon be all right. Excuse the scrawl. Best wishes."

A great deal depended upon those letters—more than Lanny could have any idea of. First result was a telephone conversation. There were no phones in the rooms of this hospital, but for a two-thousand-dollar patient they would get a long cord and run it from the hall. This was Baltimore, Maryland, calling Halifax, Nova Scotia, and that might be assumed to be important. The voice of Reverdy Holdenhurst, as clear as if he had been in the room. "We are getting ready for our cruise, and don't you want to change your mind and come along?"

"I'm afraid it's going to be some time before I can do any traveling, Reverdy." This from a man with legs that might have weighed fifty pounds apiece.

"We'll wait for you if you'll say yes. Nothing would give us more pleasure, and you'll have a complete rest and change; everything will be warm where we are going."

"Somehow or other I've lost my fondness for the sea, Reverdy. I don't enjoy thinking about it."

"A yacht isn't an airplane, and we choose our route carefully. The hurricane season will be over where we are going, and there isn't the slightest danger. We'll have a physician on board to take care of you, and we'll provide every comfort. We'll get one of those surgical carts such as they have in hospitals; and, as you know, we have an elevator on the *Oriole*. You can be taken from your cabin to the deck, and you can have sunshine or shade, whatever you prefer. If you stay where you are you'll be indoors all the time. Just think, the Caribbean, and Panama, then the South Seas, Samoa and Tahiti, and then South China, and Bali and Java. When you are able to sit up we'll have a wheel chair, and when you begin to walk we'll have a man to help you. Think it over!"

It was hard to say no to such a proposal. The father didn't mention that he had a daughter; if Lanny had any doubts whether Lizbeth would go, he could ask, but he didn't. All he could say was: "You are too kind. They don't give me any idea how long it will be before I can be out of these casts, and I couldn't think of putting you to such inconvenience."

"The casts don't make a bit of difference. We have plenty of strong men on board the yacht, and they can move you. I'd offer to come to Halifax for you, but I don't suppose they'd allow a yacht in those waters."

"It would be far too dangerous."

"Well, Robbie can have you flown, say to Miami. That's a pleasant place, and I'd wait there as long as you wished. No trouble at all for anybody."

It was a princely offer; the way the very rich treat their friends. Lanny knew exactly what it meant. The Baltimore capitalist was saying: "Come and marry my daughter. Your wounds and damages don't make any difference. Come and court her while we sail over warm tropic seas and marry her in any port you choose. Forget your cares and impossible duties, and come to the land of the Lotos-eaters!"

> A land where all things always seem'd the same!
> And round about the keel with faces pale,
> Dark faces pale against that rosy flame,
> The mild-eyed melancholy Lotos-eaters came.

X

At other times Lanny had thought his friend's importunities in bad taste, but now that he was a cripple and couldn't expect to be an active man for some time, the offer became a kindness not to be undervalued. Lanny could only plead: "I have duties, Reverdy, which I am not free to talk about. You expect to be gone six months, and I hope that I shall be fit for duty again in less time than that."

"All right, if that happens, we won't try to detain you. Whenever you feel that you are well enough, you can take a plane by way of Honolulu and San Francisco. I suppose you don't expect to give up flying for the rest of your life. What I want to do is to help you to get well in the quickest and surest way."

Lanny's final word was: "I'll think it over and let you know. I'll have to ask the hospital people."

He did this; and they told him he was free from fever, which meant that the knitting of his bones was proceeding satisfactorily. To move him in the casts would be difficult, but with care it could be done. In a week or two he should have enough strength to stand a journey. "That is," added the head surgeon, "provided you stop having nightmares." Lanny was doing his best, but it was a hard task to keep atomic formulas from racing through his mind.

This matter was so important that Robbie Budd took another weekend off. Said he: "Reverdy told me of his invitation, and we all think that's the thing for you to do, Lanny. So much better than lying here indoors in winter weather. It gets cold as the devil up here; you can feel it in the air already."

"Listen, Robbie," replied the son, "there's no use making any bones about it. Reverdy wants me to come because Lizbeth wants me to marry her; and if I take this trip, it practically means an engagement."

"That's an exaggeration, Lanny; no man has to marry unless he wants to, and I take it you haven't committed yourself."

"Surely not; but when a girl has set her cap the way Lizbeth has, it becomes damned uncomfortable, and I couldn't have any pleasure on that yacht unless I meant to oblige both father and daughter."

"Esther and I have talked about it a lot, Lanny, and we wish you would think about Lizbeth more seriously. We can't imagine a girl who would make you a more suitable wife; and surely you have taken time enough to look around. Tell me once more, and frankly: Is there some other woman?"

"There are several women I know with whom I might be happy. Lizbeth is one, and Peggy is another. But I have a duty which I can't reveal to any woman, and I couldn't make any woman happy while hiding such a secret from her."

"You haven't got up-to-date in your thinking, son. The fact that you had two passports and are some sort of government agent is surely being whispered about this military and naval port. There are bound to be German spies here, and for you to go back into Germany after this has happened would be a form of suicide. Surely you have to bring yourself to realize that!"

"I have thought about it a lot, Robbie; but my assignment is so urgent that I shall have to take a chance. I simply cannot quit!"

X I

Robbie talked with the doctors and then went back to Newcastle and phoned to Charlie Alston. "Lanny won't tell me what it is that is eating him up, but I am making a guess that you know something about it."

"I might find out," admitted the "fixer" cautiously.

'Well, here is the situation. It will be several months before he is able to be active again, and he is making it longer by his worrying. The doctors are having to give him sleeping drugs, and they don't like that and neither do I. He has nightmares and cries in his sleep; he recites long formulas, as if it were chemistry or mathematics. Now he has an invitation to take a yachting trip to the South Seas, which will give him a complete rest and make him fit for work again. But he won't go, because he insists that he has a duty and that he must get up—with both his legs still in plaster casts."

"I'll talk to him," said Alston. "Perhaps I can help."

So now it was Washington calling Halifax, and once again the telephone extension cord was plugged in. "Hello," said a voice, "this is your Paris employer. Hard luck, old scout!"

"I'm soon going to be fit again—"

"What I called up to tell you, that assignment is dead. We have got the information. The other party found a way to get it to us, and everything is jake."

"Oh, can that really be true, Professor?"

"I talked to the Boss and he says you have a furlough. You are to think about nothing but getting well. He won't see you again for six months, unless it's a purely social call."

"I believe you are kidding me!" exclaimed the P.A.

"I give you my word, I am repeating exactly what the Boss said. 'Tell him to put everything out of his mind but getting his health back; and thanks a million for what he did.' Those were his words."

"Well, of course, that's a great relief. If you really don't need me—"

"Put your mind at rest. We are going to win, not the faintest doubt about it. And you have done your share. Take it easy!"

XII

So there was Lanny, on this bed from which he had not moved for more than a month; he looked at the bare white walls which had been his landscape and the ceiling which had been his sky for that period, and he thought how pleasant it would be to look at something—anything—else. Lying on your back can become an agony; you have to try it for a while to realize how loudly every muscle and nerve and bone cry out in protest. He lay there and stifled his groans. He exercised every muscle he could without moving from one spot. He counted the days which the doctors said must elapse before they would break off the casts and let him at least turn over on his side.

He recalled to mind the trim white yacht, the *Oriole*. Some of the happiest months of his life were associated with yachting trips; first on the *Bluebird*, namesake of Ezra Hackabury's kitchen soap, and then on the *Bessie Budd*, brought into being by Johannes Robin's speculations in German marks. On those two shining pleasure craft the grandson of Budd Gunmakers had visited all the Mediterranean shores, and those of the North Sea and the Baltic; he had sailed into the fjords of Norway, and crossed to Newfoundland and down to New York. But the farthest east he had ever traveled was Odessa and the farthest west was Hollywood. The places that Reverdy had named were strange to him, and certainly worth seeing. They would be warm—and Lanny found that he had the same dread of the cold as his would-be host, the skipper of the *Oriole*. Lanny couldn't recall much about that dreadful night on a rubber raft, but he still felt the effects of it, and wanted never in his life to be cold again.

He thought of Lizbeth, and to an invalid she wore a different aspect from what she had worn to a well man. Here in his helplessness he decided that he had been brutal to her in his strength; he had humiliated her, and failed entirely to appreciate what she offered him. Just to be alive, to be taken care of, to be saved from pain—these were blessings he was able to appreciate for the first time in his life. If she was willing to help him, to take the chance of restoring him to normality, what more could he ask of love and life?

Little by little he began to realize the implications of what had happened here in Halifax, and of what Alston had told him over the phone. He was no longer a presidential agent. F.D. had put it tactfully—he was "on furlough"—but all the same, he could never go back to Hitlerland, at least not until he wanted to throw away his life. Some German agent in this British naval and military base would surely have passed the word to the Nazi spy center that was Yorkville, and from there it would have been cabled to Berlin. The Führer's personal friend, *Der Dicke's* art expert, had been revealed as a secret agent, traveling to Britain on two passports! The Nazis would surely blame him for the failure of Hess's mission, the trapping of the Führer's Deputy and most trusted friend. They would blame him for everything that had ever "leaked," whether or not he had had anything to do with it. They would hate him above all other Americans—those who had never pretended to be friends.

So, he would have to find another job! And meantime he was free —to rest, to get well, to have a wife if he wanted one! So there revived the old question: what sort of wife did he want? Right now it appeared that Laurel Creston had faded into the background; she was an intellectual, and his mind had gone into a coma. What he wanted was to escape any more pain; and the thought of Lizbeth's soft arms about him seemed the very height of bliss. He didn't put it in that crude way, and might have resented it if anyone else had done so; he just drifted along in a sort of half daze. He was exhausted, and didn't want to think; even the conversation of Cousin Jennie Budd didn't bore him, because she didn't try to make him think. And when he drifted to the island of the Lotos-eaters, it was Lizbeth who sat by his side and held his hand. She would comfort him, treat him like a sick child, help him to learn to walk again.

He had been invited to take this journey with no conditions attached, and he could leave whenever he wished. After all, he didn't have to sign a contract to marry. He could go as any other guest and see how he got along with the skipper's daughter. Maybe she wouldn't want to marry him when she discovered how good-for-nothing he was. Maybe he would never be fit to marry anybody. He saw himself gently dismissed, and again as nobly renouncing. In case of need, he could think of several polite pretexts.

Yes, that was the way to look at this cruise. He would have a chance to try out Lizbeth's mind. He would no longer have to conceal from her the fact that he was a Socialist in his sympathies; not using that alarming word, of course, but leading her gently to a sympathetic understanding of the sufferings of the poor, the indignities of the lowly. After all, she wasn't to blame for her upbringing; the fact that her mother and father hadn't succeeded in spoiling her was proof of what a sweet and gentle nature had been her endowment. He had never known anything wilful that she had done, unless you counted her determination to love Lanny Budd. And that was something not too difficult for a man to excuse.

XIII

Robbie, shrewd intriguer, had told Cousin Jennie about Lizbeth and the proposed trip. So this maiden lady was full of questions about the heiress: What did she look like and what did she do and say? Lanny had to tell how he had met her at Emily Chattersworth's villa, and had visited her in Green Spring Valley, and about her home and her parents and the servants and country club and what not. A decorous New England lady would never ask if he had kissed her, but she could hint gently that Lanny seemed lacking in ardor and wonder secretly if there was some other woman in his life. Cousin Jennie went walking and found a bookstore and brought back travel books about the West Indies and the South Seas, about Bali and Java. She read these aloud to her patient, and sighed at the thought of being able to visit these lands of wonder. The Magic City! The Pearl of the Antilles! The China Seas! The Spice Islands! Lanny, who had been raised on the Côte d'Azur, ought to have understood the device of making up fancy names for the tourist trade, but his critical faculties were less active at this time.

The owner of the *Oriole* called again. "We are ready to leave in three days, Lanny. What do you say?"

"I don't believe the doctors would let me go that soon, Reverdy."

"I renew my suggestion that we wait at Miami. There is an excellent harbor, and plenty to entertain us. Robbie tells me he will arrange to have you flown there. You can wait for good weather, and there are airports all along the coast, so it's not at all like flying to Iceland. What about it?"

"I hate to say no, Reverdy. But I think of all the trouble I shall cause you, how helpless I am—"

"Forget it, Lanny. We have people on board with nothing to do but holystone the decks and polish the brass. As for myself, what have I to do but give my friends pleasure? I will take you into my confidence and say that you are the one who will be doing the favor.

Lizbeth says she will come if you do—and you know how much I wish to have her."

"If you put it that way! But I must point out—Lizbeth has never seen me in my present condition, and she may not like it."

"Lizbeth has been told about it, and she says for you to come. Her mother doesn't think it is proper for her to do the inviting—"

But evidently there was a difference of opinion in the Holdenhurst family. No receiver clicked, so Lanny could guess that Lizbeth had been on an extension phone, or that she had taken the receiver from her father's hand. "Nonsense!" came her voice. "Come on, Lanny! We'll have a lovely time."

What could Lanny say but "All right"? Then he added: "When you see this poor wreck you may wish you hadn't spoken!"

BOOK SIX

Like Gods Together, Careless of Mankind

———————— o ————————

21. Pretty Kettle of Fish

I

WITH returning strength Lanny found it easier to write, and this was one way to pass the time. He wrote letters to his clients and his friends, telling them that he was on the way to recovery and where he expected to spend the next few months. Among these persons, naturally, was Laurel Creston; he owed it to her to let her know that he was out of danger, and since he was no longer a P.A., he could write more freely than before. "I have had to give up the duty I had undertaken, and I fear it will be some time before I can take on another. I am obeying the doctors and trying to put all cares out of my mind. I am a burden to myself and to everybody, and it is extraordinarily kind of your uncle to take me on his yacht."

Lanny thought that was putting it tactfully; if a lady fictionist had any tendency to feel slighted, this was letting her know that he was no good to anyone, herself included. He didn't mention Lizbeth, and perhaps Laurel wouldn't know that her ·cousin was going on the cruise; she could find out, of course, but at least Lanny had indicated that he didn't consider the matter of any importance. He was taking this trip for the sake of his health, lured by the warmth of the tropic seas. "By the time I return," he wrote, "you will be well on with that novel, and I promise to be your first reader." He signed this "Bienvenu," as much as to say that while he was no longer a secret agent he might become one again. It wasn't melodrama to suppose that the chambermaid who cleaned Laurel's room or the janitor who burned her trash might be in the pay of the Nazis.

Reverdy telephoned again. It was the first of November, and the yacht *Oriole* was about to depart from her Baltimore basin. On board would be himself and Lizbeth, his man secretary and her woman tutor —Lizbeth was going to improve her mind, and counted upon Lanny to help. Also there was the woman doctor, bound for her post in South China, and a Miss Gillis, whom Lanny vaguely remembered as a frail gray-haired lady. All wealthy families have impoverished relatives or school friends of the wife, who perform light duties, such as shopping, helping the social secretary, making up a four at bridge, or looking after a child who has eaten green fruit. "I'll phone you from Miami," added Reverdy. "We'll wait there and go fishing until you arrive."

The doctors said they would be willing to take off the casts in another week, and that seemed to fit the schedule. There was more telephoning, and Robbie undertook to send a two-engine plane with room in the cabin for a single bed. Budd-Erling didn't make such a plane, but Robbie would get it; if you asked how, he would give a sly smile and a wink, and remark: "A lot of people want what I've got, so now and then they have to give me what I want." The father himself didn't come; he was frightfully busy, but would send a man to stay with Lanny from the moment he left the hospital until he was safe on the *Oriole*. Also Robbie would send the promised check to the hospital.

II

The breaking off of the plaster was accomplished, and—oh, blessed relief!—Lanny could roll over in bed. He indulged in that luxury for hours, and slept at night as he had not done for weeks. Instead they put on him what they called "short-length braces," made of molded leather and steel, and extending from his ankle-joints to his knees. Also as an extra precaution, he would use crutches for a few days.

In the morning word came that the plane was at the airport. He wrote a check for the faithful Cousin Jennie, who was returning by train. He presented twenty-dollar bills to the nurses, since he couldn't go out and buy them presents. Robbie's man didn't have much to do, because there were so many hospital people eager to help. The patient's journey to the ambulance was a sort of triumphal progress, with everybody lined up to smile and say good-by. From the ambulance he was carried on a stretcher to the plane and there laid on a bed. Robbie's man sat on a camp chair beside him, and away they went.

The weather was promising, and they were making a flight to Southern Florida, a distance of some eighteen hundred miles. Robbie's injunctions were to break the journey at the Washington airport and spend the night. Lanny might have an ambulance and be taken to a hotel if he wished; but Lanny said there was no sense in that, his supper could be brought to the plane and he could sleep right there. He was cheerfully interested in the first careful tentatives at lifting his legs. His escort was an employe of the Budd-Erling plant; he was interested in talking about it, and Lanny in listening. They passed the evening, and at dawn were off on the second leg of the journey.

An ambulance was waiting at the Miami airport, and the traveler was driven to a pier where the elegant 212-foot yacht had been laid alongside especially for this event. From first to last Lanny never had a moment's discomfort; that is the way the rich are treated in this world, provided they have the sense to stay within their own sacred circle and not go wandering off on secret arctic missions with false passports. Reverdy Johnson Holdenhurst never did anything like that, but took care of himself and his family and friends if they would let him. Reverdy declared that the legend, "three generations from shirtsleeves to shirtsleeves," was true only of the wastrels and fools; it certainly wasn't true of those who had the sense to put their money into city real estate, like the Astors and Vanderbilts and Rockefellers —and the Holdenhursts of the Monumental City.

There were yachts and speedboats in this ample harbor, a winter playground of the rich. But many of them were no longer "private"; they had been turned over to the Coast Guard to be used for patrol and escort duty in a public emergency. Some had been equipped with guns, and others were doing the best they could with small arms. There were persons who thought the *Oriole* ought to be in this service; they had annoyed Reverdy with their suggestions, and he saw that they didn't get a second chance. His privacy, and the state of his health, were matters which he considered his first concern, and now he was anxious to get away from American waters before some damnable bureaucrat took it into his head to say that it was not permissible for a pleasure yacht to cruise in the Pacific.

III

All the passengers and some of the crew were lined along the rail when the ambulance came out on the pier. The invalid was transferred to a surgical cart, one of those little beds on rubber-tired wheels which are used in hospitals to carry patients to and from operations. A convenient thing to have on board, Reverdy said, and he'd have got it sooner if he had thought. Lanny might sleep on it all the time if he wished; but Lanny said no, he was soon going to be walking. To show how smart he was, when the vehicle reached the deck of the yacht he sat up so as to shake hands with the friends who gathered about.

He was happy as a bird let out of a cage. Such a wonderful thing, to be able to look around you, and to feel sunshine on your face and hands! He was pale from six weeks' confinement, but the sun would soon fix that, he could feel the process already under way. Imagine feeling the cold of the subarctic one day, and the caressing warmth of the subtropics the next! Everybody here was in white ducks or flannels, and Lanny had not failed to be provided with a summer outfit in Halifax.

Here came Lizbeth; and how pretty she looked in a yachting costume! It had been so that Lanny had first seen her in the Golfe Juan —and be sure it was perfectly tailored, also perfectly laundered by the man who was on the yacht to perform that special service. The softest light French flannel, cream-colored with blue trimmings; and to go with this, lovely cheeks that didn't need retouching, and soft brown hair that had received exactly the right kind of permanent. Lizbeth was blushing with happiness like a June bride, and possibly she thought of herself that way. She had never looked sweeter. Lanny decided that he had made a wise decision, and that this trip was going to be one of unblemished delight.

Until the owner of the yacht, after telling about the golf game he had played and the fish he had caught, remarked casually: "We won't sail until morning, because we have another passenger coming on the night train from New York: my niece, Laurel Creston."

Just so casually does a thunderbolt fall from the sky, or a parachute bomb explode after drifting down from a plane! Fortunately, a man who has been trained to be a diplomat in boyhood and who has been a secret agent for years learns not to let consternation show in his face. As it happened, Lanny had discussed with Laurel how they would both behave if and when fate brought them together in the presence of "Uncle Reverdy." After one gulp, Lanny was able to remark: "Laurel Creston? Isn't she a writer?"

"Yes," replied the other. "She has had a number of stories in magazines. One that I read I thought quite good. She telephoned that she was planning to start work on a novel, and thought that a cruise would give her the necessary quiet. So I told her to come."

"It sounds very interesting," was Lanny's casual comment.

IV

Later on he had time to think this development over, and he decided that it was a consequence of his recent letter to Laurel. The moment she had received it, she had telephoned to her uncle, asking if she would be welcome. That was clear enough; but why had she done it? It might be that she valued Lanny's knowledge of Germany, and wanted to have him available while she wrote. That was conceivable;

but staring at Lanny like the face of a jack-o'-lantern in the dark was the other possibility, that Laurel had made up her mind all of a sudden not to let Lizbeth have him to herself over a period of six months and perhaps for life!

Inner voices told him that that was the real reason, and no use fooling himself. His letter had told Laurel that he had given up the dangerous mission abroad, which was practically saying that he was free to think about love and marriage. All women are psychologists—they have had to be in order to survive through the ages—and especially is that true of one who hopes to survive as a writer of fiction for other women. The nurses at the hospital had known that a man lying helpless in bed is a shining mark for sympathetic attention; and surely the woman whose mind had created "The Gauleiter's Cousin" would be no less acute! Now "Mary Morrow" was on the train from New York, with a suitcase full of manuscripts and a couple of steamer trunks full of clothes, and in her mind the set purpose of cutting out her cousin Lizbeth and carrying off the living prize in a contest of charm!

It may have seemed egotistical of Lanny Budd's subconscious mind to be so sure; but then, a presidential agent has to be something of a psychologist too, and this one had been watching women ever since he could remember in the nursery. If there was anything unfavorable about them that his mother hadn't told him, it had been supplied by Emily and Sophie and Margy, by Rosemary and Irma and Marceline and Marie de Bruyne. In addition to these living authorities, there was *Man and Superman*, which Lanny had read and chuckled over. Yes, surely; when a woman encounters the right man for her biological purposes she goes after him. She may be ever so haughty in spirit, she may have been taught an ever-so-stiff decorum in a city whose ruling group has always been Southern and has refused to be "reconstructed." But when she meets the right man she starts spinning webs like a spider, and all other women of the eligible age become her enemies pro tem.

So this invalid lying on a pallet with rubber-tired wheels suddenly saw the cruise of the *Oriole* in an entirely new light; no longer as a sojourn in the land of the Lotos-eaters, but as a biological battleground, a jousting tournament, a duello—many such similes came to his mind. In the end he settled upon an old Scotch phrase, and the trim white shining *Oriole* became "a pretty kettle of fish!"

V

Lanny wasn't on deck when Laurel's taxi brought her to the pier. He did not meet her until next morning, when he was wheeled out into the sunshine, clad in a fresh white duck outfit. The yacht was gliding down the Miami River and out into Biscayne Bay. There was

Laurel with her uncle, he in his proper yachtsman's costume and she in a light blue summer dress. "Laurel," said the skipper, "this is my friend Lanny Budd." And then to Lanny: "This is my niece, Laurel Creston." Ladies first, always.

Both of them had studied their roles. Laurel said: "I am pleased to meet you, Mr. Budd. I have heard about you." Lanny said: "I think I have seen your work in a magazine. I am honored." Very formal, very proper—but in their secret hearts quite a tumult! Laurel would be thinking: "Will he forgive me?" Lanny was thinking: "Dare I give her a wink?"

An odd sort of intrigue, seeming-guilty yet in fact innocent. A P.A. had begun it, because he hadn't dared reveal to anyone that he had helped a woman wanted by the Gestapo to escape from Germany. Laurel had acceded to it, because she hadn't wanted her uncle to know that she had been accumulating "Red" literature in her trunk in Berlin, and had given help to the anti-Nazi underground. She and Lanny had thought it easy enough never to mention their meetings in Germany; but this simple bit of concealment had grown by accretion, until now there were large chunks of their lives which they must never refer to. Laurel might say that she had visited the French Riviera, but never that she had been a guest of Lanny's mother. And nothing about those delightful motor rides in and near New York; nor about her medium-ship, because if she did the guests would want to attend séances, and who could guess what Otto Kahn might say about past events? Whole chunks cut out of their lives! And they must always be on formal terms, always "Mister" and "Miss," at least until they had been on the yacht for some time.

Here came Lizbeth, dressed in her prettiest, and ready to give her full attention to the invalid; so it was up to Laurel to take herself tactfully out of the way, to get a book and become absorbed in it. Day and night, Lizbeth would be there, and watching like a hawk; a female hawk, which presumably has no less keen vision than her partner, and may have the double duty of keeping watch to make certain that the partner is not paying visits to any other lady hawk's perch. From the first hour it was made plain to Lanny Budd that he was Lizbeth's guest, almost her property; it was to her that he was expected to pay attention, and for any of the other females on board to divert him from this duty would be presumption, not to say treason. It simply wasn't done on board yachts, and all persons of refinement and discretion would understand it.

Lanny never ceased to wonder just how the presence of the cousin had been allowed to come about. Had Reverdy been trapped into it by a sudden telephone call? Had Laurel planned it that way, to get his consent before he had time to realize what he was doing? Or had he, manlike, failed to consider the possibility that Laurel might develop into a rival for Lanny's attention? Could it be that this solitary and easily bored man had thought of Laurel as a source of entertainment for himself? Somebody to talk to, and tell him stories, and play bridge with him? He, the conservative and old-fashioned Southerner, would surely not have read *Man and Superman,* and it might never have occurred to him that a lady of his family would be capable of trying to run off with her hostess's intended. And especially no woman who had reached the age of thirty-four or thereabouts, which in the Old South meant that she was hopelessly committed to spinsterhood, and that any sign of marital aspirations would be the occasion for gales of ridicule from all the other members of her family.

VI

So here was this invalid passenger, caught in the oddest of domestic triangles; he called it "the three L's"—Lanny, Lizbeth, and Laurel. The French had a name for it, *la vie à trois;* Lanny had been in it once before, in the Château de Bruyne, and then it had been less innocent but far more entertaining. In the present case he found that he had become a prisoner of love. Lizbeth was so sweet and so seemingly guileless that he would be unwilling to hurt her feelings, and would behave as she took it for granted that he must and would.

It wasn't so bad at the beginning. He had to get his strength back, and she was so happy to help. Food was important, and at mealtimes they wheeled him into the dining-saloon for company's sake; a tray was put in his lap, and everybody took an interest in making sure that he got everything he wanted. Later, after he had made certain that he could stand up with his braces and that they would support his weight, a man-servant helped him to a seat and he could dine like the others. He had to do a lot of sleeping, so Lizbeth made no objection when he retired to his cabin, and if he stole part of his time there to read a book, she didn't know it.

What she expected was his social time. She wanted to be nurse and mother, little sister and companion. She wanted to watch him learning to get about with his crutches, and after a few days, to guide his experiments at standing and walking alone. She wanted to feel that she was useful to him, and that his success was her reward. When at last he was able to pace the deck, she wanted to hold his arm and pretend that she was aiding him. They stopped to lean on the railing and look over the dark blue waters of the Caribbean Sea. Flying fish rose from the ship's path and scudded away close to the surface; she wanted to be the one to hear him explain that this was their way of escaping from pursuers. What a strange thing to think of, the infinitude of life in that sea, each fantastic kind preying upon the others to the best of its powers; a whole universe of cruelty without a single moral sentiment that any mind could detect!

So Lanny philosophized, and apparently Lizbeth had never heard anything of that nature. They stood at the yacht's bow, watching the porpoises diving and swinging this way and that in the water. He told her that this was play, and that the play spirit was all through nature; it was practice for living, an overflow of energy. He told her that these creatures were not fish, but mammals, which suckled their young; that seemed to her slightly shocking, but it was natural history, and doubtless that made it modest. He told her about this sea water, that it was full of all kinds of minerals, and on the coast of Texas a huge plant was being built for the extracting of magnesium from the Gulf of Mexico. She decided all over again that he was the most widely informed man she had ever known, and altogether wonderful.

It was the same when he turned the dials of the radio, which perforce took the place of newspapers on this cruise. She would have preferred the latest jazz tunes, and, as he grew stronger, to dance with him; but he wanted to listen to news about battles in the snows of Russia, and she sat by and tried to be attentive. Lanny appeared to take an aloof attitude to the struggle; it didn't make much difference who won, so she wondered why he cared to hear so many bloody details. The Germans were in the very suburbs of Moscow, and everybody seemed to think they were going to get all the way in; but suddenly they began to retreat, and then it was dreadful, because there was deep snow and bitter cold, and how anybody could live there was a mystery. How glad Lizbeth was that they were in this safe and warm place!

Secretly she consulted the globe which stood in the yacht's library, and found European Russia, and there was Moscow near the middle of it. She really wanted to understand these matters and be able to open her lips without making some "boner." She was familiar with her father's opinion, that the Communists were the greatest menace that had ever appeared in the world, and that anybody who was trying to put them down should have American sympathy. But apparently Lanny looked at it as an art expert; he remarked casually that Europe had always had wars, and one more didn't matter much.

Others would listen to these broadcasts, and generally Laurel was among them. She would sit with her lips tight, never discussing any political subject; and on that very account Lizbeth suspected her of unorthodox thoughts. Laurel had left the family nest and gone off to New York; Laurel wrote things which she apparently didn't care to show her relatives; she made remarks which were supposed to be witty, and then Lanny would laugh and Lizbeth would feel uneasy. More and more in her secret heart she was coming to distrust this cousin, and to wonder why her father had let her come. But of course she had to be polite.

VII

The southward course of the yacht took them past the Bahamas and between Cuba and Haiti; but they did not stop to see any of the sights of these places. Reverdy explained: "Althea is overdue at her post, so we plan to take her to China, and then loaf on the way home." He added to Lanny: "If that is agreeable." Of course Lanny said it was entirely agreeable.

Althea was the medical missionary, and Lanny asked what port was her destination. The answer was: "Hongkong." The name, like the sound of a bell, rang with that effect in Lanny's mind. For something over three years the name had had a special meaning to him. In Munich at the time of the settlement between Chamberlain and Hitler, Lanny had happened to make the acquaintance of a young Rumanian who called himself an astrologer and had been honored by the Nazis in their peculiar way—which was to arrest him, shut him up in an elegant suite in the Vier Jahreszeiten Hotel, feed him on the fat of the land, and order him to prepare horoscopes of the Führer and his entourage.

Lanny didn't have the slightest belief in astrology, so he hadn't been worried when this mystical personage had taken his hand, gazed into his eyes, and declared: "You will die in Hongkong within three or four years." Lanny had argued that he hadn't any interest in Hongkong, or reason for going there; to which Herr Reminescu had responded firmly: "You will go." Naturally it gave Lanny something of a jolt to be told now that he was going. He was especially attentive to the subject of precognition because of what had happened in the North Atlantic. He had disregarded one warning and wished he hadn't; and could it be now that he was going from one doom to another? Could it be that he had provoked the fates by escaping, and that they were on his trail? Or was it all *one* doom? Certainly it was true that if he hadn't met with the accident in the North Atlantic he would never have been on the way to South China.

He didn't say anything about the matter to Reverdy, because this was a pleasure trip, and talk about dooms and deaths was hardly in order. The only person on board to whom he had told the story was Laurel, and he didn't know if she would remember it; some time he might ask her—if ever he had a chance for conversation alone with her. That didn't seem likely, as matters were shaping up, for everybody on the *Oriole*, even the servants and the crew, appeared to take it for granted that the one person with whom Lanny was ever to be alone was the owner's daughter. They were so pointed about it, they withdrew so obviously, that it became embarrassing; the only way to keep a group together was to play cards or turn on the radio. The polite and well-bred cousin apparently fell in with this custom; she never favored Lanny with so much as a wink or a private smile. In his mind he kept asking her: "If that's the way you are going to act, why on earth did you come?"

VIII

They approached Panama, and a plane high overhead must have radioed the news, for an armed speedboat met them before they were in sight of land. Their papers were inspected and instructions given, for this was one of the most carefully guarded pieces of property on earth. If an enemy could knock it out, the American fleet would be cut into two halves, and neither half would be big enough for any military purpose. The Army now took charge of all vessels entering the Canal, and passengers and crew had to be below decks while the vessel was being towed through the locks. The passengers might come out and have a look at Gatun Lake, but that was just one more tropical lake with jungle-covered hills around it. The day happened to be hot, and the cabins were air cooled, so stay in them and read a book—or have your hair dressed if you were a lady.

In the town of Panama they stopped for a load of Diesel oil, and the passengers, excepting Lanny, went ashore and were driven about to look at four-hundred-year-old ruins. Reverdy said it was one of the few ports at which it would be safe to stay ashore after sundown, because the Army had got rid of the mosquitoes. Reverdy's mind was full of odds and ends of facts, and he pointed out the strange one that the Atlantic end of this canal was farther west than its Pacific end. Also, he said that the level of the western ocean was nine inches higher than the eastern, an effect of the earth's eastward revolution. Items of information like that were one's reward for traveling around the earth once a year.

The travelers bought picture postcards and wrote messages to their friends at home. They sat in a night club—there were scores of them —and listened to a "spigotty" band playing the same hit tunes they had been getting over the radio, all the way from Baltimore south. The dancing was the same as you would see in the night spots of American cities, for nowadays the merchants of entertainment were combing Mexico and Cuba and points south for forms of sensuality to stir the jaded tastes of their patrons. The guests of the *Oriole* came back early and assured their invalid that he hadn't missed much.

There was a ten-thousand-mile journey before them, and they would take it pretty nearly straight, except for refueling and the restocking of their larder. The yacht had a cruising speed of nearly twenty miles an hour, which was unusual—but then Reverdy was an unusual man, who wanted what he wanted, and had had it made exactly to his order. Their round trip would be about equal to circumnavigating the globe at its equator. In earlier years, Reverdy had gone all the way around, and that was how he had come to show up at Cannes. But now he had to make what he called "a dog's journey," there and back, and he hated the war for causing this inconvenience. Reverdy would have liked to see a part of the earth set apart as a dueling ground, where nations that wanted to fight could go and have it out, and leave the high seas to American millionaires in search of health and recreation.

IX

The guests settled down to an agreeable routine. Every morning Lizbeth studied with her tutor, that same middle-aged teacher of art whom she had employed in Baltimore. Since the pupil was a sociable soul they studied on the quarterdeck, under an ample awning, and with a steward bringing them iced fruit juices now and then. They studied different subjects at different hours, just as in school, and if at any time Lanny cared to join them it would be lovely; Miss Hayman would fall silent and let Mr. Budd do the talking, since obviously he knew so much more about everything.

Thus a prospective fiancé had opportunity to investigate the mind of his almost-intended, and he observed that it was a literal mind; education consisted of storing up a set of facts, to be used later in cultured conversation. A young lady acquired "accomplishments," and after she had got herself a husband she never used them and quickly forgot all but a few phrases. Lizbeth was supposed to have acquired a full quota before her debut, but she had picked an especially fastidious man and now was laboring to come up to his requirements. It seemed to the man pathetic in the extreme, and he would have liked to say: "My dear, that isn't the way to do it!" She would have countered: "What *is* the way?"—and what could he have told her?

Laurel had her coffee and toast brought to her cabin, and seldom appeared before lunchtime. She had a typewriter, and if you passed her door you would hear it clicking busily. Lanny would wonder: Was this another story about the Pension Baumgartner in Berlin? Or was it the beginning of the novel? Or might it by any chance be a sketch of life on board a pleasure yacht? This last ought to go well with any magazine editor. Lanny thought of titles: *South Sea Idyll; Lotos Landing; Caribbean Courtship.* All by "Mary Morrow," of course!

At mealtime, and when she was in company with the others, Laurel's manner was one of careful courtesy. She made no effort to shine in conversation, and displayed none of that sharp wit by which Lanny

had come to know her in the beginning. She appeared to have no special interest in "Mr. Budd," and rarely looked in his direction. She
deferred in all things to her uncle, and if her opinion was asked on any
subject having to do with politics or international affairs, she would
say: "Uncle Reverdy knows so much more about these matters than
I do." On that basis, anybody could get along on a private yacht!

Dr. Althea Carroll was somewhere in her late twenties, Lanny guessed
—that was as near as any gentleman would come. She had a round,
rather pale face and wore spectacles; her disposition was serious. It
was explained that her mother had been a schoolmate of Mrs. Holdenhurst and they had kept up the friendship. Her father was a physician
in the interior of China, and Althea had studied, first at Johns Hopkins
University and then at the Medical School to fit herself as her father's
assistant. She was a devout Episcopalian, and reported that her church
was far too worldly and too little interested in missionary work; she
loved the Chinese people, and meant to do what she could to help both
their bodies and their souls. She had a supply of medical books and
magazines which she read whenever it was permissible.

She was extremely careful never to be alone with the genial Mr.
Budd, and Lanny had no conversation with her except when Lizbeth
was present. There was a special reason for this, which he found out
before long: the money for the support of the mission came in part
from Lizbeth's mother, and Althea owed her education to this chari-
table lady; therefore Lizbeth's lightest desire was the woman doctor's
law, and she was careful to give no offense to anyone. The care of
Lanny's health had been assigned her as a duty, but she did not offer
to make any examination, and the advice she gave was in Lizbeth's
presence, and with Lizbeth as intermediary. "You must see that he
doesn't walk too far and that he rests in between walks."

X

Lanny observed with especial interest the habits of the owner of
this floating winter resort. The wireless operator brought him market
reports every day, and Reverdy studied these; he had elaborate charts
which showed the movement of stock values over long periods, and
apparently he never got tired of keeping these up-to-date. If he ever
sent any orders, Lanny didn't know it; perhaps he made imaginary
investments, a purely intellectual exercise like a game of chess. He
took his duties as skipper conscientiously, and every morning made
a tour of the yacht, accompanied by the master; he pried into every
corner, including the refrigerators and storerooms, the kitchen, the
engineroom, the chartroom; he gave orders for the menus of both
guests and crew, the course for the day, and many other details.

Those duties done, he sat in a steamer chair on deck and read a mystery story, a "Whodunit." There was a murder, and you were kept guessing until the last moment, and then were surprised to discover that some innocent-appearing person was a dangerous criminal. Lanny had sampled a few, and had made note that the murdered man or woman was always a person of wealth and social importance; the purpose of the criminal was to get hold of some property—a jewel, a chest of gold, a will, or whatever it might be. There was a detective who spent his life solving such mysteries, and the reader put himself in this brilliant person's place and thrilled with every step of his progress toward a solution.

The world of the "Whodunits" was a world absorbed in property, the getting of it and protecting of it. The writing and publishing of such stories was a department of business; it, too, was a way of getting and keeping property, with the help of the copyright laws. Lanny thought he had seldom met a man so absorbed in property as Reverdy Holdenhurst, and it was easy to see why he was fascinated by the idea of crime. Did he put himself in the place of the murdered man, and imagine somebody murdering him, and wonder who it might be? The innocent-appearing Lanny surely didn't want to be the one, so he was careful not to ask questions about how the cruise of the *Oriole* was financed; whether there was gold in the safe in the owner's cabin, or whether it was done by express checks, or by credit established in places where the yacht had been putting in for many years.

In the afternoon there was a siesta period, advisable in tropic climes; then came iced drinks, and they played cards on deck unless the breeze was too strong. This activity likewise had to do with property, and was a source of wonder as well as of boredom to Lanny. That people who owned millions of dollars should be trying to win one another's pennies had always seemed to him slightly fantastic; but they did it, everywhere in the leisure-class world. They were so completely dominated by the motive of money-making that when they had exhausted themselves in the battles of reality they invented play forms of the same thing. Reverdy kept the score, and there was always a settlement at the end; he found satisfaction in winning a dollar or two from a guest while spending one or two hundred dollars a day entertaining him. A mad world, my masters!

XI

Reverdy showed Lanny their route on the globe. It would have been pleasanter to travel by way of Hawaii and westward along the line of the temperate zone, but the distances between ports were too great for a yacht's fuel capacity. Farther to the south, just north of the equator,

was a belt some three thousand miles long which had been mandated
to the Japanese; they were under pledge not to fortify it, but everybody knew they had done so, and they made matters extremely unpleasant for visitors. Thus the only practicable route lay south of the
equator, dotted with groups of islands under British, French, or American control. The weather would be hot, but Reverdy had come for
that; those who didn't enjoy it could stay in the air-conditioned interior until the sun had gone down.

They passed the Galapagos Islands, but not near enough to see them.
Reverdy had been there, and reported that they were disappointing;
their surface consisted for the most part of volcanic lava, with edges
so sharp that they cut your shoes. The giant tortoises were almost ex-
tinct, and it was against the laws of Ecuador to take them. There was
some fertile land in small valleys, and settlers had tried to live there;
cattle and donkeys, pigs and dogs had escaped, and now formed a
wild fauna, extremely unpleasant and sometimes dangerous. Reverdy
had accumulated a set of scrapbooks about all the places he had visited,
and he read aloud to the company a magazine article about a couple
of back-to-nature enthusiasts who had tried to establish themselves in
a fertile glen, and of their futile struggle to fence out the fierce invaders. The man in this episode was a German scientist, embittered
against humanity; one of his measures in preparation for the simple
life was to have all his teeth out and a stainless steel set made. Lanny
thought that an odd way of getting back to nature.

Steadily the trim white *Oriole* plowed her way through these vast
and lonely waters. Her course lay straight into the sunset, and every
evening when the great golden ball dropped into the sea it was something like a half hour later—which meant that the yacht had covered
between four and five hundred miles. This seeming-easy progress
would continue for a matter of three weeks, not counting the time
off for stops. Lanny's birthday came, his forty-first, and they celebrated it with an elaborate cake and a special bottle of champagne. He
proposed a toast—to victory and peace before the *Oriole's* return.

Each day the invalid practiced walking, at first unsteadily, then with
returning strength. By advice of the doctors, including the young
lady on board, he took many short walks, and little by little made them
longer. And with this physical recuperation came activity of mind;
Lanny Budd was able to stop brooding over atomic formulas and the
months he had wasted in learning them. He wasn't at all sure that Alston had been telling him the truth about the information from Germany; but Lanny knew that he had done his best, and that sooner or
later he would find some new way to help in the war against Nazi-
Fascism. Meantime, whenever he turned on the radio, he wondered if
he was going to hear that New York had been destroyed by an atomic

bomb. Or would it be Berlin? He could not speak one word on the subject.

The yacht would never be out of reach of short-wave radio during the cruise; the passengers learned that the Russians were holding out, and apparently were going on fighting through the winter. That meant more time for America to produce supplies and find ways to get them to both Russia and Britain. Lanny would pick up scraps of news here and there and put them together and form conclusions which he was careful not to express. Reverdy told his guests what to think about the wickedness of Bolshevism, and he would have been greatly upset if he had had the idea that he had a "radical" or anything of that sort on board. He wanted Britain to win without having the Soviet Union win, and how to arrange this was a problem that Lanny passed on to him.

XII

The affair between the invalid and the owner's daughter continued to develop, and those on board watched it with increasing interest. A "romance" was their name for it, and they proved the saying that all the world loves a lover. All the world of the *Oriole* stood aside for a pair of lovers, and made things easy for them. It was taken for granted that when Lanny walked, Lizbeth should walk with him; that when he read, he should read aloud to her; that when he played bridge, she should be his partner. It was exactly like being married, except that now when he went to his cabin he could be alone, whereas when the knot was tied he would be expected to go to her cabin and stay there.

At first, when he was weak and sick, this idea of "steady company" was pleasant enough; but the painful fact was that every day as his strength returned it became less so. Lizbeth could meet his bodily needs, but she could not meet those of his mind; and the more his mind became active, the less tolerable he found it not to be alone. What on earth was he to talk to her about? Hear her recite lessons, and supplement the efforts of her tutor? When he had met her in Baltimore there had been many people, and she had chatted happily about what they had said and done. But on the yacht nothing happened, and one day was the same as the next. Pretty soon she had told him everything she knew about everybody on board, and after that the only alternatives were to play shuffleboard or bridge, or try to get some jazz music on the radio and dance in solemn languor.

He knew only too well what she wanted, which was for him to make love to her. There was a splendid tropic moon and a soft warm breeze and the sound of the yacht's prow splashing the water. Late at night, instead of going off to his cabin, he ought to sit and hold her hand, and then put his arm about her. Little by little she would yield in perfect bliss; they would murmur sweet nothings, and her heart would begin to pound and the blushes mount to her cheeks. Presently she would tell her father, and he would tell the others, that at last they were engaged. At the next port, they would go ashore and find some missionary, or the "resident," or whatever the governor of a Polynesian island was called, to make them man and wife; and after that Lanny would live the rest of his days as he was living now, doing what was expected of him, and bored beyond endurance.

Many times he had thought that he might "educate her" to his way of thinking; but now that he faced the prospect of beginning, he saw that he didn't know how. His first words would have to be: "You must promise me not to say a word to your father about what I am going to tell you." And what would that mean to Lizbeth's mind? She adored her father, and had probably never once thought of the possibility that he might be wrong. Lanny was proposing to reveal to her a set of political and social ideas which would be utterly beyond her understanding, and which she had been taught by both her mother and father were wicked, not to say sacrilegious. It could only throw her mind into a turmoil, and make her think that her adored Lanny Budd was some new sort of wolf in sheep's clothing—a Pink wolf, or even a Red one, something more terrible than had ever been known in the folklore of any people.

Well, that might be one way to break off with her; a painful way, but Lanny couldn't think of any way that was going to be pleasant. Lizbeth was leaning more and more toward him every day, and she was bound to be wondering why his arms were not held out to her. The tension was increasing; and how many more times would he bid her good night before she would catch at his hand, or have tears running down her cheeks—or worse yet, before she would start weeping in her father's presence, and force Reverdy to come to the reluctant lover and ask him what was the matter? Lanny thought: "I am in a mess, and I ought to remind Reverdy of our bargain, and get off at the first place where I can get a plane back to the States."

XIII

But that wasn't altogether satisfactory either, for he became aware that what he really wanted was to talk to Laurel Creston. Day by day as his bodily needs decreased and his mental needs increased, Laurel took the place of Lizbeth in his thoughts. He wasn't in the slightest doubt as to what he wanted to talk to Laurel about, and there was little possibility that they would run out of subjects. He could say to her what he really thought, and without any preliminary education to make certain that it didn't shock her. What a preposterous situation, that they had to pretend to be strangers, and could not take any steps to become friends! And this was supposed to continue for six months, without any chance of alteration.

Again and again he went over the problem in his mind. Had she come because of a sudden impulse? Or had it really been true that she wanted to concentrate upon a novel? Was it that she didn't care anything about Lanny Budd, except as a source of information about Germany? If this last was her motive, she was certainly being thwarted; and how long would she submit to that? Another possibility—could it be that she thought Lanny was really in love with Lizbeth, and that she was loyally keeping out of the way? Or was she waiting to let him make up his mind and give some sign as to his choice? If that was the case, what would she be thinking about him? Nothing very good, Lanny could guess. Probably that he was marrying a yacht and an estate in Green Spring Valley!

He had never given Laurel the least hint that he was interested in her cousin, or she in him. So it was possible that Laurel had come on board in ignorance of the situation existing. But, on the other hand, she might have got the facts from some member of the family, or some friend; she might have come for the studied purpose of confronting Lanny with the intellectual life, of letting him see the superiority of mind over matter, of brains over beauty. It all depended upon whether she really wanted him for herself. She had never let him know; and all he could say was that if she did want him, she was taking a large chance by her present aloofness!

All this turmoil was to be charged up against the tiresome and persistent subject of sex, which wouldn't let either men or women rest, and kept upsetting all their plans and pleasures. All that Lanny wanted, he told himself, was to enjoy intellectual conversation with a woman writer; he wanted to know what was emerging from the rattle of typewriter keys in her cabin every morning. He wanted to give her such help as his well-stored mind could supply. But he couldn't do it, because —to put it in plain language—a young female at the age for motherhood wanted him to be the father of her children.

That was a proper purpose, of course; it was the way Nature's program was carried on. And maybe Nature was wiser than any of her creatures. Lanny could wonder whether, in that spirit world about which he had done so much imagining, there might be unborn souls floating about restlessly, seeking opportunity to enter into life. A strange field for speculation, indeed! Did those souls—or minds, or egos, or personalities, or whatever name you chose to give them— exist now? Or did they only begin to exist after a missionary or resident or governor had pronounced a formula and made an entry into a register, thus officially authorizing a male sperm to make contact with a female ovum? If it was true, as many philosophers insisted and as the physicists were now agreeing, that time was a form of human thought, then the souls that were going to exist must exist now. Were they conscious of their destiny; did they know where they were coming?

And one more curious idea: when a man was trying to make up his mind whether to marry or not, did the souls know about the problem? If so, Lanny Budd must be causing considerable confusion in that shadowy vestibule. It might even be that there were two sets of souls— the Lanny-Lizbeth set and the Lanny-Laurel set, hovering at the gates of being. And would they fight one another for precedence? And could that have anything to do with the emotions that were now agitating the bosoms of two ladies on earth, or that would be agitating them before this duel of the three L's had been fought to a finish?

Another aspect of this "life in threes" was frequently in Lanny's thoughts; he was interested in psychic research, a subject that had nothing to do with sex. Laurel was a medium, and just now Lanny had a problem he was longing to investigate. This business of his going to Hongkong and what was going to happen there! Even apart from any question of his personal concern, he would have liked to try a few séances. What would Otto Kahn have to say about the matter? And would Great-Uncle Eli come, or Zaharoff or Marcel Detaze or anybody else with warnings? All that Lanny wanted was to be able to sit quietly with pencil and notebook and watch while Laurel went into one of her trances. But there was no place where it could be done on this yacht except in her cabin or Lanny's; and imagine what excitement would have been among souls both born and unborn if he had ventured upon such an enterprise!

XIV

Disturbances in the hearts of passengers had no effect upon Diesel engines, and the *Oriole* drove rapidly westward. The Pacific Ocean justified its name, and day after day there were low swells upon the water and steady blazing heat in the air. They came to the Marquesas, the first large group and Lanny's first glimpse of a region about which he had read much colorful writing. The islands loomed up gray on the horizon, and gradually became purple, and when you were near they were a tender green, like velvet upholstery which you might like to stroke. Volcanic cliffs rose out of the water a thousand feet, and behind them were steep mountains; streams made lacy waterfalls, and white birds flew in swarms about the peaks. Here and there were indentations, with native villages amid palm trees. With glasses you could watch the natives running to their canoes, preparing to come out to the yacht if it stopped.

Reverdy had visited here on every trip, and he stood by the rail with Lanny and watched the outrigger canoes of the pearl divers. Here were some of the finest pearl-fishing grounds in the world; from them came black pearls with a marvelous greenish luster, also black mother-of-pearl. The native divers plunged into the water without diving suits or helmets, and sometimes they worked as deep as seventy feet. They piled the shells into baskets which were hauled up by rope. Sometimes they were mutilated by octopi or sharks, but they carried sharp knives and were expert in using them.

The owner of the *Oriole* was fascinated by the subject of jewels, and Lanny wondered whether that was a cause or a consequence of his reading so many mystery stories. Reverdy said that on the way back they would stop and make purchases—it was an amusing form of speculation. Lanny didn't know anything about the qualities of pearls, but he said politely that he would be happy to learn. Mostly the gems were bought by Chinese traders, who were experts in values; but if you dealt with the natives you might pick up extraordinary bargains. With Reverdy the practice had begun as a diversion, but then the idea had occurred to him that by registering the yacht as a trading vessel he might charge off the costs of the cruise as a business loss in his income-tax reports. One of his complaints against the war was that this device had been rendered dangerous, and the *Oriole* had become once more a pleasure vessel.

At the large island of Nukuhiva, the scene of Melville's *Typee*, Reverdy knew the French resident and the storekeepers by name. He had notified them in advance of his coming, in order that they might have a supply of fuel on hand for him. They would charge him double prices in wartime, and he would grumble to his secretary and his male guest, but never in the presence of the ladies, bless their delicate souls!

The yacht was laid alongside a pier made of cocoanut palms, and a wheezy pump went to work; meantime the guests would step ashore, and Lanny would have his first good look at the Polynesian people. He didn't see so much as some earlier travelers, because the missionaries had put all the women into long mother hubbards, which may have improved their morals but surely not their looks. Both men and women had straight black hair and put red hibiscus flowers behind their ears. They knew a few French words, enough to sell fruits and trinkets; both men and women helped in carrying stores onto the yacht and they sang as they worked and showed gleaming white teeth when they smiled.

The tourists bought souvenirs, as all tourists do, and Lanny had his first experience of eating a mango. The one he tried was the size of an orange with a satiny reddish skin, and so full of juice that it was hard to break the skin without being deluged. Lanny said that when he ate his second he would be in a bathing suit. The steward of the yacht bought quantities of bananas and other fruits, fresh fish and shell fish, and also some breadfruit, because visitors were always curious about it. After they had tried it boiled they agreed that they preferred hot biscuits, "flannel cakes," and other Maryland delicacies prepared by their colored cook from home.

X V

The yacht resumed her course. Their next stop would be Samoa, a couple of thousand miles west-southwest. When you looked on the chart you saw it liberally peppered with islands, but when you looked on the sea you might see no island for days; so you realized the vast distances of the Pacific, and the quantity of water that was available for the extraction of magnesium and other minerals. It was the rainy season, and showers appeared from nowhere and vanished to nowhere. The vessel sped through sheets of rain, and they cooled the air; but it soon grew hot again, and the ladies, remembering their complexions, stayed in the shade of the awnings and in midday retired to the interior. Storms came, and they stayed in their cabins and sometimes lost their appetites. Lanny cheered them with the assurance that it was a good way to reduce, and already Lizbeth had reached the point where she thought about this. She had the same weakness for the cream pitcher that Lanny had observed in his darling mother since childhood.

They were two weeks out from Miami, and Lanny was walking now; also, he was impatient, because he had talked about everything he could think of with Lizbeth, and he wanted to enjoy his own thoughts. He took to reading in his cabin, and came up to stroll late at night after the other guests had retired. It was cool then, and beautiful; the yacht was kept brightly lighted on account of the possibility of a German raider. The stars were clear bright lamps hung in the sky, just as the ancient Egyptians had believed them to be. Everything that moved on the sea made phosphorescence, and the pathway of the *Oriole* was black and gold, like the colors of the Baltimore bird.

Lanny had his future to plan, and it took a lot of thinking. Did it occur to him that Laurel Creston might experience the same need? Writers of stories have to work out their next scene, and sometimes they like to stroll while doing it. Some day a novelist might want to describe a tropic night as it appears from the stern of a fast-moving vessel. Then, too, it might occur to a keen psychologist that a male guest might weary of the same feminine society, and crave solitude and a chance to commune with the stars.

Anyhow, it happened that when Lanny stole out of his cabin and up to the quarterdeck, which was reserved for the guests, there was Laurel standing by the taffrail and gazing out upon the black and gold water. All Lanny's interest in the stars vanished suddenly and he went to her side and said in a low voice: "Good evening, Laurel." It was his first real chance for a talk alone since their last drive together in New York.

She was startled, and whispered: "Oh, Lanny!" Then she added quickly: "We must not be seen together."

"Why not?"—somewhat hypocritically, it must be granted.

"You know perfectly well." She stopped abruptly, as if she had meant to say "Lanny" again, but she did not repeat it during the talk. "It would make somebody else unhappy and ruin the cruise."

"Listen," he said. "I want you to understand, once for all, I am not under any obligation in that quarter." He was taking her hint and not speaking names.

"Do you really mean that?"

"I mean it most positively."

"Well, certainly someone has a different idea."

"If she has that idea, it is because she has made it for herself. More than a year ago the father asked me in plain words to state my intentions, and I did so. I said that the nature of my work made it impossible for me to remain at home long enough to make any woman happy. My 'no' was as positive as politeness permitted."

"Well, probably they assume that your accident will have changed that."

"If they assume it, they have certainly had no confirmation from me. I have at all times made plain my status as a friend."

There was a pause; then Laurel said: "I don't know what to say, except that there is going to be a terrible unhappiness."

"When I accepted a generous invitation, I said that my affairs might compel me to return before the cruise was over. Do you think I ought to leave at Samoa, or some other place where I can get a plane or a vessel?"

"I could not give such advice. That is something you have to decide. All I can say is that you and I ought not to be seen talking together."

"There is no one about at this hour."

"Some member of the crew may be passing, and the gossip would be all over the ship. We will both be considered to have been acting dishonorably."

She might have turned and walked away, but she didn't, and Lanny took it as an opportunity for one more question. "Tell me, if you don't mind, what you are writing."

"I have started on the novel I told you about."

"And don't you think you ought to have my help?"

"I should be more than glad to have it, but not while we are guests under these strange conditions."

"Might it not be possible for you to slip me a bundle of the manuscript? I could keep it locked up and read it in my cabin and write you comments that might be useful."

Again a silence, while she thought. Then the reply: "All right, I will do that. And now, good-night. Don't think me rude or uncordial."

"Assuredly I will never think you either of those things; at least not unless you call me a troglodyte, as you did the first time we met!"

He heard a little laugh as she turned and vanished in the dimly lighted saloon.

22. *How Happy Could I Be!*

I

ONE of the books which Cousin Jennie had read aloud to her patient was *Vailima Letters;* and so what Samoa meant to Lanny Budd was Robert Louis Stevenson. That is the advantage a writer has over other men; his imaginings outlast the labors of statesmen and kings. It appears that mankind likes its imaginings to be sad; and so the story of this romantic storyteller, seeking refuge from the tubercle bacillus upon a lonely Pacific isle, has touched the hearts of men and women all over the world and made his personality as popular as his books.

Reverdy said that Stevenson's home and grave were in the western group, which had been mandated to New Zealand, but that small country didn't seem to relish its share of the white man's burden. He said that the *Oriole* would pass that island but not stop until they were on the way back. He said furthermore that romantic writers had given the public an incorrect idea of life among the white shadows of the South Seas. It was supposed to be a lazy and carefree life, and that might be true for white people who came with money in their pockets and could employ servants; but it certainly wasn't true of the natives, who had to work about as hard as mechanics and small farmers at home. To speak of living on cocoanuts and fish sounded attractive—but only to people who had never opened a cocoanut and had no conception of the hard work it required. As for fish, you had to catch them, and that meant paddling a canoe to where they were. In tropical lands if you wanted to eat them every day you had to catch them every day, for you couldn't keep them overnight.

Laurel ventured the guess that at least the fish were always there, and the cocoanuts; whereas at home the mechanic might be out of a job, and the farmer was at the mercy of the market. That was a mistake, for it touched off her uncle and made it necessary for the company at the dinner table to listen to a discourse to the effect that the so-called unemployment problem was in great part the invention of political demagogues. The men who were out of jobs were the least competent, and those who suffered did so because they had failed to save their money against a time of depression. Reverdy explained that if you helped them you destroyed the incentive to frugality and began that process of demoralization which had destroyed ancient Rome.

Everybody listened respectfully, including Lanny Budd; he watched Lizbeth, and saw the filial devotion in her eyes, and realized that she had been absorbing such doctrine since childhood, and how vain was the idea that anybody could change her way of looking at the world. He did not dare even to glance at Laurel, for fear there might come a trace of a smile upon his lips or hers. Life on board the *Oriole* exemplified the old-time saying: "Whose bread I eat, his song I sing"—or, at any rate, his song I hear!

II

Their destination was the large island of Tutuila, and its port of Pago-Pago, pronounced for some unknown reason Pango-Pango. This had become an American naval station, and the island was ruled by a naval officer. Proceeding along the shore, and close to it, the yacht tooted its whistle and the inhabitants of a village came streaming out to wave to them. That was the home of Chief Lilioukao, whose friend Reverdy had become years ago; always they paid a visit to him, and took him presents, and he gave them a feast. With the glasses you felt yourself so near that you could almost talk to this tall old man, wearing a flowered cloth, a *pareu* about his loins, and nothing else but a gray mustache. There was his daughter, and she had a baby in her arms, and the baby was new. The whistle tooted some more, and the people and the dogs raced along the beach, dancing with delight.

The yacht entered the harbor, and found a United States cruiser there, and a destroyer. The yacht was made fast to a pier, a hose was connected up, and oil began to flow into the tanks. Meantime the guests went ashore, and this time Lanny was able to go along. They inspected a half-primitive and half-civilized town, and bought a few knickknacks, as all tourists do. Later, as the sun began to go down, Reverdy hired two motorcars to take them calling upon his Polynesian friends.

All these Pacific islands are volcanic in origin, and those which are not coral atolls are masses of mountains; the natives live in the valleys, and the roads, except along the shore, are mere tracks. Heavy showers fall almost every day in the rainy season, and the vegetation is astonishing to visitors from colder lands. Reverdy explained that the people were warm-hearted and extremely courteous; always you took them gifts, and if you showed the slightest interest in any of their possessions, they would insist upon giving it to you. In the old days simple trinkets had delighted them, but nowadays they had come to know what was good. Lizbeth had gone on a shopping expedition in Baltimore, buying such things as shawls and ornamental slippers for the women, neckties and cigarette lighters for the men, and candy for the children. Everyone in the village would receive something, even if it was only a ten-cent package of gumdrops.

In a valley cut by a swiftly flowing stream and shaded by cocoanut, banana, and plantain trees, the seven guests of the *Oriole* were welcomed by three or four score of these primitive people. The men were tall and handsome; the women, called *vahines*—vah-hee-nays—had put on their best finery for the occasion. Everybody had been preparing for the expected visit; the children had gathered green cocoanuts for the drink, and huge banana leaves were spread on the ground in the grove where the feast was to be. The dishes were clean shells, and you ate with your fingers and wiped them on a damp cloth when you were through.

These people knew some French words, and Reverdy knew a few of their native words and had taught them to the other guests. In the Marquesas, food had been *kai-kai;* here it was *ai-ai.* The first course was raw fish, caught since the yacht had been sighted and then cleaned and soaked in lime juice. Then came roasted chickens; the native oven is a small pit filled with hot stones; the food is wrapped in wet green leaves, and it comes out with a delicious flavor. Each course is washed down with cocoanut milk, sweet yet sharp in taste. There were yams and taro; and then came the crowning glory, a procession of half a dozen girls, each bearing a great shell containing a young pig, roasted whole, and with the scorched leaves still shrouding it. This was a laughing ceremony, with a native playing a tune upon an accordion, and all singing English words in honor of their guests. The tune and words were: "I am a soldier of the cross," which presumably they had learned in some near-by mission. It wasn't exactly appropriate, but it didn't spoil the taste of roasted pig.

Later they sang native songs and danced for their guests. The moon came up and shone through the palm fronds, many of them more than a hundred feet in the air; the leaves rustled softly and their shadows wove shifting patterns over the dancers and the swaying spectators. For this ceremony the women wore their old-time grass skirts, and Lanny thought the scene one of the loveliest he had ever witnessed. The parting was sorrowful, and the guests drove back to the yacht loaded with poi pounders, sewing baskets, calabashes, mats of woven straw, tapa cloth, and bonita hooks carved from pearl shell and used for trolling.

III

The yacht resumed its course to the westward. A day or two later Lanny happened to encounter Laurel Creston in one of the passage-ways. She was carrying a manila envelope of manuscript size and she slipped it into his hand. He went back to his cabin, and thereafter for an hour or two was lost to the world of the Baltimore *Oriole*.

Yes, she was going to have a novel, made up of what she had seen in Germany and what Lanny had told her about the insides of the Nazi soul. It was the story of a girl, the daughter of an American pro-fessor of literature in a middle-western college. The father had studied at Heidelberg in his youth, and being a poet and something of a dreamer, he did not know much about what had been happening in Germany during the twenties and early thirties. He still thought of the Fatherland as the home of *Gemütlichkeit* and the other old-time virtues, and he had told his daughter so much about it that she had decided to follow in his footsteps in search of her Ph.D.

There was enough of these early scenes to make the reader ac-quainted with America and its naïve idealism, and then he traveled with Paula Seton to Heidelberg and its *gleichgeschaltete Universität*. Lanny knew that Laurel had studied at Goucher College, so that part was easy enough, but she hadn't been to any German university, ex-cept perhaps as a tourist. Evidently she had done a lot of reading in the public library, and she had got off to a good start with her German professor's family; its father dominant at home, subservient as a Party member; its devoted slavish mother and its Nazified children—all but one unhappy son, who obviously was destined for a love affair with Paula and for some heart-breaking tragedy.

There were details that Lanny could find fault with, but the char-acters came alive and he perceived that the story was going to reveal the sharp contrast between Nazi and democratic ideals, now so obvi-ously headed for a conflict. He found a chance to murmur to his friend: "It is good!" Then he shut himself up in his cabin and spent a lot of time making notes for her.

This time had to be stolen from Lizbeth, and she missed it and asked, poutingly: "What are you doing all the time?" He couldn't say: "I am revising your cousin's manuscript." He had to say: "I have not been feeling well. It may be something I ate at that feast." He knew that Lizbeth hadn't enjoyed eating food with her fingers. She thought of primitive people as she did of the Negroes at home.

When the notes were done, Lanny watched for a chance to slip them to Laurel; and of course when she had read them she had to thank him, and to answer some of his points and ask questions about others. It was really quite annoying that they couldn't have a heart-to-heart talk; the business of writing notes and then looking about to make sure there was nobody watching made them both appear guilty and even feel so. Manlike, Lanny found it exasperating to be unable to do what he wanted. He felt less kind toward the skipper's daughter, and this was certain sooner or later to show in his manner.

Even without this new factor, the discontent of Lizbeth was bound to increase. She didn't want mere politeness from Lanny; she wanted love, and wasn't getting it. She had the sense of being watched by the world of this yacht; and while it was a small world, it was as important to her as if it had been large. Sooner or later the guests would know the exact situation, for Lizbeth would have to confide in some woman, and that one would tell the others. Lanny wondered: would it be Dr. Carroll, or Miss Hayman, Lizbeth's teacher, or Mrs. Gillis, the family friend. This last, a widow in her fifties, paid her way by making herself useful to Lizbeth, not taking orders but anticipating them. If they were going to play cards it was Mrs. Gillis who got the cards and the score sheet and pencil; if there was a bell to be rung she rang it and if there was an order to a servant to be given she gave it. Sooner or later, Lanny guessed, Lizbeth would break down and tell this lady about her humiliation; and then, would Mrs. Gillis take the place of Lizbeth's mother and come to Lanny about it? Damnation!

IV

Another five days of hot sunshine and frequent cloudbursts, and they were in the Solomons. Here was a quite different region, not Polynesia, but Melanesia. The inhabitants were blacks with masses of kinky hair; they had been cannibals, and in the interior no doubt still were. A forbidding land of impenetrable jungles and swamps, full of snakes and disease-carrying insects. Glad indeed the guests were that they didn't have to go ashore on these immense islands, whose tangled vegetation came down to the water's edge and whose hills appeared to be always steaming and shrouded in mists. A dozen deadly diseases lurked there; Jack London claimed to have collected no fewer than nine on his famed cruise of the *Snark*. His book was in the yacht's library, and Lanny read it, well satisfied to be on a larger vessel and to survey the cannibal coast through a pair of field glasses. The book warned him to be careful not to get any scratch or cut while on the islands, because it would turn into what was called a "Solomon sore"; it would spread, and sometimes eat all the way to the bone. A sea captain's remedy was to apply a poultice made of ship's biscuit soaked in water; and this was an interesting example of how folk medicine frequently anticipates science. At this time men in the laboratories were working upon the discovery that moldy bread nourishes an organism called *Penicillium notatum* which astonished them by its power to stop the growth of harmful bacteria.

Also in the yacht's library was a pamphlet in the language of this region, and Lanny found it an amusing subject of study. It is an odd lingo called *beche-de-mer*, representing what the blacks and the traders have made of English. A man is a "he fella" and woman is a "fella mary." The pamphlet in Lanny's hands contained Bible stories prepared by the missionaries for their pupils, and it was curious to see how the Garden of Eden appeared in Melanesia. After Adam had eaten the apple, he became aware of the fact that Eve was naked, and, according to the story, "This fella Adam he say along this fella mary: 'Eve, you no got calico!'"

The Solomons are laid in two columns, and between them is a wide passage. The names of the islands Lanny read from the chart and they were all new to him. He had heard of Bougainville as an explorer, and knew that the beautiful flowering vine which covered the walls inside the court at Bienvenu had been named for him; but he didn't know there was a Bougainville Island, nor yet a Florida Island, and he had never heard anywhere the names of Savo, Rendova, Tulagi, Guadalcanal. Perhaps if he had been in position to try a séance with Laurel, there might have come some warning from the spirits, some intimation of the history that hovered over these nightmare jungles, awaiting its time to be born. Perhaps Sir Basil Zaharoff would have come, reporting the crash of heavy guns and pretending—old rascal!— that although he had made these shells and bombs he had never expected them to be exploded. Perhaps Grandfather Samuel Budd would have come, quoting the Old Testament Jehovah calling for the extermination of His enemies. Perhaps Laurel's paternal grandfather, who had been a Navy man, would have hailed the heroes who were destined here to make their names immortal. Too bad that a séance couldn't be tried!

Lanny, having no trace of the psychic gift himself, stood by the taffrail of the *Oriole*, looking down into this dark blue water, and did not know that this passage was "The Slot," and that before half a year had passed it would be black with oil and red with the blood of dying men. He saw the dark fins of sharks cutting the surface, and did not know that they were soon to be fed upon shiploads of Americans and Japanese. He watched the yacht glide into the splendid deep harbor of Tulagi, capital of the island group, and no hunch told him that a great enemy fleet would be wrecked here, and the shores and bottom sprinkled with steel hulks of all sizes. Just so on his honeymoon with Irma had Lanny steamed into the harbor of Narvik in northern Norway, and got no hint of battles to be fought there. He knew about them now, and marveled at the impenetrable veil which hides the future from the eyes of men. Perhaps it is a mercy, and they will do themselves a disservice if they ever succeed in breaking through it.

V

These were British islands, and Tulagi, the government seat, was headquarters of a number of trading firms. In addition there was a Chinese settlement, and these traders went out in shallow-draft sailboats into waters too dangerous for the whites; their boats had showcases on deck with a glass cover, so that the natives who came aboard could inspect the trinkets without being able to touch them. With one of the white firms Reverdy had an arrangement to hold a supply of Diesel oil for him each winter; he took the same meticulous care of the yacht that he took of himself, and never let the tanks get more than half empty, for in these wartimes you couldn't be sure what you were going to find at the next port.

While fuel was being pumped aboard, the passengers went ashore and visited the home of an official, a fine bungalow with a wide, screened veranda with green matting and wicker chairs. He was an Australian, and like all the others from whatever part of the world, was counting the weeks or months or years before he would go home. All the white men wore khaki shirts and shorts, and many had bandages around the calves of their legs—Solomon sores! The trader presented Lizbeth with a young megapode, a small black bird, round and comical in appearance, which he said came from Savo Island near by. These birds lay one egg almost as large as themselves, and bury it three or four feet deep in the warm sand; the natives watch the procedure and then dig up the egg for food. Lizbeth was told that she would have to feed the creature small pieces of fish at frequent intervals, and she fully intended to do it. But she found it too inconvenient, and the megapode died very soon. Then she was remorseful.

The yacht put out to sea before sunset, to avoid the mosquitoes and other disease-carrying insects. That was one way to keep out of trouble in the tropics; and another was to watch the vessel's course day and night and keep away from the narrow channels between the islands, where swift unpredictable currents are perilous. In these volcanic regions small islands appear suddenly; others sink beneath the sea, and then the infinite numbers of tiny coral flower-animals go to work and build them up, and they become atolls, or reefs with sharp points full of deadly danger. Charts become out-of-date, and the only way to be safe is to restrain your curiosity and keep to the well-established trade routes where you have sea room in case of storms.

Reverdy kept all these matters in his mind, and did not trouble the guests with them. He had seen to it that the refrigerators were stocked with fresh vegetables which could not be obtained in the tropics; now and then they would stop and buy fish from fishermen. The owner kept on board a supply of trade goods, and apparently plenty of money, or he knew where to get it. Also, he had plenty of time and never let anything hurry him; one place on the sea was much like another, and the *Oriole* had proved her ability to ride out the worst storms the Pacific could produce.

VI

So the guests on board the yacht had no cares, and it was assumed that they were perfect models of contentment. But it has long been the practice of humans who have no troubles to set to work and make some; and so, alas, it proved in this case. Here was a presidential agent who had been released "on furlough" and ordered to take a long rest; but he was discontented because he wanted to talk to a lady novelist and wasn't allowed to. Instead of leaving it for her to work out her story in her own way, he kept thinking of ideas which might be of interest to her, and he wanted to tell her about them. After several days he worked himself into a state of irritation; one afternoon when he discovered her sitting under the awning in a steamer chair, peacefully reading a book, he drew up another chair beside her. "I have a suggestion about your Professor Holitzer," he remarked casually—as though they were two ordinary people who had the right to sit side by side and discuss the manners and morals, costumes and dietetic habits, vocabulary and *Weltanschauung* of university professors in Nazified Germany!

She looked at him, startled, as if he had come waving a red flag of revolution. After a pause she said: "We really ought not to do this."

"I've been thinking it over," he declared. "I think it's just too silly that I shouldn't be able to talk to you."

"We can't change the facts. The only question is, are we prepared to pay the price?"

"So far as I am concerned, the answer is yes."

"It will be disagreeable for both of us, you must be aware."

"I am concerned only about being fair to you. Do you feel yourself under a moral obligation in the matter? And do you value what you might lose through being my friend?" He was being careful not to name any names.

"Let us get it exactly right. There is going to be a great disappointment for somebody. That is inevitable, from what you have told me."

"Yes, that is certain."

"The question then is, whether you alone are to be blamed, or whether both of us shall take a share. In the latter case, my share will be much greater. You know that is the fate of women."

"I see what you mean, and perhaps it is too high a price for you."

"I have not said that. I am just facing the facts, as I understand you always prefer to do."

"By all means, yes."

"I am an independent woman. I earn my own living and I do not need gifts or family support. But, on the other hand, I am a guest, and that means that I have voluntarily accepted certain obligations. I ask myself: Is it enough that I shall have a good conscience? Or should I not avoid the appearance of evil?"

"The evil being to be my friend?"

"The evil is to appear to be cutting someone out of the thing which she wants more than anything else in the world."

"But which she is not going to get!"

"She doesn't know that and nothing could convince her of it. She will be seeking in her mind for an explanation—and suddenly I will supply it. Never so long as we live could I convince her that I am not guilty."

That was stating the case with scientific precision. He sat returning her clear, honest gaze, and deciding that he liked people who spoke in that straightforward way, even when their conclusions were inconvenient. He wished to deal with her on that same basis, and ventured: "Tell me, why did you come here?"

"Because you wrote me that you were coming, and I thought it would be a pleasant trip."

"You wanted my help with the book?"

"Of course; you had offered it so generously. But also I thought it would be fun to be with you."

"You didn't know how matters stood with me and the other person?"

"I had heard hints, but I had no idea it was so serious."

"And if you had known it, you wouldn't have come?"

"I had no way to find out, except by coming. This cruise won't last forever; and if we meet afterwards, that won't shock anybody as it would now."

Lanny saw that it was time to move, and did so. He had hardly taken a dozen steps before Lizbeth appeared in the doorway of the saloon. He wondered if she had been watching them through a window; he resented having to feel guilty, but he was too trained in self-control to show it. He joined his would-be fiancée and invited her to walk. They could talk about the last port they had been to, and the family they had called upon. In class these persons were far below any she would have met in Baltimore, but cruising in the South Seas was like "slumming." She wanted to know why their last host had called himself an "A*stry*lian," and Lanny explained that the colony had been settled by cockney emigrants, many of them convicts. Hearing that, the daughter of the Holdenhursts crossed "A*stry*lia" off her visiting list.

VII

The next destination of the *Oriole* was the Philippines. The course led between New Britain and New Ireland, and here too were great harbors, Rabaul and Kavieng, soon to be prominent in the world's news. But Lanny continued in his insensibility to the future; his thoughts were perforce taken up with the woman question. Frequently he had in mind the familiar old English song: "How happy could I be with either, were t'other dear charmer away"; he had now decided upon a revised version: "How happy could I be with Laurel were Lizbeth away." He had definitely made up his mind that brains were more than beauty, and that he couldn't imagine what he would talk about on his next stroll with the skipper's daughter.

He hit upon a procedure which might have seemed malicious, but he told himself that it was a psychological experiment. He would find out whether Laurel was right in her idea of how her cousin would behave under the spell of the "green-eyed monster." There were three other ladies available, and Lanny selected Dr. Althea Carroll, not because she was the youngest, but because she was the most interesting to talk to. He had conceived a regard for this earnest young woman, who had not a frivolous cell in her organism. He was sure he couldn't do her any harm, for she would never dream of standing in Lizbeth's way. Besides, they were due to part in ten days, and the chances of their ever seeing each other again were slender.

All right! Lanny drew his chair close alongside that of the lady doctor, who spent her time in a quiet spot studying medical publications. Lanny engaged her in conversation concerning the diseases which they had observed among the natives in the Marquesas, Samoa, and the Solomons. That dreadful elephantiasis, for example; people's arms, legs, or other parts grew to enormous size, and the sight had almost destroyed the appetite of the guests at the Tutuilan feast. The doctor explained that the trouble was due to the clogging of the lymphatic glands, and there were two forms of the disease, one caused by microscopic thread-like worms; that was known as filariasis. The other form was more obscure; it might be due to cancerous material, or tubercular. All very learned, but, you must admit, hardly elegant, hardly in accord with the standards of Miss Emily Post.

In the midst of it, Lizbeth showed up on deck; she invariably did so whenever Lanny was there, and he wondered if she kept a vigil by the clock. The psychological test required that he should display the utmost politeness, so he arose and offered her his chair. "Dr. Carroll is telling me about the diseases of China," he said—they had taken a jump of a few thousand miles. He drew up another chair, and the doctor went on talking; this was her hobby, honestly come by, and there was nothing she knew or cared so much about.

If you have a hobby, and are so fortunate as to meet people who are rich, you cannot avoid having in the back of your mind the thought that they may be willing to put up money to enable your work to go faster and farther. Of course the rich people know it, so as a rule they try to keep away from the hobbyists. Like the war between armor plate and gun, between battleship and airplane bomb, so is the war between the safety-deposit box and the betterment of humanity. Young Dr. Althea was thinking of all the ragged, undernourished, and suffering people who stood patiently the whole day long at the door of her father's clinic. She told about beri-beri, a disease of malnutrition, and about tuberculosis, which has malnutrition as a preliminary stage. She talked about syphilis, and yaws, a variety of it. She talked about the opium habit, which the Japanese were deliberately fostering in the conquered parts of China, both for the profit they made out of it and the impotence it produced in their subject populations. She told about women who bore sickly babies with no medical attention whatever, and explained that she had taken special courses in obstetrics in order to be able to open a school for midwives.

In all her life Lizbeth had never heard anybody talking like that. She had never dreamed that any woman would talk so in the presence of a man. She became more and more restless, and finally broke in to remind them of a radio broadcast they were accustomed to hear. When she was alone with Lanny she exclaimed: "What on earth got Althea to talking about stuff like that?"

He had to be fair to the hard-working doctor, so he hastened to say: "I asked her. We are going to China, and we ought to know about conditions there."

"I don't want to know about such conditions anywhere," declared this daughter of privilege. "There's nothing we can do about such things, and why should we make ourselves sick thinking about them?"

VIII

That was only the beginning of the experiment. For several days thereafter this devil in polo shirt and tennis trousers availed himself of opportunities for conversation with an authority on Chinese manners and morals, costumes and dietetic habits, vocabulary and *Weltanschauung*—though of course they didn't call it that. Their name for it was the *Lun-Yii* or *Analects of Confucius*, a sage of twenty-five centuries ago who had taught them to face the bitter realities of life with courage, understanding, and patience. Infinite patience one had to have in order to exist in an overcrowded land, as China had been even in Confucius's time. The world was very old, and growing older, and human beings were far from perfect and growing no better. Learn to protect yourself with wisdom, and manifest benevolence when possible.

Lanny was surprised to discover that this was a very intelligent young woman indeed. She had been so quiet and tightly shut, like a white camellia bud; now under the warmth of his interest she blossomed into flower. He understood, of course, that her eloquence was due in part to the fact that she knew the Budds were rich people, perhaps as rich as the Holdenhursts. Grandfather Samuel had supported foreign missions, and so had other devout members of this old family. Lanny guessed that it might be possible to interest some of the new generation in what was going on in the antipodes.

Althea had probably never taken any courses in psychology, and so failed to realize what was happening to her friendship with the Holdenhursts while she was cultivating the Budds. Lizbeth was cooking herself into a stew of vexation. She didn't want to sit and hear that kind of talk, and she couldn't understand why Lanny persisted in inviting it. Was it just to tease her? Or was he trying to get away from her? She understood only too well the inadequacies of her conversation, but that didn't salve her wounded feelings. When he suggested that China was as important a subject of study as art or literature, and that Lizbeth and Miss Hayman might become pupils of the learned young doctor for a while, Lizbeth was annoyed beyond endurance. She listened to Miss Hayman because Miss Hayman was a teacher, and was paid to talk; but who had asked Althea to set herself up? The truth was plain enough that Lizbeth didn't really want to listen to any female's talk; she wanted to listen to a man's.

The next time he invited her to sit in at such a tête-à-tête, she said sharply: "No, thank you," and went off and settled herself to reading a book. But she couldn't keep up that bluff, and presently got up and went to her cabin. Lanny did nothing about it, because at the moment he was especially interested in what Althea was telling him. Her father, it appeared, was something of a liberal, and besides teaching young Chinese about American medical science, he had taught them about freedom and self-government. He had been a friend of Sun Yat-sen, the great republican leader, and had had something to do with the drafting of the Three People's Principles which were the foundation of the republican movement of that vast inchoate land. Sun was dead, but his widow lived in a suburb of Hongkong, and her home was a sort of shrine to which liberals from all nations repaired. The Japanese, of course, were doing all they could to wipe out the movement, for they did not want a free enlightened China but a mass of ignorant and helpless slaves.

Lanny said: "You interest me greatly, Dr. Carroll. Do you suppose Madame Sun would receive an American art expert?"

"I am sure it would please her greatly," was the reply.

"You must explain to her that I am not a political person, but I am interested in understanding the Chinese people and their art, which is bound to be influenced by this new renaissance."

"Indeed that is true, Mr. Budd, and it is fascinating to see Chinese artists using their old techniques upon modern themes. In New York I met a young Chinese who was painting American subjects such as strike scenes, with the idea of sending them back to his homeland, but Americans are so interested in his work that they buy it up as fast as he can produce it."

IX

In the midst of this conversation Lanny overlooked entirely the possibility that the skipper's daughter might be weeping in her cabin. When he thought it over afterwards he decided that his psychological researches had been successful. The next time he met Laurel alone he stopped long enough to whisper: "I have been trying an experiment, and you were dead right about what would happen."

She didn't need to ask what he was referring to. She had devoted her mind to the subject of psychology, and was observing everything that went on in this little sea-bound world. What she said was: "Oh, how cruel!" Lanny went off chuckling, and wondering whom he had been cruel to—Lizbeth, Althea, or possibly Laurel Creston.

It was like being married into the Holdenhurst family, so the man decided. If he became Lizbeth's husband, she would make him a little world exactly like this. It wouldn't always be sea-bound, but would be bound by the limits of her understanding and interests. She would love him with absorption and watch him with the jealousy of a tigress. She would know that she was his intellectual inferior, and would fear all persons, men or women, who might claim to be his intellectual equals. If such persons got his time and attention, she would hate them; her feeling for her husband would come to be half love, half hate, that strange ambivalence which is so common and so little understood. Some day, sooner or later, Lanny would say: "I never really loved you, and I cannot stand hating you, so good-by."

This while they were crossing the Bismarck Sea. They might have headed northwest, direct to Manila, but the course would have taken them across a corner of the Japanese mandate, and this they had been advised to avoid. They proceeded westward, along the coast of New Guinea, but not in sight of it. Here, too, were names of towns and villages, Lae and Buna, Aitape and Hollandia, which would soon be of interest to historians. When they had passed the 134th degree of longitude, they turned toward the north, across the equator. From that time on, each day would find the weather a trifle less hot, and this would please them; even Lanny had had enough of being parboiled, and the laundryman on board was working overtime to keep their linen immaculate.

One person to whom the weather made slight difference was Laurel. Every morning she stayed in her air-cooled cabin and hammered on the typewriter; she read and revised and tore up and wrote again; she was living in a dream world of her own creation, and the characters in that world were fully as real to her as the physical beings around her. At any rate she tried to keep it that way, and reported to Lanny that she was succeeding. They exchanged a few sentences now and then, as any gentleman might who passed a lady sitting in a steamer chair. Before they reached Davao, in the southern Philippines, she handed him another bunch of manuscript, and the notes he wrote about it made her eyes sparkle. He had a lot to say, and no typewriter on which to say it; the little portable which had served him for many years was somewhere at the bottom of the cold North Atlantic.

This odd literary intrigue went on under the noses of the host and his daughter. The conspirators carried it on with secret smiles, but they well understood that it was a serious matter; the case of Althea had shown them that there would be no peace aboard the *Oriole* if Lizbeth discovered what was going on. She would be much angrier with Laurel, a member of the family, than with a woman doctor whom she considered wholly out of the running in the matrimonial sweepstakes. Lanny had dropped his sudden interest in Chinese affairs, but Lizbeth was still restless and miserable, waiting for him to behave as an eligible man is supposed to behave when he reclines in a steamer chair under a large yellow tropic moon.

X

The port of Davao was out of their way, lying at the head of a long gulf; but the cautious skipper had been told that he could get fuel there, and he took the precaution. They stopped for a few hours and drove about in a hot town whose suburbs had been well laid out by the Americans. Hemp and copra were the main products of the region, and the roads were populous with crude carts drawn by carabao—creatures whose one idea, when they got loose, was to wallow in mud. The people had been taught in American schools and seemed more contented than any whom the *Oriole's* passengers had so far encountered.

This archipelago had been promised independence in another five years, and there was a lot of speculation about it. Reverdy was of the opinion that the people weren't ready for it; they had been conquered by one power after another through all their history, and if the Americans moved out the Japs would surely move in. Already they were on hand, having a large and busy settlement in Davao. Reverdy said that the success of the independence movement was owing to the fact that American growers of sugar beets and other products wanted to get rid of Filipino competition, and were glad to get their little brown brothers outside the United States tariff enclave.

Lanny had reason for being interested in the Philippines, because of a story which Great-Uncle Eli Budd had told him in his youth. Eli's elder brother had happened to visit the islands just after the war with Spain, and had been shocked to discover American troops engaged in suppressing the efforts of a primitive people for freedom and self-government. He had started a protest, and because of his family position had been able to make quite a stir; he hadn't been able to stop the war against Aguinaldo's forces, but he had perhaps helped to meliorate their treatment, and to set up the American public-school system in the country when the fighting was over. That was the way with reformers, Eli Budd had said; they appeared to fail, but little by little their ideas change the world. Lanny didn't say anything about this to the skipper of the *Oriole*, for the word "reformer" was a fighting word to him—or, at any rate, a talking word, and when he got started it was hard to stop him.

XI

Southward out of the gulf, and then northward along the coast of the large island of Mindanao. Presently they were in the San Bernardino Strait, narrow and deep pathway of many ships. Here again fierce battles were to be fought and great vessels were to go down, but no echo of guns was heard by the guests on the *Oriole*. They might have gone straight to Hongkong and saved time, but Reverdy had ordered mail sent to Manila, so they headed for there. The air grew cooler, and they watched the traffic of the South China Sea, with junks and native fishing craft of many designs. It was a crossroads of the world's traffic, and with airmail and newspapers to look forward to, they felt that they were coming back into civilization.

Pleasant indeed to glide into the broad shallow bay of Manila, with a well-informed skipper standing by to point out the landmarks; on the one side Bataan Peninsula and the island of Corregidor, heavily fortified, and on the other side the naval base of Cavite. Undoubtedly we should keep these points, declared Reverdy; and the Japs would get a warm reception if they came. The naval battle which had been fought here was recorded in all the guide books and required no psychic powers to reveal. The skipper of the *Oriole* could imagine himself in the role of Admiral Dewey, surveying the Spanish fleet through his glasses, and remarking to his subordinate: "You may fire when you are ready, Lanny."

Pleasant, also, to go ashore and hire a comfortable car and be driven about a modern city with fine buildings and all the conveniences. The first destination was the bank where mail for the yacht had been sent; there you were treated as distinguished guests, and escorted to the directors' room; a sack of mail was dumped before you, and you had a grand time sorting it into piles. Then to sit and run through it, each guest with his or her own chair and his or her own secrets, joyful or sad.

Lanny had his generous stack, including newspapers and magazines which would keep him interested for many a morning on deck. There was a letter from Robbie which had left Newcastle, Connecticut, only six days ago, and had been flown almost halfway around the world. No particular news; everybody was well, and business booming; what the end would be no man could guess. Lanny must be sure to cable from Manila; they would be awaiting word about his health. Lanny would do so, of course; he would cable Beauty and Rick and little Frances.

Also he would go strolling in the compact old Spanish city called Intramuros, which was Manila's glory. He would stroll into shops and buy many things of which he had been discovering the need during the past month. The steward of the yacht would renew its stock of canned goods and many sorts of fresh foods. The primitive world is picturesque and entertaining, and picture postcards of it are fun to send to your friends; but in the long run what you want is civilization, and a pocketful of money so that you can command its benefits.

Even the cheap ones! Even a morning newspaper, which costs only

five cents—and yet you would pay five dollars for it if you were where
you couldn't get it! The radio does not take its place, as you soon
learn. The civilized man has got used to depending upon his eyes, and
perhaps he needs the headline writer to work up appreciation of events.
From the *Manila Times* the son of Budd-Erling learned that the Russians were fighting furiously on their snowbound steppes and in their
shell-blasted towns; the enemy had been driven back from the suburbs
of Moscow and had not quite got into those of Leningrad. The British
were holding out at Tobruk, and the Germans had not managed to
break through to Alexandria and the Suez Canal, as everybody, including Lanny, had feared they would.

XII

It was the forenoon of the 4th of December, 1941, when the trim
white *Oriole* retraced her course out of the harbor of Manila and round
the point of Bataan Peninsula. The distance to Hongkong was given
on the chart as 631 miles, and they were due to arrive on the morning
of the 6th. Lanny looked forward to spending most of the interim
catching up with his newspapers and magazines; but the fates had
something else in store for him.

Driving to the dock where the yacht lay he had observed something
peculiar in the manner of the skipper's daughter. Never did she meet
his eyes, and she appeared to be in a state of nervous agitation. He
wondered if she had had bad news from home. But it wasn't up to
him to ask questions, any more than it is up to a man sitting on a pow-
derkeg to strike matches. No, let sleeping dogs lie, and let lovelorn
ladies keep their own counsel as long as they consent to do so. Lanny
went to his cabin, saying that he had seen enough of Manila Bay, and
had letters to prepare for mailing in Hongkong.

At dinnertime, in the dining-saloon, Lizbeth had little to say. Lanny
watched her, but only in brief glances. Usually she had a good appetite, but now she left half the food on her plate. Could it be that her
eyes were red with weeping? He wasn't sure, but when she excused
herself before the coffee he knew there was something wrong. He
hadn't misbehaved, and he wondered if Laurel had, or Althea.

As the guests went up to the main saloon for the customary game
of bridge, Lanny found reason to linger, and so did Laurel. She stopped
just long enough to whisper: "Meet me on deck at eleven o'clock."

He knew she would never have done that unless there was an emergency. He said: "There is some trouble?"

The reply was: "Lizbeth has had a letter from Emily Chattersworth."

When you say: "Oh-ho!" and accent it on the second syllable, it
means pleasant surprise, even triumph. But when you accent it on the

first syllable and let the second die away, that means something has gone wrong. Lanny excused himself from the card game on the plea that he hadn't finished with his mail. He went to his cabin and thought hard, and the longer he thought the more clearly he realized that the beans had been spilled and the fat was in the fire, the cat was out of the bag and the horse had been stolen from the stable—think of all the metaphors, tropes, similes, metonymys, analogies, catachreses, and synecdoches you can, and still you will not exaggerate the confusion which the châtelaine of Les Forêts and Sept Chênes had caused by a few casual words on paper. Lanny could imagine them without asking any questions; for example: "Give my regards to your cousin Laurel. I enjoyed so much meeting her when she was a guest at Bienvenu." Something like that! Maybe it would be in a letter to Lizbeth's mother, which the mother had forwarded, perhaps with an appended inquiry: "Did you know that Laurel had met Lanny Budd in Europe?"

It had been natural enough for Emily to write, for she and Millicent Holdenhurst had been school friends. It would be natural for her to mention Lanny and say kind things about him, for she had done her best to promote a match between Lanny and Lizbeth. It had been possible for her to write, because Washington was maintaining diplomatic relations with Vichy—curse the luck!—and mail, though censored and delayed, eventually came through. Of course Emily, at Cannes, would have had no means of knowing that Lanny, Laurel, and Lizbeth were all three going on the cruise; her letter would have come to Baltimore and been forwarded. Emily, the least malicious person in the world, couldn't have had any idea of the pretty kettle of fish she would be cooking up for her near-foster-son!

XIII

Promptly at eleven that evening Lanny strolled out to the quarter-deck. The vessel was brightly lighted as always, for a German raider might be a possibility, even this close to British ports. Laurel was standing in a shadowed spot, and Lanny joined her. She said: "Lizbeth received a letter from her mother, enclosing a letter from Mrs. Chattersworth in which she mentioned having met me when I visited Bienvenu. Lizbeth, of course, is in a terrible state of excitement, and accuses me of having come on this cruise in order to break up her chances with you."

"What did you tell her?"

"I told her the truth as far as I could. I said that I was writing stories about the Nazis which were satirical and would make the Nazis very angry; that you were Göring's art adviser, and had told me that it could do you harm if it were known that we were friends. So I promised not to mention that I knew you. She wanted to know how I had come to be at Bienvenu, and I told her that your mother had invited me at a time when you were in America, and that you came much later. That is true, you remember."

"Of course. Did it satisfy Lizbeth?"

"I doubt if anything will satisfy her, except the one thing she wants and which you are not disposed to give her. She is casting about in her mind for an explanation of your coldness, and this letter comes as an answer to all her wonderment."

"What do you intend to do about it?"

"I told her that since I was a source of annoyance to her, I would leave the yacht at Hongkong."

"But, Laurel! That will knock out your work!"

"I am afraid I couldn't keep my mind on work very well, with my hostess in her present state."

"I must tell you this," said Lanny. "I had about decided to tell your uncle that I was going to fly back to the States from Hongkong. It was our agreement that I should have the right to go."

"It will have a very disagreeable appearance, if we should both leave at the same port, Lanny."

"We can travel by different routes, if that is necessary to satisfy Mrs. Grundy."

"We could never get anybody to believe that we didn't contrive to meet again."

"Well, I hope we don't have to give any promise against that, Laurel. I am deeply interested in the family of Professor Holitzer, and also I am interested in the lady who is telling about them." Even in the midst of this grave complexity, Lanny permitted himself the luxury of a smile.

But Southern ladies rarely smile over family "situations." They have been taught to take families seriously, and even if they try not to, the families have the last word. Laurel said with unmistakable firmness: "It would be a scandal if we both left the yacht at the same port, Lanny. If you are going, I shall have to stay."

"But that will be pretty miserable for you. Lizbeth will be sure that you drove me away, and she will not forgive you."

"The decision rests with you. One or the other must stay."

He couldn't keep from seeing the humor of this. "If you go and I stay, Lizbeth will eat me alive. She may get into a position where I feel that I have compromised her and have to do the honorable thing. You had better hang on and protect me!"

XIV

They had got themselves on the horns of a dilemma; but, as it hap-pened, they didn't have to make the decision. Had the owner's daugh-ter chosen this moment to relieve her nervous tension by a walk on deck? Or had she suspected that the guilty pair were keeping a ren-dezvous? They were standing with their faces toward the door of the saloon, so that they might not be taken by surprise if anyone came out. When she appeared, Laurel, not wishing her to think they were hiding, spoke quickly: "We are talking about you, Lizbeth. Come over here."

When she was near, she did the talking, as was her right, being the hostess. Her voice was low, and trembled slightly. "I want to tell you both that I mean to behave properly. I have been thinking it over, and realize that you have the right to be in love with each other, and that I have nothing to do with it."

"Lizbeth," said the cousin, breaking in, "I have told you that Lanny has never spoken one syllable of love to me. I give you my word that this is so, and he will do the same."

"Indeed yes, Lizbeth," added the man, no less promptly. "I explained to your father a year or two ago that my position does not permit me to think about love or marriage. I have been Laurel's friend as I have been yours. I have been interested in her writing as I have been inter-ested in your studies, and I have tried to give a little help with both."

"That may all be true," replied Lizbeth. "I have no right to doubt it, but I believe that you are in love whether you know it or not. What I want to say is, it's none of my affair, and I have no right to make a fuss about it and break up the party. I have talked to my father, and it will upset him greatly if either of you leaves, for he depends upon your companionship more than he has let you know. So please let us be friends as we were before, and Lanny is perfectly free to talk to you, or to Althea, or to the others, just as he pleases—and you and he don't have to steal up on deck at night in order to talk about what Laurel is writing, or about me, or anything else."

She got that far, a little speech which no doubt she had rehearsed more than once. At this point came a little choking sob, and she burst into tears and ran quickly back into the saloon.

There was nothing they could do after that but take her at her word. This was what the world calls "good society"; its members are "well bred," and don't show their emotions in public—or, if they lose their tempers, they owe an apology and pay the debt. Lanny whispered: "That's decent of her!" and added: "Better than I expected."

Said Laurel: "I suspect that Uncle Reverdy put his foot down. Anyhow, it's all we can ask, and I suppose we have to stay, at least for a time."

So that was the way the matter stood next day, and all the way across the South China Sea. Of course Lizbeth would tell Mrs. Gillis, who was practically a member of her family, and the only woman member on board; and of course Mrs. Gillis, being human, would tell the teacher and the doctor. These three would watch for every sign of emotion, sad or mad or bad—there could hardly be any glad, for that would have been indecent. The three observers would meet in one another's cabins and fan themselves with a breeze of gossip. Just how red were Lizbeth's eyes, and just how far was her nose out of joint? And what could be the matter with the amiable Mr. Budd that he didn't fall in love with any of the three eligible ladies on board? Did he perhaps have a broken heart? Or a lady love in one of the numerous capitals of Europe which he visited? Or possibly more than one, for, after all, morals there are not exactly repressive. And as for Cousin Laurel, was she in love with him, or with whom, and what was this mysterious manuscript which she kept so carefully locked up in her steamer trunk? The Filipino boy who did the cleaning avowed that he had never had a glimpse of a single page of it.

When there are only seven guests on a yacht, only two of them males—and one of these an elderly valetudinarian self-excluded from the primrose path of dalliance—there really isn't much food for gossip, and it is up to the ladies to make the most of what a kind Providence may afford.

23. *Smoke of Their Torment*

I

ALL the way from Baltimore to Miami to Panama, and from there westward, people had been talking to Reverdy Holdenhurst about Japan. They considered it injudicious of him to venture where there was so much danger. Why couldn't he winter in some of the many places that were safe? When he asked them where, they would say, well, Florida, or Arizona, or New Mexico. This to a man who owned a beautiful yacht, and loved it, and was bound to get his money's worth out of it!

Reverdy had always had his own way, ever since he could remember, and as a result he was a stubborn character; he made up his mind what he wanted to do and then he did it. He had taken this cruise year after year; he knew the places, and had friends in each and paid them duty calls. Just so in the old days fashionable ladies had ridden in two-horse carriages in state with coachman and footman, leaving "calling cards" at one house after another. Reverdy felt that he had abandoned one half of the world at the behest of the Führer and Il Duce; he didn't feel like abandoning the other half for the Emperor of Japan.

He discussed the subject now and then during the cruise. The Japs had got themselves tied up in China, and were having no easy time of it; was it likely that they would wish to take on the might of the British Empire and the United States? Surely not until they had made their position in China secure, and had developed their sources of supply! Reverdy had visited Japan more than once, and had talked with leading statesmen; he knew them to be shrewd observers of the world scene, well able to weigh the forces they would face if they challenged the Anglo-Saxon peoples. Certainly they weren't going to begin by interfering with a harmless private yacht, whose manifest and storerooms they were free to examine at any time. Reverdy possessed letters from Japanese personages in which these polite gentlemen expressed their high regard, and he kept these in a pigeonhole of his desk, on the off chance that some Japanese lieutenant might some day step aboard from a vessel of war.

In Manila the warnings of Reverdy's acquaintances had become vigorous. What, going into Hongkong when you didn't have to, and when everybody that could get out had done so? Didn't the skipper of the *Oriole* know that all American women had been ordered out, and all British women who didn't have urgent duties? Reverdy said: yes, he knew, and he had no intention of staying in Hongkong. All he was planning to do was to put ashore a woman doctor whose father was a physician in the interior and who wished to rejoin him.

"But what an idea!" exclaimed the advisers. "Don't you know the Japanese lines are drawn tightly all the way around the Hongkong territory? Nobody can get into the interior from there!"

Reverdy smiled a tolerant smile. "My woman doctor knows the situation well. The Japs have been there for three years or more, and there are plenty of ways of getting past them. You get a launch or a sampan and go up the coast a short distance at night and land in some cove; there are Chinese guerrillas who take you in charge and escort you wherever you want to go. Especially if you are a doctor, willing to help their people—they take care of their friends."

The Baltimore capitalist had influence, and had been able to get the passports for this trip. It was still a free country, he said, and added, slyly: "If you know the right persons!" There was nobody in Manila charged with the duty of preventing a yacht owner from sailing the high seas. Reverdy discussed the matter with his guests and assured them that the stay would be very brief; while on shore they must keep in touch with the yacht and be ready to leave at any sign of trouble. He would replenish the fuel and attend to a couple of business matters, and then they would be off to the southwest, all the way to Bali and Java, where the Japanese would surely not venture—unless they were prepared to commit suicide.

"If I were a betting man," said this knowledgeable host, "I would offer ten to one that if the Japs are planning to strike at any place, it will be Vladivostok and the railroad north of Manchoukuo. There is their real enemy, and believe me, they have the sense to know it."

II

Lanny listened to these discussions, and walked the deck and pondered them. Prominent in his thoughts was the old sentence spoken to him in Munich: "You will die in Hongkong." The P.A. had told himself that astrology was a pseudo-science which had been long since discarded; but that hadn't kept him from remembering the warning. He was like a man who watches a thunderstorm gathering, sees the lightning on the horizon, and wonders what the chances are of being hit.

He might have gone to his host and said: "Reverdy, I don't think it prudent to take these ladies into a danger spot. Why not approach the coast a bit farther north, behind the Jap lines, and use the launch to put Althea in the cove where she wants to be?" The host would have acceded to this suggestion, especially if the doctor herself had supported it.

But Althea had promised to introduce Lanny to Madame Sun Yat-sen, and that was something he looked forward to. Moreover, he was really curious about the prediction. An old-time psychic researcher, he took it as a challenge and would have been ashamed to run away from it. One more chance to find out if precognition is a possibility! Plain curiosity played a part in this; he wanted to know what, if anything, was supposed to happen here. This characteristic is one which humans share with many of the animals. A bear moving along a trail and hearing a strange noise ahead will not delay for a second; he will swing off the trail and get away from there both quickly and silently. But a deer, hearing the same sound, will stop, prick up its ears, and peer in the direction of the sound; if it is a man standing on his head and kicking his legs in the air, the deer will come nearer, trying to make out the meaning of the strange phenomenon. That is one reason why the death rate of deer is so much higher than that of bears.

III

Hongkong is an island of granite hills, eleven miles long, lying in the entrance to a deep indentation that might be called an estuary or a gulf. A hundred years ago the island had been the haunt of pirates; the British had taken it, as a place where they could carry on trade and be safe from the exactions of local government. Now it was a "crown colony," called "the Gibraltar of the Far East," and was one of the centers of the world's trade. Even the fact that the Japanese had seized Canton, eighty miles distant up the river, hadn't stopped the activities of the port; for the new conquerors had to have supplies, and they were even willing for the Chinese in the interior to have supplies, provided that "squeeze" was distributed to the right Japanese officials.

The British territory included all the shores of the harbor, and the country around it for a distance of twenty or thirty miles. In this district lived some fifteen thousand white people and perhaps a hundred times as many Chinese; it was hard to say exactly, for they kept coming and going. During the four years of the Japanese invasion they had been coming, and the British had had to put them to work constructing mass shelters. Across the harbor from the island was a peninsula called Kowloon, and the refugees had filled this, and spread out into the rice fields and vegetable gardens beyond. In the harbor they lived on board sampans and junks, making a floating slum. Reverdy said you could never have any idea what poverty was until you saw China; there and in India you learned to think of human beings as of maggots in a carcass, and for the first time you realized how completely civilization depends upon the practice of birth control.

The harbor is long and narrow. The *Oriole* came in slowly, through a swarm of junks and other native craft of every shape and size: wonderful, picturesque, with sails of brown and yellow tints, patched to the very edges, over and over; steered usually by a woman or girl with a long pole, skillfully turning the craft out of the yacht's course. The good humor of the sailors and their women was delightful; when they came close to the yacht the passengers would throw coins and the natives would catch them in a little net at the end of a long pole. They were very skillful and hardly ever missed. The *Oriole* found a safe anchorage. Owing to governmental red tape, there would be delay in the fueling, and meantime the passengers went ashore in the launch. They found themselves in a modern city with luxury hotels, department stores, theaters, banks—everything they would have found in London or New York. The white residents were wealthy—why else would they have stayed here? The merchants had built themselves villas on a high hill called "the Peak"; they were crowded together and could not have so much in the way of gardens, but there was a sea breeze and they could be more comfortable in summer. In December it was cool and the men wore sweaters and tweeds.

The visitors were rolled around in easy-chairs on rubber-tired wheels called rickshaws; the Chinese who pulled them were called "boys," although they were men and looked much older than they were. It was a job which wore them out quickly and when they developed varicose veins and couldn't run any more, nobody knew what became of them and few thought to inquire. Overpopulation had its unpleasant features, but also its conveniences; there were plenty of servants, and your "Number One Boy" who ran your household ruled them with a rod of iron. The "old China hands" who had lived here since the days of the Empire took everything for granted, and laughed you down if you talked about improving anything in this part of the world. East was East, and so on. All their troubles went back to the missionaries, who had started the business of "educating these beggars" and talking to them about "reform"; as a result, all China was in chaos, and of course the Japs were taking it over—what could you expect?

I V

A person like Dr. Althea Carroll would hardly have been appreciated by the hard-boiled plutocracy of Hongkong, whether British or American. Lanny and Cousin Laurel would have been welcome, but they had chosen to give their time to the widow of China's revolutionary saint. Reverdy was an old friend of the recently appointed governor, and when he telephoned of his arrival he received an invitation to dine at Government House. That included his daughter, and it might have included his niece and the son of Budd-Erling Aircraft if Reverdy had dropped a hint about them, but he didn't.

Lanny was well content to have it that way, for he had dined in many official residences and knew what dull affairs they could be. Whatever Sir Mark Aitchison Young might have to report about the political and military situation, Reverdy would retail it during the trip to Bali; and meantime Althea would get busy and arrange for the call upon Madame Sun that evening. Lanny and Laurel would be free to do what they hadn't been able to do in Berlin or Bern, in Cannes or London or New York—to wander about the streets and look at the sights to their hearts' content.

What interested them was the Chinese quarter—or perhaps one should call it the Chinese ninety-nine-hundredths. The hills were steep, and looking down the narrow canyons you saw vistas of the bay and the hills on the far side. The streets and sidewalks were swarming with pushcarts and stands, not to mention men, women, and children, so that it was difficult for even a rickshaw to get through. Most of the shops were open to the streets, and behind them were living quarters —dens might have been a better word. Behind the tourists followed starveling children, whining a singsong. Long ago somebody must have taught it to them for a joke, but they would never know it as such; for the rest of Hongkong time they would chant: "No mammy, no pappy, no whisky-soda!"

The pair stood on the esplanade called "the Bund," watching a Chinese funeral go by. It was a long affair, entirely pedestrian. The coffin was borne by pall-bearers, who worked in relays, and the idle four of them chewed some sort of seeds, and spat frequently and made jokes with the spectators. Many of the mourners were barefoot; they had been hired, and some of them carried large bedraggled banners, rented for the occasion. Women mourners bore a sort of stretcher loaded with paper flowers. There were many bands wearing faded uniforms, and making loud noises which had no relation to music in Western ears. The oddest feature of this long procession was people with large wads of raw cotton hanging over their heads and bumping against their cheeks; other mourners kept poking at these wads with dirty cloths, and who could guess what that was supposed to signify? When they asked Althea she explained that the wads represented tears of grief, and the extra mourners were wiping them away.

V

The doctor joined them, and they had dinner in one of the restaurants patronized by the well-to-do Chinese, of which there was a large group on the island. Here, as everywhere, there was abundance for those who had the money. Althea had arranged for them to go that evening to call upon Madame Sun, and she spent the mealtime telling them about this remarkable lady, and about the Chinese silk merchant, Mr. Foo Sung, who was coming in his car to fetch them to the lady's home.

Dr. Sun Yat-sen, founder of the Chinese Republic, had been the son of a poor farmer; he had been educated in a Christian school, and had devoted his life to teaching ideas of freedom and social justice to his people. He had spent a good part of his life in exile, a fugitive from the various warlords who ruled the Flowery Kingdom. He had traveled to America and to Britain, getting support of the Chinese there for the Kuomintang, the Republican party. He had organized the revolution which had overthrown the Manchu Empire, and had laid down a sort of political charter for the future of his countrymen.

The "Three People's Principles" were, first, Nationalism, which meant freedom and independence for all Chinese; second, Democracy, which meant government by the will of the people; and third, Socialism, which meant the production and distribution of goods for use and not for private profit. Needless to say, Dr. Sun had not lived to see these principles put into effect among his four hundred million countrymen; but his ideals were cherished and taught by clear-visioned souls, not merely in China but elsewhere throughout a tormented world.

There were three ladies of China known as the Soong sisters, daughters of the wealthiest banking family in the country, all three of them Christians educated in American colleges. The best known of them, Mei-ling, was the wife of Generalissimo Chiang Kai-shek; the second, Ai-ling, was married to Finance Minister Kung of the government; the third, Ching-ling, had become the secretary of Sun Yat-sen and had married him in his later years. She had imbibed his doctrines, and although she had been sixteen years a widow, she still made them the guiding light of her life. The Kuomintang had become a political machine, and had made its terms with the wealthy exploiters—or so, at any rate, Ching-Ling believed. She was the "radical" of the Soong family, the "parlor Pink." Lanny, who had played that same uncomfortable role in his youth, could sympathize with her position; but since he had not yet decided what he was going to do with the rest of his life, he continued wearing his camouflage of art expert, a non-political personality.

VI

Mr. Foo Sung called for them at the restaurant with his limousine. He was an elderly gentleman wearing a long white goatee, gold-rimmed spectacles, and a Chinese costume of black silk; he was very dignified, very courteous, and informed about art both Oriental and Western; he spoke English, not perfectly, but easily to be understood. After he had listened for a while to Lanny's polished discourse, he invited the visitor to inspect his own collection and give him an opinion as to the genuineness of a Holbein for which he was thinking of making an offer. Lanny said that Holbeins were mostly in museums, and the likelihood of one turning up in Hongkong seemed slight. Mr. Foo replied: "I have, what you say, pedigree for him." Lanny promised to see what he could do on the morrow.

Madame Sun lived in Kowloon, the city on the mainland across the bay; you went on a little green-painted ferryboat, and there was time for cultured conversation. Mr. Foo, one of those rare persons of wealth who rise above their class interests and are willing to take their chances in a democratic world, was a great admirer of the lady they were going to visit. Lanny wondered: would he have admired her so much if she had not been a member of the richest family of the country? Human motives are mixed, at any rate as Lanny had observed them in the Western world, and he guessed that this might be true of the still more ancient Orient.

The widow of China's George Washington lived in an unpretentious Western-style cottage in the suburbs. She was a small, frail person in her fifties, looking surprisingly like her more famous sister whose picture Lanny had seen in the papers. She wore a close-fitting gown of light blue, and her black hair was pulled back from her forehead and formed a knot in back; she wore no jewels. Her English was excellent, her manner smiling and serene. She was tireless in serving on committees for the aid of war refugees, orphans, and workers' co-operatives.

She assumed that these visitors had come because they wished to understand the problems of China, and she talked about them freely. She did not mention any of the other members of her family, but pointed out what she believed were the errors of the regime. Of course it was necessary to expel the Japanese invaders, and to do that China had to have order and discipline; but not even war could suppress the struggle between the people's interests and those of the exploiters. Even in wartime profits would be made; and who was to get them, the speculators and great monopolists, or the co-operatives, which had shown so well their ability to produce the necessities of both war and peace? The co-operatives were now being stifled by the Chungking government, and worse yet was the blockade against "Red" China; even the medical supplies donated by America were not allowed to cross the line. When a political party which had been formed for the purpose of building up the people's power changed gradually into a group of politicians selling the privileges of government to the highest bidder, it became necessary to make that fact known and to keep it before the people.

Lanny, lover of peace, asked what she thought could be done about the problem of Japan. The reply was that it was the same problem as in China; the great families made use of both militarists and statesmen to increase their wealth and strengthen their hold upon the people's means of life. The people did not want wars; the people were willing to work and produce, and asked only to retain the fruits of their labor. But those who exploited labor had to increase their holdings, to protect themselves against rival groups; they had to find markets abroad, because the masses at home did not have the money to buy the products of industry. "Our hope lies in the co-operatives, Mr. Budd, and in the co-operative method of production and distribution."

Lanny would have liked to say: "I agree with you entirely." But with the caution which had become second nature, he told her: "What you say is extremely interesting, and I promise that I will investigate the subject."

The "Pink" lady replied: "There is a great co-operative movement in your own country, but it is an unfashionable affair, an achievement of the plain people, and it probably does not get the headlines very often in your capitalist press."

VII

Lanny had promised to keep in touch with the yacht, and he had left word where he and the two ladies were to spend that evening. Now the telephone rang and it was Reverdy, asking if he might speak to Mr. Budd. "I thought you would want to know that we are to leave the first thing in the morning. Sir Mark takes a very serious view of the situation and does not think that any vessel having women on board should remain here. He tells me that the Japs have just doubled their forces in Indo-China, and also that a battlefleet has been observed near their mandated islands, very close to where we passed. Sir Mark thinks they are contemplating some move against British positions. He has arranged for us to have a special permit to get fuel tomorrow morning."

"O.K. by me," Lanny replied. "Our party will be leaving for the yacht within an hour or so."

"I'll be staying a while longer with the Governor. Lizbeth has gone with one of his aides to a dance at the Peninsular Hotel, which is in Kowloon. You might go there and join her, if you like. She is being taken in a government launch, and you three can be brought to the yacht in that."

"I'll ask the others," said Lanny, "but my guess is they'll prefer to return as we came. We have been sightseeing all day, and you know it's usually pretty late before those dances break up. And besides, we aren't dressed."

"As you please," replied Reverdy. "Be sure you reach the yacht by daylight."

Lanny reported this to the company, and they discussed the Governor's information. Mr. Foo declared it was difficult to forecast the actions of the Japanese, because the Army and the Navy were separate groups, and independent to an extent unimaginable in Western lands; they did not always tell the government what they were planning, and sometimes they didn't even tell each other. The great Kwantung Army undoubtedly wanted to cut the Trans-Siberian railroad and squeeze the Russians out of Eastern Asia; the Navy undoubtedly wanted to get hold of the Dutch East Indies, with their fabulous wealth of rubber and oil and tin. Why they should be reinforcing their troops in Indo-China was hard to imagine, unless they were aiming an attack upon Singapore. Why they should send a battlefleet to their mandated islands so far to the east was even harder to explain—unless they were mad enough to be contemplating a raid upon Australia.

So it was that amateur strategists speculated and debated, not merely in Hongkong but in every spot on land and sea where there was a radio set and people to turn the dials. That Saturday night was Friday on the other side of the world; it was December 5 in "the States," and December 6 in Hongkong and Manila. Everywhere there were groups of sober-minded people asking with fear what was going to become of their world; and everywhere there were larger groups of light-minded people and the young, dancing to the pounding of drums, the moaning of saxophones, and the blaring of stopped trumpets.

VIII

Laurel, always tactful, suggested that they might be keeping their hostess too long, but Madame Sun said that she was enjoying their company. When Lanny mentioned the dance at the hotel, Mr. Foo remarked that it was being given for the benefit of the Chinese-British Bomber Fund, and he thought it might be a good thing if Ching-Ling were to show herself there, if only for a few minutes. Madame assented, saying: "I have to keep in touch with my rich friends. I am able to shame many of them into giving for our causes."

She excused herself for a few minutes, and came back wearing a handsome Mandarin gown of black silk with embroidery of gold. There was plenty of time, Mr. Foo assured them, and they drove to the Peninsular Hotel, an immense structure facing Hongkong about a mile across the bay. The Chinese city surrounded it, with shopping streets built with arcades, so that you could walk for a mile or two sheltered from sun and rain. The streets were so crowded that it was hard to walk there at all, but a skillful Chinese chauffeur was able to deliver them to the hotel, and they went up to the second floor, where two great ballrooms were thronged with dancers.

Hongkong was proud of its social life, and made it a point of prestige to continue it in spite of all opposition, whether of nature or man. The fact that there were fifty thousand Japanese troops forming a semicircle about the territory, as close at some points as fifteen miles, was no reason why smart society should give up breakfast parties followed by horseback rides, luncheons followed by sailing parties or bridge, dinners followed by dances. Then, too, there was the horse racing at the Happy Valley track; and between all the other doings there were whisky-sodas! To have given up any of all this would have been to lose face with one's Chinese allies, and with the servants. News spread with the speed of lightning in the crowded arcades, and when in this region you had lost face you had nothing left. Hongkong, Gibraltar of the Far East, must never know fear!

Madame Sun went in, and her friends crowded about her. The three Americans, not being properly costumed, stood in the doorway for a few minutes, watching the picturesque scene. Many of the men were in uniform, British or Chinese; many of the ladies wore costumes which were a compromise between the styles of the two countries. The Chinese girls wore their hair loose; it was slick and shiny, and floated behind them in black cascades. War was coming, and this might be their last chance of happiness. Lanny thought about the ball in Brussels on the night before the battle of Waterloo and which he had read about in *Vanity Fair*. To the American observer the strangest thing was to see British and Chinese dancing to that music which was called "modern," and which had come out of the jungles of Africa and been refashioned in the dives of Mississippi river towns and of New York's Harlem.

Lanny observed the daughter of the Holdenhursts dancing in the arms of a tall young man in a British Army lieutenant's uniform. He was handsome and blond, with a trim little mustache. Lizbeth bore every sign of being happy, and Lanny thought perhaps this would be the great romance of her life; this gallant warrior would whisper into her ear, and promise to come to Green Spring Valley when the war was over; if this were so, the rest of the cruise of the *Oriole* would be happier for the son of Budd-Erling. He did not know whether she saw him now, and took care not to intrude upon her dream.

On with the dance! Mr. Foo invited them to have supper in the hotel dining-room, and when they were through it was midnight. They went upstairs for a final glimpse of the dancers, and to say good-by to Madame Sun. As they stood in the doorway the music stopped suddenly, and there was a man standing in the balcony, calling for silence. Later on they learned that he was Mr. Wilson, head of the President Line of steamships and a prominent figure socially. He waved a megaphone, and when he got silence he spoke: "All men connected with ships in the harbor report on board *at once*. All men belonging to the reserve report for duty *at once*."

So that was the end of the festivities. There were very few white men in Hongkong who didn't belong to one or the other of these categories, and they faded suddenly out of the picture, leaving the women to gather in little groups, pale in spite of their war paint. There was only one thing it could possibly mean—the Japanese enemy. Where was he, and what was he doing or threatening? Mr. Foo said: "Madame will know," and went to ask her. She, as sister-in-law of the "Gissimo," would have the right to share military secrets; and presently the elderly merchant came back and reported: "Big fleet Japanese ships near. All ships in port ordered leave tonight or next night. Very bad situation. You go to yacht quick."

IX

That was indeed a serious matter, and they wasted no time in discussion. Madame Sun would be taken home by other friends. Mr. Foo would take the three passengers in his car. Dr. Carroll, who was not going on the yacht, would spend the night at Mr. Foo's home. They hurried down to the front of the hotel, where a press of people were calling for their cars, for taxis or rickshaws. After some delay they found their host's car, and made their way to the Star ferry, as it was called. There they found a long line of cars waiting. Mr. Foo said: "We never able to get car on board next boat. You walk more quick. Other side, you get taxi."

That was obviously good advice, so Lanny and Laurel said a brief farewell to the other two. "Some day you come again," said the elderly Chinese, and the doctor promised to write to Lanny at Newcastle when possible. They hurried to join the waiting crowd, getting close to the front, and when the ferry came in they crowded on board. A heavy fog had drifted over the harbor, something common at this season; foghorns and whistles sounded from near and far, and the little green boat crept ahead with caution.

It would be a good night for escaping, if a vessel could find its way out to sea, everybody agreed. There were ship's officers here who meant to try it; they talked freely—the presence of danger broke down the customary reticence. Information was scarce but speculation plentiful. All seemed to agree that Hongkong could withstand a long siege, but the business of ships was at sea and not locked up in any harbor. Among the landsmen, every one had his post; if any one of them had a doubt or a fear he kept it in his heart.

In a time like this it was natural for the men to assume that their jobs were more important; they rushed off the boat and grabbed all the waiting taxis and rickshaws, and Lanny, whose legs still had to be treated carefully, walked off with his lady and found the street bare. They started along the waterfront, and it was some time before they were able to find one rickshaw and then a second. At long last they got to the pier where the launch of the *Oriole* was to be, but there was no launch. With sinking hearts they made certain, and then seated themselves to wait. Lanny said: "Perhaps the launch is taking Reverdy to the yacht." Laurel's reply was: "Would he have stayed this late with the Governor?" It really didn't seem plausible.

They sat gazing out into the fog, so heavy that they could not see a light the distance of a city block. The air resounded with the horns and whistles of ships; evidently there was much movement going on, but those on shore could only guess about it. Laurel asked: "Do you suppose the launch would have trouble in finding this pier?"

"They couldn't very well miss the whole waterfront," was the reply. "When they step ashore they can find out where they are, and would surely send somebody here for us."

They debated the idea of going out to search for the yacht at her anchorage. They could hire a sampan or rowboat, but it would be extremely dangerous in this fog, and once out of sight of the dock they would be lost. They would have little chance of finding the yacht, and afterwards would have still less of getting back to the same spot. They had precise instructions; this was the place, and there was no chance of mistaking it; if they went off looking elsewhere, the launch might come and miss them. Reverdy had given them until daylight, and that was a long time off.

X

There was nothing to do but sit still. Fortunately it was warm. The busy labor of the Chinese docks went on by night as by day, in war as in peace; a ship was being loaded farther out on the pier, and trucks rolled by them, piled high with boxes and sacks. "Trucks," in a Chinese port, did not mean motor vehicles; it meant a low platform on wheels, hauled by perhaps a dozen men with straps across their shoulders. You saw them going uphill and down in Hongkong streets. Here on the pier none of these sweating laborers paid the slightest attention to a white "missie" and her man.

There was only one subject to talk about, and they had already said everything—except one thing which was too painful to be voiced. But as the slow hours dragged by Lanny became fixed in his conviction, and finally he said: "I am afraid the *Oriole* has departed. We are not going to see her again—at least not in Hongkong."

"Oh, Lanny, such a dreadful idea!" exclaimed Laurel. "I can't bring myself to face it."

"How else can you figure it? Lizbeth was with a member of the Governor's staff at the dance. Is it conceivable that when an alarm was given, a staff member wasn't the first to be told? They had a government launch and they bolted for it, and of course their first job was to deliver Lizbeth to the yacht—they must have agreed to do that when they borrowed her. And Reverdy was due to be there—he surely wasn't going to sit chatting with Sir Mark a minute after the alarm came. It wouldn't take him more than a few minutes to get from Government

House to this spot, and he would find the launch here, but no Lanny and no Laurel. What would he do?"

"I suppose he would fume and fret for a while, but then he would be taken out to the yacht."

"He would find Lizbeth on board, or she would arrive soon afterwards; and then what? Let us say that he sends the launch in again— no simple matter in this fog. Would he possibly fail to put a time limit on it?"

"It would be a dreadful decision to have to make, Lanny."

"He would say: 'I give them one hour. If they aren't there by that time, it's their hard luck.'"

Laurel had to find some excuse for her uncle, even in this imaginary scene. "He would have to think of the other people on board, the crew as well as the passengers."

"Do you really think he would think about that, Laurel?"

This brought her up short, and she hesitated. "I think he would think that he was thinking about it—if that is not too complicated."

"I am guessing, of course. He may have been told by the Governor that this fog offers him his one chance to get out, and that every minute he waits he is reducing that chance. My guess is, he has weighed anchor, and the *Oriole's* siren is one of those sounds we are hearing, though we can't recognize it."

Every minute that passed brought this theory more to the fore. The only argument to oppose it was that Uncle Reverdy was a Southern gentleman, and wouldn't desert a lady, especially one who was a member of his own family. Laurel suggested that the fog was so bad and the night traffic so thick he dared not send the launch ashore until daylight. Possibly he himself had gone to the Hongkong Hotel for the night. Possibly he had been told that the cruiser and the destroyer in the harbor would convoy a fleet of vessels out by daylight.

"Possibly, but surely not probably!" was Lanny's reply. "The Japs have an airport at Canton, and if they mean trouble they may go to work at dawn this Sunday morning."

Nothing to do but sit and wait! He asked if she didn't want to take a nap, but she answered that she was too keyed up. He asked whether she was worried about the loss of her manuscript; she relieved his mind on that point by telling him that in Manila she had mailed a copy to her friend in New York. He wanted to know if it hurt her to talk about the idea of her uncle going off and leaving her; to this she replied: "I try to see it from his point of view. If he had to weigh Lizbeth's safety against mine, naturally he would favor hers."

"What I am wondering is how much our recent misconduct would weigh against us in the balance."

"Oh, Lanny! Surely not that!"

"I won't talk about you, since it might be painful. But consider *my* standing." There was a smile in Lanny's voice—he didn't mean to give up smiling, even in darkness and danger. "I was his prospective son-in-law, and I rejected the honor, and in a particularly inconsiderate way. I came aboard the yacht under false pretenses, I wrote to my lady friend, telling her that I was coming. Of course Reverdy wouldn't know whether I suggested your coming, or whether that was your own bright idea. Most probably he suspects it was a conspiracy between us, and that I decided to come with the idea of enjoying the pleasure of your society. Certainly I had been keeping from him and his family the fact that I had known his niece for three years or so, and that she had been a guest in my mother's home. Don't you think that in view of all this, there might be a strong tendency to say: 'All right, they wanted to be together, and now they have it, and don't have us to bother them'?"

"Lanny, that is a horrid thought. I simply won't face it!"

"All right; and maybe when the fog lifts, and we see the trim white *Oriole* resting at anchor, I'll be ashamed of having said it. We'll tell ourselves that all this is a nightmare, and it will be very romantic that we sat out all night on a Hongkong dock with coolies stumbling over our feet!"

XI

There was a subject of conversation which had been in his mind ever since Reverdy's telephone call. "Laurel," he said, "do you remember what I once told you, about an astrologer who predicted that I was going to die in Hongkong?"

"Indeed, yes," she answered. "I wondered if you had forgotten it."

"I have thought about it off and on. I wanted very much to try a séance with you and see if anything came. It was one thing which made me so impatient on the *Oriole*—that there was no way we could arrange it."

"It is silly of me, Lanny, but I begin to tremble every time I think of that prophecy. Of course I tell myself there cannot possibly be anything to astrology."

"There is nothing to astrology, but there might easily be something to an astrologer; he might be a medium, and have some psychic gift, no more to be understood than your own. That young Rumanian held my hand, and I asked him why he did it; he said he didn't know, he sometimes got things that way. I just don't know whether there is such a thing as the power called precognition, but there seems to be a lot of evidence for it, and I keep an open mind about it, in spite of what anybody says. If I'm going to die in Hongkong, I may know it a few minutes ahead of time, and that will interest me greatly."

"Don't joke, Lanny! I am so deeply concerned."

"I'm not joking. We all have to die some time, and we might as well learn to take it with an easy mind. Death is as much a part of our being as birth, and one seems to me as odd and unbelievable as the other."

"I don't want to die and I don't want you to die; we both have too much to do. Most of all I am horrified by the idea that if you were to die, the blame would rest on my uncle."

"If I were you I wouldn't worry over that, Laurel. I have been thinking the problem over in the last few hours, and I tell you that if I had the free choice at this moment, to be in his position or my own, I'd choose to be here."

"You think the yacht is in that great danger?"

"We get certain thought patterns and find it impossible to change them, even when we consciously try. As far back as men have been going to sea, they have had the certainty that if they could get beyond the horizon, they were safe from a pursuer. Now they forget that the Japs have planes, and carriers, and long-range bombers, to say nothing of submarines. If the Japs are going to attack this port, they will know perfectly well that ships will be stealing out tonight, and they will have made plans accordingly."

"What a hideous idea—the *Oriole* being sunk!"

"They might sink her, and again they might have use for her; put a crew on board and take her to Formosa."

"What would they do with the passengers and crew?"

"Intern them, I suppose. On the other hand, if they haven't time or the men to spare, they might sink her with one shell. What I am saying is, if I had to choose, I believe I would stay in Hongkong—in fact I thought of suggesting to you that we should refuse to go on the launch. In the first place Hongkong may hold out, and the siege may be relieved; in the second place, we may find a way to escape with Althea, and have a chance to see Free China. Surely a lot of people are going to get out, by one route or another; and she and Mr. Foo and Madame Sun will know as much about the routes and the disguises as anybody in this place. So if you have any impulse to despair, take my advice and don't!"

The woman said: "I am thinking about Lizbeth, and the awful things that may be happening to her!"

XII

Dawn came as a slow diffusion of light through the fog. First it was possible to see that it was fog; then it was possible to see that it was moving slowly, broken by light breezes; presently there were clear stretches of water, with a patch of sail revealed, then hidden again.

The two watchers strained their eyes toward where the yacht had been, and little by little increased their certainty that the place was empty. There were glimpses of the opposite shore with its hills; there were freighters at anchor and many small boats moving; but no trim white *Oriole*.

It was possible that the yacht had been moved to the refueling depot; but surely some messenger would have come to this pier where the guests were waiting. They debated these ideas until it was broad daylight, and they could see the whole harbor, with many ships—but fewer than on the previous day. This was the time when the Jap planes would come, if they were coming that Sunday morning; but they did not show up, and the stranded pair wondered, could it have been a false alarm? Could the enemy fleet that had been sighted be bringing merely normal supplies for the troops in Canton, or farther south, in Indo-China?

The sun was well up in the sky before they decided that there was no longer any use sitting on the bulwark of a pier. They had agreed that their next move was to get in touch with Althea, for she might be leaving at any time and they would depend on her advice. Lanny got rickshaws, and they were taken to the nearest hotel—not the fashionable Hongkong, because Laurel declared she looked too seedy. The hotel was crowded, so she sat in the lobby while he went to the telephone.

There were several Foo Sungs in the book, but the hotel clerk could tell which was the wealthy and well-known silk merchant. Lanny called, and a voice answered in Chinese. All Lanny could say in that language was "Doctor Carroll," and this he kept repeating until at last he heard the voice of his friend. When he told her what had happened, she cried out in dismay, then said: "Please wait. I will speak to Mr. Foo." Coming back, she reported: "Mr. Foo begs you to come to his house. It will be a great honor. He will send his car at once." Lanny accepted for both of them, with due gratitude.

The place was in the center of the island, reached by a winding road through the hills. The home of a well-to-do Chinese is always a compound; you enter by high much-carved gates, and there is a central area, large or small, and buildings completely enclosing it—buildings with far-hanging, curved roofs. There are stables and pens for various animals, and quarters for many servants; if the master is rich, there is a wall separating all this from the residential part; if he has become wholly or partly westernized, he has a Chinese and a Western wing of his house, each in its proper style.

That was the way with Mr. Foo; his drawing-room might have been in Grosvenor Square or on Park Avenue, and when he escorted Lanny to a bedroom, there were classical Poussins on the walls, and lovely figure pieces by Corot. Lanny found this surprising, but he reflected that an elderly Chinese would have the same interest in scenes of the *ancien régime* that a wealthy Frenchman would have in scenes of the Ming dynasty. In costumes and architecture these periods were different, but in their inner essence, the psychology of the ruling class, they were much the same.

The courteous host informed them that this would be their home for as long as they cared to stay. They had breakfasted at the hotel while waiting for the car, so now he suggested that they should sleep, and later they would have a conference. Meantime, through connections in the city he would make certain that the yacht was no longer in the harbor; also he would learn what he could about the alarm of last night and what it meant. He assured them that there was no need for haste; the monkey men—so he called the foes of his country—were assuredly not going to break into Hongkong in the next few days, and there would be plenty of time to work out plans. That was comforting, and Lanny slept soundly on a good spring mattress.

XIII

In the late afternoon, when the promised conference took place, the elderly Chinese reported that the *Oriole* had undoubtedly departed— although of course she had not been seen in the fog. Many ships had stolen out, and a large convoy was to leave this night. What happened to the yacht would not be known for some time, since assuredly she would not use her wireless until she was far away. A Japanese convoy, including various warships, was approaching the harbor of Hongkong. It was probably bringing reinforcements, and what these were for was anybody's guess—an advance into the interior, or an attack upon the port. "We soon know," said Mr. Foo.

Althea was eager to persuade them to travel with her and visit her parents at the mission, which was in the province of Hunan. They would see this ancient land, and they could get a commercial plane to Chungking, from which capital they could be flown out to India, and from there home. But first they would have to wait and see what the Jap convoy was up to; their way of escape lay across its path, and they must give it time to get out of the way. Lanny would do more walking and strengthen his legs; also he would look at paintings!

The art expert was surprised to find in this home a dozen or more examples of English and French painters, mostly portraits. The silk merchant had traveled, and he had not taken the word of dealers but had bought what pleased him. Like *Der Dicke*, his taste ran to ladies, but, unlike the roistering Nazi, he insisted upon having them clothed. No decent Chinese would have had naked women in his drawing-room, even painted ones. In the dining-room he had a Whistler, and in his breakfast nook, very oddly, several Gibson girls, tall and tightly corseted. Lanny asked about the Holbein, but that was in the city, and no doubt would be hidden now. The visitors were destined never to see it.

Later on the host took his friend into the Chinese part of his home, where he had a series of landscapes of Tibet by the Russian Nicholas Roerich. There, also, he brought forward what he called his Number One wife, an elderly wizened figure as different from a Gibson girl as could be found on earth. She had had her feet bound in infancy and hobbled on two stumps; she did not know any English, but bowed and smiled like one of those tiny figures of mandarins which are made with a round base and a weight in it so that they cannot be upset but go on bobbing when you touch them. She had learned Lanny's name, and said it several times as if proud of the accomplishment. "Mista Budd! Mista Budd!"

XIV

In the course of the evening the guest found a chance to say to Laurel: "Is there any reason why Althea and Mr. Foo shouldn't witness a séance?" She thought for a moment and said that she had no objection. So Lanny told them about this strange faculty which Laurel had discovered in Germany, but didn't say she had made the discovery in Adolf Hitler's Berchtesgaden retreat!

Lanny outlined the procedure, and was interested to observe the reaction of these two friends from opposite sides of the world. The woman doctor had never taken psychic research seriously, and was not to be influenced by the fact that the Bible is full of such phenomena; that was far in the past, and belonged in the field of religion, not open to experiment, and apparently never to be repeated—until, perhaps, the Second Coming. Mr. Foo said that all Chinese were taught that the spirits of their ancestors survived and exercised a guardian influence, but among westernized Chinese the idea was allowed to recede into the background of the mind. However, he had no prejudices against it, and there are few persons who would reject the idea of a free show, right in their own drawing-room.

Laurel lay back on a couch and drifted into her strange trance, and Lanny sat by with notebook and pencil. Presently there came a gentle murmur, which said it was the voice of the late Otto H. Kahn. But it wasn't a very convincing Otto; he seemed to be out of sorts, perhaps bewildered by a strange environment. Some day, perhaps, the scientists will know how to manage these subconscious forces, but until that time psychic research remains an uncertain and frequently vexatious task. The spirits in the vasty deep refuse to come when you do call to them;

they choose their own time, and just when you have invited your friends and are most anxious for results they absent themselves, or misbehave and embarrass you greatly.

Perhaps it is the psychic atmosphere that is wrong; they require faith and love, and do not respond to a cold scientific attitude. The ideal master of ceremonies, as Lanny had observed, was Parsifal Dingle, who never had the least doubt that every spirit was exactly what he or she claimed to be; he talked to them with warm friendship, and they blossomed out and revealed their inmost secrets. But with Lanny it was "that old telepathy." He kept wondering, and in his secret soul trying to reduce these shadowy beings to the low status of subconscious automatisms. No matter how much he tried to imitate Parsifal's voice and manner, they did not get the same psychic help from him.

Whatever the reason, Otto Kahn said that he didn't know anything about a Rumanian astrologer named Reminescu, and never had anything to do with quackery like that; the whole idea was silly and boring. He said that Laurel Creston's grandmother was a sweet old lady, but she didn't have many ideas and objected to her progeny getting mixed in wars. He said, yes, there were a lot of Chinese spirits, all talking at once, but presumably they were speaking Cantonese, a dialect which he didn't understand very well. This, presumably, was an effort at humor in the urbane manner which the international banker had affected on earth; but when he said that Lings and Lungs and Sings and Sungs sounded all alike to him, he was being somewhat less than gracious. When Lanny introduced him to Mr. Foo, he apologized and said he could see that the elderly merchant was a cultivated person, and that if he would name some spirit who spoke English, he, Otto Kahn, would endeavor to make contact with him. But when Mr. Foo named his former business partner, the best the control could do was to describe his costume, and say that his English speech was difficult to make out.

All very disappointing; and when Laurel had come out of her trance the best Lanny could do was to tell their friends some of the remarkable things which had happened in Germany and at Bienvenu. But that isn't convincing to other people; they say they believe you, and perhaps they believe that they do, but it isn't the same as seeing and hearing for themselves. Even then, as Lanny had observed, few people can believe even what they see and hear; it is all so contrary to received opinion. Since infancy they have imbibed the idea that each and every mind in the world is a separate enclave, shut off from all other minds and forced to communicate by light waves and sound waves and other physical media. If there could be such a thing as direct contact of mind with mind, how would anybody ever keep any secrets, and without secrets how could he live?

And if there were such a thing as foreseeing the future, how could you stand it? Said the skeptical woman physician: "If you could foresee it, you might change it, and then it wouldn't be the future." To which the speculative art expert replied: "If we were able to foresee the future, it would be our future that we should foresee the future and change it the way we wanted it." You can see how many complications this would introduce into the intellectual life. It would be worse than relativity!

X V

Discussing thus like Milton's fallen angels the mechanism of the universe—"fix'd fate, free-will, foreknowledge absolute"—they passed a pleasant evening, but they did not get the least hint as to what was being prepared for them at that especially fateful hour, nor did Lanny Budd get any further data as to the chances of his dying in Hongkong. Not by the mysterious psychic medium, which appears to be independent of both time and space, but by plain ordinary sound waves traveling at their customary rate of one thousand and eighty-seven feet per second, was the visiting American to get that information. They partook of a late supper and went to bed soon after midnight; Lanny didn't know about the others, but he slept the heavy sleep of one who had spent the previous night sitting on the hard bulwark of a fog-shrouded pier and whose gluteus muscles still ached from the ordeal.

It was broad daylight when he opened his eyes. He had been having a dream—he was in a thunderstorm and trying to hide from the lightning; this dream mingled with his waking state, so that he wasn't quite sure which was which. There were heavy, thudding sounds in his ears, and he didn't have to lie very long and speculate about them. He had heard them too many times in the course of twenty-five tragic years: first in London, during World War I, then in tormented Barcelona, Madrid, and Valencia; more recently in London again and in Paris, and worst of all, during half a dozen dreadful days and nights off the beaches of Dunkirk.

He had become an expert in the different sounds, having had them explained by those who were in the business. Ack-ack makes a sharp cracking noise, both when the shell is fired and when it explodes in the sky; bombs make a dull, heavy sound. Bombs, dropped from airplanes, were detonated when they hit the ground—or some other object such as a ship or a house. When Lanny heard their thump, he saw with his mind's eye a great burst of black smoke, and the debris of a house flying in every direction—bricks and stones, beams and pieces of furniture and human bodies.

He slipped into his clothes and ran out into the passage. There were the two ladies, in borrowed dressing gowns; presently their host and

several of the servants joined them, all wide-eyed with fright. They
had never heard such sounds before, and it was up to the expert to tell
them what he knew. He guessed that the explosions were three or four
miles away, but he couldn't be sure, because big bombs sound nearer
than small. Could it be that the British were indulging in target practice? Mr. Foo said it was most unlikely, for the British had very few
planes here, and the flyers got their training before they came. He
went to the telephone; but apparently a great part of Hongkong had
the same idea at the same moment, and he could not get a connection.

XVI

It was Monday, the 8th of December, Hongkong time, and Sunday,
the 7th, at Pearl Harbor. The latter place being to the east, its time is
ahead of China's; already the American battleships lay at the bottom
of the harbor, and the great airfield was a mass of smoldering ruins.
Mr. Foo turned on the radio and got the news of the attack—though
of course the extent of the damage was concealed. They sat staring at
one another, unable to realize what it meant, that America was actually
in the war. Would it by any chance bring help for Hongkong?

It wasn't long before the radio was telling them what had been happening here. Japanese bombers had attacked the Kai Tak airfield on the
Kowloon peninsula just back of the great hotel in which the Saturday
night dance had been held. That dance had been for the benefit of the
British-Chinese bomber force—and now there was no such force, at
least not in the Hongkong territory. The radio didn't say that, for they
wouldn't give any information to the enemy; they just said that bombs
had been dropped, never what had been hit.

That was the way in this modern war; the first move of every enemy
was to paralyze his opponent's means of attack. Never again would
there be a declaration of war, and always the first target would be the
enemy's airfields. In this case the Japanese had a field at Canton, and
the distance was seventy-three miles; they would fly back and get
another load, and they would keep that up all day long; you could
pretty nearly figure when you would be hearing more of those "crump-
ing" sounds. Regularly, for the next eighteen days the Japanese planes
came at two- or three-hour intervals. Since night bombing wasn't ac-
curate, they would let everybody have a night's rest, and come again
at dawn, fog and storms permitting.

After Lanny had listened to the second relay, he said to his friendly
host: "I hate to say it, Mr. Foo, but if the British have no way to
oppose this enemy air force, your splendid city will not be able to hold
out very long. It was command of the air that enabled Franco to destroy the Spanish republic; it was command of the air which enabled

Hitler to destroy first the Dutch and Belgian Armies, and then the French; it has been a slender margin of air power which has enabled the British to hold out against him."

In past times it had been the practice of kings to chop off the heads of heralds who brought bad news; but this wise old Chinese was a modern man and knew a fact when it was set before him. He said: "It is bad, but it not destroy China. Canton and Shanghai stand it, we stand it too."

Lanny was interested in the reaction of the others to this accumulation of tragedy. Said the woman doctor: "If there is going to be a siege, I can be just as useful here as at home, so there doesn't seem much sense in moving." She said it in her quiet matter-of-fact way—it was obviously so, and no false heroics.

Laurel Creston, who hadn't been brought up to face wholesale pain and sorrow, looked at this girl who was so plain and unprepossessing, and who wore spectacles. Laurel forced herself to smile. "What shall we do, Lanny, stay and see if there is anything to astrology?"

He, the magnificent male, the charmer, the much-desired, couldn't fail to meet a challenge like that. "Let's stick it out for a while," he replied. "Whatever happens to me, I'll say it was telepathy or clairvoyance. I'll never admit that the stars had anything to do with it!"

24. Supped Full with Horrors

I

THE Japanese air force did not confine their efforts to the Kai Tak airfield. They bombed oil depots, arsenals, and barracks, and of course vessels in the harbor; they blasted and sank the Clipper which was loading up for a flight to Manila; incidentally they dropped a bomb squarely in the middle of the Central Market and killed or wounded some eight hundred Chinese. When this news came over the radio, Althea said it was time for her to go and help. Mr. Foo said he would send her in his car.

Laurel suggested: "Perhaps they would take me as a nurse. I will go and offer." Lanny might have said: "I am doing important work for my government and have been forbidden to take unnecessary risks." Possibly it was his duty to say that; but instead he asked: "Do you suppose they would let me drive an ambulance?"

It wasn't so hard for the doctor, because she had been trained for this sort of thing from childhood. But what training the other two had got they had had to give themselves; all they had got from the world was to have good manners, to be properly dressed, and to have what they asked for and do what pleased them. It took considerable moral effort to step into that limousine and be driven to what they knew would be scenes of terror. Bombs were falling as they drove, and there were other sounds which Lanny recognized as gunfire. The enemy ground forces were attacking all around the perimeter of the "New Territories," a matter of some fifty miles, and that was far too great a front to be held by the few regiments of British and Indian troops on hand. The Japs would know how many there were, but Lanny couldn't be sure, so he said nothing. He braced himself for whatever ordeal might come, to himself and to these high-spirited women.

The doctor was the only one among them who possessed belongings, hers having been brought off the yacht. She now wore a surgeon's white coat and carried her kit. When she reported at headquarters, they told her where to go, and that was all there was to it. Laurel said: "May I help her?" and they answered: "Surely." Lanny said: "I thought maybe I might drive an ambulance; I have driven a car several hundred thousand miles in my life." They told him to go along.

Within half an hour they were at the Jockey Club, which had been the center of Hongkong social life, and now had been cleared out and turned into an emergency hospital. In a few minutes Althea was performing an operation upon a Chinese woman whose leg had been blown off and tied with a tourniquet. Laurel, who had never even seen an operation before, was instructed how to administer the anesthetic; she began her new career by taking one glance at the chunk of raw and bloody meat, and then fainting. When she came to she wept with embarrassment, and proceeded to grit her teeth and do what she was told.

As for Lanny, he explained that he could drive but couldn't lift weights or jump about, on account of his recently damaged legs; also, he didn't know where anything was in Hongkong, except the big hotels and the American Club. They gave him a Chinese who spoke English of a sort, and a truck, which the British call a lorry. It was his duty to drive as fast as possible to places where the bomb blasts were reported, and there to make the best guess he could as to which persons had a chance to live long enough to reach the dressing station. He would use the authority conferred by his Anglo-Saxon features and good clothes to command some of the spectators to load the wounded into the truck, and the Chinese would translate his orders and perhaps make them more emphatic. If Lanny was too liberal in his estimate as to the life expectancy of people without hands, or feet, or faces, the

doctors would correct him and he would do better next time. He
would drive, tooting his horn vigorously, and trying not to make more
casualties on the way. He would hear the shriek of planes power-
diving over his head, and each time would say to himself: "You will
die in Hongkong!"

II

This attack had been foreseen many years, and the British authorities
had built air-raid shelters. When enemy planes were sighted and the
wavering sirens blew, the people on the streets, regardless of race,
creed, or color, would dive into the nearest tunnel and the streets
would be clear. All except the drivers of ambulances and military
vehicles; they were supposed to continue and take their chances. Now
and then, caught in a traffic jam, Lanny would have a chance to look
up and see the black bombers and the poisonous "eggs" dropping from
them.

They were bombing only "military objectives," for reason that they
felt sure of taking the city; but their bombing was often inaccurate,
and in the course of the next few days Lanny witnessed many dreadful sights, such as he had got used to in the victim cities of Nazi-Fascism
in Britain and on the Continent. The shells were of the fragmentation
variety, intended to kill people rather than to wreck blocks of houses;
he saw human beings blasted and blackened by bombs, blown through
doors and windows, buried under debris, suffering unimaginably dreadful wounds. He had many hard decisions to make: he had been told to
favor the white people, and he had to tell himself that this was a necessary decision, because they were in charge of affairs and possessed the
knowledge of how to run them. But it made him rather sick to listen
to the scoldings of stout ladies in the fashionable hotels, objecting to
the Chinese mob crowding in upon them during air raids.

When the blessed relief of darkness came, Lanny would have dinner
with his two women friends, and twice the blessed old Chinese came,
bringing some delicacy and begging them to come to his home and
spend the night. They were pale and exhausted, living on their nerves;
but there was always more work to be done, and they would insist on
doing it. The place was now full of wounded soldiers: English, Scot-
tish, Canadian boys, also Indian Gurkhas. A life hung upon your
efforts, and how could you turn your back? Althea was relentless with
herself, and Laurel would die before she would show herself weaker.
Telephone calls would come, and Lanny would climb into his lorry,
even though he was a bit dizzy.

Here and there they picked up items of news and traded them with
one another. In the first day's air raid, the Japs had knocked out all but

five of the planes at Kai Tak; these five had been dragged out by the crews from the burning hangars and towed by tractors away from the field. Quite an adventure story: where street signs or other obstructions barred the way they had been flattened by the tractors, and the planes had been dragged into rice fields and camouflaged with care. There was still a small strip of the airfield that was usable, and when darkness came the planes were brought back and flown away to Chungking with important passengers. They came back for three successive nights, and the enemy wasn't able to get them.

Who were these passengers? Madame Sun was one, Lanny learned; others were persons who had influence, and could persuade the British authorities that they were important. An American art expert would hardly have rated; but if he had presented himself as the son of Budd-Erling Aircraft, a powerful factor in lend-lease, he might have got by. And surely the niece of Reverdy Holdenhurst, who had dined at Government House only last Saturday evening! But Laurel put her foot down; she wouldn't go, at least not while Althea stuck it out. She thought that Lanny ought to go, because of the importance of his work; but Lanny said: "I am surely not leaving you."

III

The Japanese troops pressed the fight all around the perimeter. They had been especially trained for this campaign, and of course they had had spies all over the place. Traitor Chinese led them by paths through the hills, and they showed up behind the pillboxes which were supposed to stop them. It was as Lanny had foretold to Mr. Foo—their planes machine-gunned the British in the trenches and bombed the supply depots behind the lines. Once more it was proved that armies on the ground cannot operate unless there is air power overhead to protect them. In three days the Japs had broken into Kowloon—and then there were dreadful scenes, for the Chinese masses began looting ahead of the advance, and the whites were helpless to protect themselves.

The greatest weakness of this Gibraltar of the Far East was its water supply. The reservoirs in which water was collected were conspicuous, and the enemy did not fail to bomb the outlets. Pretty soon there was not enough water to put out fires, and it became evident that there wasn't going to be enough to keep a million and a half human beings alive. The Japs brought heavy guns into Kowloon, and from then on the people of this island knew what a military siege really was. The shells poured in by night as well as by day, three every minute; and whatever target the enemy aimed at he hit. The agents of the puppet Chinese government which had been set up in Nanking were everywhere. They would climb to a roof and signal the Japs on the distant

hills, and then they would dive down into the crowd and there was no
way to find them. A few minutes later would come the shells. So the
naval dockyards were blasted, the power plant, the radio masts on the
"Peak."

Lanny was sent to bring supplies to the "Battle-Box," the communi-
cations headquarters of the Army. It was sixty feet underground, and
supposed to be bombproof. Its location in the heart of the city was a
secret closely kept; Lanny had to take an oath not even to mention that
he had been there. But evidently the Japs had found out about it, for
several shells exploded near, and as Lanny came out, a near-by building was struck and the blast knocked him twenty feet or more and
flattened him against a wall. There was a minute or so right there when
he thought the astrologer's prediction had come true.

He was taken to a first-aid station in his own lorry, but all he had
to do was to lie still for a while. He had been lucky, but he knew that
he couldn't draw upon that bank forever. The British lines were being
forced back all around the semicircle, and now the enemy was landing at night on the island itself. Demands for surrender came, but the
British refused, and the censors allowed nothing to go out but op-
timism. Nevertheless, Lanny made up his mind that the end was coming
soon, and he told his two ladies. Mr. Foo came to see them, riding in a
rickshaw; he had turned his car over to the government and was staying
in town. When he saw how exhausted all three of them were he begged
them to come to dinner with him and talk things over; you could still
get food in restaurants, although the quantity was strictly rationed.

I V

In a private room of the same Chinese restaurant where Lanny and
Laurel had celebrated their arrival in this ill-fated city, the four people
sat and discussed their future. For the elderly merchant there was, obviously, but one choice; he would stay with his family, and whatever
the conquering "monkey men" handed out to them they would take.
But for the three Americans it was different; there was still time to get
away. A few were trying it every night; what was happening to them
of course could not be known. But the decision must be made. "You
go now—or then you don't go," said Mr. Foo.

It appeared that the decision depended upon the doctor. Lanny was
willing to quit, and they all agreed that he could be considered to have
done his duty by the island of Hongkong. Laurel was willing, except
that she couldn't bear to desert Althea. It was this conscientious soul
who had the scruples, her professional honor being involved. She
could name one patient after another whose life depended upon her;
and she didn't believe that the triumph of the Japanese would make

much difference in her ability to help. Even "monkey men" would respect a doctor, and they would need her services, perhaps for their own wounded. For a physician, and especially one who was a devout Christian, war was something different from what it was to the ordinary person.

Lanny's comment was: "Surely you will find plenty of people who need your help in the province of Hunan. Does your Hippocratic oath oblige you to prefer this group over that?"

She replied: "It is just that the situation here is so acute."

"Yes, but it may very soon be acute in your home province, and you won't be able to get to it. You will be a prisoner of the Japs, and whatever your services are, they will be performed in a concentration camp."

"Japs get Hongkong, they soon go north," broke in the Chinese. "They cut railroad to Hankow, they go through Hunan."

Laurel said: "Lanny, I think you ought to give Althea at least a hint about your own position."

"I am under pledge not to talk about that under any circumstances. But I suppose I can say that I am doing some important service for our government. I was told to take a six months' furlough, and if I count the time I spent in hospital, that is more than half up. I hope to return to duty."

"Let me add this," put in the woman writer. "Lanny has never told me his secret, but I have been watching him for the past couple of years and I am pretty sure that I have guessed it. If you help him to escape you may be sure that you have rendered an important service to our country. And don't forget that our country is now in the war."

"Am I really needed for your escape?" demanded the doctor. "Mr. Foo can give Lanny a guide who knows some English, and who can be trusted."

"You know Madame Sun, Althea, and you understand her cause. You know how to speak to the Chinese partisans, and tell them what I have just told you. They will do things for you that they would never do for a wealthy stranger—or so they would consider Lanny."

"You go, Doctor Carroll!" commanded the elderly Chinese. "You go help Chinese people. You don't let monkey men get you. You remember Nanking!" He spoke for a minute or two in his native language—things perhaps too terrible to say in English—or perhaps he didn't know the words.

So at last the doctor gave way. "I'll have to leave my kit," she said. "If I sent for it, they would know I was going away. There are spies everywhere."

"You come my house, we talk," said the merchant. At last report the enemy had not got there, and if they did, he declared, he would know how to hide his friends. He would get some sort of conveyance to take them to the place, and he would make all arrangements for their trip. When Lanny tried to thank him, he replied: "You friend Madame Sun." Evidently that was going to be magic.

V

In this comfortable home they rested, and thought with grief about what might be coming to it. They had seen so many fine buildings, so much of human comfort and convenience, go up in smoke and dust and rubble. Guns were going off all around them, but they were still a mile or two away at the nearest. It wouldn't take a tank many minutes to cover that distance, but their host assured them that he could put them where the Japs would never find them. He had already discussed the flight with a fisherman, owner of a junk and member of "the Party," a man who could be trusted. For three hundred American dollars he would stow them away in his hold. "Bad smell!" said the old gentleman, grinning.

They would steal through the East Lamma Channel, and after they got by Hongkong and other islands, they would turn northeastward along the coast. It must be a night of heavy fog, for the Jap Navy was on patrol against just such escapes. They would have a chance of freedom, and if they were captured—well, they would be in the same position as all the other people of the territory.

Meantime there was nothing to do but rest, and they needed it. They had learned to sleep through gunfire, and to eat food when they could get it, and to simulate cheerfulness always. They had learned to face even the ghastly idea that the American battlefleet was at the bottom of Pearl Harbor. Did this mean that the great naval base was going to share the fate of Hongkong? Did it mean that the Japanese would be able to invade California? Radio JBW—"Hongkong calling!"—was still working, but it played mostly Christmas carols; the news, obviously, couldn't be frank, since the enemy was listening in. People sat and guessed, and believed the best or the worst according to their temperaments. The son of Budd-Erling, considered an authority because of his father, could assure them that America was building many planes and would build whatever number it took; assuredly President Roosevelt would never make terms with a government of assassins.

Old Mr. Foo found this comforting, and said: "Tell them we got plenty men for fight; all we need is guns."

"It is hard to get anything to China now," Lanny replied. "The distances are such that it may be easier to take Japan than to get supplies to China." That must have sounded like wild talk here in doomed and shell-torn Hongkong, but Mr. Foo was too polite to say so. Lanny added: "I have heard my father discuss it with air-force people, and that is what they were saying."

They had to consider the problem of money for their trip. All three of the Americans had some with them, and American money would be good even in the interior of China; certainly in any town there would be someone to exchange it. Chinese money varied from district to district, and Mr. Foo suffered when he thought how they would be cheated. As for silver, it was so heavy that coolies would have been needed if they were going to carry enough. Mr. Foo would provide them with some gold, and he suggested that the ladies should carry it well hidden—they might be less apt to be robbed. He would pay the fisherman; this reliable "Party member" would receive one half in advance and the second half when he returned.

Lanny brought up the question of how to repay these sums. Mr. Foo said: "You know China War Relief Association in San Francisco?"

"No doubt I could find it," replied the other.

"You pay them thousand dollar. You tell them it come from Mr. Foo Sung in Hongkong."

"I'll pay them two thousand, if I get there," said the liberal-minded traveler—and Mr. Foo said that was quite all right with him. Lanny added: "I will get a receipt and mail it to you when the war is over. On the chance that I may not get back, I will give you an order on my father, who will surely make it good." He wrote a draft on the President of the Budd-Erling Aircraft Corporation, Newcastle, Conn., instructing him to pay to Mr. Foo Sung, silk merchant of Hongkong, the sum of one thousand dollars. To the merchant he explained: "I won't say what it is for, because that might get you into trouble if the Japs got hold of it. You can tell my father when you write."

VI

That was all, and they had nothing more to do but wait, and offer prayers for fog to whatever gods they believed in. The sound of the guns seemed to be coming nearer, and they speculated about this. Mr. Foo told them that his household was in a panic and wanted to run away—but where to? He had his Number Two wife put on her best robe and brought her in to meet the foreigners; she was young, pretty, and painfully embarrassed, but maybe that was because of the guns. With her came three small children, and they, too, were shy, and hardly dared lift their eyes to the tall, white-faced and light-haired apparitions. Mr. Foo had two sons by the Number One wife; they were safe in Chungking, he thanked his gods.

Next for their entertainment, the host produced a copy of a four-page newspaper, printed in the Cantonese language. He read them the name, *Tin Yin Yat Po;* that meant, he said, the *Heavenly Discourse Daily.* It was Jap propaganda, and he amused them by translating some of it for them. Then he had one of his servants bring in the birds, for a Chinese with money to spare does not keep dogs—they eat too much in a crowded country; he keeps beautiful singing birds, and he will pay fancy prices for well-trained ones. Mr. Foo had half a dozen, one of them a small black creature called a myna; it was a talking bird, and had been taught a dozen or more Chinese words, and one American— or is it two?—"O.K.!" One bird was named "Voice of a Thousand Bells," and the owner would take it out into the court when the sun shone, take the cover off the cage, and sit for a couple of hours listening to the song.

At the same time he would smoke his pipe and meditate upon the maxims of ancient Chinese sages. That had been his idea of a happy life, but now, he feared, it would soon be no more. The sages had had much to say about the uncertainties of fortune, and the need of the wise man to prepare himself to bear reverses. In proof thereof Mr. Foo quoted Liu Chi, who had been servant to the Emperor Hung Wu, first of the Ming dynasty six hundred years ago. When asked about the possibility of divination, this ancient one had replied:

"In the space of a day and night, the flower blooms and dies. Between spring and autumn, things perish and are renewed. Beneath the roaring cascade a deep pool is found. Dark valleys lie at the foot of high hills. These things you know; what more can divination tell you?"

Lanny's comment was: "I suppose that is my answer to the question of whether I shall die in Hongkong."

VII

They sat in this comfortable drawing-room, in which the sound of machine-gun fire had now been added to that of cannon. They had heard that it was in this part of the world that explosives had first been invented, but not applied to the killing of men. This, too, led to learned discourses; Lanny listened for a while, and then, when there came a lull, declared: "Mr. Foo, I have a special favor to ask of you. At first it may seem to be rude, but there is a reason for it."

"I am sure you never rude, Mr. Budd," said the old gentleman. "My house, all I have, is yours."

"What I wish to ask is that you and Dr. Carroll leave me alone with Miss Creston for a while. The reason is that I wish to ask her to marry me."

The effect of this was as if there had been a pin in the seat of the venerable Chinese; he leaped up. His race has been blessed with a keen sense of humor, and Lanny's remark delighted him beyond measure.

He clapped his hands together like a child; his rather wide mouth spread into a grin, and he cried: "Oh, good, good, good!" Apparently he couldn't think of any other word. "Very good! Very good!" He turned his enraptured smile upon Laurel. "You take him! He very nice man. You take him quick! What you say?"

Laurel's usually pale face had turned bright pink, and she was in a state of confusion; but still, she was a Baltimore lady, even on this under side of the earth. "He hasn't asked me yet, Mr. Foo."

This was more than a hint, and the delighted old man held up his finger to the woman doctor. "Come," he said. "We go."

Lanny sat gazing at his friend, and smiling almost as broadly as the Chinese. He did not speak, and finally she exclaimed: "Lanny, what a thing to do!"

"I waited," he said. "But what chance did I have?"

She might have said: "You have it now," but being a Baltimore lady, she said nothing. It was up to him.

He took her hand and led her to a sofa where he could sit by her side. Still wearing his teasing smile, he began: "We are going on a long journey, and it may sometimes be embarrassing. We may not be able to get separate rooms."

"Is that the reason you want to marry me?"

"There are many reasons, and I am beginning with the more obvious. Time and again I have wanted to try séances with you, but always it would have been a scandal. Think how nice it will be to be able to experiment all we please!"

"Lanny, stop joking!"

"I am not joking at all; these are solid, sensible facts. Another is that I may really die in Hongkong, and you may survive. I have earned quite a lot of money at my profession, and while I have wasted much of it in fashionable living, I still have some left. My father has my stocks and bonds in his safe-deposit box, and if anything happens to me I should like you to own them."

"You don't wish to leave them to any member of your own family?"

"There is no member who needs them. All my various fathers and mothers have begged me to get married, and they will have no ground of complaint if I take their advice."

"In order to talk about marriage, Lanny, it is necessary that something should be said about love."

"I am coming to that, dear. I have quite a discourse in mind, and we don't seem to have anything urgent to do until darkness falls."

"I am ready to hear whatever you have to say." Usually it was Laurel who did the teasing, and she could hardly complain if for once he had taken a leaf out of her book.

"I must have seemed a reluctant lover, and I beg you at the outset to believe that this has not been from choice."

"I have understood your circumstances, Lanny; at least I have guessed at them. But I had no means of guessing which of your various lady friends you would choose if you were free to choose."

"I admit that I have taken time to make up my mind; but then I had the time, and what was I to do with it? Speculation was all that was allowed me. I did that off and on, whenever I felt too lonely."

"Tell me honestly: were you ever in love with Lizbeth?"

"The phrase 'in love' is a dubious one, and I find myself reluctant to use it. I was 'in love' when I was young, and I remember it vividly; it denotes a state of complete absorption in passion, a suspension of the judgment that can lead to blunders and cruel suffering. I don't think that a man who has just passed his forty-first birthday ought to let himself be brought to that state—and still less ought he to desire it."

"I see that you have indeed quite a discourse prepared." Laurel had recovered her self-possession, and was perhaps ready to take the teasing role away from him.

"Believe me, I had at least a month on the *Oriole* in which to work it out in my mind. I could not say it, I could only think it, and I thought about every aspect of the problem."

"Ever since you made up your mind that Lizbeth bored you too much for endurance?"

"Precisely then. You must understand that I was under heavy pressure to think about marrying Lizbeth. First my mother and all her friends, and then my father and my stepmother in Connecticut picked her as the proper person for me, and did everything they could to get us and keep us together. My father had business reasons, for Reverdy has become his heaviest stockholder. When I first met Lizbeth she seemed to me very sweet and lovely, and it was possible to think of making her happy. Apparently she fell in love with me from the first and never gave it up; in the end it became embarrassing, because I realized that she had no interest in my ideas."

"Nor in any ideas," said Laurel decisively.

"But there was a time, at first, when I thought: She is the only sort of woman I could marry without having to hide her. You understand, my job required me to be a near-Fascist and to go among people of that sort. If I married a woman of my own way of thinking, I should have to hide her, and that is a wretched way of life. I tried it once, and I know that it is hardly possible for either the man or the woman to be happy under such conditions."

The lady from Baltimore was looking at him curiously. "You are apparently referring to something that I do not know about."

"It is something I am starting to tell you about. A year or more after my divorce from Irma I was secretly married to a woman of the German underground. Nobody knows about it except my friends Rick and Nina, in England. Her name was Trudi Schultz, and I had known her for years in Berlin; she and her husband were fighting the Nazis, and the Nazis got him. I helped Trudi to escape, and she lived in Paris. I used to visit her there clandestinely; it would have ruined both of us if our connection had been known. Finally she disappeared, and I learned that the Nazis had her in a château they had rented near Paris. I pretty nearly finished myself trying to save her, but I was too late."

"What happened to her?"

"They spirited her away into Germany. Later on I was able to trick Rudi Hess into finding out for me that she had died in Dachau concentration camp. That was all over before I met you."

"What a dreadful story! I begin to see why you do not talk lightly about a third marriage."

"I could not bring myself to ask you to share such a life as I was obliged to live. It would have ruined my work to be known as the husband of 'Mary Morrow,' or even as her friend on any terms. You must have been annoyed by all the precautions I took, but I assure you they were necessary."

"Let me tell you something, Lanny, before you go any further. I am not hinting for an answer, and you don't have to say a word. I just want you to know that I have a guess concerning that trip to Poughkeepsie, and what it was about."

"I told you that it was on picture business."

"You did, and of course you have to go on saying it. However, I sat in a dark theater, looking at a very silly movie, and I thought: He isn't going off to sell pictures just a day or two before he leaves on a dangerous mission. There is only one man in this part of the country important enough for him to be visiting; but of course I have to pretend that I haven't guessed. Please understand that I have never opened my lips on the subject to any person but you, and I never shall."

"Let's leave it there," he said, "and come back to the subject of love."

VIII

Laurel Creston could have guessed the greater part of that "discourse" which he had prepared in his mind, but no woman wants to guess it, she wants to hear it, and she is never bored by it—at least, not if it is the right man speaking.

"I have had five love affairs in my life," he told her, "and some day I will tell you about them. Two of the women died, and the other three left me for what they thought was a higher destiny; one became a stage star, and the others became countesses; I couldn't have helped any of them on their chosen paths. From the two real and unselfish loves that I enjoyed I learned a lot, and you may have the benefit of my knowledge if you wish. It may be useful to you as a novelist, if not as a wife."

"By all means tell me," she responded.

"I don't think of love as a devouring flame or anything of that extravagant sort. It may be that, but I don't want any of it. I think of it as a partnership in some worth-while undertaking, and I believe that the basis of it is honesty and good faith, and mutuality of interests, or at any rate, respect for each other's interests, whatever they may be. I think that love can be made, in much the same way that you make a cake, provided that you know the recipe and have the right ingredients. A man and a woman agree to help each other, to take care of each other, to try to understand each other's needs and tastes—and if they do, and are honest and frank about it, love will grow between them. True and enduring love is mainly shared experience."

"In other words, Lanny, you are trying to tell me that you don't love me now, but that you will be able to if you try?"

"Nothing of the sort, dear. I mean that I am not putting the icing on the cake until after I have mixed and baked it. Many times I have wanted to love you, and many times I have said: 'No; you haven't the right to think about it. You haven't the right to suggest the idea to her. You haven't the right to torment yourself with the idea. You haven't the right to have a wife so long as you are—' well, what I have been."

"You're not that any longer?"

"I am on a furlough with three months still to run, and it may be longer yet before I can get back to the job. I doubt if, after what happened to me in Halifax, I can go back into Naziland again. Of course I'm going on fighting Nazi-Fascism, but it may have to be in some different way, and it may permit me to have a wife and to cherish her, and not have to hide her as if she were a criminal."

"And so, you haven't loved me yet, but you might begin if you would let yourself."

"Let's not quibble about words, dear. I think that you are a lovely person. You are wise, and you are kind—"

"No, not kind, Lanny! I have a sharp, satirical tongue."

"Yes, but you aim your shafts at my enemies. We agree in our ideas, and I have seen you tried in the fire. I know that you could make me happy. The question is, whether I could make you happy. Is that better?"

"Much better," she admitted.

"All right then; and now it's your turn."

"I want to be wooed, Lanny. I want to be told all sorts of wonderful things about myself. And above all, I want to hear that I am needed."

He perceived that she had succeeded in turning the tables and now was teasing him, but he didn't mind. He had learned long ago that love is a game. He asked: "Then I have your permission to woo you?"

"Oh, indeed you have!"

"I don't know if we are going to escape, but even if we don't, love in a concentration camp will be better than no love at all. If we do escape, we have a long journey before us, and we'll make it a honeymoon journey, and practice enjoying every moment of it, even the hardships. I promise that I won't stop making love to you when the wedding vows have been pledged. I will woo you with every word, every glance, every thought. I will be gentle and kind. I will think first about your happiness, and I will guard you as the most precious jewel in all Cathay—the Celestial Kingdom, the Flowery Kingdom, the Dragon Kingdom. Is that the way you want me to talk to you?"

"That is the most delightful talk that a Baltimore bluestocking ever had offered to her."

"We will get you stockings of pure China silk, and golden slippers with pearls on them, and we will dance all the way from the South China Sea to Outer Mongolia. And every day I will tell you all the lovely things I have dreamed about you, and every night we will make the dreams come true."

"Did you really have dreams about me, Lanny?"

"I said that I wouldn't, that I had no right to—but then I did."

"And all the time I was giving myself up for a hopeless old maid!"

"Old maid?" he exclaimed, for he knew what a dreadful thing that was among Southern-minded people. "You are seven years younger than I am."

"Why, Lanny, how perfectly outrageous! How did you find that out?"

"Bless your heart, you told me yourself."

"I never did anything of the sort! Wild horses couldn't have dragged it out of me!"

"You told it, while you were in trance."

"Oh! You asked me such questions!"

"On my honor, I did not. You volunteered it when we were experimenting with age regression. You told about political affairs when you were sixteen years old. I knew it was a direful secret, so I kept it locked in my heart."

"And still you say you want to love me! And when you might have had one who was only twenty-one!"

"It would have taken her at least thirteen years to find out what I was talking about—and then she would have disapproved of it heartily."

IX

So they played at courtship, after the fashion which Laurel had been taught in her girlhood, by that same grandmother who now came to her in the spirit world and scolded her for not making proper use of her opportunities. "Mary Morrow" had conferred this art of coquetry upon the heroine of her partly completed novel, to the great bewilderment of the German lad in the university town. It didn't bewilder Lanny, because he had had the advantage of reading the manuscript; also, there had been plenty of flirts on the Coast of Pleasure, beginning with Sophie Timmons, whose technique he had watched in childhood, and coming down to his half-sister Marceline in recent years.

He ventured to take her hand. "You haven't told me yet if you will marry me," he objected.

"Are you sure that you have asked me yet?" she countered.

"I ask you now. Will you marry me, Laurel?"

"I wonder—how does one get married in Hongkong?"

"One can't—it takes two."

"Three, I am sure. Somebody has to say the words."

"Mr. Foo will be able to tell us. We might have a Chinese wedding; they ring gongs and shoot off firecrackers and carry 'happiness banners.'"

"But no guns, Lanny. You will have to have this battle stopped. I couldn't bear to be married while other people are being killed."

"I will have to see the Governor about that. But seriously, darling—will you marry me?"

"This is so sudden, Lanny! I was brought up to look forward to a proper wedding, with veils and a trousseau, and at least four bridesmaids."

"When I was a little fellow—"

"You must have been a delightful little fellow, Lanny!"

"I heard a song about a bicycle built for two. Somebody was wooing Daisy, but it might as well have been another flower. Laurel, Laurel, give me your answer, do! I'm half crazy, all for the love of you! It won't be a stylish marriage—I can't afford a carriage—and so on. I don't think I could get even a tandem bicycle here; but we might find the rector of this parish, or perhaps his curate. I don't know what the law is, but maybe Althea can tell us, or find out. But first of all, you have to say that you will marry me."

"Oh, Lanny, I'm not just playing! I am frightened—just as much as if I were a schoolgirl."

"I wonder," he said, "what would happen if I were to kiss you?"

"I really can't tell. You might try and find out."

So he tried, and his lips met hers and stayed there. He put his arms about her and she put hers about him, and pretty soon there was no doubt about the answer. The blood mounted into her cheeks and the tears came into her eyes, and when they broke off the embrace she was sobbing a little. "Oh, Lanny, I am so happy! I have wanted you for so long!"

"Is that really so, dear?"

"I oughtn't to tell you! You will discover how much I love you, and all my defenses will be gone!"

"Don't worry, I am not that sort of man. I want to be loved and I want to be trusted."

"I am different from you, Lanny. I don't have to make my love like a cake. I am 'in love'—or will be if I dare."

He kissed her again; he kissed her several times before he troubled her with any more similes or philosophical discourses. He hadn't been sure whether she cared for him, she had been such a rigidly proper lady. But now he made sure, and he let her know beyond peradventure that he was a serious and ardent lover. The next time he asked her: "Will you marry me?" she answered, promptly and humbly: "Yes, Lanny." So he kissed her again to seal the bargain and make sure she wouldn't change her mind.

X

Mr. Foo had thoughtfully closed the drawing-room door; now Lanny got up and opened it. He clapped his hands and called: "Yoo-hoo!"—which he assumed might be Chinese for something. The others came quickly, and he told them that the answer was yes, and the old gentleman could not have been happier if it had been his own Number Three wedding. He wrung Lanny's hand and then Laurel's—it wasn't "ladies first" in the Middle Kingdom. Althea kissed Laurel and was as pleased, good soul, as if she were the lucky one.

Then came the problem of weddings. There was a Church of England chapel not far away, and Mr. Foo knew the clergyman; Althea, who had been to Hongkong before, had met him. She said that he would probably be ministering to the wounded, but perhaps they could go to him. Laurel, whose defenses were gone, said: "Tell him we shall take but a few minutes of his time."

Althea tried the telephone and found that it was still working. Hongkong was dying slowly, but clinging to life up to the last moment. There was no response from the clergyman's house; at the host's suggestion she tried other places and finally found him in a near-by country store which had been turned into a hospital. There was a discussion, and Althea said: "It is an emergency, for a reason which cannot be explained over the phone." She, the good Episcopal lady, a physician who had been helping at the Jockey Club, had a right to be believed; also, a Chinese merchant who was wealthy and did many charities was a person to be obliged. The clergyman, who still had his car, promised to be there within the hour.

So now began a great flurry; for of course you can't just stand up and answer "yes" a few times and let that settle it. There is no part of the world where there doesn't have to be excitement over a wedding. Mr. Foo's household would have to be present, and must have time to put on festival clothing; there must be flowers in the room, and also something to eat—no time to bake a cake, but there would be wine, and sweet wafers, and candied fruit, whatever could be found in cellars and storerooms in a hurry. There were servants rushing this way and that, bowing to the blushing bride, and she having to be told what to do, and feeling rather dizzy, because it really was "so sudden."

There was one serious trouble, which Althea mentioned with hesitation. "I have been told that you are a divorced man, Mr. Budd; and Mr. Notting may not feel that he is permitted—you know, the practice of the Church of England is very strict."

"That's all right," said Lanny soothingly. "I can explain everything to him if he asks."

XI

There came a very proper young English priest, wearing his black costume and round clerical collar; he was thin, stoop-shouldered, pale, and like everybody else on this doomed island had been working himself to exhaustion. Lanny explained the situation: the lady in the case was an American spinster aged thirty-four; he himself was an American widower aged forty-one. They had been left behind from the yacht *Oriole*, having missed it in a fog. They were about to make an effort to escape by sea, this night if there was fog; they would have to travel through the interior of the country, and manifestly this would be awkward if they were not married; the lady would be hopelessly compromised. She was a most respectable person, a niece of the yacht owner, Mr. Holdenhurst, who had dined with the Governor the night before the Japanese attack. She had known Lanny for three years and it was in all ways a proper match.

Since Lanny described himself, quite truthfully, as a widower, Mr. Notting had no thought of divorce and did not mention that subject. The trouble, he said, was with the ordinances of the territory of Hongkong; a license was required, and before it could be issued, the parties must give two weeks' notice to the Registrar of Marriages. Furthermore, in order for a marriage to be legal, all British colonies require a civil ceremony to precede the religious. And furthermore, the ceremony was not permitted to be performed in a private home; it had to be in a building licensed for the purpose.

Lanny had to think fast to get over that set of hurdles. Said he: "If you should marry us without a civil ceremony, and in a private home, that marriage would be valid in the eyes of God, would it not?" When the clergyman admitted that it would, Lanny added: "We could presumably have a later ceremony in some place and under some circumstances which would be legally beyond controversy. Would that be enough for you, Laurel?"

Somewhat to his surprise she answered promptly: "It would."

So the prospective groom set to work to undermine the scruples of this conscientious gentleman on the subject of a license. Englishmen are not accustomed to the idea of remaking laws to suit themselves, or interpreting them according to their own convenience. But Mr. Notting could not deny that transportation on this island was almost unobtainable and the roads pitted with bomb craters. If anyone got into the city, he might not be able to get out again. The Registrar might be serving as a fire warden, or his office might have been bombed out of existence. If the island had to surrender, who would file any records, or trouble to take care of them? Surely there must be some point at which a state of emergency could be recognized, and the laws of God take precedence over those of men!

So argued the free-lance American—anarchistic as most of them are. The fact that he, and the bride also, were foreigners, and were going to remove themselves from the territory at once, certainly seemed to provide a case about which the government would hardly need to concern itself. Also, the fact that both parties had been baptized into the Episcopal Church gave them a right to appeal to Mr. Notting. Lanny wasn't making anything up when he said this, for he had been christened in the American church in Cannes—Emily Chattersworth had seen to it and become his godmother. He had about forgotten it, but didn't mention this detail. Laurel had been brought up an Episcopalian, and was quite clearly the sort of person who belongs in that Church. Also, it was evident that she was in fear of the shooting that was going on simultaneously with this discussion; she had a right to be—and perhaps the clergyman was also. Anyhow, he gave way, and said that under the special circumstances he would unite this pair in the holy estate of matrimony and take his chances of being exculpated by his government.

He put on his canonicals, and in this elegant drawing-room, which in a few hours was to be a smoke-blackened ruin, the couple took their stand before him. Althea and the members of the Chinese family constituted a congregation, respectful and much impressed. Mr. Foo had put on a ceremonial jacket of brocaded black silk over a blue gown, and his two wives also lent splendor to the occasion.

In a voice somewhat larger than you would have expected from such a frail figure the white-robed priest addressed the mixed company:

"Dearly beloved, we are gathered together here in the sight of God, and in the face of this congregation, to join together this man and this woman in Holy Matrimony; which is an honorable estate, instituted of God Himself, signifying unto us the mystical union that is betwixt Christ and His Church."

And so on, until he pronounced the terrifying invitation: "If any man can show any just cause, why they may not lawfully be joined together, let him now speak, or else hereafter for ever hold his peace." Lanny could imagine Althea Carroll standing up and saying: "This is a divorced man." His heart skipped a beat or two during the pause; but she kept silence, now and thereafter for ever. Perhaps she too recognized that war creates emergencies, or perhaps she wouldn't take the chance of having to travel through Southern China with a couple living in sin.

The clergyman turned to Lanny—this was another case where gentlemen came first. "Wilt thou have this Woman to thy wedded wife, to live together according to God's law in the holy estate of Matrimony? Wilt thou love her, comfort her, honour and keep her in sickness and in health? and, forsaking all other, keep thee only unto her, so long as ye both shall live?" Lanny replied promptly that he would, and when the question was put to the lady, she said the same. Lanny pronounced his formula: "To have and to hold from this day forward; for better, for worse, for richer, for poorer; in sickness and in health; to love and to cherish, till death us do part, according to God's holy law; and thereto I give thee my troth."

Then came Laurel's turn; Althea "gave" her, and she said her little piece. Mr. Foo had produced a fine gold ring, his wedding gift. The ceremony was completed and they were man and wife, whom God had joined together and whom no man was going to put asunder. Lanny took the clergyman aside and put the proper envelope into his hand, and blue-clad servants came hurrying with hot brown rice wine, and cookies known as "phoenix and dragon." Mr. Notting ate and drank quickly, for all through this service the guns had been banging and rattling, and they always seemed getting closer. No one could guess at what moment the enemy might burst into this compound. The clergyman shook hands quickly and hurried away, saying that he must get back to his wounded men.

XII

It lacked but two hours of darkness, and Mr. Foo reported: "Fog coming up. You may be lucky." He reported also that the Tommies could be seen on a little ridge not far from the compound; they were digging themselves in for a stand. The trouble was, the Japs had a way of infiltrating as soon as darkness came; they might be sneaking up the gullies on this estate. They might take the compound as a defense point, or the Tommies might fall back upon it, in which case it would become a shell target. "More good you hide," said the host; and they were willing.

He led them outdoors, inside the compound. The buildings formed a complete wall about it, except for the entrance gate, and a small hole known as the Door of Compassion through which food was passed out to the poor. He took them to one of the buildings, which appeared to be a combination of toolhouse and storeroom. In one corner was a pile of sacks which might contain grain or charcoal. A servant followed the master, and the latter said: "This is Ho. Good man, long time I trust him. He take you to boat." Now the trusted Ho dragged the sacks away, and there was a trapdoor which he lifted, disclosing a small black hole.

"Not very nice," said the master, "but safe. You stay two, maybe three hour, then boat come."

"Fine," replied Lanny. "But what about your family? Don't you want to hide them?"

"Jap come, he find family gone, he make search, he find family sure. He mad, he act bad. More good whole family stay, give him wine, give him food, smile, look friendly, he maybe not bad. He say he want China friend, he make what he call Greater East Asia Co-prosperity Sphere. Everybody hate only white man."

That did not accord with what Lanny had read about the behavior of Japanese troops in Nanking, Canton, and other cities; but possibly they had now realized their mistake and would enforce discipline. Anyhow, it was no time for discussion, when at any moment troops of either side might be banging on that much-carved gate. Mr. Foo would go himself and open it, bow low, and hold out a bottle of wine in one hand and a plate of rice in the other, symbolical of friendship and submission.

Meantime, he put into his male guest's hands two objects which the guest had observed and wondered about. They were made of canvas, with canvas straps at their four corners; their shape was extraordinary, bulging in the center like a pillow and tapering to flatness at the ends. They looked to Lanny like enlargements of objects he had picked up on the beach at Juan, and which the fisher-boys had said were shark's eggs, though he didn't know if that was true. The objects Mr. Foo gave him were soft, stuffed with cotton batting carefully quilted; when they were put into Lanny's hands he discovered that they were heavier than he had expected.

"These for ladies wear under dress," explained the host; and his face wore a happy grin as he saw the bewilderment of the three. "Big part in front, straps behind. People see, think ladies pregnant."

"Glory hallelujah!" exclaimed the new bridegroom. He had heard of bustles, but never one to be worn over the belly.

"Chinese man think have baby very honorable. He think you very rich man, important, you travel two wife. Both wife pregnant same time, he think you powerful man, great respect. Jap, too, he maybe don't bother pregnant woman. Number One wife fix these for you."

"Pray, thank your Number One wife on behalf of both the ladies," said Lanny, recovering his *savoir-faire*.

"Plenty gold sovereigns sewed inside. You open little cut, take out one, two maybe, sew up again. About eight hundred American dollar. You don't get gold in America, I hear."

"No, indeed; we have to turn it over to the government."

"You come China for freedom!" chuckled the old merchant.

The servant Ho had carried two waterproof duffelbags, containing various necessities of the journey, collected by their host. Included were two ladies' costumes in the Chinese style, loose jackets and what in America were called slacks. "More good for travel," said he. "People think more proper. You keep extra clothes for getting wet. You got parasol for sun and rain."

"I don't know how we can ever thank you, Mr. Foo!" exclaimed Laurel.

"Some day we beat bad enemy, you come China, maybe I come New York. We have good time, we laugh, how you bride gone seven month pregnant in one hour. Now you go down quick, keep very still, no laugh, no talk. You fix self all ready. Boat come, you go quick; maybe monkey man near shore, nobody know."

XIII

Lanny went down the ladder, the bags were handed to him, and the women followed. The cellar was about eight feet square and six feet high. There were several boxes and on these they sat. The trapdoor was closed and they heard the sacks being moved over it. Then the place was pitch dark, and so the women could set about their dressing. They could not keep from giggling over the extraordinary appearance they were going to present to all China. In the Middle Ages in Europe crusaders setting off to the wars had devised what were called "chastity belts" to put upon their wives and lock fast. Presumably what this pair were now putting on might be called "unchastity belts," though Lanny wouldn't venture that jest until he knew them better. He kept a proper silence and pretended not to know that the women were shaking with laughter.

Laurel groped her way to him and sat by his side. He put one arm about her, and with his other hand he took one of hers; that was their honeymoon, just to sit there, and know that one problem at least was settled for life. They wouldn't have to play any more games, or practice more coquetry. She was his, and he was hers, and it was wonderfully soothing and pleasant. Now and then he would think of that odd attachment to her costume, and would grin unseen; he wouldn't for the world make any move to investigate it, for though she was his lawful wedded wife she was still the decorous Southern lady. He was, however, privileged to press her hand and to hold her closer to him, and this he did. It was a way of repeating the words she had been so determined to hear; words so simple and obvious, yet which never become a cliché: "I love you."

Now and then they would feel the earth shake beneath them. They were closer to it than they had ever been before, and these artificial earthquakes went through them as if they were a part of the earth, never individualized, never set free. Each time he felt the shudder pass through her body, magnified by her nervous system. After an especially heavy explosion she whispered into his ear: "Lanny, promise me something."

"What is it, dear?"

"Whatever happens, you won't try to resist."

"No, of course not. I have no weapon."

"I mean, whatever they do to me. They would kill you if you did."

"You know what they may do to you, dear?"

"I know. But whatever it is, you must not move, not even speak. Without you I do not want to live. Promise me."

"All right," he whispered. His thoughts were grim; for to rape the women in the presence of the men had been one of the methods whereby the Sons of Heaven had been manifesting their superiority to the white race.

Perhaps half an hour passed, and they heard sounds overhead. The sacks were being dragged away, and the trapdoor opened. It couldn't be time for the boat; could it be that the enemy had come? They did not move, they hardly dared breathe—until they heard the soft voice of their friend the silk merchant. "Paintings," he said, and by faint light Lanny saw the reliable Ho sliding a large roll into the opening. Lanny took it, and found that it was wrapped in strong cloth and tied.

He understood that the old gentleman had had his precious paintings taken out of their frames and rolled up. He eased the burden gently down to the ground and rolled it into a corner. "O.K.," said the host, and the trapdoor was let down again.

After that there was no way to keep track of time. They were in the hands of fate—or was it the stars, as the ancient Greeks and Egyptians had imagined? Lanny, who had always proceeded on the theory that it was better to be happy than sad, used the time to supply that deficiency which the lady from Baltimore had noted in his conduct. He had her hand, and the hand is a means whereby through uncounted ages the human organism has conducted investigations and made discoveries. The gentlest pressures can reveal the most intimate secrets; and when Lanny put her hand to his lips and kept it there, she wasn't left in the slightest doubt as to what he meant. It wasn't a marriage of convenience, and it wasn't just a preliminary to psychic research.

Althea had politely seated herself as far away as possible inside an eight-foot square. Being a qualified doctor, she knew all the facts of life, but that made no difference in the proprieties. This innocent little courtship had to be carried on without the faintest trace of sound: not a murmur, not a sigh, not a movement of the lips—otherwise Laurel would have been disturbed by the thought that Althea would be disturbed. Those laws of modesty, of reticence, of propriety, were harder than any steel. But hand can move upon hand without betrayal, and a man's hand can touch a woman's breast and tell it all the things he has neglected to tell in times past. Both of them knew that his hand might be shot off within the hour, that her breast might be pierced by sharp steel; but these few minutes were safe, and precious with a loveliness which Nature had been preparing for hundreds of millions of years, so that her purposes might not fail of accomplishment and that life might be renewed even in the very presence of death.

XIV

Time passed, and the earth shaking grew more violent; the explosions were surely nearer. But there was nothing they could do about it. If that shed caught fire, could they manage to lift the trapdoor with the sacks on top? Lanny doubted it. The cellar would gradually grow hotter, and they would be baked alive. They put their trust in Mr. Foo; but suppose that he was killed by a shell? There was nothing to be done but to draw a little closer and hold each other a little tighter.

At last, sounds over their heads again! The sacks were being moved. Once more it was the question: friend or foe? The door was lifted, and the voice of Mr. Foo said: "Come quick!" They went up the ladder, the two pregnant ladies in Chinese trousers and jackets, and then the man. Night had come, but their host had a small flashlight, and Lanny got a glimpse of the two female forms, and he saw it was a perfect illusion. Evidently the Number One Mrs. Foo had also known the facts of life, and they were the same here as in the western half of the world.

"Fog very good," declared the old man. "Boat come soon. You follow Ho, he take you quick. Very quiet, may be anywhere monkey man."

All three wrung his hand and thanked him. He said: "I am old man, you young. Go quick. Good luck."

The reliable servant tucked one of the ladies' bags under each arm, and Lanny carried the small bundle of possessions he had managed to accumulate while driving the lorry in Hongkong. They went, half running, through the beautiful gate—"To and From the World Gate" was its name—and struck out across a field. Presently they were following a hedge row; the man in front stopped now and then to listen, and they all held their breaths. The fog was thick, and drifting slowly; you could feel it cool against your face. Other creatures were moving that night, but whether they were friend or foe, or perhaps animals, could not be known. The fugitives moved, lifting their feet carefully; the women were wearing Chinese canvas shoes, their leather shoes being in the bags.

Presently they came to a gully, and after listening, they slid down into it. There were many stones, which made hard walking; but there was a trace of a path, and they followed it by putting a hand on the shoulder of the person ahead. Much stopping and listening, and suddenly the guide whispered: *"Yat pun jai!"*—which means Japanese dwarfs. He led them to one side, where they crouched against the side of the bank, partly hidden by bushes. They heard sounds of men walking, and presently there came a file up the gully, evidently trying to move silently. They might be enemy troops or they might be British —there was no guessing. They passed, and it was still again, and the journey was resumed.

Lanny guessed that this gully would lead them to the sea, and so it proved. The slope diminished, the ground became wet, and presently it was a stream, and they were following a path along its side. When they stopped to listen they heard gurgling water, and before long they realized that it was lapping waves. They couldn't see ten feet in front of them, but there was an open feeling, perhaps a matter of sound echoes; they knew they were facing the sea. They went a short way along the shore and stopped at a small platform, wet and slimy, perhaps used to haul a fishing boat upon. This was the place, and the guide took them a few feet back into the bushes, where they crouched and waited.

How any junk was going to find the spot in that dense fog was a mystery to the Occidental mind. But Lanny had read somewhere that the Chinese had invented the compass, and he hoped they hadn't forgotten its use. Anyhow, there was nothing to do but wait. Althea knew a few words of Cantonese, the dialect spoken in this part of the country, entirely different from Mandarin spoken in the northern and central parts. She translated to the others what Ho said: "Boat maybe." It seemed like a slim chance, but their lives depended upon it. If daylight found them crouching here, they would have a hard time escaping.

XV

Soon there came over the water what they took to be the sound of sails being lowered. A Chinese junk has lateen sails, which means that there are parallel strips of bamboo all the way across. When these come down they make considerable noise. Apparently this was a shallow cove, and the vessel was being poled in. There was the sound of an anchor rope being paid out, and presently a tiny skiff appeared at the platform—a craft barely large enough for one passenger and the man who poled or paddled.

This was the fisherman to whom their fate was entrusted. They saw him only as a shadowy form. He exchanged a few whispered words with Ho, and the latter put a packet of money into his hands. Lanny gave the faithful servant a proper *cumshaw*, and then got into the rickety little skiff. He was going first, so as to preclude the possibility of the junk sailing off with the two women. He climbed onto the deck and stood waiting while first Laurel and then Althea were brought on board. The skiff was lifted in, and while the rest of the crew pulled up the anchor, the fisherman signed to his passengers to follow.

Lanny could see almost nothing of this junk, but he had seen them by the hundreds in the South China Sea and in Hongkong harbor. They have curved prows and a high poop, and Lanny guessed that this was a small one, perhaps thirty feet long. They entered through a doorway so low that they had to stoop; a hatchway was lifted and they went down a companionway that was almost a ladder. They were in a part of the hold, and remembered what Mr. Foo had said: "Bad smell." He had been a good prophet. Fish nets had been stored here, perhaps for decades, and the stench was strong; the three would smell of fish for the rest of their visit to China. But then, what are a few fish or a million fish compared to all the conglomerate smells of the Orient? Nothing to sneeze at.

Some boxes were to be their bed, and behind them they could hide in case of alarm. There was a pile of nets and another of gunny sacks, and they might pull these over themselves and escape detection in case the Japs came aboard. The fisherman explained this, in words which

Althea said she was able to understand. The man added: "I am old-time Party member. You friends Madame Sun." The magic still worked!

They lay in utter darkness, and listened to the sounds of the anchor being pulled up and the sails being set. Then their bed became tilted, and they knew that the vessel was under way. They could feel the vibration of the waves hitting the planking. They could imagine a sailing vessel sliding through this black fog, and could only pray that the compass was true. Of course the fisherman would know these waters as a dog knows its own yard; southeast through the East Lamma Channel, and then, after passing the islands that lie east of Hongkong, northeast along the coast.

It was safe to talk now, and Lanny leaned toward his bride, saying: "At least the astrologer is licked. I am not going to die in Hongkong."

"Don't say that!" she whispered, still afraid of the fates. "We are not out of danger yet."

"*Near* Hongkong or *around* Hongkong, perhaps—but not *in* Hongkong, or *on* it!"

BOOK SEVEN

An Ancient Tale of Wrong

———————————— o ————————————

25. *Looking over Wasted Lands*

I

THERE were no means of guessing how long that voyage to the continent of Asia might last; and at any moment it might be interrupted by a crash upon rocks or a shot from a Japanese war vessel. There was no longer any reason for silence, so they discussed these and other possibilities: what they were likely to find when they were put ashore, what means of travel they would use, what course they would take. Althea, who knew the country, would be the captain of the expedition, and she gave them a series of lectures on life in subtropical China. When they were tired, they stretched themselves on hard planks with the duffelbags for pillows. The doctor again removed herself to a discreet distance, but this was not necessary, for it was no time or place for a bridal night.

Hand in hand Lanny and his new wife lay, and part of the time they dozed, or thought about the strange adventure of their times; they shared in mind the agony of a civilization undergoing assault from organized banditry. Long ago Trudi Schultz had remarked to Lanny that it was a bad time to be born. That had certainly proved true for her, and now Lanny confronted the possibility that the same dark fate might be hanging over the gentle and sensitive woman who lay by his side. He would be helpless to protect her, alike against the cruelties of nature and those of man: whether a storm were to come up while this sailing craft was crossing a corner of the South China Sea, or whether it were to be boarded by primitive barbarians armed with the instruments of killing devised by modern science.

Hours passed, and more hours. Lanny had his watch, and kept it wound, but he had overlooked the importance of such a small convenience as a box of matches. Perhaps the kind Mr. Foo had put some in the bags, but they did not want to unpack them in this filthy place. They did not think they could keep food on their stomachs here, especially as the junk was now beginning to toss and her timbers to creak. They clung together and talked some more; they agreed that the tossing meant they were out in the open sea, and this meant they were safer from the Japs, if not from the sea. They did not know which to fear more.

What would the fisherman do if a storm came up? What fishermen always did, Lanny said—fight for their lives. They would have to keep away from the coast, unless it was an off-shore wind. Such a wind would blow the fog away, and perhaps expose them to sight of the enemy. Lanny had heard that the British flyers now had a device by which they could see in the dark, by means of radio waves echoed back; whether the Japanese Navy had it, who could guess? Lanny, who had done a lot of sailing and yachting in his fashionable life, noted the slow pitching of the vessel from front to back, and guessed that they were running before a wind. That would speed their journey, but make it harder for them to land.

Althea, the devout soul, revealed that she was praying. She invited them to join her. They had just pledged their marital troth in the presence of the Lord, and in His name; why should they not ask Him to protect them and bring their marriage to fruition? The prayers of three were stronger than those of one; had not Jesus said: "Where two or three are gathered together in my name, there am I in the midst of them"? Althea said the prayer ordained for use in storms at sea. "Oh, most powerful and glorious Lord God," it begins, "at whose command the winds blow, and lift up the waves of the sea, and who stillest the rage thereof; We, thy creatures, but miserable sinners, do in this our great distress cry unto Thee for help: Save, Lord, or else we perish." This she repeated, and the others learned it.

To persons who had fallen under the spell of materialistic science and had never been able entirely to escape it, this seemed an infinitely strange procedure. But prolonged anxiety and the sight of death had brought them to the state of little children, and they did what they were told. Presently Althea sang, and again they learned the words:

> Eternal Father, strong to save,
> Whose arm hath bound the restless wave,
> Who bidd'st the mighty ocean deep
> Its own appointed limits keep;
> Oh, hear us when we cry to Thee
> For those in peril on the sea.

II

It has happened many times, as travelers on the sea have come home
to testify; but of course there is no testimony from those who did not
come home—therefore the testimony is not found convincing by the
devotees of materialistic science. Be that as it may, the slow pitching
of the junk gradually diminished, and likewise the creaking of her
planking and timbers. The lapping of little waves seemed like dead
silence in comparison, and the travelers sat motionless, waiting. Was
that the sound of an anchor rope being paid out? Did that mean they
were safe in a harbor, or could it be that the vessel had been captured
at sea, and that it would be Japanese who opened the trapdoor? Should
they cover themselves with the nets and the filthy gunny sacks?

While they hesitated, the trapdoor was opened and a dim light shone
in. They heard the voice of the "old-time Party member," saying the
magic phrase which men know all over the earth if they have had any
contact with white persons: "O.K., boss!"

So they handed up their belongings and climbed the short ladder.
The light was that of a dim lantern, but they could see the figure of
their deliverer, and Lanny grasped his hand and patted him on the
back and said: "Good fellow! O.K. fellow!" The three passengers were
so happy they hugged each other; that is, Lanny hugged Laurel, and
she passed it on to Althea. It was really a remarkable occasion; and
when you have condescended to pray and sing a hymn, you can surely
afford to laugh and shout for a while.

They were escorted to the open deck, and discovered that dawn was
breaking. They could see that they were in a little cove, and that there
was a flat shore. The fisherman pointed and said: "*Hou fang!*" Althea
translated: "The Rear"—which was their phrase for "Free China."
So of course they wanted to get there quickly. Lanny presented a
proper *cumshaw* to all members of the crew—three besides the captain
—and shook hands with them. He asked Althea to make plain to them
that America was now in the war on China's side. These weather-
beaten men of the sea beamed with pleasure, and said: "Come soon!"
They made it plain that they wanted none of the Greater East Asia
Co-prosperity Sphere.

The little skiff was set down in the water, and Lanny climbed in.
They anticipated no danger, but it was proper for him to go first on
chance that danger might be met. Holding one of the precious duffelbags in his arms he was paddled to a rocky point where he could step
ashore dryshod. While the skiff went back to the junk, he dived
quickly into the bag, and discovered to his relief that the elderly
Chinese angel had provided headnets and gloves against the mosquitoes

which are the curse of the tropics. In fact, the angel had put in a score of little conveniences which were plentiful in Hongkong but unobtainable in the interior—matches, a flashlight with spare batteries, an aluminum kettle for boiling water; also iodine and quinine. Mr. Foo could afford to be generous, alas, for he had to reckon that whatever he did not give to his allies would soon belong to his enemies.

First came Laurel, for the doctor, determined altruist, would always be last: the youngest, the strongest, and not married, she would insist. Lanny took his wife in his arms and kissed her shamelessly; then he stood off for the first good look at her since she had entered her seventh month. It really wasn't fair to expect him to keep from laughing, and finally she gave way and joined him. She was blushing scarlet, but had to admit that it was an ingenious way of hiding money. The Chinese had been in this war for four years, and prior to that they had been in wars for at least four thousand; so they had had to learn devices. "For ways that are dark and for tricks that are vain the heathen Chinee is peculiar!"

Althea came in due course; and they said the last farewell to their gallant preserver. "Good fishing!" said Althea, groping in Cantonese, and they shook hands all round once more. They would have stood to wave while the man paddled away—but for the facts that he had to turn his back, and that the mosquitoes were after them. As soon as Althea had put on her net and gloves, she produced her tiny *Book of Common Prayer*, without which she never traveled. She had asked a favor, and now that it had been granted she would not forget to say thanks. Standing on safe and solid shore she read aloud from the 107th Psalm:

Oh that men would praise the Lord for his goodness: and declare the wonders that he doeth for the children of men!

That they would offer unto him the sacrifice of thanksgiving: and tell out his works with gladness!

They that go down to the sea in ships: and occupy their business in great waters:

These men see the works of the Lord: and his wonders in the deep.

For at his word the stormy wind ariseth: which lifteth up the waves thereof.

They are carried up to the heaven, and down again to the deep: their soul melteth away because of the trouble.

They reel to and fro, and stagger like a drunken man: and are at their wits' end.

So when they cry unto the Lord in their trouble: he delivereth them out of their distress.

For he maketh the storm to cease: so that the waves thereof are still.

Then are they glad, because they are at rest: and so he bringeth them unto the haven where they would be.

III

There were small fishing craft drawn up on the shores of this cove, and rice cultivation began almost at the water's edge. That was one of the first things they were to learn about subtropical China; never would you find a single square inch on which food might be grown that did not have food growing. No poor peasant ever saw a flower—unless it was being grown for a rich man's market. Another thing you learned was that labor in the fields began at the first trace of daylight; it continued until it was no longer possible to distinguish a rice stalk from a weed. Already the peasants were at work, using heavy-handled hoes; their clothing was a pair of ragged blue-jeans, a pair of straw sandals, and a straw hat with an immense wide brim against the heat which the sun would pour upon them as soon as it appeared over the horizon.

Another peculiarity the strangers observed at once: these toilers had no interest in anything except their toil. Not one stopped to stare, to say nothing of exchanging a greeting. You might have thought that foreigners were landing in this cove every few minutes, and that the peasants were bored with them. But Althea said they had no curiosity, they could not afford such a luxury. Either their fields were small, subdivided again and again as families grew, or else the field belonged to a landlord who claimed the greater part of the crop. Get to work and stay!

Rice is grown in swamps, whether natural or artificial. If it is a natural swamp, floods come, and the crop is ruined, and the mud house is washed away, and the bodies of peasants are found hanging from tree limbs. When the ground is higher, the water must be brought to it by irrigation ditches or by the labor of arms, legs, and backs. One of the first sights the travelers saw was men with yokes across their shoulders from which dangled two heavy buckets made of wood or bamboo staves; they filled these at the stream and carried them up to the higher level to sprinkle the young plants. Presently the travelers came to a treadmill which carried a continuous stream of buckets down to the water and then up to a trough, where they emptied themselves and went down for another load. A patient bullock walked this treadmill, and he, too, began with the dawn. There were families too poor to own a bullock, and for these the wife and daughters did the walking. They, too, had no curiosity.

A road in South China, they discovered, is a narrow causeway between rice fields. It is paved with flagstones, and there is only one row, three or four feet wide. This is symbolical of a peculiar fact which the visitor realizes only gradually; he misses something, and at last he realizes what it is. There are wheelbarrows but no carts of any sort; everything is carried on the backs of bullocks or human beings, mostly the latter. Only in the towns does one find vehicles.

The sun came up, a ball of blazing fire, and then they were glad that Mr. Foo had included in his Christmas package three light parasols made of bamboo and paper, such as everybody carries in this region. The better grade are waterproof and serve against rain as well as sunlight. The path led along a stream which flowed into the sea, and they assumed that there would be a village at the path's end. They met a peasant wheelbarrowing a load of straw, and Althea attempted to ask him in Cantonese; but, alas, he spoke the Swatow dialect. Farther in the interior it would be the Hakka dialect, and they would have to find an official or other educated person before they could talk.

Villages were everywhere, Althea assured them, and it never did any good to ask distances, because the Chinese were so amiably polite; they would always tell you what they thought you wanted to hear, so they would say that the place was "near." The travelers needed no map in this land; it was enough to know that they must continue about a hundred miles in a northerly direction, so as to get safely away from the district held by the Japs, and then they would head to the northwest a couple of hundred miles and hit the Siang-kiang, a river near which the home of Althea's parents was situated.

IV

They came to a village; and there for the first time they met people who looked at them with curiosity and tried to answer questions. The head of the village, a very old man who put on a soiled white robe for the occasion, was able to speak a few words of Mandarin. He found nothing strange that an American gentleman should be traveling with two pregnant wives; Althea told him that Mr. Budd was an immensely wealthy American, a friend of President Roosevelt, and had come to make plans for helping China against the Japanese. She was making up this mild fib and it troubled her conscience. The old man beamed, and bowed his head to the level of his waist; he escorted them to a teahouse where they could sit in the shade—it was made of bamboo frame and hanging reed mats.

Here Althea began a ritual which was important in China, and which she as a physician took in charge. In that crowded land all "night soil" is saved and used as fertilizer, so everything must be assumed to be infected; all food has to be thoroughly cooked and all water boiled. Arriving anywhere, Althea's first duty was to go to the kitchen and fill her aluminum kettle with water and set it on a fire to boil for ten minutes. She would keep it until it had cooled, and then pour it into the leather water bottles provided for their journey.

In the teahouse a meal of chicken cooked with walnuts and rice was prepared. Lanny and Laurel had amused themselves in Hongkong with chopsticks; now they had to learn seriously, and not shock the thousands of people who would be watching them all the way across the land. "Face" is all-important, and the dignity of the great American republic must be maintained. To be seen shoveling rice into your mouth with a spoon or a fork would have been like being seen in the Ritzy-Waldorf of New York putting pie into your mouth with a knife. It wouldn't help you to tell the people in the Ritzy-Waldorf that you came from a land where all pie is eaten that way; this would make matters worse, for it would be telling the diners that all your people were as ill bred as yourself.

By the time the meal was finished the next stage of their journey had been arranged. Outside the tearoom stood three small donkeys; they had no saddles, only cloth on their middles, but there would be no danger, for they had never moved faster than a slow walk since the day they were born, and a man would walk ahead of each leading him with a rope. Apparently it had not occurred to anyone that one man might lead three donkeys in a string, both going and coming; but men were far more plentiful than donkeys, and perhaps no man was willing to trust his own out of sight.

There was the question of money, and the village elder told them what to pay. Lanny had some "Hongkong notes," and these were still good in the neighborhood. In the old days travelers had had to carry loads of "twenty-cent pieces" and "cash." These coins were supposed to be of copper, but they had been debased, and now, in wartime, they had disappeared entirely. Paper money was so plentiful that a dollar note, a "mex," was the smallest that would buy anything. Gold, of course, was almost beyond price, and the job of changing a sovereign was to be undertaken with many precautions.

The procession set out: three tourists seated with dignity, holding their baggage in place with one hand and their parasols with the other. It would have looked odd in America, but here most distinguished; nobody asked why a special envoy from President Roosevelt should bring two gravid wives with him. The sun blazed, and perspiration streamed from the bare backs of the guides, and from the foreheads and armpits of the riders; also from the donkeys—so before long there was a new odor added to that of ancient fish. If the travelers got tired of clamping donkey bodies with their knees they could get off and walk alongside, but they must still hold their duffelbags in place. No use ever to be impatient in the Orient; just tell yourself that you hadn't died in Hongkong and that every step was away from the Japs.

This wasn't to be a long trip, they were assured, and at the next village, somewhat larger, they would be able to get palanquins. The road followed the bank of the small stream, and in course of the journey they learned all about rice culture, for the paddies were at various stages. Also there was sugar cane, and another tall plant which Althea said was hemp; soil, sun, and water, and you could grow anything. Beautiful golden oranges hung from trees, and these they were free to buy and eat; but no thin-skinned fruit, for even your own hands were infected with the dust of China, and it did no good to wash them with the water of China.

The next village was larger, which meant that it was more crowded; the houses were packed together, in order to leave more land for cultivation. They had been told the name of the official to ask for and they asked, and again were received with honor. The name of President Roosevelt proved to be even more potent than that of Madame Sun. The drivers were paid off, not without much discussion; another meal was served and more water boiled, and there were three palanquins waiting. A palanquin in this region was not a straight chair as in Hongkong; it was a sort of litter in which you reclined, with only your head propped up. It was old and ragged, but had a blessed sunshade overhead, so you did not have to hold the parasol. Two men carried the palanquin on their shoulders, and walked at a steady pace; when you got used to the motion you could doze if you wished.

Apparently these lean and stringy yellow men never tired, but they wouldn't go more than a certain distance from home; they were afraid of the unknown, perhaps of robbers, perhaps of evil spirits; you had to pay them off and get a fresh outfit. Coolies, and their fathers before them, had been beasts of burden for millennia; but now, under the influence of the revolution, they were waking up. They hated the British but liked Americans; now they had learned to hate another sort of yellow people. Lanny had the fortune to draw one who liked to talk, and who pointed out sights on the way. He seemed unable to understand that the traveler couldn't understand the Swatow dialect, and Lanny didn't try to explain.

V

The sun was going down, and another village lay ahead of them. In it was an inn, they had been told; also, not far away there was an American mission. Althea had been able to glean the fact that it was conducted by the Seventh Day Adventists, and this was an unorthodox sect, most exasperating to a respectable Episcopalian. When after a lifetime of effort you had succeeded in teaching a few heathen that Sunday was the Lord's day, and on it thou shalt do no manner of work, how preposterous to have some white people turn up, calling themselves Christians and telling the heathen that the Lord's day was Saturday and that the time to quit work was at sundown on Friday!

Even so, they would have liked to visit that mission, where they could be sure of finding clean bed and board; but there was another objection, the presence of two pregnant ladies with only one man. They could not take off those belts and let the coolies or the domestics see them in their virginal state; to do so would be to start a story which would spread by the teahouse grapevine all over China. It would reveal the fact that they carried treasure, and thus would be an invitation to all the bandits of the land—and there were hordes of them! No, for better for worse they had committed themselves to the *mores* of the country—and also to its bed and board.

Even Althea hadn't realized how primitive an inn could be in this remote region. They had assumed that there would at least be bedrooms, shared only with fleas, lice, and bedbugs; but now they discovered that there was one common shelter, in which wayfarers were privileged to sleep for the payment of a few cash. A bed consisted of boards spread on two trestles, and a pillow was a wooden block if you had nothing else. The Chinese are a gregarious people, and the more there are of them crowded into a room, a street, a village, the safer they feel; their love of company includes pigs and chickens, and even safe friendly creatures like donkeys and bullocks. They are not used to white tourists joining them on equal terms; however, if such apparitions appear, they will smile and bow, and then start chattering with immense volubility. Their children will stand and stare, perfectly motionless, perfectly silent, for as long as no one calls them away.

The bones of these refugees already ached from hard boards, but there was no alternative; they were tired, and they sat down. The doctor set about her boiling water ritual; investigating the prospects in the kitchen, she came back and reported that they could have a stew made of duck and rice cooked with strong spices, provided they were willing to wait for the duck to be caught and killed. They signed the death warrant, and meanwhile quenched their thirst with tepid water from their bottles.

Among the treasures in their duffelbags was a can of insect powder and a little squirtgun, and with that they sprayed the wooden shelf on which they were to sleep; also they sprayed up their sleeves and trouser legs, inside their shirts, and everywhere else they could reach with propriety. The operation was watched with absorbed interest by the local population, and Althea said that they would probably take it for some religious rite. "Like the burning of incense!" remarked Lanny.

Althea had warned them that they must not be seen to use any medicaments, and, no matter what happened, they must never give any hint that she was a doctor. The word would be spread by their coolies, and all the sick of every village would be brought to them; they would have to use up all their slender stock and there would be no way to replace it. Said she: "The people take it for granted that any American medicine will cure all diseases, and they will take affront if we refuse to help them."

V I

The capture and execution of the duck was achieved, and they made a very good meal. This was Christmas Day, and Hongkong had surrendered, though they did not find it out until later. They counted themselves lucky to be alive, and enjoyed a well-earned Christmas dinner, watched by people who raised fowls but probably did not taste the meat thereof more than once or twice in a year. The adult population did not stand and stare, but glanced furtively, and it was evident that they were talking eagerly about what they saw. Althea said they would be talking about it for a long time to come. Laurel replied: "It is true of us, also; certainly of me." Her sharp eyes were taking in everything, and Lanny guessed that there would someday be stories about Kwangtung Province in American magazines. She would ask her woman companion about the meaning of this and that. They could talk freely, in the certainty that nobody among the spectators would understand a word. Laurel could even say "I adore you" to Lanny—this while Althea was boiling the water and arguing over the price of duck and rice with spices.

The headman of this village came to pay them a courtesy call. He was a short but dignified figure wearing a black mustache in the old drooping style. He spoke a little Mandarin, and said he was the tax collector of the district; they didn't know what his politics might be —there were many parts of the country ruled by semi-independent war lords. So the travelers used President Roosevelt instead of Sun Chingling. The official said that President Roosevelt was a great man and when was he going to send help to China? Everybody would ask that, all the way to wherever they went.

The grapevine had brought two items of news to the village. First, there was a Japanese offensive under way north from Canton, following the railroad; and second, there was a great battle being fought at the gates of Changsha, the principal city of what is called the "rice bowl of China." It lies on the railroad that runs from Canton and Hankow through Central China. The Japs were in possession of both ends of the line, and if they came down from the north and up from the south at the same time they would cut Free China into two halves, an eastern and a western.

The significance of this to the refugees was obvious. They had a map with them but didn't need to study it, having done so at Mr. Foo's. Althea's home lay close to the railroad, less than a hundred miles south of Changsha, and if the enemy won the battle, there might soon be no mission to go to. The other item of news was no less disturbing, for if the offensive from Canton succeeded, the Japs would cut across the route the Americans were proposing to take. At present they and the Japs were moving northward on parallel lines, the Japs having the advantage of a railroad and two rivers, whereas the Americans had only country roads.

They mentioned this fact to the tax collector, Mr. Feng, and his almond eyes twinkled. "You forget," Althea translated, "Japanese have armies facing them at both ends of line. American gentleman and ladies have only friends in all China, help them along fast!" He went on to mention that Changsha had been taken once before by the Japs, but they had been forced to abandon it, and this might happen again. In the end the foe might succeed in taking the entire railroad, but it would not be very soon.

Mr. Feng said that the grapevine had brought the news about the attack on Pearl Harbor, and they understood that the Americans were their full allies at last. Why didn't they come at once? Lanny had to explain that they could not come for a long time, for the Americans were a peaceable people like the Chinese, and it would take time to convert their industry to the ends of war. "Tell him that China must hold out!" To this Mr. Feng replied that China would do so, but it was very hard, because of the scarcity of everything, and their money losing its value.

The official invited them to his home, where they could be made more comfortable; but Althea replied that they had made arrangements at this inn, and if they were now to leave, it would be taken as a discourtesy, a criticism of the service they had received. The other admitted that this was true, and he was impressed by their willingness to live like the Chinese people and share their hardships. He told them the good news that from here on there was a canal. Waterways had been for hundreds of years the principal method of travel in Kwangtung and the boats were comfortable. With this assurance they slept soundly, and to their surprise forgot the hard couch.

VII

Their attentive friend had taken their passports, and next morning he came again, returning these, and with them an official-looking paper with Chinese printing and writing on it and those rubber stampings which are common to all lands. It was, he said, a military permit for the three to travel to Hengyang; it would be impossible for them to continue without it. China was at war, and was compelled to keep watch against spies of the Tokyo government, and of its puppet, the Nanking government, and sometimes, alas, of the Yenan government. How Mr. Feng had got this document he did not say, but he dropped a hint that it was not in his own department, and that he had had not a little difficulty in arranging matters. The doctor whispered to Lanny that Mr. Feng would expect some material thanks, and that one thousand depreciated dollars ought to be about right. Lanny took the gentleman aside and everybody's face was saved. They were glad to have this document, for many times they were stopped by gendarmes and required to show it, and several times they had to stop at police stations and fill out questionnaires.

The journey continued. They were being very aristocratic and having a boat to themselves. It was about fifteen feet long, flat-bottomed; lean, active yellow men propelled it with poles, and never once lost their balance or their amiable expressions. One of them remarked to Althea with a grin: "Beat Japanese Army!"—so evidently Mr. Feng had enlisted their patriotic sentiments. The passengers, reclining luxuriously on wooden couches, surveyed the fields of Kwangtung Province, green in winter.

Rain came up, and at noon they stopped under the shelter of a bullock shed, generously shared by these patient animals. The boatmen ate the bowl of rice which they carried and drank the rain water which they gathered in their hats—a simple process of turning the hat upside down and standing under it with their mouths wide open to catch the dripping stream. Lanny asked the medical lady if the rainwater of China was apt to be infected with the bacillus of dysentery, and she said no, but the hats surely were. She explained why the coolies did not all die—that those who were subject to the disease had been dying off through the centuries.

The rain ceased, and the sun came out, and then they missed the rain on account of the heat. They adopted as their practice to start the long boat ride at the first streak of dawn, and at noon to find a teahouse or other place where they could rest and perhaps doze under the shelter of reed mats, resuming their journey when the afternoon was half over. They blessed the Chinese teahouses, which are, as the coffeehouses were in old London and the corner drugstores are in America, places of congregation and refreshment, where you can meet the people and hear talk. Those in China are larger, because there are more customers; unlike the peasants in the fields, the townsmen appeared to have plenty of leisure, or at any rate they took it. In the shops you would always find more clerks than customers—and far more clerks than articles to be sold, according to Laurel, who hadn't yet got adjusted to life in a world at war. Lanny assured her: "When we get back to America, we may be surprised to discover how much like China it has become!"

They wondered what was happening at home; they wondered what was happening in Britain and in Europe, in Manila and Hongkong and Singapore. But they didn't have much chance to think about it; their time and thought went to just keeping alive, to holding themselves above the level of discomfort on which these people lived. Speaking as a physician, Althea said that very few among this human mass were healthy; she pointed out the signs of overwork and undernourishment, and of the painful infections which flourished. To see the people smiling, and grateful for the smallest kindness, was infinitely touching; the superior beings who were passing through, skimming the surface of so much human misery, felt themselves guilty, charged themselves before the bar of their own conscience.

VIII

All this time the newly married couple had no privacy whatever. Even when they got a separate room, it was only one, and there was no way to explain that a traveling lord didn't want both his wives in the room with him. To put one of them away by herself would have been to humiliate her, to excite gossip; possibly it might have been unsafe for her. When she went to boil the water, she established herself as Number Two wife; and meantime the lord would sit on a plank beside his fair-haired and very lovely Number One, and smile upon her and say: "I love you." The watching audience could interpret the smile correctly.

"Darling," Lanny would plead, "accustom yourself to public life. You are acting in a play, and the audience is completely absorbed in it."

Hard for a lady from Baltimore, but she realized that it is no fun traveling unless you conform to the customs of the country. So, when they entered a crowded tearoom—men only—she would bow in stage-queen manner and give them a smile of royalty. Then, while the Number Two went about a servant's duties, she would entertain her lord and master with cheerful conversation. When he asked: "Are you happy?" she would reply: "I am alive, and so is my husband." When he asked solicitously: "Are you feeling all right?" she would say: "I am getting tough. In a little while I'll be ready to take up my bag and walk."

But of course that wouldn't have done in China. Not even a bandit's lady would have behaved so. "And especially not in your condition!"

Lanny would say. He ventured to make jokes about it, for after all, she was his wife, though as yet in name only.

Little by little she accustomed herself to the idea that the most public place can be private, if you don't recognize the difference. If Chinese men enjoyed seeing the lovelight in the eyes of a lady from the opposite side of the world, what harm could it do? Maybe it would send them home to be kinder to their own wives. The horror of footbinding was pretty much ended in China, Althea assured them, but the manifold exploitation of women went on everywhere throughout the Orient. So this pair continued their gentle wooing from one town of Kwangtung to the next, and the spectators gave every sign of finding the performance to their taste.

The land rose as they got farther from the sea, and so they parted from their genial boatmen. The weather stayed almost as hot, but there was less moisture in the air and the mosquitoes were not so numerous. The gentle slopes of the hills were carefully terraced, and the bright green spread of teaplants delighted the eye. They took to "chairs" again. They rode for a while, then walked for a while; their human beasts of burden walked all the time, and seemed to find it unprecedented that people should use their own legs when they were paying good money for other people's legs. Doubtless the well-to-do Chinese would have told the visitors that they were setting a bad precedent, demoralizing the livery service of the land. The doctor said that missionaries heard the same complaint; they were accused of spreading ideas and stirring up the people—the same charge which had been brought against Jesus, in another land where riches and poverty had dwelt side by side for ages. The complaint against the missionaries was brought with special bitterness by the "old China hands," the whites who had come here to make money and stayed to make more. These held the missions to blame for the revolution, the Reds, and all the turmoil of the past quarter century.

IX

In the distance they could see the blue Nan-ling mountains, which form the boundary between Kwangtung and Hunan Provinces. They were told that from the next town a bus line went through these mountains. The bus was always crowded, but in China the poor were put off, and the rich and important traveled; it had always been that way, and apparently no one thought of changing it. The three had to show their precious military permit; and after it had been inspected and stamped, and they had paid enough paper dollars, a bench was assigned to them, just wide enough for the three to squeeze into. The bus rattled, but it ran; and they were glad, because they had been told that they would have had trouble in finding coolies to take them through the mountains. Not that the burden bearers minded the climb, but they were afraid of bandits, also of demons, which swarm in the wild places.

The foothills were bare of trees and appeared to be grazing land, though there was plenty of rice wherever water was available. They came to a town which appeared as one great market for chickens, brought in from all the countryside. Processions of coolies went by them, laden with baskets and crates full of live hens and roosters: the cackling and crowing in the town added a new note to the racket which is apparently necessary to the happiness of the Chinese populace. The travelers feasted on chicken and rice at a stopping place, and again the bus set out, climbing steadily.

The mountains are not very high, but there are many of them; the trip took a full day, and they saw no bandits, only a squad of government soldiers who had been hunting deserters and were leading a string of them bound with ropes, very miserable-looking fellows. They heard more about the recruiting process; soldiers swooped down on a village and all able-bodied men ran to hide, but some were caught and carried off. The travelers were pained by this sight; a Chinese who didn't love the Chungking government explained that the rich were allowed to buy their way out of military service, and the poor were drafted even when they were not liable by law.

They were surprised to find that there were still forests in the mountains of South China, but the process of stripping them was going on continually. Timber was being cut, and the cutters didn't in the least mind felling a tree across the road and obliging a bus to wait until the debris had been cleared. Cool mountain streams tempted the travelers, but the stern warden of their health forbade them to drink even this water unboiled. For an hour or two they enjoyed bracing cold, and then they were going down into Hunan Province and it was warm again. Twenty-seven million people lived in this province, according to the statistics, but Lanny doubted if anybody had counted them, ever from the beginning of time. In the highlands the peasants grew wheat, groundnuts, and a little tea; lower down it would be rice again —they were on the way to the "rice bowl." To add savor to this number-one food, long trains of bearers carried baskets of coarse salt out of the hills. A stream flowed through the pass, and presently others joined it and there was water enough to float logs. The trees cut higher up had holes chopped through the end, and were dragged with ropes by a dozen coolies. That was the way you got a telephone or telegraph pole into your rice bowl!

X

A town of some size, and a teahouse with a wonderful rare treasure—a radio set! It was old and produced many extra noises, but you could hear broadcasts from Chungking, and Althea translated the news of the world. America was calling for an army of ten million men, and President Roosevelt had promised fifty thousand airplanes—many thousands for China. Hongkong had surrendered, and Manila was being attacked; so also the Dutch East Indies. Of more immediate concern, Chungking claimed a great victory at Changsha, the capital city of Hunan Province; the large and well-mechanized army of the Japanese had been routed and was in part surrounded. Also, the enemy offensive north of Canton had been checked. There was no longer any reason why the tourists should not head westward into the river valley which led to Althea's home. They might even be able to get a ride on the railroad which the Japs weren't going to get for some time!

Another crowded bus took them into the valley of the Lui-ho. This was almost civilization compared with the remote country they had crossed; but they found it no improvement, rather the opposite. They were in the backwash of war; endless trains of coolies carried supplies southward to the Canton front, while refugees and wounded men came from it; the sights were the most pitiful they had beheld. Food was scarce, prices higher, shelters more crowded. The river was low and even the smallest boats couldn't get through. As for the railroad, their first look was terrifying, the trains were crowded with passengers, inside, outside, and on top. But Althea said: "This is China. We'll get aboard!"

First they had to report to the military authorities and have their pass checked. Apparently it was in order, and everybody was very polite. Next they found the telegraph office. A curious thing: the operator did not know a word of English, but he was expert in sending the letters of the Morse code. China had an excellent telegraph network, and messages would go by radiogram from Chungking. Lanny filed a cablegram to his father, telling of his escape from Hongkong and his marriage, and asking him to notify Beauty, Irma, Rick, and Alston. He wasn't sure if the message would ever arrive, but later on he learned that it had. Althea sent a message to her parents, which, oddly enough, failed to arrive.

They found a good inn, where they got plentiful buckets of hot water and took real baths. In the morning they were "chaired" to the railroad station, and Althea conferred with the official in charge. She told him about the important American emissary and paid him the proper *cumshaw*. It was an ancient custom, and when the jampacked train came in, the station master spoke to the conductor, who came to the American lady and got "his." Apparently he had a compartment which he kept vacant for such emergencies. They were put into it, and the aged train staggered on its way.

With every *li* of the slow progress the air grew cooler, and also the crowds denser. The railroad was comparatively new, but the river had been here for ages, and the villages had been strung along it, sometimes with buildings overhanging the banks and always jammed one against the next. Paralleling the river was a highway, less than a dozen feet wide, hardly able to accommodate the human pack-animals going both ways. A town seemed to go on forever, and perhaps it was more than one town—there was no way to be sure. Sitting by his wife's side, looking out upon all this, Lanny exclaimed: "What a curious thing! You remember I told you about the scenes of China that I watched in a crystal ball?"

"Yes, very well."

"Well, these are the scenes. They are so familiar, I can't get over the feeling that I've been here before."

"When did this begin, Lanny?"

"About three years ago. I stopped experimenting with the crystal ball because I couldn't get anything but China, and I got tired of it."

"That was after the astrologer told you about dying in Hong-kong?"

"It was soon after, and of course I thought that might account for it —my subconscious mind had got a powerful impulse, and proceeded to put together everything I had read about this country. Now the correspondences keep striking me: these roads crowded with traffic, and the loads hanging from men's shoulders; the carved gates across the road, the houses with curved double roofs, the square watch towers, the tall pagodas, like one roofed building on top of another. I even saw some of the men crippled and wounded."

"But you knew that China was at war, Lanny!" She was so anxious that they should not fool themselves.

"I know. We can never be sure about it. But it's so vivid, I can't get over the feeling."

"Yes, but it's that way with dreams. Think how often our subconscious mind makes up elaborate fantasies, and when we wake up we have a hard time realizing that it didn't happen. I have spent half a morning trying to convince myself that some unpleasant thing was entirely imaginary."

"Help me to wake up now!" he replied with a smile.

XI

The overloaded train delivered them after dark at the overloaded city of Hengyang, formerly Hengchow. A heavy rain had come up, but they disregarded it because they were so near their destination. They had a roll of money, and "money will make the mare to go," and likewise all her Chinese substitutes. Six "chairmen" were found, marvelous beings who took them along at what was almost a dog-trot, shouting to those who blocked the narrow way and sometimes elbowing them. The language was Mandarin now, and Althea said they were commanding: "Make way for the American lord!"

They had bought themselves Chinese gowns made of quilted cotton, as protection against the chill of night—for this was the month of January, and cold winds sometimes came from far-off Siberia. When the robes got wet they became very heavy and sagged out of shape, but the travelers refused to seek shelter. Althea had not seen her parents for several years, and was greatly excited. The coolies raced, because they knew the neighborhood and could be sure that a hot meal awaited them at the mission. "Me Christian man," said one of them, proudly; Althea told her friends sadly that he was probably a "rice Christian," one who professed religion in order to be fed.

They trotted up the slope on which the mission was situated. They arrived long after dark, so Lanny saw only the vague outlines of several buildings. In front of the cottage which had been Althea's home since childhood she raised a shout, and the door was opened and light streamed forth, and there came running a thin, gray-haired lady and clasped a soggy bundle of daughter in her arms, crying with relief and happiness—they had given her up for lost in Hongkong.

A tall elderly gentleman followed, carrying a flashlight, and they all came under the shelter of the porch for introductions. While the father put on his raincoat and led the coolies to another building where they would be fed and sheltered, Althea and Laurel were led upstairs to divest themselves of their raiment. A sorry sight they were, with clothing out of shape and wet hair straggling into their eyes. A funny scene, too, when they divested themselves of their "unchastity belts" and explained the phenomenon to the startled mother.

There was a bathtub in this house, and they took turns. Lanny had a shave—he had grown a beard, and looked comical to himself, and alarming to his bride. Then, clean and warm in comfortable dressing gowns, they had a hot meal of American foods—no rice, please! While eating they took turns telling their adventures. The parents had received a letter from Althea in Baltimore, saying that she was coming on the *Oriole;* they had heard nothing since. They had heard the name of Laurel Creston, but never that of Mr. Lanny Budd, who now turned up as a bridegroom of one lady and rescuer of both. Being old-fashioned people, they gave full credit to the man.

There could hardly have been a happier party in all China than in the home of Dr. John Taney Carroll that night. He was a Carroll of Carrollton, it appeared, and the name was on the Declaration of Independence. He was a sternly conscientious man—one didn't come to a part of the world like this without deep convictions; he worked a ten-hour day at a clinic here and at another down in the city, and whatever reward he received would have to be in Heaven, surely not in Hengyang. The mother was a devoted soul who shared her husband's every thought, and had brought up three children to follow in his footsteps. In short, it was a Christian home in the good sense of a much-abused phrase. Lanny wished there might be more of them in various parts of the earth that he had visited. He told himself that he would be willing to accept the Thirty-nine Articles of the Church of England, if men couldn't find any other basis for practicing brotherhood.

XII

The bride and groom having been married by Episcopalian authority, it was proper that their union should be consummated under the same auspices. For two weeks they had never been alone; now they found themselves in a guest-room with lace curtains in the windows, covers on the tables, a "splasher" on the wall behind the washstand—in short, all the little elegancies of a middle-class home of thirty years ago, including freshly ironed sheets and pillowcases on the bed. To that place of almost unimaginable luxury Lanny led his newly-won treasure; he sat by her side, took her hands in his, and looked into bright brown eyes which revealed the intelligence behind them—and also now a little fear.

"I will be gentle and kind," he said. "I will find out what makes you happy, and I will do that and nothing else. That goes for tonight and all other nights and days as well." This was a sort of supplement to the marriage service, what the churchmen call a work of supererogation.

On that long journey Lanny might have sought occasion to claim what the world called his "marital rights"; but it would have distressed his bride greatly, amid the dirt and discomfort of a primitive world. He had known this, and his consideration had touched her deeply. Now she answered: "My heart is yours, Lanny. I trust you as I have never trusted anyone since I was a child—when I trusted everybody."

"Tell me this," he continued. "Do you want to have a child?"

"I always thought that I never would; but I should love to have your child."

"It will interfere very much with writing," he warned.

"I can arrange it. I have thought about it a lot."

"You will find that America is at war—all-out war, be certain. Help will be hard to get."

"I'll find somebody, don't worry."

"Darling, I must be honest with you. When I get back home, some job will be assigned me. I have tried to figure out what it will be, but I can't. It may take me away from you for long periods; and it may be dangerous."

"That is all the more reason for having your child, and not delaying about it. Let us be happy while we can."

He kissed her, and put his newly-shaven cheek against hers and whispered: "Gather ye rosebuds while ye may, old time is still a-flying." The rhyme was "dying," so he didn't complete the stanza; instead, he told her: "I have found the right woman, and I am going to make her happy."

"You must be happy, too, dear," she countered. "I don't want to be a selfish wife."

"Don't have any worry about that," he answered. "I have been lonely for a long time, and now I have exactly what I want." He smiled, close to her lips, "All you have to do is to guide me, and I will be the perfect lover!"

XIII

In the morning they inspected the mission plant. There was a school, a dispensary and small hospital, a dining-hall and kitchen, a laundry, and cottages for those in charge and dormitories for the men and the women workers: a little unit of American civilization picked up and deposited in the middle of this ancient neglected land. *Chung Hua Sheng Kung Hui* was its name. Lanny had heard the missioners sneered at because they lived according to American standards; but having tried the other course, he was certain that no American could live as the Chinese masses lived and at the same time carry on intellectual or professional work. He soon observed that all these people were thin; with the rise in prices, their small salaries were losing value and nobody was getting enough to eat.

Lanny talked with some of the Chinese, and wondered how many of them were "rice Christians." He couldn't enter into their hearts, of course, but he could see that they had learned English more or less well, and many could read it. They had learned to keep clean, and to use modern machinery. They didn't have to be taught to work hard, for everybody in the Far East did that, excepting the very rich and the depraved, the opium addicts, the gamblers, and other parasites. The mission converts learned that there was such a thing as an ideal of altruism, and they at least paid the tribute which vice pays to virtue.

The visitor's greatest surprise came from the political atmosphere which he discovered prevailing in this mission. He was used to thinking of the Episcopal Church as a refuge, perhaps the last refuge, of a gentle and refined conservatism. It had been that in Newcastle, and still more on the French Riviera; all the "best people" attended, together with their doctors and lawyers and trades people—often for business reasons—and their carefully selected governesses and secretaries and maids. Hardly anybody else attended, and if you had taken these away there wouldn't have been any church. But here Lanny discovered that the prevailing tone of the mission was Pink and there were spots of bright Red. He wondered, had the ancient Chinese succeeded in teaching their teachers? Or could it be that daily contact with the poverty of the East had brought the Church of Jesus back to the state of mind of its Founder, who had Himself lived under much the same conditions?

Whatever the reason, the bishop of this diocese, with headquarters in Hankow, had become during forty-two years of service an out-and-out sympathizer with the masses in their revolt against landlords and moneylenders. He had become convinced that the so-called "Christian generals" who had been chopping off the heads of thousands of Communists were not ideal representatives of the lowly Nazarene. Bishop Roots had retired three or four years ago, but his portrait, showing a rotund, bald, and very determined cleric, still hung in the main hall of the mission and his spirit still dominated the institution. He had announced himself a "Christian revolutionary," and had invited so many of the hated Reds to take shelter in his home that his enemies had dubbed the place "the Moscow-Heaven Axis."

XIV

The priest of this mission was an elderly Chinese, Dr. Yi Yuan-tsai; a kindly, wise, and devout maker of Christian converts. To him Lanny explained the circumstances of his marriage in Hongkong, and his desire that it should have that legal validity which had not been obtainable under the guns of the Japanese. Dr. Yi assured him that under Chinese law he possessed full authority to perform the ceremony, and that its validity would be recognized by the allied government of the United States of America. So the couple stood up in the home of the Carrolls, and in the presence of that family renewed their pledges. Lanny sent another wireless message to his father, explaining the circumstances—for Robbie was the one who must have this matter clear,

in the event that the fates which had missed Lanny in Hongkong were
to get him anywhere on the way home.

They had a short-wave radio set at their service now and could get
the news of the world and be sure of it. Always when he turned a dial,
Lanny's first thought was of the atomic bomb. Would it be Berlin, or
London, or New York? But no, it was just the old routine, the operation of the military meatgrinder. The Germans had had to give up
efforts to take Moscow that winter, but they had taken Rostov, at the
eastern end of the Black Sea, and that was serious because it was so
close to the oil of the Caucasus. The Japanese were coming down on
Singapore, amazing the world by the speed with which they moved in
what were supposed to be impenetrable jungles. They had taken the
Solomons, those cannibal islands through which the *Oriole* had passed;
the cannibals wouldn't be of any use to them, but they had that fine
harbor of Tulagi, and were on their way to Australia, or Pearl Harbor,
or both.

Their armies in China had been definitely checked at Changsha in
the north and on the Canton front in the south, which meant a respite
for the missioners. But it could be only temporary, for manifestly the
Japanese had to have that railroad, the only north and south line
through the country. They would continue to send reinforcements,
and to attack. The missioners confronted the dreadful prospect of having to leave this place and emigrate to the west. How were they to do
it, with such poor means of transport? Some fifty million Chinese
had already done it, leaving everything except what they could carry
in wheelbarrows or on their backs. There had been no such mass migra-
tion in history—and it was still going on, impelled by the continuing
atrocities of the Japanese.

XV

In Lanny Budd's Pink days, a dozen years ago, he had been browsing
in the Rand School bookstore and had picked up *Daughter of Earth*,
by Agnes Smedley, of whom he had heard. He read the extraordinary
life story of a child born to a large family of American poor whites,
and dragged from one part of the land to another in unending wretched-
ness. She had managed to pick up bits of education and had become a
schoolteacher, and then a rebel propagandist and friend of the op-
pressed of all lands. Traveling to China as a journalist, she had made
the cause of the Chinese workers her own, and had traveled with the
Red Army and broadcast its story to the world.

Lanny and Laurel had already heard about this army from Sun
Ching-ling: how the workers and peasants had risen against the landlords and moneylenders and established a government according to the

Three People's Principles. The Kuomintang government under the control of Madame Sun's brother-in-law, the Generalissimo Chiang Kai-shek, had set out to put this rebel government down by mass slaughter; the result had been the famous Long March; a great army had emigrated to the northwest, a distance as great as across the United States. Now they were established just south of the Great Wall, and there was a truce between them and the Chungking government while they fought the Japanese. The Reds were known as the Eighth Route Army; and in the library of the mission was another book by Agnes Smedley, *China Fights Back*, telling the story of her travels and adventures with this army in the early campaigns, now four years in the past.

Althea, being a consecrated soul, had gone to work without even one day's rest; but the other two were leisure-class people who had a right to play—and besides, they were on their honeymoon. What more pleasant way to spend it than to read about other people's heroism? Agnes Smedley, with a seriously injured back, always in pain, had walked or ridden on horseback through a region where the most elementary necessities were not to be obtained. "There are no nails, no oil or fat, no salt, no fuel for fire. I shall be writing in the dead of winter without a blaze to warm me. And (need I tell you?) without sufficient food. Our food even now in the autumn is rice, or millet as a base, with one vegetable. Today it was turnips, and yesterday it was turnips. Sometimes we have no vegetables at all."

Such was the price which the masses of China were paying for freedom, and which an American sympathizer paid in order to report their sacrifices. A woman with an injured back carried her typewriter strapped to it because she was afraid to overload the one horse and one mule which carried the supplies of her party. "If my horse or mule should die, I am lost," she wrote; and concluded: "I am not complaining when I write all this. These are the happiest, most purposeful days of my life. I prefer one bowl of rice a day and this life to all that 'civilization' has to offer me. I prefer to walk and ride with an injured back that would take six months to heal even if I should stay in bed."

Lanny and Laurel took turns reading the book aloud; and when they finished, the bride said: "We ought to go and see those things, Lanny; it would be a crime to be so near and pass them by."

"It sounds near, but it isn't, darling. It's as far as from New York to Chicago, and there are no railroads for a good part of the way."

"I know, but we ought to get there. Somebody ought to write about what's happening now." They knew that Agnes Smedley's health had broken under the strain and she was back in her native land.

"It would be a hard journey," he warned. "Conditions can't be any better than they were four years ago. They are probably worse."

"Yes, but we could take supplies. I suppose there is some way you could draw on your bank at home. We could get warm clothing. Many people have taken such trips, even in winter."

"It seems a dubious sort of way to start a baby, darling."

"It would only be a question of the first months. We wouldn't have to stay long—I am quick at getting impressions and making notes of what I need."

"And what about your novel?"

"I won't forget it. I'd just write a few articles about China. Maybe I couldn't get anything printed, but I'd like to try."

"I hate to take you into any more danger, Laurel—"

"I know—you bold brave man, you want to walk into danger yourself and leave your delicate charmer at home. But you call yourself a feminist, and that means that women demand their share of the bad as well as the good."

This was hardly to be disputed, and Lanny said: "All right. If that's what you want, we'll talk it over with the two doctors and see if they think it can be done." He meant the father and daughter, with whom he had already discussed the idea of going out by way of Chungking. It might be that as far as danger was concerned there wasn't much to choose between the two routes. They would have to fly from Chungking, and that means over the "Hump," the most dangerous bit of air in the world. "If we go by the north," he suggested, "we might get a plane to Russia."

"The Moscow-Heaven Axis in reverse," smiled Laurel.

The husband, swapping wisecracks, remarked: "I have a title for your first book. *The Red Honeymoon!*"

26. *Hope Springs Eternal*

I

THE elder Dr. Carroll threw buckets of cold water over the project of a trip to Yenan. "Utterly out of the question!" he said, and explained that the difficulties were not so much of distance and weather as they were military and political. Free China was divided into two parts: the Communists, in the north, known as the "Border Government," and those at Chungking, the "Central Government," headed by the Generalissimo Chiang Kai-shek. There was a truce between them while they fought the Japanese enemy, but it was like a forced marriage and nobody could guess how long it would endure. The group of money-minded men about the Generalissimo hated and feared the Reds, and could not endure to see them win a victory, even over the foreign foe. The Gissimo kept several hundred thousand of his best troops deployed along the border between the two governments, maintaining the strictest sort of blockade.

"If you go to Chungking," declared the doctor, "you will surely not be permitted to travel to Yenan; the mere request would cause you to be marked as dangerous characters, and you would probably not get to travel anywhere. Nor can you travel toward Yenan from here; you would be halted at every military post."

"Couldn't we get up some pretext that would take us near Yenan?"

"Even if you did, you couldn't cross the border."

"You mean there is no intercourse whatever?"

"No trade is allowed; but sometimes there is officially-sanctioned exchange of products. They need our rice, and we need their oil and other products."

"What would happen if we were caught trying to get smuggled across?"

"The Chinese who helped you would be promptly shot; and you yourselves would be taken to the headquarters of General Hu Tsung-nan. He is a very charming little gentleman—was one of the Gissimo's fellow-students at the Whampoa Military Academy and commands his choicest crack troops—so precious that they have never yet been used against the Japs."

"And what will he do to us?"

"He will no doubt have delightful chats with you, since he is interested in the outside world and misses it in the lonely barren country where he is stationed. He will consider you two greatly misguided souls, and will endeavor to persuade you of the error of your notions regarding China. But I hardly think he will put you in one of his reform schools."

"Oh!—he has reform schools?"

"A polite name he gives to his concentration camps. He is disturbed because so many of the young people from our best families have heard about the work the Border Government is doing, especially the universities for both boys and girls. They want to go there and study—even if they have to walk all the way. General Hu's soldiers catch them and they are put in schools and taught what wicked ideas the Reds hold, and they are not let loose until the authorities are convinced they are completely cured."

"A curious thing," remarked Lanny, "how the world has become the same everywhere. I know of labor schools in several parts of England and America, and some of our best families would like to do exactly that with sons and daughters who take an interest in them."

"It would appear that the same forces are at work," replied the other. "I don't know much about politics myself. I don't have time to study it."

"Tell me this, Doctor. What will General Hu do if he should find that he cannot convert us?"

"He will doubtless send you to Chungking, and they will make another attempt."

"And then?"

"They are polite to Americans, and especially to those who have money and might command publicity. They will let you stay, and set spies to watch your every move. Anybody who talks to you will be marked for life; so pretty soon you will ask to be helped on your way and they will help you."

"That doesn't sound so very bad," commented Lanny. "What do you say, Laurel?"

"I want very much to try it," remarked the spunky lady. "We must promise never to tell anybody that Dr. Carroll gave us encouragement."

There was a twinkle in the doctor's tired gray eyes.

II

They spent a couple of weeks at the mission, resting and discussing the problem of their next move. It was a great temptation to choose the easy way. There was a commercial airline to Chungking, and they could take a plane, fly out by way of Calcutta, and be at home, perhaps in a week. No more dirt, no more discomfort, no more water boiling! But Laurel wanted to see the future, and make sure whether it really worked. She wasn't satisfied with the suggestion of the two doctors, that she visit some of the Red "islands" which were closer to them. These were great tracts where the Japs had never penetrated, and where the Communists held complete sway; one was near Hengyang, another near Canton—they had passed along its borders. But the writer said, No, to get any real material she would have to visit headquarters, the intellectual center. She was lured by the fact that no journalists had been there for a couple of years; and also by the fact that Lanny thought he could get into the Soviet Union.

Little by little the son of Budd-Erling discovered what it was going to be like, having a literary lady for a wife. She wasn't going to give up her work; apparently that possibility hadn't crossed her mind. She was a "born writer," and went to her job in the same way that a humming bird goes to flowers, or to a saucer of sugar water if one is provided. A mission of the Protestant Episcopal Church of America in the ricebowl of China was a large platter to her, and she was on the wing all day. The students and teachers, the nurses and other workers, were glad to talk with her; the Americans were reminded of home, and the Chinese wanted to practice English; all were made happy by the idea of being written about. "A chiel's amang ye, takin' notes"—a female chiel in this case, and in faith she would "prent it." She shut herself up in a room with one of the mission typewriters and typed out the notes. One set she would put in an envelope and entrust to Althea to be mailed to New York—for mail was still going, by way of Chungking; the other set she would carry on her journey. She asked Lanny to help recall the details of life in Hongkong and on the way to the mission, and he typed that for her. She had more than one use for a husband, it appeared.

Lanny didn't mind, for he had more than one use for a wife. He had been brought up as a little ladies' man, and thought it was all right being managed when he had the right manager. He found what Laurel wrote worth while, and he was pleased to look at China through her keen eyes. In fact, this was what he had been asking for; he had seen Germany through her eyes, and the Coast of Pleasure, and London and New York; he had imagined himself looking at the whole United States, going to and coming from Hollywood. Now he would look at Red China, then at Red Russia, and it would all be according to plan. When he had recited the marriage service, for better, for worse, he had really meant it—but of course he meant it for better!

Althea's mother, keeping the dark secret, cut open those "unchastity belts" with her own scissors and took out the gold coins. She had to admit that the idea was a clever one, so she made a clean specimen for Laurel to wear on the new journey—deducting only a few coins which the newlyweds insisted upon paying for their bed and board at the mission. Lanny got more money by the simple device of giving Dr. Carroll, senior, a check on a New York bank; in view of the war situation the physician said that he would rather have his savings in his home country. Lanny agreed that if he reached New York before the check came through, he would put the money to the doctor's account and stop payment on the check.

III

They announced that they wished to try the venture, and so the elder doctor undertook to find the right sort of Chinese-speaking guide. Presently he produced a wiry black-haired little fellow of thirty or so, by the name of Han Hua. He spoke English of a mixed-up sort, and was obviously intelligent; the doctor said he was honest and would do whatever he agreed to.

Lanny and Laurel proceeded to interview him to find out if he was the proper person for them, and presently they realized that Han was interviewing *them*, in order to judge whether they were proper persons to be received by the Border Government. Lanny, experienced in intrigue, decided that he was some kind of agent; he never did tell what he was doing, but they guessed it had something to do with propaganda. The Gissimo's friends resented the fact that the Reds carried on propaganda within Central Government territory, and they called it a violation of the truce. But Han said that the Chungking crowd was carrying on only a halfway war against the Japs; their troops didn't know what it was all about, and had to be kidnaped and forced to fight. The Border Government educated its people, and anybody who absorbed its ideas became a volunteer, ready to give his life for the cause of true and complete freedom. Wasn't that helpful, even among the Gissimo's own men?

Lanny guessed that a dossier was being prepared upon himself and wife, and he went back to the manners and language of his old Pink days. He told how he had helped to finance a labor school on the French Riviera, and another in Berlin; how he had been put out of Italy more than seventeen years ago for trying to send out of the country the facts about the murder of the Socialist Matteotti. He said that he was a personal friend of President Roosevelt and was going to make a report to him on present conditions in both Red republics. He guessed that Han wouldn't believe this, but he would know that it was a good story, calculated to grease the wheels. By a happy thought Lanny mentioned that he had read *Daughter of Earth* some years ago, and they had just been reading aloud Comrade Smedley's newest book about China. By the time he finished this discourse, the Chinese Red was completely warmed up, and said he thought it would be "good good thing" if this American couple would learn to know the new world of the north, and report it correctly to the American people.

"But how can we get a permit to travel to the border?" demanded Lanny.

Han wasn't so discouraging as the elderly doctor. He said that the underground had various ways of arranging such matters; their representatives had to travel, and they did. Of course it wouldn't be so easy with white people, who couldn't be disguised. It might be a question of buying a permit from some local official of the Chungking government. Han explained that the Communists had abolished corruption, by applying the death penalty; but Chungking was riddled with it, and, naturally, the Reds took advantage of the fact, in defending themselves against the cruel blockade which kept out even American medical goods. Han said at a guess that for two thousand Chinese dollars he could get them a valid permit to travel to South Shensi, where the

Reds could take charge of them and smuggle them across the border by night.

Lanny was agreeable to this proposal, and added that he would be glad to pay this class-conscious agent another two thousand to act as guide and interpreter on the trip. That wasn't any bribe, for Lanny assumed that Han would be acting with the approval of his superiors, or of his group, which, no doubt, was working in Hengyang at risk of life.

Han returned after a couple of days and reported that his "friends" had approved the proposal and that the travel permit could be obtained. So then came a busy period of preparation. They bought long sheepskin coats with wool inside, and woolen underclothing and socks. They filled their duffelbags with all the comforts needed for a long and uncertain journey. In the great city of Hengyang you could buy anything, it appeared, if you knew where to go and let a Chinese do the bargaining. Generally the price would be cut by two-thirds, but don't imagine that you could do that offhand, and without a lot of arguing back and forth.

Their kind host provided them with a letter to the head of a mission in Hupeh Province, more than half way to their goal; this would serve as "cover," in the event that their purposes were closely questioned. The doctor said that the Hupeh mission might be able to provide them with some pretext for continuing on in the territory controlled by the polite and cultured General Hu Tsung-nan. "Do whatever Han tells you," said the elder Dr. Carroll, with one of those eye twinkles they had learned to recognize. "He has very useful connections."

IV

Bright and early one morning toward the end of January the expedition set forth. Althea and Laurel dropped tears, for they had become warm friends; they promised to write to each other as soon as it was possible, and Laurel promised to take over the water-boiling ritual. All supplies had been provided, all debts paid, and a new life was beginning, a new world opening up. Laurel looked picturesque in sheepskin trousers, seated in her palanquin; the whole mission turned out to see her off and shout and sing good-by. She had made people love her, and they were certain that by the power of her pen she was going to bring American aid to China immediately upon her arrival.

The first stage of their journey was by a small steamer down the Siang River, and their first destination was the mountain resort of Hengshan, close to the river. Lanny didn't wish to forget entirely that he was an art expert, and he wanted to be able to produce evidence of such activity when questioned by the military. There were ancient art objects at Hengshan, which had been the favorite resort of the highly cultivated poet-emperor, Chien Lung, of the eighteenth century. A bus carried them up to the place, and they spent that night in a comfortable inn.

They were on their way into the rice bowl. Changsha lay less than a day's journey ahead, but that city had been wrecked and was still being bombed by the frustrated Japs, so they would turn off to the northwest, by the shores of the great lake of Tung-ting. This lake and a chain of others form a sort of reservoir of the Yangtse River which cuts across China from east to west. The river and the lakes form the rice bowl; their marshy shores are like the delta of the Nile and that of the Mississippi. In rainy weather the causeways called roads are all but impassable; you would slip off them or get stuck in them. That was what had defeated the Japanese invader in the great battle of Changsha which had just been fought. Those storms which had made things so uncomfortable for the American trio had saved the rice bowl for Free China.

Now the sun smiled on them, and they took off their sheepskin coats and laid them across their laps. The bus was the best they had yet seen in China, and while it was jammed, the polite passengers showed their respect for President Roosevelt by avoiding to crowd the American tourists. They gazed on endless rice fields—nearly always small plots, cultivated with the endless personal care of a land where human labor is the cheapest of all commodities. Each step they took carried them farther from the equator and nearer to the Arctic ice cap; for that, too, they could find compensation—the big black mosquitoes would be fewer, and soon would be gone entirely.

Many rivers flow into Tung-ting, and all those on the south and west had to be crossed. At the biggest river they changed busses; the passengers crossed on small ferryboats, using sails, poles, and long four-man sculls; it took a lot of time and also of yelling. The Chinese apparently could not work together without a great deal of noise, and making it seemed to be one of their greatest pleasures in life. They all wanted to talk to the Americans, and Han was eager to assist. One of the early Christian fathers had said that when he was in Rome he did as the Romans did; and on this principle Laurel would carry on conversations with the interpreter's help. Han would talk loudly, for the benefit of the whole bus, and Laurel did not rebuke him, because she saw what pleasure it gave to all. When she asked the man why the Chinese always shouted, he told her the custom had been started by an emperor who was suspicious of his subjects and decreed the death penalty for anybody observed to be whispering.

V

Han Hua was a part of China, and they studied him all the way. He was incessantly talkative, and delighted to tell the story of his life. He had been born a peasant in the south, a district where the wealthy land-lords had named the magistrate. Little Han had heard of the concept of justice—he called it *cheng yi*—but he had seen very little of it in action. At the age of thirteen he had joined the Red Army, and there had begun to pick up an education. He had learned to read and write, and since then had read every scrap of printed material he could get hold of. His present employers soon realized that one of his reasons, perhaps the principal reason for taking this job, was the chance it offered to improve his English. It wasn't long before Lanny was say-ing to his wife—in French—that the only fault he had to find with the Red regime of China was that it caused Han Hua to ask so many ques-tions.

Truly embarrassing questions! Was everybody in America as rich and beautiful as in the movies they sent to the Far East? And was it true that everybody had a vote—or were there Negroes who weren't allowed to vote? And was it true that the police ever beat up strikers, after the fashion which Han had seen in Old China? And why was it that the South, most revolutionary part of China, was the least revolu-tionary part of the United States? And why had the Americans sold scrap iron and oil to the Japs when it had been so obvious that the Japs were going to use the stuff against America? And how did it happen that the Americans had no language of their own? And why were there so many strange ways of spelling words? How could it be that "through" didn't rhyme with "rough"? To say nothing of "plough" and "cough" and "hiccough"! Lanny had to admit that many things in the Englishman's language could have been improved. Han said he was glad that matters had been arranged more sensibly in Mandarin.

This secret agent of revolution would get hold of a newspaper in towns through which they passed. (Lanny was astonished to learn that there were some sixteen hundred newspapers published in Free China at war.) He would read a paragraph and then turn round and tell his employers what it said. If it was news from home he would explain it, and if it was news from abroad he would ask them to explain it. Sit-ting in an inn waiting for their food, he would require Lanny to draw him a map showing the states of the United States, and he would write down populations and data such as that; he would cherish those scraps of paper to study. But why did American states have such queer names as Massachusetts and Connecticut? And why did Americans eat so much food? A Chinese worker could get more out of one grain of rice than an American could get out of a handful of wheat.

In short, here was the proletariat in process of awakening, in the rice bowl of China as in the bread basket of the Ukraine and among the sharecroppers of Arkansas and Oklahoma. "Workers of all countries, unite! You have nothing to lose but your chains; you have a world to win!" Han Hua was Red China in miniature; and as he came to know his employers better and to understand that, fabulously rich though they were, they were yet willing to see the land owned by those who worked it and the tools of industry owned by those who used them, he opened his heart and provided "Mary Morrow" with so many stories and picturesque phrases that she couldn't find time enough to jot them down.

Six times in one day, at bus stops, the vehicle had to wait while gendarmes or officials inspected that marvelous document which Han Hua had obtained for two thousand of the dollars called "CN"—for "Chinese National"—equivalent to a hundred real dollars at the start of the journey and to less at its end. Once the three had to fill out elaborate questionnaires—the bus didn't mind waiting. Lanny, of course, was the art expert from Connecticut, U.S.A., a refugee from Hongkong, and deeply interested in the ancient art of China. He had found a book in Hengyang, and provided himself with a list of the treasures he hoped to inspect in the districts to which he was traveling. Nobody ever failed to be polite, especially to the so obviously pregnant wife. Both husband and wife got used to the routine of inspection, and took to keeping the score; before they dived underground in the mountains of South Shensi, they had produced their passports and permits a total equal exactly to the number of weeks in that year!

VI

They were approaching the great Yangtse River, called the Son of the Sea. The river comes down from the western highlands through a great chain of gorges, and at the foot of the gorges is the city of Ichang, where in old days all freight had had to be trans-shipped into special vessels built to run the rapids. Now Ichang was in the hands of the Japs, and all efforts of the Chinese to retake it had failed. Below the city were stretches of the river across which smuggling was continually going on, but Han said he would be afraid to take his party across by that route. The Japs took no prisoners in this war, and they would especially enjoy getting some Americans to torture.

The Americans agreed that they preferred to face the perils of nature. They hired a Ford car of the "tin Lizzie" era and headed to the west, into the mountains through which the great chasm has been cut:

mountains denuded of trees, and terraced wherever there was a drop of moisture to be found. Han said that the farmers caught the rain in cisterns and ladled it onto their plants at night. Rains came now, most inopportunely; they drove with care on slippery mountain trails along the edges of high cliffs. There was traffic everywhere in China, it appeared, and when there was no room for passing, Han would sternly command the other parties to back up, and they would obey. Later he revealed that he had issued the commands in the name of the United States of America!

They came in sight of the famous gorges, and here was one of the most extraordinary spectacles that had ever confronted the eyes of the much-traveled Lanny Budd. It was as if a giant machine had come and cut a huge crevasse, half a mile deep and a hundred miles long, through these mountain masses; and then a swarm of human ants had come and covered the walls with themselves and their constructions. Where the wall was too steep for them to climb from the surging river they had come down from above. They had cut pathways along the cliffs and dug caves in them. Wherever there was a lump of earth they had built a wall about it and planted food. Where there was no earth they had brought it in baskets and built or dug rock basins to hold it. The caves were their homes, and outside they toiled every hour of daylight, constructing vegetable patches where you would have expected to find the nests of eagles and fish hawks. When the travelers came into sight of this gorge they looked across to the opposite face and saw it like a city turned up on end. The trails which led up into passes through the mountains had been planted on the sides, and looked like shafts of green, even at the beginning of February.

The party descended through such a trail, and when they came to the bottom they found a town strung along the water's edge. As soon as the high waters of summer receded, the peasants rushed to the new soil and planted it. If there came an unseasonable flood their labor would be swept away, and they, too, not infrequently. Few Chinese of the peasant class knew how to swim, and Lanny doubted if many of them had ever heard of such a possibility; if they fell into water and there was nothing to catch hold of, they drowned. Han said that in the old days of commerce through the gorges there had been special boats going up and down to pick up the corpses; they would tie a rope around the neck of each and tow it; when they had accumulated a sufficient bunch they would tow it to the burial grounds.

The Japanese command of the foot of the gorges had caused the direction of traffic to change and it was now crossways to the river. At the town strung along the water's edge they found crowds of people waiting for barges or junks to take them across the fast stream. When Lanny saw the number who intended to pile onto such a craft he refused to trust the life of his partner to it, and insisted in plutocratic fashion upon hiring a private barge. He and Laurel sat in a dirty and depressing tea-house while Han carried on the shouted negotiations which were necessary to this deal; Lanny had told the guide to pay the price and save time, but apparently this was a violation of conscience to a Chinese. A proper bargain had to be struck.

At last they were loaded and cast forth upon the tide. Six sturdy yellow men, naked save for loincloths, sculled and rowed with long oars and desperate concentration. They were swept far downstream; when they reached the opposite bank the men produced boat hooks, caught whatever objects they could find, and toilsomely pulled the craft foot by foot against the current. That was the way the gorges of the Yangtse had been ascended ever since men had discovered them and before they had discovered the power of steam.

The travelers were put ashore at the proper spot, the agreed price was paid, and they hired another car which chugged painfully up a steep trail. They spent their first night in the province of Hupeh very uncomfortably in a stone hut, along with goats and donkeys and all the smells of China. A good part of the fleas of China were present, also, but the humans had magic against these and kept themselves well powdered. The peasant who maintained this so-called inn told them through the interpreter many fearsome tales about the wizards who dwelt in these Lan-shan—the second word meaning mountains. It had been an especially powerful wizard who made the gorge which they had just crossed; he had done it by blowing with his nostrils, and that was why it was known as the Wind-box gorge. It was these wizards who sent the floods and destroyed the works of man; they were in league with the great water dragons which had their palaces in the deep pools and under the black rocks of the river bed.

VII

There are many mountains in the province of Hupeh, and the farther north the explorers went the more they needed their sheepskin coats. Their backs became toughened, and they grew used to being swayed back and forth by the bumping of an aged car. They learned to eat what they could get, mostly rice, eggs, and stored vegetables, washed down by tea made from their boiled water and no sugar. Presently they came to another great east and west river which had to be crossed; it was called the Han, and they asked playfully if it had been named for one of their guide's ancestors. He grinned and informed them that "Han" was an alternative word for "Chinese."

Just north of here was the mission to which they had a letter. It proved to be a small place, but it made them welcome and afforded them an opportunity to get clean. They took their hosts into their confidence; these people had no sympathy with the Border Government, but accepted the statement that their fellow-countrymen were getting material for a report to Washington. They thought it a strange mission for a pregnant woman—and Laurel did not share her secret with them. They gave the party a letter to another mission farther north, and warned them that after that stage they would be approaching the territory of General Hu, and it would be imperative for them to travel only at night.

From the next town there was a bus line, going north; and so they rolled on through the dirt and misery of war-torn China. "Beyond the Eight Horizons," was the native phrase. This country had been fought over, back and forth, ever since the overthrow of the Manchu Empire a generation ago. This was the China that Lanny had read about: bare deforested mountains and dustblown slopes of yellow loess long since deprived of fertility. Peasants still toiled for an existence in the hills, but the wealth was confined to the river valleys, and these were exposed to incessant floods.

They came to the next mission, which proved to belong to the unorthodox Seventh Day Adventists. The party had the bad luck to arrive on Friday evening, when men and women had become gloomy and were walking humbly before their God. But that did not prevent them from receiving the travelers, feeding them, and giving what advice they could. All shades of political opinion were the same in the Lord's eyes, they reported, but this was not so in the eyes of General Hu, therefore they requested anyone who was bound for Yenan to leave the mission before morning.

Han set forth to find some friends of his, meaning, of course, his Party's underground committee; he came back to report that he had a safe hiding place. They set out before dawn, and were led into a mountain gorge, and in its recesses they found caves with peasant families. The Americans had been assured that caves, if they were dry, could be warm and comfortable; this one had the customary *k'ang* along one wall, an earthen shelf on which they could sleep and wait for the next night. A Chinese family continued its life as if there were no visitors present.

From that time on the party belonged to the Red underground. They traveled only by night, over all sorts of country, including steep mountain trails where they trusted their lives to the instincts of tough little ponies. Many travelers were on these trails, most of them with heavy loads. Mysterious figures appeared and disappeared in darkness. Perhaps they were smugglers, perhaps soldiers; nobody asked any questions. Han would produce some local guide, and that guide would deliver them at a place where they and others would spend a day sleeping and eating, but doing very little talking. Han would report to his boss that he had paid so many paper dollars for various services— a cup of tea cost two dollars now—and Lanny would hand him another bundle. Han would report that they were so many *li*—about a third of a mile—nearer to Yenan, and Lanny would take the liberty of not being certain about that.

VIII

At last they were in North Shensi, which was Red territory, and outside the reach of the cultivated General Hu—whom they were never to see. They became creatures of the daylight again, and surveyed this neglected land which the new occupants were in process of restoring. Han explained to them how each unit of the Eighth Route Army had been obliged to go to farming and become self-sustaining— since the scattered half-starved peasants had nothing to give them. The visitors were received at an army post, and were fed in a mud hut with a thatched roof—this was a "club house." They sat outside on a still night, amid a throng of gray-clad soldiers, and were entertained by Chinese boxing, patriotic speeches, and the singing of the *Guerrilla Marching Song.*

Hitchhiking on a rice truck, they followed the valley of the Yen River, and so came, weary and sore, to their long-sought goal, the city of Yenan, three thousand years ancient, according to their guide. The syllable *"an"* means "peace," but it had been a futile hope through all those thirty centuries. On one of the hills stood a tremendously tall pagoda, supposed to exert a spell against invaders; but that hadn't worked against the Mongols and wasn't working now against the Japanese. They had been bombing the city unhindered for a matter of four years and a half, and there were few buildings with walls standing; when you entered these you generally discovered that they had no roofs.

The city lies in a flat plain, not too wide, and the hills rise abruptly; so the citizens had retired to the suburbs and dug themselves caves. The soil is of loess, good and hard, and when you have dug far enough you are safe from bombs of any size; you are cool in summer and warm in winter and dry at all seasons. You and your co-operative friends can cut a street, ascending slowly along a cliff side, and so you can have a whole row of dwellings; or it may be a hospital, a factory, a university for young men, or one for young women. There were thousands of caves—apparently nobody had ever taken a census of them.

Such was Yenan, and the American visitors fell in love with it at the first contact. Most important of all, it was the cleanest community they had come upon. Perhaps that was because it was new, and perhaps because its citizens were young; the soldiers were young and their commanders not much older; the students were young and their teachers not much older. Everybody was hard at work, everybody was doing something novel and exciting; the place gave you a sense of exhilaration, the like of which Lanny had not encountered since he had gone visiting among the "radicals" in his early days. Those hadn't been able to do anything but dream and talk, whereas these people were constructing, they were making their dreams come true.

Americans were scarce in Red China, and the arrival of this unannounced pair occasioned great interest; everybody wanted to meet them, and to shake hands—they had adopted that western custom, and did it with alarming vigor. The visitors were taken up by Yenan's best society—which meant precisely everybody in the place. Socialist equality was their bright dream, and everybody felt himself on the same plane, from the poorly dressed ex-peasant, Mao Tse-tung, Party chairman and government head, to the youngest *hsiao-kuei*, which means "little devil," and is the name for the small boys who follow the army and make themselves useful to the soldiers. When civil wars have gone on for a generation, there is a plentiful supply of boys who have no homes, and if you feed them they will work and grow up to be soldiers.

The Budds were put up at the Guest House, which meant that they had a private cave. It contained two cots, a small table and two stools made of local wood, a water pitcher, a basin and a *pot de chambre* made of local clay, a couple of blankets and a couple of straw mats—all products of the co-operatives. That was more than most people had and all that anybody needed. The first time Laurel had met Lanny, she had called him a troglodyte, a cave-dweller; now here they were, two of them, and the jokes they made were many.

They and their guide would have their meals in a communal dining-room, and they would eat what everybody else ate—rice, millet, boiled vegetables, and once a week a little meat. The first person they met in the dining-room was a scholarly Englishman who had been teaching at Yenching University in Peiping when he had got news of the attack on Pearl Harbor, and had made a quick dive to the Red guerrillas who were in the near-by mountains. He was in Yenan for only a short visit, he said: he was going back to the armies to help them with radio, which was his hobby. Next to him sat an American doctor who had been several years in this new world and liked it so well that he had taken a Chinese name; you addressed him as Dr. Ma. He was the happiest American they had met in a long time, having only one serious complaint, that his hospital had no medicines.

IX

After spending a couple of days on the back of a Chinese pony scrambling up mountainsides and along the edge of precipices and over dubious suspension bridges, a delicately-reared lady would have been glad to lie down and rest for a day or two. But everybody wanted to show her things and tell her stories, and this was what she had come for. So she climbed the side of cliffs and inspected the new institutions of a new-old land. The co-operatives were not peculiar to the Red part of Free China; there were several thousand of them, in a score of provinces. They were the answer of the whole land to the move westward and to the desperate needs of war. This population—soldiers, workers, and intellectuals—had never seen western and northwestern China before, and had hardly known that it existed. They had come to a raw, almost abandoned land, and had applied to it the techniques of social effort which had been worked out by revolutionary theorists of Europe and America and which had received their first trials on a nation-wide scale in the Soviet Union.

Some of these leaders had studied in Russia, and so their movement called itself Marxist; but Lanny Budd quickly decided that they weren't really Marxist, they were early American Utopian. They were Brook Farm and New Harmony, Ruskin, Tennessee, and Llano, California; they were Robert Owen and Bronson Alcott, Edward Bellamy and J. A. Wayland. Lanny had read about them in the library of his Great-Uncle Eli, and now it was one of the strangest experiences of his life to discover their theories and techniques bursting into flower here on the dustblown hills under the Great Wall of China.

Here was the communal life; here were the communal kitchens and dining-rooms, the communal nurseries where children were cared for; here were the co-operative production and distribution, the socialized medicine, the socialized teaching. Here was the old idea of students supporting themselves by part-time manual labor; here was a medical college where the students brought spinning wheels out into the open in good weather and spun cloth for three hours every morning. The old New England spinning wheels which had clothed Lanny's forefathers, and which now brought fancy prices from collectors of antiques! Here, too, was the old New England practice of community help in house-raising, corn-husking, and other farm tasks—the name for it here was "labor exchange."

Even more important than all these economic devices was the social spirit. Here were the vision and the dream, the ideal of brotherhood and mutual aid; hope springing eternal in the human breast; faith in the perfectibility of man, in the possibility of building new institutions and having them right this time; the casting off of old habits of greed and self-seeking, the setting up of a new code of group awareness. "Solidarity forever!" had been the slogan of the "Wobblies"; that of the Chinese co-operatives was: *"Gung ho!"*—meaning work together. The American Dr. Ma was as happy as a schoolboy. "For the first time," he said, "here is a medical world without professional jealousy. Nobody is making money out of the sick; nobody is trying to be richer or more famous than his colleagues; we are all trying to find out the causes of disease and prevent them before they start."

Lanny had visited Leningrad and Odessa, and had seen a bit of this dream in action; but Laurel had only read the books, and had only half believed in the possibility. Naturally a critical nature, prone to see human weaknesses rather than virtues, she was moved by this torrent of faith and enthusiasm. She forgot all about her stiff back and aching thighs, and went from place to place, asking questions for hours. Lanny went along, an amused spectator, and Han blossomed forth as the proud propagandist, scoring the great success of his life—for had he not been the one to discover these wealthy and important Americans and to bring them safely through many perils? Who says that the collective life will destroy all initiative?

X

The Japanese planes came now and then, seeking for something they could destroy. They hated this place above all others in China, for it was not only the capital of an enemy country, it was the headquarters of an idea and an ideal more dangerous than any government or any army; something which threatened, not merely the Japanese government and army, but its social system; a challenge to the wealthy clique which owned Japan, and made slaves of the Japanese people as well as of the Chinese. One of the most interesting discoveries the American couple made in Yenan was the Japanese People's Emancipation League, composed of prisoners of war who had elected to espouse the cause of their captors, to receive the Red education, and to aid the guerrillas in undermining the morale of the Jap Armies. This was the familiar Communist technique; and Laurel said: "Perhaps it is the only way that war will be ended in the world." Her husband replied: "Watch out, and don't be seduced by Red propaganda!"

Yenan was the center from which all this propaganda went out to four hundred million Chinese. Yenan was the capital of the Border Government and the headquarters of its army. Lanny had come to realize what tremendous forces that movement had; not merely the Balu Chün, the regular Eighth Route Army, but the irregulars, the guerrillas, well organized and keeping up incessant resistance in every province of this immense land. The Japs were supposed to have the whole of northeastern China, but it wasn't so; they had only the ports, the navigable rivers, and the railroads, plus as much territory as they could reach by short marches; all the rest was in the hands of the Chinese partisans, who were continually raiding, sabotaging, destroying. The Japs would send punitive expeditions, which would wipe out whole villages; as soon as they left, the peasants would start rebuilding —and meantime the partisans would be raiding at some other spot.

"Where do they get the supplies?" Lanny asked. The answer was that everything came from the enemy; arms, ammunition, food—they even got a tank now and then. The Japs could not guard every place, and the little handful they left behind would be overwhelmed in the night. "Everything they have becomes ours," said one of the generals.

The reason this could go on was that the whole peasant population was with the partisans; for the first time in the history of this land, the people had an army which they regarded as their own. The armies of the war lords had plundered even their own provinces, and had been hated and feared by their own people; but the Red Army educated as it went. "So it can never be put down," said Mao Tse-tung, its cool-headed political leader, chairman of the Party. "It may be scattered, but it will reassemble. It may be wiped out, but it will spring up again."

XI

Mao had assented readily to the desire of the two visitors to pay a call upon him. Like everybody else, he and his family lived in caves, but there was a compound in front where his bodyguard stayed—he was a man ardently sought by the enemy and there were many prices upon his head. The interview was at night, and the visitors were driven to the place in a rather rickety truck. The high gate of the compound squeaked on its wooden hinges, and Han, proud and happy, gave the password; they were escorted into the reception room of this cave, which had a red brick floor and whitewashed walls. The room was lighted by only one candle, set in a cup.

When their host rose, they saw that he was a large man, with a full face, thick black hair, and a kindly expression. He wore baggy homespun trousers and jacket, and during the interview he smoked bad homegrown cigarettes. The visitors thought that they had never met a more unassuming person. He did not speak English, and had his own interpreter; he would wait until a question had been translated, and then he would reply, one short sentence at a time, pausing until that had been put into English for the guests. He was a very serious man, and quiet as a Buddha; he had no nervous gestures and his tone was low and mild. Sitting in the shadows, he had the aspect of an oracle.

He explained the revolution to which his Party was dedicated. Three-quarters of the Chinese people were peasants, and they had been in the grip of landlords who took from half to three-quarters of their produce; that was virtual slavery, and the Party was pledged to restore the land to those who worked it. After that had been accomplished, they were a Party of democracy complete and without reservation. Yes, they were willing that the former landlords should have votes, on equal terms with everybody else. "The landlord vote will never carry an election," said Chairman Mao, with a smile.

First of all came the task of driving out the Japanese invader; that was another and even worse kind of landlord, and there would never be any peace in East Asia until the Japanese peasants had abolished landlordism in their country and set up their own people's party. Mao wanted to know how well, if at all, this fact was understood in America; for a while he became the interviewer, and Lanny and Laurel answered questions. Lanny explained that there was the same struggle going on in America; there were landlords there, too, and they dominated politics and political thinking. "Of course with us land means natural resources, coal and oil and minerals—"

"With us, also," put in the other.

"The Republican Party is the party of those vested interests, including the great industrialists, those who control the corporations which own the land and its natural wealth, the patents, all the secrets and the machinery of production. The Democratic Party is groping its way to a solution of this problem, but it is very far from sharing or even understanding collectivist ideas."

"Does President Roosevelt understand them?"

"He has such an active mind, I should hesitate to say there is any social problem he does not understand—with the help of his wife, perhaps. But he is more or less a prisoner of the politicians from the southern part of our country, which is governed by a land-owning aristocracy very much as you had here in China. That is why his administration will send help to Chiang Kai-shek, but will look upon your movement with suspicion."

"And yet they call themselves Democratic?" inquired the Chinese leader.

"In our country," explained the visitor, "we draw a sharp distinction in the spelling of that word. When it is spelled with a capital letter, it means a group of respectable capitalist-minded politicians. When it is spelled with a small letter, it means something very dangerous, and the large-letter politicians would put it in jail if they could."

Said Mao Tse-tung: "When I was a peasant child and was told that the world was round, I assumed that the people down there must be standing on their heads. And now it seems that perhaps the child was right."

XII

The thing which interested these visitors most in Yenan was the educational system, which had made it the cultural center of the nation. In this poor and backward province of Shensi alone there were now more than a thousand mass-education schools, and in Yenan were several high schools and universities, besides technical academies, and —of all things in the midst of war—an art school. At all these the Budd couple were honored guests, and their fame spread from one to another.

The *K'ang Ta* means "University of Resistance," and its students were learning to fight Japanese imperialism while at the same time encouraging the Japanese people against their oppressors. This university had been greatly reduced in size, Lanny was told, because the Central Chinese Government had made so much trouble for the students trying to get to it. Now there were only two thousand students in Yenan, while the rest, about ten thousand, had been moved to the "occupied" parts of China; that is to say, to the guerrilla-held "islands" of the northeast. What a topsy-turvy situation, that students preparing to fight a foreign foe would be more afraid of their own government than of the foe!

Most fascinating to Laurel was the Nü Ta, the women's university. This occupied about two hundred caves, extending all the way around two mountains, with a highway serving it, and stairs here and there leading to the valley below. Edgar Snow, who had visited it a couple of years previously, had called it a "College of Amazons." Now it had close to a thousand students, and taught them everything from the care of babies to the complexities of English spelling. All around were terraced fields, and in these the students worked for two hours daily, rising at dawn.

They all wore blue cotton uniforms, straw sandals, and army caps. Lanny saw no rouge or lipstick in Yenan, and he did not miss it. Many of the women were married, but they were only allowed to be with their husbands on Saturday nights; the other nights they studied. Most of them were daughters of workers or peasants, but there were a few playfully known as "the capitalists." One was pointed out as the daughter of a Shanghai millionaire who had made his fortune out of "Tiger Balm," a patent medicine which was supposed to cure all the ills that Chinese flesh is heir to.

Everything was free at this university except bedding and uniforms.

The cost to the government of maintaining it—reckoning in American money—amounted to about forty cents per student per month. Lanny had never seen such serious young folk, and he contrasted them in his mind with American students as he had known them—their minds occupied with football and jazz, petting parties and fraternity politics. His wife suggested: "Perhaps we are going to find that the war has made some difference at home."

XIII

In the shelter of their guest chamber the two troglodytes discussed the sights they had seen and the conclusions to be drawn from them. Was this Communist stage one through which all civilizations had to pass? Or did it apply only to the backward peoples? And if so, what were the advanced peoples going to make of it, and how were they to get along with it? Lanny said: "Yenan poses a problem to the capitalist world, and it won't be settled by this war. If the powers permit this to succeed, the news of it will spread to India, to Burma, Indo-China, Java—all the places where the dark-skinned peoples live in poverty and toil for the benefit of white masters."

"Are you afraid that I will become a Communist, Lanny?" asked his wife, abruptly.

"Get the facts, and make up your own mind. But I hope you won't become fanatical, as I fear my sister Bess has."

"I gather that you haven't been able to make up your own mind altogether."

"I am like a man who looks at one side of a coin and then at the other, and they are different, and he can't decide which is the coin. I see co-operation, and that delights me; then I see repression, and that repels me. Which is the coin?"

"These people don't seem repressed, dear."

"I know; but you forget the people who aren't here, who were killed or driven out. Those we meet are doing what they believe in; but there is no room for any who believe differently and might like to say so."

"Do we want to go off to some blissful tropic island and live until this class struggle has been fought out?"

"No, but I can't help wishing that political and economic problems might be settled by free discussion and majority consent. At least I feel bound to advocate that method for my own country, and for all others which have established the democratic process."

"Of course, but you're not in any of those countries now: you're in China, which apparently has been governed by despotic emperors and war lords as far back as anybody's memory goes. You are going to Russia, where some of the tsars were insane and most of them cruel, so far as I can learn."

"I know, and I tell myself that I can't have fixed principles, I have to judge each situation on its own merits or lack of them. I say: 'I will be a Red for Yenan and a democratic Socialist for the United States.' But the Communists won't have it that way, and neither will the Socialists; both sides have come to hate the other worse than they hate the capitalists. I have known Socialists so exasperated by Communist dogmatism and arrogance that they have been driven completely into reaction; they still think they are Socialists, but they never say anything about how to get Socialism, they spend all their time denouncing the Reds."

"The longer I watch things, the more I realize that the world is in a mess," said the wise lady whom this philosopher had chosen for his wife. "Let us make up our minds that we are going to try to understand all sides, and not expect to find it easy."

"This war is going to be hard," replied the husband; "and unless I am mistaken the peace will be harder. World capitalism is going to be even less willing to let the Chinese people go Red than they were to let the Russians go Red after the last war. The whole British Empire will be at stake, and the Dutch, the French, the Belgians—whatever else there is. If the flames of revolt are not extinguished they will spread to the Arabs, and to Africa, North and South."

"Haven't we shown how to help a backward people in the Philippines, Lanny?"

"Yes, and I think that would be the answer; but can we get the other great powers to learn from us? And will our own capitalists let us teach them? Won't we be sending American money and arms to help Chungking put down Yenan, and to help the British and the Dutch to maintain their empires?"

"Let's win this war first, Lanny!" said the wife.

27. The Desert Shall Rejoice

I

THE time had come for Mr. and Mrs. Budd to be moving on. The diet deficiency was beginning to affect the health of both of them; Laurel's cheeks were pale and she was losing weight. It was a tuberculosis diet, and few white people could live on it; many of the Chinese suffered from the disease. Lanny recalled the case of Thoreau, who had preserved his independence at the expense of his nutrition and had paid this same penalty. There was no sense in paying it unless you had to.

One of Lanny's first moves upon arriving in Yenan had been to make the acquaintance of two wide-awake Russians who represented Tass, the news agency of the Soviet Union. They received news from their homeland by wireless and transmitted it to the newspapers of China by the national mail system, which was still working in spite of war. Lanny guessed that the pair would be in contact with the Soviet authorities by way of Ulan-Bator, capital of Outer Mongolia.

He explained to them that he was the nephew of Jesse Blackless, Communist deputy in the parliament of the recently deceased French Republic, and now serving as adviser on French affairs to Narkomindel, the Soviet Foreign Office, located in Kuibyshev, to which the government had moved. Also he was brother-in-law to Hansi Robin, the violinist, and half-brother to Bessie Budd Robin, his accompanist, both of whom enjoyed the status of "honored artists of the Soviet Union," and had gone to Moscow after the attack by the Hitlerite bandits, in order to express sympathy for the Soviet people and give them what encouragement they could. All three of these persons had urged Lanny to come to the Soviet Union, and Jesse Blackless had said that he could obtain the necessary permission. It was for this reason that Mr. and Mrs. Budd had taken the long journey from Hongkong to Yenan. Lanny further explained that his father was the President of Budd-Erling Aircraft, whose planes would soon be going to Russia under lend-lease—if they were not already there.

What he desired was to inform Jesse Blackless that his nephew was in Chungking and desired to enter the Soviet Union. The agents informed him that they had no sending apparatus. They took him to the head of the New China Agency, the Communist news network, who agreed to put a news item on the air, with the reasonable chance that the Moscow monitors would pick up the broadcast. Certainly it was news that the son of Budd-Erling Aircraft had escaped from the Japanese at Hongkong, and had traveled all the way across China and was now in Yenan. His wife, the New York writer who used the pen name of Mary Morrow in the *Bluebook* magazine, was also news; and likewise the fact that they desired to visit Mr. Budd's uncle. It was to be expected that the Moscow monitoring station would take the trouble to inform the uncle of the recording of such a broadcast.

II

Lanny knew that bureaucratic wheels grind slowly in all lands, so he didn't expect an answer for some time. He was agreeably surprised when three days later one of the Tass men handed him a message: "Congratulations will endeavor to arrange transit visas will report Jesse Blackless." Then, for a couple of weeks, silence. Lanny had about made up his mind to approach the Yenan authorities and ask them to intervene, when at last came the decision: "Invitation extended come Ulan-Bator transportation from there will be provided Jesse Blackless."

The Red uncle may not have realized what a task he was setting the newlyweds by his three words of instructions: "Come Ulan-Bator." This capital of Outer Mongolia lay a thousand miles to the north. First you had to cross the Great Wall, and then you had to cross the Gobi desert, from which came the dust storms that drove everybody in Yenan into hiding in their caves. With every step of the journey you would be moving into greater cold, until, when you finished, you would be almost in Siberia. It was now the end of February, but spring comes late in that region, and to make such a journey would require an expedition.

Their only chance would be to fly; and this Lanny discussed with the Yenan authorities. They had a crude airfield here, but only one small plane that had not been smashed by the Japs—and that one was not in order. Chungking had planes, and sometimes brought in supplies under the exchange arrangement, but they wouldn't have any dealings with private parties. There were several commercial airlines within Central Government territory, but they were never permitted to cross the border into Red territory. Lanny visited the airport, and with Han's help questioned those in charge, but nobody knew of any plane that was for hire, or of any way to fly to the capital of Outer Mongolia.

The couple might, of course, go out by way of Chungking; Lanny might send a wireless message to the American Embassy, appealing for help, and doubtless the embassy would arrange for the pair to be brought out on the return trip of some government plane. But then they would miss Russia, and it would be an admission of defeat. The Chungking officials would scold them, and would confiscate all Laurel's notes about Yenan, and probably those about the rest of China, on the ground that she had shown herself a hostile person, and had broken Chungking's stringent regulations.

Lanny began inquiring about camels, and supplies needed for a crossing of the Gobi. Laurel still had most of the gold sovereigns sewed up in her belt; but how could one get in touch with the Mongolians, to hire a camel train, and to find out if their government would permit an expedition to pass through? And what were the chances of the Japs raiding across any part of the route? How far could they be helped by the Yenan government? And so on.

At this point there came, quite literally, a windfall; at any rate an airfall. One of Laurel's student friends told her that a strange plane had arrived on the previous evening, and Lanny hurried to the airport to find out about it. Sure enough, there was a two-engine plane, apparently a small transport; he couldn't be sure, because soldiers were guarding it and wouldn't let anybody near. Lanny tried to question one of the airport men who knew a little English, but the man wouldn't talk. All very hush-hush, and Lanny wondered, could it be an enemy plane which had got lost and run out of gas?

He got the story by appealing to one of the military officers whom he had met on the evening of his speech about the T.V.A. The plane was flown by a Frenchman who claimed to have saved it from capture in a raid of the Japs in Hopeh Province. According to the man's story, he had been flying for a commercial concern, and they had stored the plane until the time when business might be resumed. Hearing that enemy raiders were approaching the place, the Frenchman had thrown some extra tins of fuel into the plane and taken off in a hurry. He had tried to land at a field in Central Government territory, but had been fired upon, and so he had decided to try Yenan. The authorities here were dubious about him, suspected him as a spy or saboteur, and had locked him up for the present.

Lanny got permission to interview the man, and found him a typical product of the Paris boulevards; cynical, clever, aware of all the worst facts of the world. Jean Fouché was his name, and he was, of course, delighted to meet someone who knew his *argot* and could talk about old times. Lanny made sure that he really was what he claimed to be, a man without the slightest interest in Chinese politics, who had flown all over the country for high pay and with no thought but to get back to Paris with the money in his pockets. He took Lanny for the art expert and rich man's son, and asked what he thought these Red

salauds would do to him, and would they confiscate the plane? Before
the talk was over he suggested, with a sly wink: "Wouldn't you like
to buy it, Mr. Budd?"

Lanny's answer must have surprised him. "If I bought it, would you
be able to fly me to Ulan-Bator?"

III

Lanny took the problem direct to Mao Tse-tung, who denied that
he was a dictator, but who might have something to say about it all
the same. The American explained that he had no idea what would be
the attitude of the Border Government to a refugee plane, whether
they would confiscate it or buy it; all he wanted out of it was a trip
across the Gobi desert. He wanted to get to Moscow without having
to ask favors of Chungking, and without risk of having his wife's
precious notes confiscated. If she reached New York with those notes
intact she could write articles whose propaganda value to Yenan would
exceed the price of many planes. Lanny Budd, old-time Pink, knew
how to put matters to the Party chairman of a People's government.
He added that he had such sympathy with that government that he
would expect to pay a generous fee for the service.

The People's Council, or the General Staff, or whoever it was that
decided such matters, took two days to debate the project. Then a
polite young official—how polite they all were, and how young!—
announced the news to Mr. Lanny Budd. The People's government
would be pleased to transport him and his wife to Ulan-Bator for the
actual cost of the gasoline, which was unfortunately very high; they
estimated it at eight thousand Chinese dollars, which was four hundred
American dollars. The young official named the sum deprecatingly, as
if he would be ready to cut it in half if Mr. Lanny Budd had shown
any sign of displeasure; but Lanny answered promptly that the sum
appeared most reasonable and he would be happy to pay it in gold. He
was asked when he would like to make the trip, and replied that he
and his wife would be ready at five minutes' notice. He was told that
the decision would depend upon weather conditions; also, that the
Ulan-Bator airport would be notified by wireless of the proposed
flight.

"The pilot and the co-pilot will be our own," remarked the official,
significantly; and this Lanny had expected. They wouldn't take any
chance that M. Fouché might like Ulan-Bator and decide to remain.
Lanny ventured to ask what was going to happen to the man, and the
reply was that he had already been released and provided with useful
work—but of a sort that wouldn't take him anywhere near the airport!
Lanny didn't ask if the man was to be paid for the plane; an old-time

Pink knew the Communist formula, "the socialization of the instruments and means of production and distribution"—and assuredly a transport plane was covered by the last word of that formula. The Yenan theoreticians had recently decided that they were fostering private enterprise in order to destroy feudalism, their first and most real enemy; but they would probably not feel bound to apply that new directive to an airplane of dubious origin.

I V

The travelers packed their few belongings—less what they gave to their friends. They had a sad time saying good-by; the faithful Han wept, and said that the light of his life was going out. Lanny gave him the Newcastle address and told him to write when circumstances permitted. Their friends all promised to write—there would be peace again someday, and Free China would build a new world, so wonderful that everybody in America would want to fly to see it!

A cart took them to the field before dawn, and with their sheepskin coats on and their blankets wrapped about their legs they settled themselves for a long flight. Their baggage included two bottles of water and a lunch consisting of boiled rice, slices of spiced mutton, and two large pickled cucumbers. As soon as there was light enough to see by, the plane took off, and they soared past the tall pagoda which was supposed to keep off enemies. Soon after the sun was up they were above the Great Wall, which they had heard about since childhood but never expected to see. It was wide enough for several horsemen to ride on abreast; from the air it looked like the parallel cables of a suspension bridge, hung from tower to tower over the unending hills of North China. They had been told that there were fourteen hundred miles of it; undoubtedly it was one of the mightiest works of man— but it hadn't succeeded in keeping the Mongols out of this country.

On the other side was Inner Mongolia, now partly in Jap hands; but they saw no enemy, and the vast sky was empty. They passed over the Yellow River, the Hwang-ho, which makes a great double bend here. Now and then they passed over villages and saw peasants working, but the peasants seldom looked up. The Chinese were moving into this country, driven westward by the Japs, and the Mongols were moving out before the Chinese. The spade was mightier than the thundering herd.

This plane had not been built for anybody's comfort, but to carry freight. It had no heating arrangements, and no fuel to waste. Its walls transmitted every sound, and the roar of well-worn engines made it necessary to shout if you wanted to be heard. Extra tins of gasoline were lashed fast to the floor, and the rest of the space was at the disposal of the passengers; they could stand and look out of the windows, first one side and then the other, pointing out anything of interest. They were over Outer Mongolia now, the great Gobi desert; bare wastes of wind-driven sand, sometimes piled into hills with rocks sticking through.

Somewhere in these immense spaces the Andrews expedition had discovered the dinosaur eggs, perhaps the most sensational event in the history of archaeology, or geology, or whatever science it is which deals with ancient eggs. That had been while Lanny was making love to Marie de Bruyne on the Coast of Pleasure; and now, even if the spot had been marked, he couldn't have seen very much from the height of a quarter of a mile. There is nothing more monotonous than looking down upon a desert, unless it is looking down upon an empty ocean. The map showed a caravan route through the Gobi, but they saw no trace of it, and no signs of life; they soon got tired of standing on their feet, and lay down and wrapped themselves in blankets against the cold.

Lanny thought, and his thoughts were not entirely pleasant. This was a two-seater plane, and on all such planes the practice was that while the pilot drove, the co-pilot took the altitude of the sun, and figured the wind drift and other factors which made up what the Pan-Am people called the "Howgozit." But up in front there sat two Chinese who looked like schoolboys, and had neither instruments nor charts. What were they doing? Just guessing? Or did they know this desert so well that they could distinguish one chain of sandhills from another? The pilot hadn't claimed any such knowledge; he had just said, with a cheerful grin: "I take you!"

Ulan-Bator couldn't be such a great city that you could see it from a considerable distance. And suppose you missed it, and started circling around looking for it? There would be a margin of daylight, for the trip was estimated to take only six or eight hours, depending upon the wind. But would there be a margin of gasoline? And suppose you had to come down in this desolate and terrifying waste? There were places that looked level, but how could you be sure what ridges might show up in the sand when you got near? And if you landed on such ground could you ever take off again? What would happen to you, with only a limited supply of food and water? Could you stand the cold of one of these desert nights? If one of the deadly sandstorms hit you, the plane might be buried and you would almost certainly be lost. They were not hot winds, such as blew from the Sahara and sometimes made life miserable in Southern France and Spain; they were winds that came from Siberia and the Arctic. Lanny suddenly decided that he had been taking too many chances with his valuable bride.

V

She was lying on her back, the most comfortable position on a hard floor. She was wrapped in a blanket, and the cold of mid-morning was not too great. Her duffelbag, partly emptied, was serving as a pillow, and her eyes were closed; he thought she was asleep, and he sat for some time watching her with loving thoughts. There was reason to believe that the great miracle of nature had taken place within her body, and Lanny thought about that, always with awe. It wouldn't be his first experience of the emotions of fatherhood; his thoughts wandered away to the other side of the world, where his first child would soon be celebrating her twelfth birthday. He had sent her a cablegram from Manila, and Robbie was supposed to have let her know the news from Hengyang.

He looked at his wife again, and saw that her lips were moving. He thought she was talking in her sleep, and laid his ear close to her lips, with the idea that she would be amused to know what she had been saying. Her tone was always gentle, not meant to compete with twin motors of a transport plane. But he could hear her voice, and somehow it sounded different. He leaned still closer, and made out the words. This is what he heard:

"I am not really malicious, and I wish you to be happy. I was not meant for him. I didn't know enough, and I suppose I was too eager. Men don't like that. Mother warned me, but I wouldn't listen. Anyhow, it doesn't matter now. Take good care of him, Laurel, he is really a kind man. He thinks too well of himself, but you can remedy that a little, perhaps."

The voice fell silent; and Lanny thought: "Oh, my God! *Lizbeth!*" Straightway, as usual, came the skeptical idea: "Or is it Laurel's dream?" Anyhow, it was a phenomenon, and an old-time psychic researcher wouldn't fail to seize the opportunity. He put his lips close to his wife's ear and said, loud enough to be heard but not enough to wake her: "Is that you, Lizbeth?"

"Yes," came the reply.

"This is Lanny. Do you want to talk to me?"

"I was always glad to talk to you, Lanny."

"Where are you?"

"I am in the spirit world."

"Are you happy?"

"I am always happy. I still love you, Lanny. It can't be wrong now."

"I am glad to hear that. I always wanted you to be happy."

"I know that. You never said anything unkind to me."

This sounded to the hearer like the standard patter of the séance room. He wanted something more evidential, so he asked: "Can you tell me what happened to you?"

"It is very tragic, Lanny, and I don't like to talk about it."

"All your friends will be anxious to know, Lizbeth; your mother especially."

"The Japanese got the *Oriole;* they sank her with one shell, and we had no time to get into the boats."

"Everybody on board was lost?"

"Everybody. They steamed away and left us."

"When was this?"

"The morning after we left Hongkong. They sank many ships."

"Is your father with you?"

"Yes. Tell mother that we are both well."

"Is there any special message for your mother? Something that will convince her it was you speaking."

"Nothing will convince her, I fear; but you can try. Tell her that the mice have made a nest in the rag doll that used to be my playmate and that is now in the old gray trunk in the attic."

"Will you come to your mother and speak to her, Lizbeth?"

"I will try, but I am not sure I can do it."

"Will you come and talk to Laurel some more?"

"I cannot promise. I am very tired now. I have been talking a long time."

The voice faded away; and Laurel sighed gently several times, as was her way in coming out of a trance. This was, so far as Lanny knew, the first time she had ever gone into a spontaneous trance; but of course it might have happened many times without her realizing it. He was curious to know if she would realize it now; he chose to take this as a problem in psychology, rather than to reflect upon the tragic story he had heard. Just now was surely not the time to tell Laurel such news—if it was news.

When she opened her eyes, he leaned to her ear and asked: "Were you asleep?"

"I suppose so," she replied. She was always slightly dazed after a trance.

"Did you have any dream?"

"I don't know. I don't remember any."

"Lie still for a while and see if you can recall anything."

He let her alone, and thought about that strange experience. It was the old story with him; he couldn't be sure whether to think this was actually the spirit of Lizbeth Holdenhurst or whether it was a product of Laurel's own subconscious mind, playing with the problem of what had happened to the yacht. It was a fact that not a day had passed since the eighth of last December that his wife hadn't said to him something to this effect: "Oh, what do you suppose has happened to the *Oriole?* And when shall we be able to find out?" He had told her that they might find wireless service from Ulan-Bator; so no doubt she had the subject prominent in her mind. The idea of a shell from a Japanese war vessel and what it would do to a yacht had been discussed by them many times. The words supposed to be spoken by Lizbeth were in character; but why shouldn't they be? Laurel had known her cousin from the cousin's infancy; and if Laurel the author had set out to write a dialog with her rival for Lanny Budd's love it would certainly have been "in character." When the dream mind has a mind to, it can be just as realistic as the literary mind; and apparently the trance mind is equally well endowed. Lanny had read much about "spontaneous trances," and knew that some mediums went into them frequently.

Now he said: "Can you remember any dream?"

"I can't recall a thing," she answered. "Why do you ask?"

"Your lips were moving, and I thought you must be having a dream." He said no more, for the roar of the engines took all pleasure out of conversation. He wrapped his blanket about him and lay down, closing his eyes and going over every word the "spirit" had said, so as to be sure of retaining it.

VI

The Chinese schoolboys were better guessers than Lanny had feared, and none of the passenger's forebodings was realized. Shortly after noon the pilot turned and shouted, and they leaped up and ran to the front. "Ulan-Bator!" Sure enough; through the clear air over the snowbound landscape they could see far-distant buildings. The passengers stood watching the welcome sight draw steadily closer. It was much more of a city than they had expected; they had looked for a scattering of conical Mongol tents called *yurts*, and there were these in great numbers, but also modern buildings, including a theater capable of seating several thousand persons. The Soviets had been here—and wherever they came you would find means of entertaining and instructing the masses.

There was a large airport, with planes in revetments. The arrival circled once, so as to give those in control an opportunity to observe the plane through glasses and make sure it was the one which had been scheduled. A year or so ago there had been a treaty between Russia and Japan, by which it was agreed that Outer Mongolia was in the Soviet sphere; but doubtless the authorities wouldn't take chances, and the pilot apparently didn't want to take any either. They circled, and waggled their wings in friendly fashion.

They came down to a three-point landing, skidded slightly in the snow, and then came to rest. Men came running, some of them soldiers. They saw the door open and two travel-worn tourists appear in the entrance, raising their clenched right fists and announcing: *"Amerikansky tovarische!"* When the questioning began they shook their heads vigorously, exclaiming: *"Nyet, nyet Russky!"* That probably wasn't right, but it was what Lanny recalled from visits, one a decade ago and the other two decades ago.

A gangway was brought for them to descend on, and presently an official came who spoke a little English. Lanny produced his credentials, in the form of the telegram from Kuibyshev instructing him to come here. The official knew nothing about it, but since they were Americans it was doubtless all right. Americans were a privileged people, likely to drop down out of any sky; and now they were allies in the war on the Hitlerite bandits. *"Amerikansky tovarische"* would get them anything they wanted in the People's Revolutionary Republic of Outer Mongolia.

Lanny put presents into the young pilots' hands and thanked them in the name of the people's cause. Farewells were said, and then the travelers were put into a much-worn car and driven to a government office where they told their story. No instructions had come, but they wrote a telegram to Uncle Jesse, and doubtless others were sent by the officials. Meantime the Americans were put up in a reasonably clean hotel room, and made the discovery which has become legendary among Americans traveling in Sovietland—the plumbing didn't work. Lanny said it wouldn't matter so much with Mongolians, for he had been told that they were the least-washed people in the world; water was applied to them only twice in a lifetime, first when they were born and second when they got married.

Naturally the couple wanted to see all they could of this unexpected new city of Central Asia. Ulan-Bator Khoto means "Red Knight City"; before that it had been Urga, the palace, the holy place, residence of the Living Buddha. When the last one had died, the Soviets had not permitted the customary reincarnation to occur, and the former residence had become a museum. The desire of the *Amerikansky* to view it was appreciated. They would have a "guide," who would also be a police guard, but that wouldn't trouble them, since they had nothing to hide. He was a yellow man, but politically Red, and knew a few words of what he thought was English and used over and over.

Later, when the authorities got word from Kuibyshev, they realized that they had important visitors and supplied them with an "intellectual," a young woman of Mongolian race who had studied English in Moscow and now served as translator in one of the offices of what she insisted was the entirely autonomous People's government. She wanted to show them every modern improvement in the community, including the university, the veterinary college, the medical college, and the wonderful theater with the revolving stage; she appeared chagrined when they told her that they had seen such things in America, and that after the museum they most desired to visit a real *yurt* and see how the primitive Mongols lived. Milk and curds were their food, together with blood which they drew from the legs of living cattle and horses and drank while it was warm. They bundled up their babies, all but a small opening at each end, and never unbundled them except as they grew and needed a larger chrysalis.

She took her charges out into the desert and showed them not merely a group of *yurts*, but also a high school, including a snow-covered spot which she said had been a truck garden, and would be again. "They even had flowers," she remarked, proudly; and Lanny quoted to her: "The desert shall rejoice, and blossom like the rose." She thought that was lovely, and asked who had said it. When he told her Isaiah, she looked blank and asked: "Who is he?" When the visitor replied: "He is one of the prophets in the Jewish Old Testament," she was disconcerted. He told her: "You ought to look into them; you'd be surprised to see what good comrades they were!"

VII

Instructions came: the travelers were to be flown to Ulan-Ude, a station on the Trans-Siberian railway, where they would be picked up by a westbound passenger plane. They were back in civilization; there was a regular airline between the two Ulans—Mongolian for Reds. The plane would be heated, so they would no longer have to wonder if they were going to freeze to death in a storm. If you think you don't like civilization, just get out of its reach for a few weeks!

In Ulan-Ude they had to wait, and nobody could say for how long. The Soviet Union at war could not spare a plane to transport private passengers a distance of four thousand miles, and there were no commercial planes anywhere within its borders. Here everything was concentrated upon the one task of repelling the Hitlerite invader. (That was the name they gave him, the worst name they could think of; as a rule they reserved the name "German" for the "people," with whom they insisted they had no quarrel.)

Machinery had been brought here from the western front; brick factory buildings were arising, and soon products would be pouring forth. What the products would be nobody told the travelers, and it was not good form to ask. They were guests of the local soviet, and were taken about and shown all the modern improvements. Lanny found a bookstore and obtained a pocket dictionary, and they diligently studied the more important words—those which had to do with something to eat.

During this period of leisure Lanny told his wife the words she had spoken while over the Gobi desert. She was deeply shocked, and tears ran down her cheeks. "Oh, Lanny, those poor people! How perfectly dreadful!"

"Don't forget, dear, it may not be true. It may have been just a bad dream."

"I believe it is true," she declared. "I don't have any idea how it happens, but I have become convinced that my mind gets things. And that sounds so like Lizbeth. Poor child!"

She made Lanny repeat every word that he remembered; and then, of course, she wanted to try another séance. They did so; but the effort produced only Otto Kahn and his playful courtesy—he said he didn't have the pleasure of the young lady's acquaintance, and in the spirit world no gentleman would speak to a lady without a proper introduction. Laurel tried half a dozen times, but her husband never again heard the gentle voice of the girl from the Green Spring Valley.

VIII

There came a westbound transport plane with two vacant seats, and at a half-hour's notice the passengers were hustled on board. Now they had comfortable seats, and presently were flying over the wide Lake Baikal—only they couldn't see it, because all the curtains were drawn. That was the case whenever they were passing over military secrets. Lanny guessed that it might be the new railroad which had been built around the foot of the lake; in the old days there had been a great ferry, and passenger and freight cars had had to be shuttled across. They could talk now, because this was a passenger plane, with sound-absorbing walls; their seats were side by side, and they did not get acquainted with the other passengers, most of whom were in uniform. One was a prisoner, handcuffed to his guard. They did not ask what he had done.

All day they were privileged to look at the snowbound wastes of Siberia, with a few towns, all with factory chimneys smoking. At nightfall they came to Irkutsk, but didn't see anything of it, because the curtains again were drawn. At the airport they had only time for a meal, and to stretch their legs, and then they were off for the long night journey. They had to sleep sitting up, but that was a small matter after the discomforts they had been experiencing. Lanny, the much-traveled, remarked: "If you want to appreciate an airplane, travel across all China before you get on board!"

The journey took the rest of the next day. They had no map, and weren't even told the names of the places at which they stopped. They were like a consignment of freight, tagged for Kuibyshev, for reasons not known to those who handled the shipment. They were glad to be warm, and to be able to get wholewheat bread and cabbage soup (with small pieces of meat) at the stopping places. They were grateful for the Russian custom of tea-drinking, which provided a huge samovar full of boiling water at all stations.

Their only fears were that they might be put off in favor of more important passengers, or that the Arctic might send a snowstorm and force them down. But the all-powerful Soviet government had weather stations all along their northern coast, and even in the ice-bound islands beyond; and apparently somebody in authority at Kuibyshev wanted to talk to the son of Budd-Erling. The bridal pair stayed on the plane, and the plane stayed on its course, and on the evening of the second day it settled down on a runway well spread with ashes, and they were told one word which they could understand. It was the name of a wheat and cattle town on the middle Volga which had once been Samara, and had been changed in honor of a prominent Soviet commissar named Kuibyshev.

There in the airport was the shrunken and wrinkled old gentleman who had once been an American painter on the French Riviera, and later a *député de la république française*. He was wrapped in a shaggy bearskin coat and had a hat to match—for you can't go about with your old bald head entirely bare when the temperature is far below zero. He had just had an attack of influenza, he told them—but he was determined to stick it out and live to attend the funeral of Adolf Hitler. He must have been homesick, for when he set eyes on his nephew he gave him a Russian bear's hug and kissed him on both whiskery cheeks. Lanny hadn't had a chance to shave, and looked like a Mongolian herdsman who had been married for several months.

But Laurel was Laurel, and had managed to get her hair in order on board the plane. Uncle Jesse took her two hands in his and looked her over carefully. "My new niece!" he said. "You look all right, but you are undernourished."

"We have been living on rice," remarked Lanny. "It will be up to you to feed her."

"I'll do my best," replied the old man. Then, still giving his attention to the lady from Baltimore: "You are a clever little minx, and you have a sharp tongue. I should hate to be your enemy."

"Quite true," said the niece, amused. "But how do you know it? Are you psychic?"

"I leave all that rubbish to Lanny. I have read your stories."

"You found them in Russia?"

"No, hardly. But this government doesn't make any mistake about the people it lets into the country. The clippings were ordered by cable and came by air in a diplomatic pouch. I was told about them, and asked for the privilege of reading them. You have already made several friends among our literati."

"Certainly that is a pleasant way to greet an author, Uncle Jesse, and I appreciate it."

" 'The *Herrenvolk*' has already been translated, and will be published on the back page of *Pravda* if you give your consent."

Laurel was so pleased she couldn't keep the tears out of her eyes. "Of course I give it," she said. "And I give my heart to the Soviet people at war!"

IX

Jesse had got them a room, the most priceless of all possessions in this river town which had once been a wheat-shipping center and now suddenly had become a world capital. "One of your admirers is sleeping on my sofa," he told the wife, with a chuckle.

They got some food in the airport restaurant, and then somebody's car took the author of "The *Herrenvolk*," together with her duffelbag and husband, through the snow-paved streets of Kuibyshev. Lanny perceived that he was going to be a mere appendage so long as he stayed in the Soviet Union, and perhaps elsewhere; that pleased him, for he was proud of his new treasure, and pleased to have his literary judgment confirmed. Only one thought troubled him, again and again; he couldn't get over his habit of trying to keep his secret from the Gestapo, and now he would find himself whispering to himself: "Good Lord, what will the Führer and the Reichsmarschall make of this! What will Kurt Meissner make of it!" They had seemed so far away, but now they were near again—and they were sure to have spies in this town.

Everybody wanted to know about Yenan: the number of its caves and their size; the progress of its schools and the number of the pupils; the state of its morale, the size of its armies, and every word they could remember that Mao Tse-tung had spoken. Laurel had notes? Oh, wonderful! Would she produce them and read from them? And would she permit the leading Soviet journalist Ilya Ehrenburg to prepare an interview with her? The story would go to America, and would greatly increase the price which a woman explorer could demand for her work in New York. She couldn't say No, if only out of gratitude for a warm room to sleep in and nourishing food to eat. More and more clearly her husband saw that a presidential agent's goose was cooked—and might as well be eaten hot!

With the help of his uncle whom the censors knew, Lanny sent off two cablegrams: one to his father, reading: "Arrived safely from

Hongkong via Yenan with wife Laurel Creston Reverdy's niece stop what news concerning Oriole sailed from Hongkong December eight love to all reply Continental Hotel Kuibyshev Lanny Budd." The other was to Charles T. Alston at his Washington hotel: "Escaped Hongkong traveled via Yenan wire instructions stop if wanted Washington please facilitate travel self and wife married writer Laurel Creston fellow-passenger yacht Oriole stop yacht left Hongkong December eight kindly mention news if available regards reply Continental Hotel Kuibyshev Lanny Budd."

After that a distinguished author's husband had nothing to do but wander about and look at the temporary capital of the Soviet Union at war, and accept the hospitality of all who wanted to invite them. For years Lanny Budd had been known in New York and London as Mister Irma Barnes, and now he was Mister Mary Morrow and didn't mind it a bit. They went about in their stained and battered sheepskin costumes, and it was perfectly all right, because everybody knew they couldn't have got new clothes if they had tried. And anyhow, the costumes were like military service stripes. On the streets people would look and then say: "Those must be the *Amerikansky* who have traveled through China! Wonderful people, the *Amerikansky!* How soon will they send us help?"

Lanny had read many times that the Russian people were not permitted to talk with foreigners, or that they were afraid to, and seldom invited them to their homes. He and Laurel did not find it so, but they realized that perhaps they were a special case; the fact that they had come from Yenan, and the fact that Lanny was a nephew of Jesse Blackless and Laurel an anti-Nazi writer—these facts put them in a different class from persons in the pay of capitalist newspapers who came and pretended to like the Russians, accepted their hospitality, and then went away and wrote things about them which they considered insulting and often downright inventions.

The American couple walked the wide streets of this river port, which in many ways made Lanny think of the frontier towns of the American West. The snow was piled in ridges, there being neither time nor labor to remove it. The shops had nothing on display, and there were long queues waiting wherever there was a chance of anything inside. The people were poorly clad, and you saw signs of undernourishment, but nothing compared to conditions among the Chinese; what was available was fairly distributed and there was no black market. The people were quiet, sober, and friendly; they seldom smiled, but on the other hand they showed no traces of anxiety. To be sure, the front was some eight hundred miles away, and no bombs had been dropped here, but everybody got the war news, from the papers or from radios in the factories and offices; they knew that their own winter offensive had been stopped by the Germans, and that another great Panzer drive was coming as surely as springtime.

X

Yes, the inhabitants of Kuibyshev, and of Saratov and Stalingrad and the other towns of the Volga, had reasons enough to be afraid, and to worry if they had been so disposed. But they had been born in an age of war and revolution, and excepting the old ones, they had never known a time when their country wasn't under siege. Sometimes it had been only an ideological, a propaganda siege—but that had been preliminary to political and military attack, and the Soviets had always known it. World capitalism had fought them from the hour of their birth, and with every weapon in its arsenal. Laurel was too young to remember these events, but Lanny had been part of them in his heart and mind, and even to some extent in reality.

He told her how, because of his knowledge of French, he had become secretary-translator to Professor Alston at the Peace Conference; how he had met Lincoln Steffens, who had been sent by President Wilson to Russia and had come home to report: "I have seen the future and it works." Lanny and Steffens together had taken Colonel House to meet Jesse Blackless in his attic studio in Montmartre, and there they had met three representatives of the new-born revolutionary government. It was there that the Prinkipo Conference was planned; and while it never came off, it served the purpose of teaching Lanny Budd how world capitalism worked, and how deadly it was to the cause of the dispossessed all over the earth. So now he was able to understand every pulsebeat of that distrust which filled the souls of Soviet people, and caused them to look upon every stranger as a possible spy and future betrayer.

"The madness of Adolf Hitler has made us allies for the moment," he told her, "but the Russians find it hard to realize that this is so, and they cannot be persuaded that it will last. When this war is over, America will still be a capitalist nation, the most powerful in the world. Its wealthy class will inevitably be the enemy of every Communist nation—not because it wants to be, but because of the economic forces which drive it."

"Don't forget that I have read a volume of Lenin," remarked Laurel, with a smile. "The theory of economic determinism is not strange to me."

"You will meet my father, and you will like him, because he is a kind and generous person; but if you talk to him about this situation you will find that he is economically determined, and he will tell you exactly why and how. He has a lot of men on his payroll—maybe ten thousand by now—and when the war is over he will have the devil's own time trying to meet that payroll. In order to do it he will have to sell goods abroad, and he will come into conflict with states which maintain government monopolies in foreign trade. He will consider that unfair competition and a deadly menace to his 'free enterprise system.' "

"Will he be willing to go to war to end it?"

"Social forces do not operate with clear-cut programs. 'Issues' will arise, one after another, and Robbie will always be sure that he is right. He will hire propagandists to defend his cause, and he will believe his own propaganda. Some day there will be an issue which he will call one of 'principle,' and which therefore cannot be compromised. Fighting will start over some border, and Robbie will be absolutely certain that the Communists have started it; he will also be certain that anybody who opposes him is a hireling in the service of the Reds."

"A pretty bleak prospect you are holding out for your unborn child, Lanny!"

"I don't pretend to know what is coming, dear. It is what H. G. Wells has called 'a race between education and catastrophe.' If the American people can be brought to understand the nature of exploitation and the competitive wage system, they may put their economy on a basis where they can live without paying tribute to Robbie, and without lending money to foreigners to enable them to buy our goods. But I don't know who's going to win that race."

X I

There came a cablegram from the afore-mentioned capitalist exploiter. Lanny had expected to hear from him first, because he was a prompt and business-like person, and he didn't have to consult anybody else, as would be the case with Alston. The message said: "Congratulations and best love from all to you both stop please advise concerning your plans stop do you need money stop no news whatever from yacht Oriole stop family greatly distressed wire any information Robert Budd."

When Laurel read that message she broke down and wept, the first time Lanny had seen her do that. It was dreadful news, and he couldn't think of any word to comfort her. More than three months had passed since the *Oriole* had sailed, and in that time she would surely have reached some harbor and reported. Of course there was a chance that she might have been wrecked, and that those on board were hiding from the Japs, or perhaps trying to make their way to civilization. But Laurel took her psychic message as settling the matter. "Something tells me it is true."

Lanny could only remind her that since this war had started many tens of thousands, perhaps hundreds of thousands, had gone out to sea and never come back. That would go on—who could guess how many years more? But none of those persons happened to be known to Laurel Creston, and she had not entered into their lives and the secrets of their hearts as she had done with her uncle and her cousin. "They had their weaknesses, but they were kind people, Lanny."

"I know," he said. "But Reverdy had no great desire to live, and it didn't seem to me that Lizbeth was headed for a happy life. Anyhow, you can take this comfort—if your message is true, they aren't suffering now. That is the one answer to grief." He put his arms about her and held her tightly. "Life is for the living, dear. We have our work to do, and perhaps we may be able to leave the world a tiny bit better than we found it. We cannot end death, but we may help to stop wholesale murder."

He knew that by her uncle's death she had come into possession of a considerable amount of money. He didn't know how large the Holdenhurst fortune was, but he knew what share of it Laurel would possess, because he had inspected the list of persons who received a share of Reverdy's Budd-Erling investments, under the strange tax-dodging scheme he had devised. Lanny wouldn't mention this until some time later. Now he was the lover trying to share her sorrow, and to diminish it by transferring her thoughts to himself. He was not unacquainted with that most futile of human emotions called grief; he had wept for Rick when he had thought Rick was dead, and for Marcel Detaze, and then for Marie de Bruyne, and for Freddi Robin, and for Trudi. Worst of all had been those last two cases, where he had known that the persons were undergoing torture and that their deaths were to be desired. Laurel should hope that her psychic message was veridical, and that nobody on the *Oriole* was in the hands of the Japs.

XII

Experienced in love as well as in sorrow, Lanny told his wife that he needed her, and that she had given him the most complete happiness he had ever known. She answered that he had loved so many women, and could she take the place of them all? He put in his plea that five women in a matter of twenty-six years wasn't such a bad record—considering that it had been made on the Coast of Pleasure, and in the smart society of Paris and London and Berlin and New York. In those places the record might pass as equivalent to a celibate life.

"Never forget, darling," he told her, "two of those women died, and the other three left me, so I haven't been exactly a Don Juan. Only one of the five—that was Trudi—understood and sympathized with my ideas; and she didn't know my world, and would never have been able to help me as you can. She knew that, and it troubled all her thoughts of me."

"Didn't Marie understand your ideas?"

"Marie was a conventional lady of the French provinces, Catholic and conservative. She loved me, but she was always afraid of our love and looked upon it as sin. Also, she was shocked beyond words when I caused us to be put out of Italy by trying to help Matteotti; she broke with me, and wouldn't see me for months afterwards."

He told these old stories, as a way to divert her mind. He told her that from this time on there would be only one woman in the world for him; if he ever looked at any other, it would be as a subject for her fiction, and he would report it to her promptly. He knew that this would have to be true if she was ever to enjoy peace, for that had been her upbringing. He was tireless in telling her so, and trying to wipe out his European past. He assured her that he meant every word of the Episcopalian formula he had recited: "to love and to cherish, till death us do part." They had already had some trials together; he hoped he had stood them acceptably, and he was certain that she had. Now they had work to do; they couldn't stay indefinitely in Soviet Russia, and must make the most of their days. So the lady from Baltimore dried her eyes and wiped the shine off her nose—here, as in Yenan, there was neither powder nor rouge to be had.

Such are the quirks of human nature—Lanny would catch himself thinking about Lizbeth and her father and the other people on the *Oriole,* and doing just what he had forbidden his wife to do. He had been more fond of Lizbeth than he had been willing to admit, even to himself. He had been, say one-quarter in love with her; he had thought of her intimately, and studied her closely. She had done her best according to her lights; certainly she had never knowingly done harm to anybody. And what a horrid ending to a young life, so full of hope and expectation! What a blindly cruel thing nature could be—and men, who were nature's product. How difficult to imagine reason or purpose in what they did!

And then Reverdy: he had been Lanny's friend, as much as he could be any man's friend. His wilfulness had been a reaction against his own weakness, his inadequacy to the tasks the world had set him. He had been determined to assert himself, to prove himself to others and to himself. He had tried so hard to take care of his precious person, and of his precious fortune—and how inadequate his judgment had been to that task! Looking back, Lanny could see it; but who is there, looking back, that cannot see blunders—whole storerooms full of them— memory storerooms!

And all those other people on the yacht; the three women guests,

the officers and the crew—persons with whom Lanny had lived in
daily contact for more than a month, and whose lives had been entrusted to Reverdy's fallible judgment! What had their thoughts been,
and their feelings, when the shell had struck—assuming that there had
been a shell—and when they had found themselves thrown into the dark
engulfing water? Lanny could form an idea, all-too-vivid, having been
in the same plight so recently. It was something he hadn't told Laurel
in detail; but he could never get the memories out of his own mind,
and the world would never seem to him quite the same bright and
cheerful place.

28. *Fifty-Year Plan*

I

THE second cablegram arrived a couple of days later. "Lanning
Prescott Budd Continental Hotel Kuibyshev retel delighted important
service awaits your return notify when ready will arrange air transportation yourself and wife no news concerning Oriole sorry regards
Charles T. Alston."

Lanny said: "My six months' furlough is up. What do you say?" His
wife answered: "Let's have two or three days to look around in
Moscow. Then we can go "

He took the cablegram to his Red uncle. Having been in New
York and read the newspapers, Jesse knew the name of this "fixer" for
the administration. "Lanny," he said, "you know that I have never
asked questions about your political or diplomatic job, whatever you
call it. But I was sure you had one and I couldn't help guessing. It
may be you will feel more free to talk now."

"I haven't been formally released from my promise, Uncle Jesse,
but since there's no chance of my going back into Germany, I can talk
a bit more freely."

"I have had the idea that you have access to Roosevelt."

"That is true."

"You will probably see him on your return?"

"I have every expectation of it."

"The head of my department in Narkomindel was interested in what
you had to tell about Yenan. I took the liberty of giving him the idea

that you were one of the President's confidants, and he suggested that it might be worth while for Stalin to have a talk with you. Would that interest you?"

"I can't think of anything that would interest me more, Uncle Jesse."

"You understand, it would have to be strictly on the QT."

"You ought to know by now that I am not a loose talker. I assume that I would be free to tell F.D. about it."

"Stalin would probably give you messages for him. There has been some talk of their meeting, you know."

"They ought to meet, and soon. I am sure that Stalin would be surprised by F.D.'s grasp of the world situation, and by his desire for friendship between the two nations."

"The surprise might be mutual, Lanny."

"So much the better. I will go to Moscow as soon as you can arrange the trip, and I'll wait there until you find out if the meeting is to take place."

Lanny had observed that the Russians he met seldom brought up the name of the head of their government, and when others brought it up they spoke with reserve. He was not surprised to find even his free-spoken uncle displaying anxiety now. "You understand, Lanny, this is a great honor which is being suggested for you. Stalin almost never sees foreigners, with the exception of specially accredited diplomats."

"I appreciate that, Uncle Jesse." Lanny kept his smile to himself. "I will do my best not to damage your position here."

"It isn't that, my boy; I am an old man, and don't expect to be holding my present job very long. But I am deeply concerned about stopping this spring's German drive. Our position is desperate, and we need American help the worst way."

"I agree, Uncle Jesse. I will report what I have learned here, and anything that your Chief sees fit to entrust to me."

"Will you feel free to talk to him about Roosevelt?"

"I can't imagine any reason why I shouldn't. I am sure that if I had a chance to ask F.D. he would bid me tell everything I know."

"All right," said the old Red warhorse, reassured, "I will see what can be done."

"Make it plain that I am not seeking the interview," suggested the P.A. "I imagine I'll be more apt to get it that way."

"You wouldn't have a chance to get it the other way," replied the uncle.

II

The plane to Moscow was a fast one; it flew late in the day, and four hours later it set them down on the airport in darkness. They would be under the bombs again, as they had been in Hongkong, ten thousand miles away. Their fellow-passengers on the ride were officials, mostly in uniform—no others rode in planes at present. They offered no sociability, and the Americans sat with their own thoughts.

They were taken to the Guest House of Narkomindel, which meant that they had been raised to the top of the social ladder. It is a one-time bourgeois mansion in the street called "Dead Alley." They were escorted to an elegant suite, and discovered to their satisfaction that here everything worked—not merely toilets and hot-water faucets, but bells and doorlocks and bureau drawers; the inkwells had ink and the pens did not scratch. One of their first adventures was the very grave major-domo, who presented a list of foods occupying four mimeograph pages and requested them to study it and mark those items which represented their preference.

They were extremely modest in their demands; they were judging the Soviet revolution by the standards of Yenan—but they discovered that a revolution a quarter of a century later may be something else again. All the articles of diet they asked for were provided, and the establishment insisted on adding a number of extras, enough to make four meals per diem, three of them of four courses each. They had great difficulty in persuading the old-style major-domo that they could not drink champagne with their breakfast. Russian hospitality, of which they had heard so much, threatened to overwhelm them after two or three months of rice and turnips.

The climax came when their hosts discovered that they proposed to walk out and inspect the scenery of Moscow clad in sheepskin coats which they had purchased in Hengyang and worn in all sorts of weather, riding on donkeys and sleeping on *k'angs*. The gracious and cultivated young lady who had been assigned as their escort informed them that they were to be taken to one of the warehouses where the Soviets stored their furs and provided with proper coats and hats for the month of March in latitude 56 degrees north. When they protested that they had never owned such luxuries and could not afford them, they were told in a shocked voice that they were to receive them as gifts. When they said that they could not possibly accept such gifts, they were told that if they did not do it they would greatly hurt the feelings of their hosts. When they asked what they had done to deserve such bounty, the reply was: "You have been our friends; and you will be going out by the Archangel route, which is very cold." It appeared that they must have not merely coats but hats and felt boots; and when they tried to take the less expensive sorts they were told that these were "reserved" and that they must have the better kind.

When they were alone, Lanny said to his wife: "There is a possibility that I may be asked to talk with an especially important person. I had to give my word not to name him, except to another important person in Washington. You will have to forgive me."

"I will always forgive you," she answered—and then with a twinkle in her bright brown eyes: "Provided I am certain the important persons are of your own sex, not mine."

Lanny assured her: "So far they have all been. The only exception was the mistress of Premier Paul Reynaud—and she, poor distracted soul, was killed in an automobile wreck. She was going to send me to the King of the Belgians to stop the Blitzkrieg, but we were too late. It was a suspicious-looking assignation, but old Pétain was present, so that made it respectable."

III

On the little river called Moskva which flows into the upper Volga, the ancient tsars of Muscovy had built their capital. It had started with a fortress village called the Kremlin, fronting the river; its shape is that of an isosceles triangle, and inside are crowded many government buildings, and, since the ancient rulers were all pious killers, several churches with domes in the shape of onions turned upside down. These had been covered with gold leaf that shone splendidly in the sun, but now everything was camouflage. Outside the walls was the great Red Square, with the tomb in which the body of Lenin had been preserved —but now it had been spirited away to a hiding place where the bombs could not get it. The tomb had been made to look like a *dacha*, or country house; the Kremlin walls were painted to resemble blocks of houses with shrubbery; there were huge nets across the Moscow River, with camouflage to turn it into houses and groves of trees.

Everywhere you looked were anti-aircraft guns mounted, for this was one of the most fortified places in the world, and the box barrage that went up when enemy planes were reported at night was the most tremendous that had ever assailed the ears of Lanny Budd. The Guest House had a cellar, and when the sirens gave their long wails the guests dived into it, along with the major-domo and all his staff. It was the democracy of fear.

Moscow is a sprawling city, and its notable buildings are scattered, so that it has no show streets like Fifth Avenue or the boulevards of Paris. Now it had been half emptied of its population. Its art treasures had been removed, and some of its buildings, like the famed Bolshoi theater, had been blasted with bombs. Soldiers were everywhere, fresh ones going toward the west in trucks, and wounded coming back. Long lines of carts carried supplies to the vast armies which had been attacking or retreating with very few intervals for eight or nine months.

The military defenses of the capital were secret and the visitors did not ask anything about them. They were taken to the only theater that was going—most of the shows were with the troops. They inspected the beautiful subway stations, of which all Muscovites were so proud; but now they were air-raid shelters and very dirty. They were driven through the Park of Culture and Rest—covered with snow and closed to the public. If they had asked to see the great Stalin truck factory, the favor might have been granted, even in wartime; but the son of Budd-Erling had seen all the factories he wanted in one life.

I V

What they liked best was to go out and wander about the streets of Moscow under siege. These streets were snow-piled and litter-strewn, and the people in them were shivering, ill-clad and unwashed; yet there was about them an atmosphere of quiet endurance, of firm patience, of determination you could feel without understanding a word they spoke. "I wish I could get at their souls," Laurel said—but of course that was not possible. When you talked to them through an interpreter they would be thinking about that third person, and saying what that person would expect; if they didn't say it, the interpreter might put it in anyhow.

"They have been promised a new world for a quarter of a century," Lanny reminded his wife. "They have been clinging fast to that hope through all their sufferings."

"Are they any better off than they were?" she wondered.

"In wartime, not much, I imagine. But they have the hope, and that is what human beings live by. And at least they know what they don't want—to be ruled by Hitler."

"I try to see the good side of this system, Lanny; but I shrink so from thoughts of the terror. It seems to me these streets must smell of blood."

"Yes, darling; but you must remember, it's very old blood. The tsars ruled by terror, ever since we have any record of them."

"But does it have to go on forever? Communism promised to bring peace and fraternity."

"The Soviet revolution was a mild affair at the outset," explained the husband who had watched it. "Many of the Old Bolsheviks were gentle idealists, who hoped to convert their opponents. There was no terror until the attempt on Lenin, and later the assassination of Kirov."

Laurel had never heard the name of this friend and right-hand man of Stalin, who had been shot by a Soviet official with "White" connections. It had been that deed which had let loose the terror and the series of purges. "God knows I hate killing," declared Lanny; "but I didn't make this world, and I have to start from where it is. I face the uncomfortable fact that France and Belgium and Norway and the Balkan countries all went down before Hitler because he was able to find quislings who hated their own governments so much that they were willing to sell them out to an invader. But you don't hear anything about Soviet quislings—and why?"

"They were shot, I suppose."

"They were shot in advance, before they had a chance to do any of their quisling. Much as it hurts me, I have to face the fact that if Stalin hadn't purged his pro-Nazi elements, including his generals, there wouldn't have been any Soviet Union at this moment; Hitler would have the whole of this country, and that means he would have the world. If he is able to get Russia's resources, and make slaves out of the workers as he is now doing with Poles and Frenchmen and the rest, we could never beat him—not in the thousand years that he talks about."

There seemed to be no answer for that. Laurel said: "Of course we have to take what allies we can get."

"We have to pitch in and help win this war; then, when we lift the fear of invasion from the hearts of the Soviet people, we can hope they will discover the advantages of freedom, just as we have. The people we see about us are little different from ourselves; they want the comforts of civilization, they want knowledge, and the chance to apply it to living. Karl Marx predicted that the state, as a part of capitalism, would wither away under Communism; it was his belief that the state existed for the repression of subject classes, and that once there were no such classes, the state would become an agency of co-operation, a menace to no one. We don't see much signs of that in wartime, but we may be surprised how quickly the change would come if we could get peace and a system of world order."

V

Hansi and Bess were out of town, and Lanny was afraid he was going to miss them; then he learned that they were scheduled for a concert in Moscow, and they showed up, having been brought by plane. They came to the Guest House, and what a time they had exchanging reminiscences! Lanny and Laurel had traveled something like three-quarters of the way around the earth for this meeting, and Hansi and Bess had traveled the rest of the way. Neither of the musicians had ever heard of Laurel, but now they read her story in *Pravda* and were in a state of excitement over the honor done to an American writer. When Bess had listened to an account of the Yenan visit she put her arms about Laurel and exclaimed: "For years I have been hoping for this to happen to Lanny. My dear, you are just the right woman for him, and I am happier than I can tell you."

The two couples were driven to the concert together. Hansi had got himself a pair of fur-lined gloves to protect his precious hands from the cold, and when they got to the concert hall he soaked them in hot water for several minutes. Then they went onto the stage of the immense Tchaikovsky Hall, and all of a sudden Laurel had her wish granted —she got at the souls of the people of Moscow. They stood up to welcome these two American artists, whose coming was not merely a musical but a political event, symbolical of the aid that was promised from overseas. The audience listened entranced while Hansi played Russian music which they knew, and then American folk music which he wanted them to know.

Laurel listened, too, and now and then stole glances at the rapt faces about her; so she learned what was in the hearts of the ill-clad and hungry people whom she had been watching on the streets of this war-torn city. They wanted beauty, they wanted love, they wanted the fire of the spirit, the dreams and the glory—all the gifts which Hansi Robin had been laboring for thirty years to put into his music. When he finished they hailed him with such a tumult of applause as Laurel had never heard in any concert hall; they would have kept him there all night if he had not played the *International*, with which his wartime concerts were concluded.

Next day there came to the Guest House a uniformed officer of the Red Army, who requested an interview with Mr. Budd alone, and identified himself as being on the staff of Premier Stalin. In precise and proper English he inquired whether Mr. Budd would be prepared to meet the Premier that evening at twenty-three o'clock. Mr. Budd replied that he would be completely prepared, and gladly. The officer informed him that he would be on hand with a car at twenty-two-thirty precisely, and Mr. Budd promised to have on his new fur coat and fur-topped boots at that hour.

He told his wife about the appointment, assuring her that the important personage was a member of his sex and not of hers. "He could not be more important if he tried," said Lanny—and while this wasn't telling her, it was certainly giving her a good chance to guess. He left her to the company of a group of her colleagues, male and female, who had read "The *Herrenvolk*." Soviet intellectuals like to sit up all night discussing world literature—while the head of their government and army sat up discussing world statecraft.

The car came, an American Cadillac, and Lanny entered it and was driven to one of the Kremlin gates. The car was searched, to make sure there was nobody in it but the persons who were supposed to be. The Soviet Union wasn't taking any chances with the head of its government and army. Lanny learned later that they had taken the precaution to cable to Washington and ascertain whether the son of Budd-Erling was what he claimed to be, and whether President Roosevelt considered him a person worth the Marshal's time. Since the White House staff didn't know anything about the aforesaid son, they had referred the question to the President, who had replied that Mr. Budd possessed his complete confidence and that the Marshal should talk to him as if it were the President himself. If Lanny had known this, he would have been less surprised by what was now to happen.

VI

They were driven to one of the buildings within the historic enclosure. At the door a soldier flashed a torchlight upon them; the soldier spoke a few words and they passed in. Lanny had read that Stalin lived in a simple apartment in one of these buildings, and he wondered if he was to be taken there. Or had the head man of Russia built himself a magnificent reception room, calculated to intimidate the visitor after the style of Mussolini and Hitler?

Without the formality of a knock, the visitor was led through an anteroom into a ground-floor room in one of the ancient Kremlin structures; a room of moderate size, oval in shape and with a vaulted ceiling, its walls partly paneled in white oak while the other parts were of smooth white plaster. There were three windows which gave upon the yard. A narrow carpet led to a flat-topped desk with an empty armchair, and beside it another armchair which the guest was invited to take. In a smaller chair near by sat a youngish, slender man with dark hair and eyes; he rose, but was not introduced. Lanny guessed that he must be the interpreter.

The guest took his seat, and used a minute or two of time to inspect the room. At the right of Stalin's chair was a small stand with several telephones, of different colors to distinguish them. The desk was pretty well covered with books, and against the wall was a bookcase containing the works of Lenin and two sets of encyclopedias, the *Soviet* and the *Brockhaus*. Near the entrance was a glass case containing the death mask of Lenin; beside it stood an old-fashioned grandfather's clock in a case made of ebony. On the walls were portraits of Marx and Engels with their heavy whiskers. Through an open door Lanny could see a room with a long table and maps on the wall; doubtless it was the council room where the defense of the Soviet Union was discussed.

The officer went to a closed door and tapped gently. In perhaps half a minute the door was opened, and there entered a personage whose statue was in every school in the Soviet Union and whose portrait was

in every home. In foreign lands, people who read magazines or newspapers had come to know these features as well as those they saw in
the looking glass.

In the portraits Stalin had somehow looked like a large man. Perhaps
he didn't have large people about him, or perhaps it was the general
tendency to assume that all Russians were large. He was five feet five,
which was several inches shorter than Lanny; stockily built, but not
fat. He was dressed informally, in a dark blue blouse and trousers
tucked into boots. His hair and heavy mustache were both iron gray.
He had a large head, and his complexion was sallow and marked by
smallpox. His left arm was slightly shrunken, a defect he shared with
the last of the German Kaisers.

He was a serious and busy man, and had little time for humor and
none at all for formality. Lanny had risen, and they shook hands as if
they were two Americans. Stalin said, in Russian: "Happy to meet you,
Mr. Budd," and the translator at once spoke the words in English.
Stalin took the chair at his desk, and the interpreter placed himself in
front of it; by turning his head slightly, he faced one and then the
other speaker. The staff officer excused himself, and without further
preliminaries the interview was on.

VII

Djugashvili was the name of this statesman's parents, and when they
had had him christened they added Josef Vissarionovich Ivanovich
David Nijerdse Chezhkov. It was Lenin who had suggested that he
adopt the name of Stalin, which means steel, and is much easier to say.
His father had been a drunken cobbler in the Georgian city of Tbilisi,
which we call Tiflis. At great sacrifice the widowed mother had sent
her bright little boy to a church school and then to a theological
seminary, intending to make him a priest. But instead of concerning
himself with the next world the bright little boy had taken up the notion of changing this one. He became a social revolutionary and scored
a record: eight times imprisoned, seven times exiled, and six times
escaped. He was not among those who retired to Switzerland or London and spent their time studying in libraries and expounding theories;
he was a man of action, and came back to the battle again and again.
Among his actions, according to reports, was the holding up of a truck
carrying funds for a bank—this as a means of financing his revolutionary party.

Now in his early sixties Stalin had fought his way to the control of
his party and his country, including an army of some four million men
and growing fast. He had a deadly enemy who had attacked him without provocation and had crashed three or four hundred miles into his

country, killing several million soldiers and civilians and dragging the able-bodied survivors off into slavery, after a fashion unknown in Europe for many centuries. Josef Stalin's whole mind was occupied with the problem of defeating this enemy and hurling him out of Russia. He had sent the greater part of the government to safety, but he himself had stayed under the bombs. He hadn't summoned Lanny Budd in order to meet a charming playboy or to hear a story of adventure, but to glean every fact that might conduce to the success of Soviet arms.

At the Peace Conference, and on other occasions since, Lanny had been annoyed by persons who spoke Rumanian or Armenian or what not, and would pour out floods of eloquence without giving the interpreter a chance to get in more than a sentence or two. But the master of the Soviet Union was not among these futile ones. He spoke in a quiet, even tone, and when he had said a sentence or two he waited until the interpreter was through. Lanny followed the same technique, and was interested to observe that while he, Lanny, was speaking, Stalin was apparently staring at the pit of Lanny's stomach. This continued while the interpreter was speaking, and only when Stalin spoke did he raise his eyes to his auditor's. Then he seemed to be boring into the auditor's soul. Manifestly, he was a judge of men and a stern one; he was a prober of secrets, and if Lanny had been a Russian with secrets to hide, he would have been uneasy in his mind. But Stalin couldn't do any harm to Lanny, and all Lanny had to think about was that he might do some good to Stalin.

There were cigarettes and a tobacco box on the desk, and the host offered them. When Lanny said he did not smoke, Stalin proceeded to stuff a large and well-worn pipe. Thereafter, when he was not speaking, he puffed—but Lady Nicotine did not exercise her supposed soothing effect upon his mind. He pressed the visitor with questions: why had Hongkong fallen so quickly, and what had been the attitude of the Chinese there, and what were food conditions in the interior of the country, and to what extent was Chungking keeping its truce with Yenan? Now and then he made a note on a pad. A P.A., no stranger to diplomatic subtleties, wondered if this was a pretence, and if a recording was being made of this interview.

VIII

Lanny told what he had seen in Yenan, and whom he had met. How was Mao Tse-tung getting along, and what had he said about his prospects? Lanny described the circumstances of the interview, and repeated everything the head of the Border Government had spoken. Lanny had heard many stories about the operations of the Chinese guerrillas, and these were important, because Stalin was training great numbers of Russians to operate in that way against the Germans; supplies would be dropped to them by parachute, information would be sent by radio codes, and they would cause a steady draining of German resources.

The Premier brought up the subject of Budd-Erling. He had heard about its product, and was pleased to have one of America's industrial achievements described to him. Lanny said: "You must understand, I am six months behind the time. I have no doubt that since Pearl Harbor the enterprise has been growing like a mushroom. For many years my father has been telling me that the future of the world would be decided by airpower, and now he is having the chance for which he has been asking."

"Your father used to make planes for the Nazis, I am told," remarked the Red chief, with studied casualness.

"Understand, I don't defend his course. I pleaded with him against it, but he took the stand that he was a businessman, and offered his wares in the open market. The Germans kept his enterprise alive for several years."

"I am familiar with the point of view, Mr. Budd. Business is business."

"I repeat what my father has told me many times: it is not the planes which are important, but the power to produce planes; and that remains in America."

"It is the planes which are important to us at present." This with grim decisiveness.

"I can only tell you what my father and his experts were discussing last September, before I left home. The problem as regards your country is not so much the making of planes as of their delivery. If we ship them by way of Archangel, the submarines will get most of them. If we ship them by the Persian Gulf, it is difficult to assemble them in the midst of desert sand. There seemed to be general agreement that the solution of the problem must be by way of Alaska and Siberia."

"It is too cold, and there are too many fogs, Mr. Budd. If we are to use the northern route, it would be shorter to fly over the North Pole."

"You are speaking of bombers, sir; but the Budd-Erling is a fighter plane, with short range. We already have bases in Alaska, and I take it for granted that we are now constructing a chain of them. If you could do the same from the Chukotsky Peninsula westward, the problem would be solved. It is my father's opinion that the losses would be small, compared to those which would be inevitable over the Archangel route. My father does not like that route, and I doubt very much if our government does either."

"We are considering the matter from every point of view, Mr.

Budd. My understanding is that Admiral Standley is coming here as ambassador, and doubtless he will bring a technical staff with him."

IX

Now and then, as this interrogation went on, the visitor would be wondering: "Does he know that I have been a friend of the head Nazis?" It seemed unlikely that Stalin's efficient secret service would have failed to unearth such a fact. Lanny had decided that he wouldn't bring up the subject; he could suppose that Uncle Jesse might have taken the liberty of passing on his guess that Lanny had been a secret agent of President Roosevelt working in Germany. In any case, Stalin would have his suspicions; there had been an old saying among Russians: "Lenin trusts only Stalin and Stalin trusts nobody." And the record showed that Lenin had distrusted Stalin!

Perhaps that was the basis of the great man's next remark. "I should like to ask you, Mr. Budd—how does it happen that the son of a great American capitalist is sympathetic with the Soviet point of view?"

"I must be frank, sir, and inform you that I am a Socialist, not a Communist. But I am against Hitlerism with all my soul, and I welcome every ally in that fight. It was my mother's elder brother, Jesse Blackless, who gave me my first push toward the left, when I was a small boy. He took me to meet an Italian syndicalist, Barbara Pugliese, of whom you may have heard."

"I met her at international gatherings in the old days."

"She produced a deep impression on my mind, and after that I began meeting various persons of leftist turn of mind. At the Paris Peace Conference I acted as secretary-translator to Professor Charles Alston, and there I came to know George D. Herron and Lincoln Steffens, and was the means of bringing Steffens and Colonel House into touch with three representatives of the new Soviet government who came to Paris. At that time, we were all working desperately to stop the attacks of world capitalism upon your new government. We succeeded in persuading President Wilson to appoint Herron to a conference at an island called Prinkipo, if you remember."

"I am not apt to forget any of the events of those days, Mr. Budd."

"We failed, but things might have been much worse, and doubtless would have been if we had not striven so hard. The effort was important in my personal life, because I got an education out of it, and I made a few friends. It was Professor Alston who vouched for me to President Roosevelt."

"You know the President well, I am told."

"I have had perhaps a dozen long conferences with him—always at night, and in his bedroom, where he works lying down. I have never spoken of that to anyone, but I tell you about it, because I am sure the President would wish me to do so. I should prefer that you keep the matter between us—at least until I have found out what my next assignment is to be. Let me explain that I was on my way to England on an especially confidential mission when I got both my legs broken in an airplane crash at sea. I was told to take a six months' furlough, and that is about up. I am well again, and expect to have another assignment."

"Thank you for the explanation. I am greatly interested in your President, and glad to meet anyone who knows him well."

"You should meet him yourself, sir. He is one of the most delightful of companions, and his sincerity convinces everybody—except, of course, those who hate his efforts to reform our economic system."

"I should like nothing better than to meet him; but it would be a long trip for him, and I, unfortunately, cannot leave Moscow while this crisis continues."

"If all goes well, I should see the President in a few days, and if you have any message you care to entrust to me, I will deliver it faithfully."

"Tell him that we need help of every sort, and we need it now. All our information is that the Hitlerites intend to make a new onslaught within a month or so—depending on the weather."

"Do you have any idea where it will be centered?"

"It will be all along the front, and we cannot tell the main objective; it may be another try at Moscow, or it may be for the oil of the Caucasus. It will probably depend upon where they find a weak spot. Very certainly they will throw in everything they have, and we shall be strained to the uttermost."

"I understand your idea, sir, and will report it."

X

Lanny had said that his own knowledge was out-of-date; but he knew enough about F.D.'s position to understand that there would be a score of nations clamoring for armaments, and especially planes: Britain for her own shores and for North Africa; the Free French for their colonies, and the Dutch for theirs; the Chinese, the Australians, the New Zealanders—to say nothing of American generals and admirals on many fronts, and civilians in every harbor of the Atlantic and the Pacific. What F.D. would want was Stalin's political views and intentions, and especially what Lanny thought about the matter—did he mean what he said?

So now the P.A. ventured: "May I ask you one or two questions, sir? I meet a good many influential persons, and they will all wish to know: Will the Russians hold out?"

"Concerning that you may answer without any qualification: We shall fight on our present lines, and retreat when we are forced to. We shall fight every foot of the way, wherever we are. We shall fight on the Volga, and in the Urals, and in Siberia, if we have to retreat that far. Whatever is left of the Soviet system will fight Hitlerism to the last breath."

"That assurance will be comforting to some of my friends, who do not understand the difference between the two systems as clearly as I do."

The Premier raised his keen gray eyes to the visitor's face and watched him closely. "Tell me, Mr. Budd—when your friends ask you what is the difference between the two systems, what do you tell them?"

Lanny knew that that was a crucial question; but he didn't have to hesitate, having answered it many times, in his own mind and elsewhere. "First of all, I try to make it plain that the Nazi system is based upon a racial point of view—really a national one—whereas the Soviet system is based upon an economic point of view, and applies to all races and nations equally. Under your system it is possible to believe in the brotherhood of man and to work toward it; whereas the Nazis offer the rest of the world nothing but perpetual slavery and war."

Lanny could see by the look on his host's face that he had passed his examination successfully. Without waiting to get his marks he ventured to go on: "When people hear that I have talked with Premier Stalin, they will crowd round to ask: 'If he wins, is he going to try to take all the rest of Europe?'"

"What would I do with the rest of Europe, Mr. Budd?"

"You must tell me that, sir, in order that I may be able to quote you."

"You may say without qualification: The Soviet Union does not want the rest of Europe. The Soviet peoples have all the land and resources they need; they want only peace, so that they can develop what they have. Let the rest of Europe work out its own problems in its own way—subject to but one restriction, that it does not permit itself to be turned into a center of intrigue against the Soviet peoples, such as we saw in the so-called *cordon sanitaire* during the past quarter century."

"There is a great deal of talk in America about an international organization to preserve the peace after this war. Tell me what you say to that."

"We shall be for it without reservation. I point out to you what our record has been on the League of Nations. We joined as soon as they would let us and we stayed until they booted us out. But America never joined."

"Would you assent to the idea that America, Britain, and the Soviet

Union shall take the lead in forming such an organization, and constitute its nucleus?"

"I would say that if we failed to do it, we should be indicted before the bar of history."

"Is that your personal attitude, Premier Stalin, or is it the attitude of your government?"

"It is both. I am familiar with the fact that people in your country have been taught to think of me as a dictator, like Hitler; but there is no resemblance between our functions. I never act without consulting the membership of our Politburo; and if I should find that the majority opinion was against me, I should not act. I will illustrate by telling you what happened in the case of the defense of Leningrad. The majority of the group thought that the city could not successfully be defended. I had read Peter the Great's opinion that it could be defended by artillery, and I advocated that we try. The question was fought out with fierce arguments, and in the end I was able to persuade the majority. So far, it appears fortunate that I succeeded."

"The American people are disturbed by the idea of dictatorship. When they question me, I remind them of the Marxist formula, which Lenin approved, that after the victory of Communism the state would wither away. Do you still hold to that idea?"

"It would never occur to me to revise any of Lenin's ideas. I consider myself his pupil, and I ask myself one question: What would he have done in this situation?"

"One could hardly expect any state to wither in wartime," Lanny ventured.

"Surely not. You may be quite sure that when you arrive in America, you will find the state growing rapidly, and you will hear President Roosevelt being called a dictator."

"I have already heard it a hundred times," smiled the visitor.

"The capitalist state, in the Marxist-Leninist interpretation, is an agency of class repression. In a classless society there would be no function for it. As fast as people get education, they will assert themselves, and a democratic society will come automatically."

"I may say that is your ultimate aim, Premier Stalin?"

"I myself have said it many times, and so have all our theorists. But we do not use the name democracy as a camouflage for the continuation of wage slavery."

Lanny smiled again. "I perceive, sir, that you have some acquaintance with the political theories of American big business."

XI

The son of Budd-Erling was supposed to have come here to give information to the Soviet leader; but he took the occasion to explain that he would like to take information to his own Chief. He knew pretty well what his Chief would want to know; and also he could guess what ideas his Chief would like to put into the mind of the Red Premier. "Tell me, sir," he ventured, "what sources of information you have concerning my country."

"I get many reports, and also I have editorials and leading features translated from your newspapers. I know that when your Red-baiters, such as Mr. Hearst and Colonel McCormick, talk about democracy, they mean the opposite of what I mean. To them it is the defense of their class system; the freedom enjoyed under it is their freedom, not that of their workers."

"You have those gentry right, sir; but do not make the mistake of exaggerating their influence. The people read their papers but do not take their political advice. In the last three elections President Roosevelt was opposed by seventy per cent of our capitalist press, and yet he was elected."

"You would oblige me if you could tell me why your people read such vile papers."

"The reasons might be difficult for a foreigner to understand. The papers are old and long established, and people are used to their names and their format. They have huge sums of money and buy the best talent of all sorts—cartoonists, sports writers, movie gossip, and above all, comic strips. The children follow those stories and clamor for them; a large percentage of the children never grow up mentally, so they go on reading the same thing. When it comes to voting, they are frequently deceived, but in the long run the idea of their class interest does penetrate their minds."

"America is indeed a difficult country to understand—or even to believe in. You have such violent contrasts."

"We are a violent people, sir—and my guess is that both the Japs and the Nazis are going to find it out. As for Willie Hearst and Bertie McCormick, they are two spoiled children who inherited vast fortunes, and have used them according to their furious prejudices. Hearst came to Naziland and found everything to his taste; he made business deals with Hitler, and defended him with ardor, up to the point where the persecution of the Jews became too extreme, and he had to remember several million readers and a large block of his department-store advertisers. But not all our great capitalists have such predatory minds; there are men of social conscience among them, and President Roosevelt has been laboring to train a group of these in the public service."

"But President Roosevelt cannot live forever, Mr. Budd. What are we to expect if he should die?"

"He is doing just what Lenin did, and what you are trying to continue: building a party which will keep his ideas and ideals alive. One of these is friendship and co-operation with the Soviet Union. Our Vice-President, Henry Wallace, is just as ardent in holding to that idea, and I do not believe the Republican Party will ever again come back into power, except by adopting the New Deal program in essentials. You may have observed that tendency in Wendell Willkie's campaign; he made the Old Party bosses furious by the concessions he made to New Deal thinking."

"I was struck by that fact, Mr. Budd."

"If I may make a suggestion, sir, nothing will promote President Roosevelt's desires so well as expressions from you of democratic tendencies and intentions in your own country. You follow Lenin's words, while we in America follow Lincoln's: 'government of the people, by the people, for the people.' The nearer you approach to that platform, the easier it will become for our two peoples to co-operate in world affairs."

"I will bear your suggestion in mind, Mr. Budd." Could it be that there was a touch of dryness in the Red statesman's voice?

"Let me make it plain," persisted the idealistic visitor; "I am not speaking my own thoughts, but those of the President. In my last talk with him he referred to the Soviet Union, and I ventured to point out that its distrust of the capitalist powers was no phobia, but was based on historic facts. The President replied: 'I know it well, and I have a Fifty-Year Plan for making friends with the Soviet Union.' "

The Premier stared at his guest while these words were being translated, and then his stern features relaxed, first into a smile and then into a laugh, the only one during this long interview. "Capital! Capital!" he exclaimed. "He is a man of true humor." Then, after these words had been put into English: "Tell him for me that we shall try to exceed our quota, and to finish ahead of schedule." These were the technical terms, the slogans of the *Piatiletka*, the Five-Year Plan, and even the self-effacing translator grinned as he repeated them for the guest.

XII

It was an excellent note on which to close. The hour was one in the morning, and Lanny had had two hours of this busy man's time. No doubt he had a stack of documents piled on his reading table, as F.D. invariably did. He pressed a button, and in a minute or two a servant appeared, wheeling a tray with various liquors and a plate of dry crackers.

"I am going to give you a toast," declared Stalin. "In what do you prefer to drink it?"

"In what looks to be red wine," was the guest's reply. "I am afraid of your Russian firewater." The host was amused when this phrase was translated to him, and he asked, was it American? Lanny told him it was the very earliest—American Indian.

The Premier poured out two glasses of the red wine and handed one to Lanny. He held his up, and the guest followed suit. "To the friendship of our two countries!" proclaimed "Uncle Joe." "May we teach you industrial democracy at the same time that you are teaching us political democracy!"

They clinked glasses and drank. Lanny knew that custom required him to drain his glass and then hold it inverted over his head as a sign that he had done so. He complied, and his host showed that he was pleased by this conformity. He took the glass and filled it again, then filled his own. "And now, your turn."

Lanny recited: "To the health of Stalin and Roosevelt. May they live to carry out a program of democracy, with freedom of speech and religion for all men." He wasn't sure if the Soviet chief would drink that toast, but the chief showed no sign of distaste. The visitor said: "I have kept you too long, sir. I am honored by the confidence you have given me, and I will faithfully report your words."

"You are a well-informed man, Mr. Budd, and good company. The next time you come this way, I hope you won't fail to let me know."

He had already pressed another button; the young officer appeared, and escorted the visitor into the anteroom, where he donned his fur-lined coat and hat, and went out into the bitter cold and utter blackness of that city of the tsars. Only the stars far overhead were not blacked out. Perhaps they didn't know there was a war on, and that human insects on a remote obscure planet were using the forces of nature and their own minds to bring an end to one another's existence.

The presidential agent, going over the interview in his mind, was saying: "God grant that he means it!"

Printed in the United States
38674LVS00005B/17